Endorsements for *Daisy Chain*

Mary DeMuth's beautiful, lyric style of [...] you into this compelling story of hope and grief, of [...] demption found, even in the midst of suffering. Jed's journey will linger in a reader's heart, long after his story is over. *Daisy Chain* is another brilliant masterpiece by one of my favorite authors.

> Susan May Warren,
> Award-winning author of *Nothing But Trouble*, a PJ Sugar novel

Daisy Chain is a hauntingly beautiful novel in which innocence gives way to one unspeakable awful summer in Defiance, Texas. Mary DeMuth's storytelling has never been stronger, nor the stakes more desperate. This is one story that will linger long, long after the last page is read.

> Sharon K. Souza,
> Author of *Lying on Sunday* and *Every Good & Perfect Gift*

Every now and then a book comes along that weaves its way into your soul and takes up residence. *Daisy Chain* is such a book. Heartbreaking. Hopeful. And peopled with unforgettable characters—Jed, Hixon, Bald Muriel, and the irrepressible Daisy—who wind their way into your heart and won't let go. Reminiscent of *To Kill a Mockingbird*, this book will leave a lasting mark on your heart and soul. Thank you, Mary DeMuth, for writing it.

> Laura Jensen Walker,
> Author of *Daring Chloe* and *Turning the Paige*

Daisy Chain, the first book in the Defiance Texas Trilogy, is a powerful story of friendship, family secrets, and the presence and love of God in the darkest of places and through the darkest of days. Readers should be advised to clear space on their bookshelves for this emotion-packed story.

> Tamara Leigh,
> Author of *Faking Grace* and *Paying Piper*

Daisy Chain is a spell-binding, beautifully mysterious masterwork of a story that will both frighten and comfort, break your heart and mend it again. Mary DeMuth is one of our very best authors, and you will savor this novel from the first page to the last.

> Kathleen Popa,
> Author of *To Dance in the Desert* and *The Feast of Saint Bertie*

Mary DeMuth has written yet another lyrical tale of haunting secrets and lavish redemption. *Daisy Chain* is sure to steal your heart and take your breath away.

Claudia Mair Burney,
Author of *Zora and Nicky: A Novel in Black and White*

Daisy Chain grabbed my heart immediately, broke it with Jed's struggles, and healed it with the touch of Grace in his broken world. Mary DeMuth has penned a compelling tale that kept me turning pages until the surprising, yet satisfying, conclusion. I can hardly wait for the next installment from Defiance.

Janelle Clare Schneider, Author

Mary DeMuth's artistic flair for the sublime and the subtle shines in *Daisy Chain*. Painfully poignant and realistically redemptive, this is a story to savor and ponder.

Susan Meissner,
Author of *The Shape of Mercy*

Within a few paragraphs of *Daisy Chain* I found myself letting out a contented sigh. The story captured my attention from the first page, but more than that, the writing has a melody to it. If words can lull one into a story, these did. Reminiscent of *Peace Like a River*, only different, better.

Tricia Goyer,
Author of ACFW Book of the Year winners
Night Song and *Dawn of a Thousand Nights*

Mary DeMuth's latest novel, *Daisy Chain*, is a deeply moving tale of love and loss, hope and heartache. Richly drawn characters and a starkly believable southern setting paint a landscape that this reader will not soon forget. Highly recommended.

Annette Smith,
Author *A Bigger Life*

Daisy Chain

BOOK ONE

MARY E. DeMUTH

ZONDERVAN®

ZONDERVAN.com/
AUTHORTRACKER
follow your favorite authors

ZONDERVAN

Daisy Chain
Copyright © 2009 by Mary E. DeMuth

This title is also available in a Zondervan audio edition.
Visit www.zondervan.fm.

Requests for information should be addressed to:

Zondervan, *Grand Rapids, Michigan* 49530

Library of Congress Cataloging-in-Publication Data

DeMuth, Mary E., 1967-
     Daisy chain : a novel / Mary E. DeMuth.
         p. cm. — (Defiance Texas trilogy ; bk. 1)
    ISBN 978-0-310-27836-8 (pbk.)
      1. Missing persons—Fiction. 2. Texas—Fiction. I. Title.
    PS3604.E48D35 2009
    813'.6—dc22
                                       2008045581

Published in association with the literary agency of Alive Communications, Inc., 7680 Goddard Street, Suite 200, Colorado Springs, CO 80920. www.alivecommunications.com

Interior design by Christine Orejuela-Winkelman

Printed in the United States of America

09 10 11 12 13 14 15 • 23 22 21 20 19 18 17 16 15 14 13 12 11 10 9 8 7 6 5 4 3 2 1

To T. Scat who understands Jed, and rises above.

Acknowledgments

Sophie, Aidan, and Julia, thank you for your patience during the great wet summer of 2007 for giving me the space and grace I needed to finish this book. Patrick, I appreciate your cheerleading as I follow my dream, even as we've had to adjust to a different sort of dream back here in the United States. You're a man of character, integrity, and leadership. Thank you for showing me what Jesus is all about.

Life Sentence, my sweet critique group: If I could, I'd give you Lindt chocolate every day. You've been such a blessing to me, Leslie and D'Ann. Thanks for laboring through this novel alongside me.

Andy Meisenheimer, I'm thankful we met in the ACFW hallway and that you understood my desire to write compelling, well-written fiction. Thanks for "getting" me.

Beth Jusino, you're a gem of an agent, always present, full of great guidance. Thank you for your listening ear, your wise words, and, especially, your friendship.

Rob and Ashley Eagar, thanks for reading my novels, loving them, and helping me strategize ways to get them into readers' hands. I appreciate your passion for Jesus.

Cec Murphey, thanks for believing in me in such a tangible way.

Officer Ben Woodruff, thanks for helping me figure out police procedure. I so appreciate it!

Thanks to the Walker family, whose hospitality at Sabine Creek Ranch allowed me time and space to edit this novel during the rush of the holidays.

Thank you, Susie Larson, for letting me use your ditch illustration.

Thank you, prayer team, who prayed me through this book: Kevin and Renee Bailey, Lilli Brenchley, Gahlen and Lee Ann Crawford, Jeanne Damoff, Nicky Derieux, Suzanne Deshchidn, Pamela Dowd, Colleen Eslinger, Katy and Eric Gedney, Sandi Glahn, Jack and Helen Graves, Kim Griffith, Ed and Sue Harrell, Debbie Hutchison, Cyndi Kraweitz, Pam LeTourneau, Rae McIlrath, Michael and Renee Mills, Kim Moore, Marilyn Neel, Caroline O'Neill, Kathy O'Neill, Don Pape, Jen Powell, Brandy Prince, Katy Raymond, Marcia Robbins, Darren and Holly Sapp, Tom and Holly Schmidt, Carla Smith, Erin Teske, Jim and Stacey Tomisser, Heidi VanDyken, JR and Ginger Vassar, Rod and Mary Vestal, Tracy Walker, Jodie Westfall, Denise Wilhite, Betsy Williams, Jan Winebrenner, and Liz Wolf. Your prayers, I'm convinced, will help the Jeds of the world, and those who love them, find Jesus.

Jesus, thanks for enlivening this story with scraps and tapestries of Your grace. Thank You for garlanding my head with daisy chains and singing over me.

One

DEFIANCE, TEXAS

It had been thirty roller-coaster years since Daisy Marie Chance forced fourteen-year-old Jed Pepper to fall in love with her. He'd obliged her, dizzied at the thought ever since. It had been that long before Jed could walk through the ruins of Crooked Creek Church, a butterfly flitting a prophecy he never could believe, even today. It was Daisy's singsong words that gave the butterfly its bewitching manner, those same words that strangled him with newfound love. For years, he wished he'd had an Instamatic camera to capture the moment he fell for Daisy, but then entropy would've had its way, fading and creasing Daisy's face until she'd have looked like an overloved newspaper recipe, wrinkled and unreadable.

Thing was, he could always read Daisy's face. Even then. She'd looked at him square in the eyes that day in 1977, in the exact same spot he stood now, and declared, "Your family ain't normal, Jed." And because lies came easy to him, he'd thought, of course my family's normal. Anyone with eyes could see that. Daisy said a lot of words, being a thirteen-year-old girl and all, but these didn't make much sense.

Thirty years later they did. They screamed the truth through the empty field where the church used to creak in the wind.

For a hesitant moment, enshrined in the ruins of his childhood,

Jed was fourteen again. Filled to the brim with testosterone and pestered by an orange and black tormenter and Daisy's oh-so-true words.

"Your family ain't normal, Jed."

He watched the butterfly loop above the organ, never landing, like it had a thing against church music. Or maybe dust.

He sat on a rickety pew.

"Jed?"

He clasped his hands around his ears, hoping Daisy's words would run away. He hummed "A Mighty Fortress Is Our God."

She put her nose right in front of his. He felt her breathing, smelled her Juicy Fruit breath. "You in there?"

He swatted the air between them, hoping she'd disappear. "Yeah. Quit bothering me." He looked at his watch. Six fifteen. Time to go.

"But your face." Daisy sat down a Bible's throw away.

Jed touched his swollen eye. "Yeah? So? What about it?"

"It looks like it hurts." Daisy scooted closer. She reached her arm his direction.

He inched away.

"The truth, Jed. How'd you get that shiner?"

He watched the butterfly. "I was stupid. Ran my face into a corner." Thirty seconds had ticked. The watch clicked like a stopwatch, pestering him.

"Faces don't mess with corners, Jed."

"Mine did. Chasing Sissy around the house. She said it wasn't fair because I was bigger. She tied a bandana around my head. I ran after her blind." Another well-told lie, almost as good as Hap's stories from the pulpit. Six sixteen. Time to go.

Daisy shook her head. Her long blonde braid whipped back and forth like a tire swing over a swimming hole. She hated bangs, something her mom, Miss Emory, knew but hacked away at them a few weeks ago anyway, leaving them a crooked mess.

Daisy still steamed about it, but her only protest was two yellow clips with smiling daisies pulling the jagged bangs away from her forehead.

"I love you, you know."

Jed's face warmed. "Would you quit that please? There's no room for talk like that."

"Why not? This is church, right? Aren't you supposed to say *love* in church? Besides, you know what street I live on."

Jed rolled his eyes. "Love Street."

"That's right."

"I don't see how that makes any difference."

"It makes every difference. It's destiny, what street you live on." Daisy turned away from Jed, pulled her braid to her mouth. She bit its stubbled end and groaned like she was gritting teeth. Her angry noise.

The monarch flew in circles in front of Daisy, as if it were trying to lift her mood by dancing on air. It lit upon the pew between the two of them, wings folded up toward the ceiling in prayer.

Daisy bent near the monarch, but the butterfly didn't flinch. "It means something, sure enough," she whispered.

"What's gotten into you? It's tired, that's all. And it happened to sit down right there." Jed pointed his finger at the motionless butterfly.

With one tentative hop, the monarch left the dusty pew for Jed's dirt-stained fingernail. It seemed to study his face while the sun shone through its papery wings. It flapped once and then flew clear away, out one of the abandoned church's broken stained glass windows.

They sat in pew four listening to doves calling each other.

Jed checked his watch. Nearly twenty after.

"It's a sign. Jed Pepper, you're going to change the world. You've been chosen."

"You're frustrating." Jed stood.

"Am not."

"Are too." Jed scatted the air with a wave of his hand, as if doing that would erase the words Daisy spoke, an aerial Etch A Sketch.

He walked Crooked Creek Church's middle aisle backwards, like a sinner unrepentant, while Daisy chattered away. Part of him wanted to leave her behind for good, but another part wanted to listen to her forever and a year. He'd welcome her words to fill the silence of his home.

"Hey, Jed?"

"Now what?"

"You be careful."

"I will."

"Promise?"

"Did anyone ever tell you you're a pest?"

"Mama does. Every single day. Should I add you to the list?" Her voice got that empty sound whenever she spoke of Miss Emory—a longing for something her mama couldn't or wouldn't give her.

He considered his answer. Daisy's mama scatted her like she was an interrupting fruit fly half the time. He didn't want to treat her the same. "No, never mind. Forget I said it."

"I'm a good forgetter." She smiled.

He couldn't help but smile in return. "I gotta go." If he ran, he'd make it.

Daisy stepped out into the aisle, hands on hips. "I'm going to marry you someday. You wait and see."

Jed rolled his eyes. Girls.

"I'm going to put on a long white dress and you're going to wear a fine suit. We're going to tend birds. I can't live without 'em."

A dove shot through an open window, looping frantically through the church, flying crazy-winged out where it came from in a flustering of wings against windowpane. For a moment, everything was silent. Dead quiet.

"God's been here," Daisy whispered, looking haunted-eyed at Jed.

He looked away.

She tapped him on the shoulder. "And when we're married, we're going to have six kids—all girls. Want to know their names?" This time her eyes spelled mischief.

"Not hardly."

"Petunia, Hollyhock, Primrose, Begonia, Dahlia, and Buttercup."

Jed leaned against the back pew, eyeing the door of escape. "Sounds more like a garden than a batch of kids." He knew he should leave, but Daisy held some sort of annoying girl spell over him.

"Very funny."

"I need to head home." Jed turned. He opened the back door. He'd come in the side way, through a low window, and was going to leave proper this time. Besides, it was the closest way to escape Daisy's sentences. Next thing, she'd be talking about perfume or how smooth babies' skin was or going on about the butterfly's hidden meaning. Anyone knew he wouldn't change the world. Not today at least. He'd be happy to make it through one day.

Daisy followed him. "You going to leave me here alone? I traipsed all the way from town to come here."

"It's not like we don't meet here every single day. You'll be fine. How many times have you walked home from here? A thousand? Two?"

"It's a long walk."

"For crying out loud, Daisy, this is Defiance, Texas. There's nothing to be afraid of. Besides, you've got God's eye for protection."

She looked away, didn't say a word while seconds ticked

away. She took a deep breath, then let it out. "You'll regret it." The western sun shone through the church's broken-out windows, brightening the left side of Daisy's face. She looked almost like an angel, that is if angels had braided hair and prattled on and on.

"See you later," he called over his shoulder.

Jed shut the door, knowing Daisy preferred crawling out of the church like a fugitive. Ever since she read a book about Anne who holed up from Nazis, she'd taken to hiding and sneaking. He tied baler twine around the doorknob and a piece of wood sticking out from the doorframe, securing the door.

He faced his world in that moment, let its significance and fury sink into his heart. Would he change the world? Hard to say.

Two

Jed sprinted the first part of the field in front of Crooked Creek Church. He didn't look back, but his mind kept hearing Daisy's singsong words to the rhythm of his feet to the earth. He slowed until he stood at the end of the field, out of eyeshot from the church. He panted several breaths, letting his watch tick away his tardiness. He was late. In the distance he heard Sissy's holler.

Two voices tugged at him. Daisy's plea and Sissy's calling. Heeding one, he skirted the woods, ran behind Ethrea Ree's house and prepared to hurdle his back gate, but Sissy jumped in front of him behind their shed.

Jed jumped back. "You scared me to death."

She pulled a thin finger to her mouth, shushing him. "He's mad," she whispered. Her eyes seemed bigger tonight, her irises like little globes in a sea of paste, her face the color of Wonder Bread.

He looked behind him toward the church, Daisy's voice still pestering his head. "I left Daisy to walk home on her own. I should go back. Check on her." He turned to leave.

She grabbed him with spindly fingers. "Stop it, Jed. Stay. Please stay."

A perfect S. All those S words would've been difficult to say for someone who lisped, which people said Sissy did. For the life of him, he never heard Sissy's th's. She'd been called Thithy at school by bullies Jed promptly tanned.

"Listen, Sissy. I'm already late. Already in trouble. I may as well make sure she made it home safe." Jed looked at his little sister. She had a don't-you-dare-leave-me look in her eyes, a mixture of fear and anger. "Don't worry, Sissy, I'll be fine. You understand, don't you?"

A tear licked her pale cheek. "I need you here." She looked toward the back door.

Jed swallowed. He understood her face. He shook his head of the implications, then patted Sissy's head. "I'll be back quick. I promise. Pretend you never saw me."

"Wait." She snuck around to the shed's front, opened the door, rummaged around, and came back with a flashlight. "To keep you safe." A high-pitched whistle screamed through the evening air—their father's call to dinner, come hell or high water. Sissy begged with her eyes, but Jed looked away.

"It's not even dark. I'll be home in a snap."

Glancing back at the shed, Jed ran straight into Ethrea Ree's giant rosebush. A thorn scraped his cheek. He wiped away blood with the back of his hand, licking it clean. He read somewhere that warriors grew stronger when they drank their own wounds—and Lord knew, he needed strength.

Facing the bush, Jed spied clean cuts where the neighbor's roses had been given a haircut. Mama didn't garden; she pruned flowers from other folks in the neighborhood, being particularly smitten with Ethrea Ree's tangle of roses.

There were two ways Jed could get back to his and Daisy's daily meeting spot—through the open field directly south of the old church or straight down Crooked Creek, a gully usually baked dry by the sun, through the woods flanking the western side of the church. Jed chose the gully; its smoother bottom was easier to navigate than the potholed field.

There were two Defiances—the modern one west of Forest

Lane, built in the fifties, and Old Defiance that burned to the ground. His home, built after the fires, straddled the two worlds, east of Forest Lane on a country road running east and west called Dyer Lane. The only thing that didn't burn was Crooked Creek Church. The parishioners reasoned saving the church from the licks of flame was God's doing, though they abandoned it soon after when their new church with its pointy steeple and red bricks was erected in town.

Jed and Daisy spent most of their spare time uncovering relics from Old Defiance. They plundered rusted tools, old fixtures, nail files, burned-but-not-broken toys from the vine-encased ruins. The best of their finds they cataloged in hideouts in the woods between both worlds—Old Defiance and New, creating their own Defiance from the ruins of the charred one. Daisy called them both Town Archaeologists. But even Daisy, brave as she was, wouldn't do a dig in what she called the Haunted Forest, south of the new downtown, which was fine by Jed—that overgrown woods gave him the willies.

Daisy'd often sent him on what she called "treasure hunts," without maps or written clues. Instead, she'd mark a trail with silly objects until he happened on the treasure. Once it was Cheerios, paced about ten feet apart, that led him to another one of their hideouts, a series of logs that made a makeshift picnic table, where Daisy awaited him with two Cool Whip containers, two wooden spoons—the kind that came with cups of ice cream at school—a small container of warm milk, and a box of half-eaten cereal. "Well done, Jed Pepper," she'd said. "But you could've come quicker so the milk didn't sour."

Sometimes Jed wondered why they'd spent so much time digging up the past, but the diversion of it all kept his mind away from things he'd rather not think about. Daisy too. Playing house with burned remains was easier than living in his own house that hadn't been licked by fire, least not the burning kind.

Jed looked at his watch. It'd been over an hour since he left Daisy; she was probably already home eating fried chicken and peach pie, and here he was being a worrywart.

He broke through the woods and crossed the field until the old Crooked Creek Church stood tall, directly in front of him. Something about the place didn't look right, but he couldn't put his finger on it. The quiet night started to panic him, but he shrugged it off, making himself take action, be a man. He mounted the stairs and walked through the church's open door. The evening cast long, uneven shadows into the church like misshapen skyscrapers.

"Daisy? You here?"

Jed's voice echoed off the walls. A tired fly looped nearby, humming through the eerie silence. A crow cawed good night from outside. Jed wiped sweat from his forehead, forgetting his eye. He hollered when he touched it. "Daisy?"

He turned to leave and tripped over a shoe.

Daisy's shoe.

Jed picked it up, examined it. It was Daisy's all right. Dirty tennis shoe with white laces. Scuffed at the toe. He looked for its companion, but found nothing. "Daisy? Is this some sort of joke? What'd you leave a shoe for?" His voice sounded small. Jed swallowed. He looked back toward the entrance.

The doorway looked like a mouth hollering—wide and open.

Jed ran toward it, all the while wondering what its gaping meant. Hadn't he just walked through it? Daisy never used the door, said it was for folks without imagination. "Daisy? This isn't funny. You trying to spook me?"

Jed examined the door, trying to remember how he'd secured it. He held the makeshift latch in his hands, hoping it'd remind him. When he left Daisy, he'd opened the door from the inside—that, he knew. He closed it while she chattered. He remembered hearing the door shut against the frame. Then the twine.

Jed let out a shout. Like a slow-motion cartoon, he watched himself take the dangling twine and secure it across the door, shutting Daisy inside Crooked Creek Church. The only way the door could've been opened was if someone from the outside untied it.

Three

D aisy! Daisy!"
      Shoe in hand, Jed scampered down the church's rickety stairs. The field before him, the woods to his right, he made a choice, knowing her house was on the other side of the forest. He ran wildly toward the woods, hoping his feet touched her barefoot prints, trying to convince himself this was one of her spy games. Jed picked his way through the pine forest, leaped across the Crooked Creek gully, and didn't stop until he reached the road leading to Defiance and Daisy's home a block ahead of him. If he turned right, he'd head right to the rendering plant. He looked down at the gravel road.

Daisy'd constantly lamented her tender feet, how she could barely stand to walk barefoot on grass. But gravel?

Jed walked more deliberately now. He wondered if he should double back and call her name near the church again, but something kept him walking toward New Defiance. With every step, he reasoned her home. Prayed her there. Pictured her sitting behind her front window drinking a Coke, wearing one shoe and a wicked smile. "I hopped all the way home to get a rise out of you," he could almost hear her say. "I knew you'd follow me."

But with each step, his throat felt tighter. A gang of lightning bugs swirled around him in a lazy dance, ghost-lighting the street. The humid air, though cooled by the setting sun, choked him. He felt its wet warmth tickling the back of his throat. He coughed.

Daisy's words pounded his head. "It's a long walk." The statement sounded haunting, a hollow phantom of a voice, as his feet crushed gravel beneath his feet. He usually walked her home. Usually. Mostly.

The woods behind him a hundred or so feet, the road now turned to pavement. He focused on the streetlight near Daisy's house. Almost there.

"Daisy? You here? I swear if you run out from the bushes, I'll kill you. This isn't funny."

A dog barked. Jed jumped out of his skin. With the next step, Jed's left foot rose gently. He stopped, bent close to the street and touched something soft. He lifted it to his face. A sock. Daisies circled its ankle—Daisy's sock.

"Daisy Marie Chance, you come out now." Jed smiled. It was obviously another one of Daisy's crazy treasure hunts. He let out a breath.

Jed walked farther, sock and shoe in hand, now letting anger sting his voice. "Come out! I figured out your little game." The hum of a mosquito answered back. He whispered a prayer heavenward then, to Jesus. Surely Jesus would hear his prayer and answer by producing Daisy—the best answer to prayer he could imagine. But his words sounded too quiet and he wondered if Jesus even heard him. Jesus stayed quiet, just like he did when the awful men questioned and accused him. Since Jed wasn't questioning or accusing, why was Jesus quiet? Why wouldn't he answer?

A breeze blew the rendering plant's smell Jed's way. He tried to hold his breath and cover his face, but the dull odor of rotting animals seeped into his T-shirt and tortured his nose. He wished Daisy didn't have to live so near this hellhole for doomed animals.

Daisy's cracker-box house spotlighted the street. Emory Chance always kept every light on in the house. Not a soul knew why, not even Daisy. Jed ran up the stairs and stood in front of the door. He squinted under the porch light. He'd always snuck around back, hoping not to mess with Miss Emory's moods.

Jed knocked. Swallowed. The air smelled like thunder, but the sky didn't rumble.

Miss Emory opened the door in a rush. Her blonde hair was the color of Daisy's, her thin face nearly identical to the contours of her daughter's. Miss Emory seldom smiled, but she did now. Jed noticed her perfectly straight teeth, the curve of her red lips upward toward the porch ceiling, though it looked more painted on than real. Like Sissy's china doll's mouth.

"Jed. Just you?"

"Ma'am?"

"Where's my girl?"

"Isn't she here?"

"No, she's with you." She erased the painted on smile, her lips setting into a thin, hard slit.

"No, ma'am, she's not."

Miss Emory put her hands on her hips. She bit her lip. She gave Jed a once-over with her eyes, spied the shoe and sock in his hands. "Those are Daisy's."

"I found them."

"Jed Pepper, don't be fooling with me. You two always hang out. You're practically the girl's brother. Last thing she told me was she was meeting you. That was hours ago. You always walk her home."

Jed looked at his feet.

"Where is she?"

"I don't know." Jed's voice squeaked.

"Why do you have her shoe?" She grabbed it.

"It was in the church."

"What church?"

"The old Crooked Creek Church." Jed pointed toward the woods where the remains of the church stood.

She grabbed Jed by the shoulders and shook him. He dropped

Daisy's sock. "This game you're playing isn't funny." She let go, then looked up and down the quiet street. "Come out, Daisy. I'm not in the mood for your little games."

In the distance between them, the air stilled. Far away, fainter than a cat's meow high in a tree, a dove mourned. Miss Emory's eyes grew large, the whites circling her irises like an ocean around an island. Jed saw fear there. He stepped back.

She picked up Daisy's sock, held it to her chest. "There's no telling where she is. But I'll say this: you're sticking to me like Elmer's until I find out."

In this moment he first felt the strangled feeling with which he was so familiar. The props? A porch ceiling that seemed to push down on Jed. Miss Emory's blood red fingernails digging into his forearm. A too-quiet swampy night. A shoe. A sock. All he wanted to do was run as Miss Emory's grip tightened. But it was her eyes that imprisoned him.

Four

After they first met, Daisy'd pulled Jed away from his mama and Sissy. She whispered, "There's no telling what you'll get with her, so it's best we keep to ourselves." And she'd shared with Jed all sorts of things about her mama that weren't too flattering—about a hidden coffee can stuffed to the brim with marijuana and rolling papers, her leaving Daisy alone at night, sometimes 'til three in the morning, how she'd yell at her during the day and stroke Daisy's hair when she thought her asleep. It made Jed uncomfortable, especially when Miss Emory looked him square in the eyes, like she knew all the secrets between Jed and Daisy and did not approve of him knowing.

Jed tried to swallow her cold down deep, tried to look the other way. He wanted to say something, anything that cut through her icy silence while they waited for the police. But she broke the spell herself, pulling out a cigarette, lighting it in one easy motion, and blowing smoke into Jed's face. It swirled between them, then haloed her head.

Sirens whined in the distance, freeing his mouth. "I gotta find her," he said. He broke from her grip, took her stairs three at a time, and crashed out her picket gate.

Jed found his feet, Miss Emory hollering behind him. "Running away? That what you're good at?"

But Jed didn't answer. His sneakers carried him toward the

woods, away from cold-faced grown-ups and panicked questions. While pavement whirred beneath him, Jed knew Hap would soon swagger up Miss Emory's steps, thanks to a pirated police radio he listened to religiously, calling himself the Protector of the People. His '52 Chevy would idle in her driveway.

At the edge of the forest, Jed sucked in five breaths. He heard the Chevy's rumbling engine in the distance and thought maybe he should return and face the consequences of not coming home for dinner. But his feet had carried him this far; no use turning back now.

Nearly nine, no stars winked at Jed as he walked farther from Miss Emory's. Tempted to turn on the flashlight still in his hand, he decided to keep it off — for now. He walked hunched in the dried creek bed in case someone happened by, all the while wishing Daisy'd pop out from a bush and holler laughter.

No hollering, though. Just the hum of the darkening night and an occasional bark from a dog far away.

In the middle of the woods, his eyes adjusted to the dark. He kept the flashlight off. His breath boomed louder than the caw of night birds overhead.

The trees stood giant-like around him, thick enough to send a shiver right through him. He jumped out of the gully, his sneakers meeting the forest floor's softer earth. The way the dirt gave underneath him shuddered through him. What if he stepped on Daisy? And what if she was—

He told himself to think her alive, not staring at the treetops with dead eyes. But his mind had already touched that place of terror and wouldn't let death go.

With every step, he remembered the bits and pieces of death he'd seen growing up. The doe whose baby scampered away after Hap's swift bullet pierced her mama's chest. Myriad armadillos on display at Roger's Five and Dime in New Defiance. Squirrel pelts laid out like casualties on a blanket in the sun at the local swap meet. His fish Goldy belly up, then swirling around and around the toilet bowl's blue-scented water. A roadkill cat, eyes bulging, mouth open, maggots entering and exiting. He could almost smell kitty's stench.

With death stuck in his mind and the darkening night reminding him of killers, Jed fingered the flashlight, clicked it.

No light. Nothing.

Was this what life would be like for him? One mishap after another, nothing ever working right?

A branch snapped.

He looked behind him, saw nothing but shadows. His heart pounded his temples.

Another noise. A footstep?

He spun around and squinted at the charcoal forest. A hint of movement to his left kept him rooted to the ground. "Anyone there?"

Silence.

Must've been a bird. Or his imagination. Swallowing a cry, he trudged forward, praying God would give him what Hap called "traveling mercies" as he hunted for Daisy.

Another branch clacked, followed by a muffled voice. Terror and glee attacked Jed at once. Daisy! It had to be Daisy!

"Boy," a man said. Nothing more, just "Boy."

Five

The first time Jed met Hixon Jones, Old Tabernacle Church throbbed to the beat of gospel music, people jumped wildly, hollering "Jesus," frenzying themselves, and Preacher Harrison'd paced and shouted the ins and outs of the Holy Spirit. The crowd brothered and sistered everyone—"Brother Jed, Sister Sissy, Sister Ouisie." Grown-ups and children alike swooned when the preacher touched their foreheads. Sissy told Jed she thought Preacher Harrison had discovered some mystical secret spot on folks' heads, that if he pressed in just the right place, he'd faint them.

In the midst of the crowd, Hixon Jones stood stick straight, an immovable tree in the wind, while others swayed and willowed and timbered around him. Sissy'd held Jed's hand. Her hand was cold; he could feel her shivers. And Hixon Jones had smiled their way, nodding to Mama. Then Jed. Then Sissy.

It was the first time the Holy Spirit freaked Jed out, but not the only time.

Mama shushed Jed. Sissy pressed in beside him. And Hap, well, he stayed home to study the Word, while Preacher Harrison hollered and whispered it. This was during Mama's quest for miracles after pacing the shores of Lake Pisgah in search of them, yet finding them terribly finicky. "I have a feeling about this meeting," she told Jed on the way to the revival. "Jesus—He's going to meet us."

When Hixon approached the pulpit, Jed's throat constricted. The swaying people stopped their swaying. The hollering people ceased to holler. The brothering and sistering stopped. Hixon muted them all. He simply stood in front of the quieting revival crowd and whispered, "Jesus."

And stepped off the stage.

It was that same voice that said "boy." Jed spun around trying to locate the voice.

"Right here, in front of you."

Hixon stood there, black as night, his teeth shining like an upside-down moon.

Jed let out the breath he'd sucked in. "Hixon! You scared me to death. What're you doing out here?"

"Looking. Just like you."

"How did you—"

"The Good Lord whispered it to me. I was fixing a roof when he told me something was wrong. When I saw the police at Daisy's—I knew." Hixon nodded, his eyes shut. But then his eyes opened enough for Jed to thank the Good Lord for the trace of light they offered. In the darkness as Hixon stood in front of him, the moon made its face known, shining a beam of blue light on the two of them through a clearing in the trees.

"You the last one to see her?" Hixon wrapped arms around himself.

Jed nodded, then swallowed. Hearing the question niggled him. He was the last person to see Daisy Marie Chance. Did the whole town know by now?

He'd heard enough sermons fly from Hap's lips about the blessings of guilt, so he knew the voice in his head was right. He should've walked her home. Like always. Should've put up with her rambling. But he didn't, and that messed up his head.

Hixon touched Jed's shoulder.

He jerked away. His other shoulder hit a nearby trunk. Jed wanted to apologize, but he couldn't. He didn't really know how.

"It's all right, Jeddy Boy. You know I won't hurt you." He stepped clear away. "You have a flashlight."

"It doesn't work."

"If you don't mind." Hixon reached through the moonlight and put a strong grip on the flashlight. He held it to his chest. "We need more light, Sweet Jesus." He shifted the dark shaft from hand to hand three times, then handed it back to Jed. "It'll work now."

Jed took it but didn't click it. All this talk of the Good Lord and Sweet Jesus jumbled his mind. Part of him wanted to fling the flashlight through the trees, but knowing how Hap would react if he lost it, he kept it close. As they walked together, he could nearly taste Hixon's judgment over his lack of faith.

You never have faith enough, Jed. Never faith enough. May as well run naked with the heathens. Never faith enough.

Real worry hit Jed like a slap from Hap's open hand. The Chevy's presence at Miss Emory's along with Jed's unforgivable dinner-skipping rushed at him all at once like a rabid dog, ripping at his insides. Hap would yell, yes. Would hate him. Would tell him he's a sorry example for Sissy. All those thoughts whistled through his head while Hixon plodded beside him.

"God never said those words," Hixon said.

Jed shook his head, scattering his father's words to the quiet night. "What?"

"Those faithless words you listen to. God never said them."

Hixon's words brought him back to Old Tabernacle, prophecies flying, folks falling down, children weeping for their sins. Since then, Hixon'd settled on Hap's church, Defiance Community Church. But he seemed to fit in better at Old Tab—a mystery Jed never unraveled.

Jed, on the other hand, didn't know what to think of Hixon. Hap told him that Hixon was a crazy coot, talking to the sky when it didn't rain and dancing under it when it did. What if Hixon didn't fix a roof and was out in the forest tonight because he had something to do with Daisy? Jed wanted to walk till the woods ended, to be clear of the underbrush so he could put his feet on wide land. So he could think straight about Hixon Jones.

The moon slipped behind a cloud. Without thinking, Jed clicked the flashlight. It shot a shaft of light through the woods, highlighting their path. Though Jed knew he should marvel at the light's miracle, he talked himself out of it by telling himself, I must've clicked it wrong the first time.

Hixon whistled "She'll be coming 'round the mountain when she comes," and a little bit of Jed's fear left. If only that song told the truth and Daisy'd jump right out and join Hixon's melody. There were no mountains in Defiance. Only a few rolling hills here and there and a man-made dome of dirt some folks had after they dug themselves an underground house. More likely, Daisy would be coming around the corner, or around the rendering plant, or around the church.

Mid-whistle, Hixon tripped end over teakettle, his body flinging forward through the inked night. Jed grabbed wildly at his arm, but missed. Hixon thudded face-first on the path. He rolled himself over, brushed leaves from his head, and smiled while Jed spotlighted him with the flashlight. A crow cawed overhead, but Jed couldn't see it.

Hixon brushed the earth from his hands and face. Spat what must've gotten into his mouth.

The smell of Defiance dirt, half mildew, half sweet, mingled with Hixon's hard-work scent, reminding Jed of what a farmer might smell like.

Hixon laughed, his teeth whiter than the moon. "That Holy Spirit! I should've listened to Him. He told me to watch my step, but did I? No. I kept on my Hixon way and tripped over God's roots." He spat again, this time near Jed's feet.

A bird flapped and fluttered on the edge of the woods. Jed jumped, his foot landing right in Hixon's spit. He nearly cursed.

Stupid bird. He wiped his feet on the forest floor, releasing its earthiness again.

Hixon walked ahead of him, lanky legs taking deliberate steps. "Maybe my falling's a sign." He looked back at Jed. "You think so?"

Jed followed. For a moment he wondered if stepping in this man's footprints would lead him down the wrong path, but he pushed the thought away.

Hixon shot a look his way. "Jed?"

"I heard you. How could falling be a sign, anyway? Seems to me God would want you upright."

Hixon kept walking.

Jed kept following with reluctant steps.

Hixon hummed something, though Jed couldn't make it out. The man stopped. He stretched his arms horizontally, making himself into a T. He sucked in a big breath through his nose like he smelled the entire forest. "I'll tell you how falling's a sign. Because God is always up to stuff." He stretched out his arms, then pointed to the sky. "Everything in life could be a kiss from God, or a little bit of direction, or his way of preventing disasters. Maybe I fell seconds before a snake got me. This side of heaven, I'll never know." Again, Hixon reached his hands to the dark sky. "Thank you, sweet Holy Spirit, for my fall. I look forward to hearing all about it when I get to heaven." He reached for Jed's shoulder, brought him in step with him side by side as he walked along. "Now, the Spirit says we need to get ourselves to church."

The Holy Spirit still freaked Jed out, especially when Hap called him the Holy Ghost. Jed's mind went to a swirling, cloudy ghost who sucked life from its victims like a blood-hungry vampire. Hearing Hixon speak as if the Holy Spirit was a fishing buddy settled him a bit.

The woods spit them out on the field before Crooked Creek Church. Stars poked themselves through the cloudy night like glitter on black construction paper. Seeing the church, its front door wide open, jellied Jed's knees. Only idiots left girls behind in an abandoned church. Idiots like him. The words played like a scratched 45 in his head. Even if he took off the needle, they taunted.

Idiots like you.

Idiots like you.

"You go on in, Jed."

The church pulled him, like a black hole collapsing on itself. Hixon stood at a distance while Jed mounted the rickety stairs. On its threshold, he smelled Daisy. Could nearly see her in the pew as he grazed the church with the flashlight. He creaked down the center aisle, each step agonizing. He stopped at their pew. Slid in. Willed Daisy back to him.

Sitting in their place, alone, made the silence roar all the louder. Shoot, he'd even tolerate her love talk and all that nonsense about their six girl-children with flower names. Anything to have her sitting next to him. Anything.

He put the flashlight down, turned it off. He spun around. Hixon stood in the doorway but didn't come closer, as if he knew Jed needed this time with Daisy's ghost.

Jed always wondered why their pew had hymnals. None of the others had them. He didn't know if Daisy scrounged up some and placed them on this row or if it was mere happenstance. She'd always made fun of the name, *Baptist Hymnal*. "Why not call it 'Songs to Sing for Jesus' for heaven's sake?" It made all the sense in the world for Daisy to say something like that, her being a singer at heart.

Jed could hear her singsong voice in his head, clear as day. He grabbed the hymnal, wanting to hold something Daisy'd touched, but it held itself to the pew. He tugged at it until it broke free. Something slapped the floor in the struggle. He reached down and picked it up.

Jed clicked the flashlight, illuminating a white book. "Dear

Diary" it read in golden letters. Daisy's diary. Jed looked left and right, like he was Anne hiding from Nazis. When he looked behind, Hixon was no longer in the doorway.

Footsteps pounded the stairs. Jed shoved the diary into a back pocket, pulled his shirt over it.

"Who's in here?" an angry voice shouted. A swath of light scanned the church as Jed stood.

Where was Hixon?

A policeman stood in the doorway. His stance looked angry, though Jed couldn't be sure because his light flashed his eyes and darkened the man's face.

"Jed?" Officer Spellman creaked up the aisle, keeping his light on Jed's face. "Dear Lord. We've been worried sick. You know your father's looking for you?"

Jed nodded. A sick feeling crept up his esophagus. "Yes, sir."

Officer Spellman stepped closer, looked him over. "It's uncanny how much you favor your daddy. Could be his twin."

Jed felt nothing. Since he was a toddler, all of Defiance told him he and Hap were spitting images of each other.

"You come with me. I'm taking you home."

At the word *home*, Jed knew one thing about the world: his life was over. Even so, he held Daisy in his back pocket. No matter what happened, he'd never let her go.

Six

They'd first met each other because Daisy's loud singing streamed through an open window as Jed walked by her house one day. Boxes were stacked taller than Jed on the porch, evidence of Defiance getting a new neighbor. Eight-year-old Jed held Mama's hand tight and Sissy held the other when they heard that voice belting "Born to Be Wild." Mama, a shy thing battling Hap's expectations to be otherwise, cleared her throat. She marched up those steps, knocked on the door, and waited. Miss Emory answered, a half-weary smile on her face.

"Who's singing?" Mama whispered. "It's so—"

"Loud?" Miss Emory let out a laugh. "It's my Daisy. Let me get her."

Jed hated girls up to that point, except Sissy, of course. But when he saw Daisy that first time, he changed his mind. Hair tangled, feet in flip-flops, she sized him up one side and down the other and said, "You and me are going to be friends. Best friends." And they were, just as she said.

That first day, after Daisy talked his ear off about her mama, they'd played king and queen with makeshift crowns Daisy made out of construction paper, glue, and glitter. She dressed him in an old robe and gave him a crape myrtle stick (with the pink flower still attached) as a scepter. Even at seven, she directed their play, commanding him to decapitate every single one of her stuffed animals. "Off with the teddy bear's head! Treachery!" she'd said.

Hap stepped through Jed's bedroom doorway, spitting words between preacher-white teeth.

Though standing, Jed suddenly felt seven inches tall, dwarfed by the man who loomed larger than Frankenstein. Used to be when Jed stood hip high to Hap, his father would place a large protective hand on his head and ruffle his hair. But no more. Not since Jed's growth spurt. Hap's anger had also grown.

Jed sat on his unmade bed, drawing an invisible line between Hap and him that he hoped would become like a castle wall.

Hap placed a hammy foot over Jed's line, looming closer. "What on God's green earth do you have to say for yourself?" How many times had Hap sneered those words?

In times like this, Jed knew whatever he said would be evidence for more beatings. So he mumbled.

"What?"

"Nothing."

Swift as a hawk in a dive, Hap's square hand slapped Jed's left cheek. "You answer when I ask you a question, you irresponsible weakling."

Jed touched his face. "Sorry, sir."

"Sorry?" Hap sucked in a breath. "Sorry? You better be sorry—missing dinner, worrying your mother sick, traipsing around Defiance after dark, sneaking here and there like Satan roaming the earth. You know what you are?" Hap didn't wait for a response. "Worthless."

The words stung him, kick-starting the mean voice in his head—one sounding just like Hap. Irresponsible. Weakling. Worthless. You'll never amount to anything. Jed believed the words as gospel truth, the words pounding Jed's head like a runner's pulse. Jed stood, mute. He took a step forward, planting his feet square with his shoulders. Go ahead and hit me again, he wanted to say. Or maybe he didn't.

Hap backed away. One step. He took several deep breaths, no doubt counting to ten. Experience told Jed that Hap counted like this to prove how difficult it was for him to tolerate Jed rather than to stop a raging temper.

Jed raised his gaze beyond Hap and settled on a picture Sissy painted for him. It hung crooked in a crude frame, a stick-skinny girl alongside a barking dog. Sissy painted a smile broader than her face, extending beyond her cheeks, which made perfect sense considering her obsession with dogs. Under the picture she'd written, "To the best brother ever." She gave it to him after he'd tackled Bobby Farmer for calling her Thithy the first time. "Your thithter's a baby," he'd lisped in mockery. "A thilly little baby." Anger'd snapped Jed into a pummeling protector — the Hulk in a boy's angry body — leveling Bobby while Sissy watched wide-eyed, not a lisp on her lips.

Quiet footsteps rapped the floor.

Sissy darted around the doorjamb, not seeming to care a bit about Hap, not worrying a thing about what he'd do. Jed's only comfort, Sissy. She grabbed him, wrapped her spindly arms around him tight, pinning his elbows to his sides. Jed wriggled her free, pulling Sissy to the new line he'd drawn in his mind — a giant's step away from Hap.

"You scared me silly," she said.

"You knew?" Hap squinted his eyes in his angry, angry face.

Sissy slinked behind Jed.

"She heard all the commotion is all." Jed held Sissy's shaking hand.

"I've had my fill of conspiracies. Had my fill. Sissy, I'll deal with you later."

Hap's words felt like a fist in Jed's diaphragm. Now his sneaking would cost Sissy something terrible.

Sissy tugged at his shirt. "You sure you're okay?"

The weight of Hap's sneer made him want to scream, "Heck,

no!" but he dared not make the night more terrible by nearly swearing. Heck was the same as hell; everyone knew that. Joy detergent awaited the tongue of anyone who dared to forget. "Yeah, I'm fine. Don't worry." He angled a get-back-to-bed look to her.

She nodded. When she'd come in, she'd run straight to Jed, nearly crashing into Hap. As she left, she slunk away, walking a wide circle around the breathing, counting man. "'Night, Jed."

"'Night, Sissy."

"You mind explaining yourself?" Hap hissed.

Jed *did* mind. His father had a superpower way of changing Jed's good, happy words into deeds of sin and devilishness. If he said anything, he'd be doomed. He could nearly feel the belt on his backside, could hear the slash as it cut the air and landed with a snap.

He didn't know why, but while crickets chirped night songs and no one said a word in the house, he remembered Jesus. His silence during His unjust questioning. Wasn't Jesus the most pure man? Quiet Jesus?

"Answer me, son." Hap backed away a step.

Jed squinted his eyes toward the floor, willing the line he'd drawn to this time keep Hap away. He didn't say a word, didn't even breathe. Like quiet Jesus. He looked up.

Jed was silent. Hap's face twitched, twisting into something Jed dreaded more than distant tornado sirens. Cold, hard, chiseled steel.

Hap stared a hole into Jed's head, like he could see his way into Jed's thoughts—X-ray thought vision like Superman. He shook his head, slow-like, his eyes mere slits. He cleared his throat. Jed coughed and glanced at his imaginary line. His eyes burned; they wanted sleep more than anything—sleep so he could dream of a different ending to Daisy's day and wake up with pebbles tickling his window and a smiling friend.

Hap turned—his hard stare turning with him, thank God.

He turned back and faced Jed again, a monster in the doorway. "Want to know what I think? I bet you had something to do with Daisy's disappearance." His voice was cold. "I aim to find out." He looked toward the backyard where a switch was probably waiting for him to find. "I aim to find out."

Seven

Conscience!" Hap preached four Sundays ago, mesmerizing the congregation with his theatrics. "Conscience is what the Good Lord gives like a present to his children. It tells you to do good. It scares you from doing bad. Ladies and gentlemen, be assured. Having a strong conscience is a good thing. The only thing more painful is if the Good Lord takes your conscience away. Next thing you know, you're a reprobate."

Jed now knew exactly what a reprobate was, knew he sometimes embodied a reprobate's life, but when he first heard it, the word *reprobate* sounded ominous, something to be pushed against, feared. At fourteen, he nursed his conscience like a dying campfire, adding sticks and leaves and stray pieces of trash to its flicker. He had to.

Hap's cruelest punishments were the quiet ones, where Jed had to guess at them for hours and hours. The waiting, the wondering, the waiting some more punished him worse than a licking. He'd rather have the belt of truth or a pruned tree branch or a metal ruler than Hap's calculated silence. Hap seemed to know this, preferring a long, slow punishment aimed at reforming Jed's wayward ways in the most excruciating manner. It was like God had handed the supreme task of maintaining Jed's conscience to Hap—and Hap took up the charge with silent joy.

Jed stretched out on his mattress, pulled the covers up. His heart felt as filthy as his feet that shed Defiance dirt on the dull sheets. No relief, only a blazing conscience and an empty, quiet room the color of thunderclouds.

He opened the window, letting in the stale wind. He silenced himself, breathing like a mouse. In the stillness, he strained to hear Daisy's voice. Her laughter. Her songs. Only doves mourned back, sad as Jed's soul. They seemed to sing "I'm sa-aad, sa-aad, sa-aad" over and over.

Jed noticed his clothes heaped on the floor. He remembered the cross look Mama aimed his way whenever he gave in to his piles, so he jumped from between his sheets and folded his clothes.

Something thudded onto the floor.

Daisy's diary.

How stupid he'd been for forgetting. He scooped up the diary, sat cross-legged on his bed, then clicked on the nightstand light. He'd listened for Daisy's voice when all along her heart spoke from the pages of her diary. Maybe, just maybe, her book held clues to her disappearance.

Jed opened it.

A pressed daisy smiled a hello. The sticky night blew out a hot breath, floating the flower to the floor like a cottonwood blossom in the wind. He put down the book, jumped off his bed, and picked it up. Examined its petals. No words. No messages from missing Daisy. He cradled the flower in his hand, like Sissy when she caught a ladybug and sang songs over it. He placed the daisy on the nightstand.

The bed welcomed him, but not nearly as much as Daisy's book. Knees tented toward the ceiling, Jed touched the first page. The very first word was his name. Followed by a warning.

"Jed, I swear I'll kick your shins something fierce if you read this. You'll be sorrier than a horse that's eaten too many green apples, I'm telling you. Still, I know you'll read it. If you've read this far, you've already decided to violate my privacy. You're out to break my heart in seventy-eight pieces, may as well make it seventy-nine. So, I'll forgive you, after I shin-kick your sorry self. I'm warning you, though. You'll marry me someday, Jed. (Quit barfing, okay?) It's your payment for reading my diary. Sincerely, Daisy."

Reading Daisy's name, her words, he could hear her voice in his tired, aching head. The way she chirped through woodsy trails and open fields of bluebonnets. How she made up lyrics about him when he pouted a foul mood, making him laugh despite his scowling ways. He could nearly smell her hair if he shut his eyes. She'd bathed in honeysuckle in late spring, rubbing the flower all over her and decorating her ear with a sprig or two. Dear God, Daisy, where'd you go off to?

Jed sucked in. Held his breath. Battled wet eyes. Crying's for sissies, he'd told Sissy last week. When he said it, he'd crumbled inside, like a paper smashed and gripped by an angry writer. He hugged Sissy tight after saying such nonsense to a girl so full of emotion she practically bubbled tears. I'm sorry, he told her. So sorry. Cry all you want.

Jed dropped to the floor and did seventy-nine push-ups. For breaking Daisy's heart. For letting her down. For becoming a reprobate. With every up, every down, he said her name in his head like a prayer.

Daisy.

Daisy.

Daisy.

Arms aching, eyes wet, all he wanted right now was to bellow and croon like a half-starved hyena. To yelp at the ceiling. To wish the ceiling would fall on him like Chicken Little predicted. The sky was falling. All around him. And Daisy wasn't there to hold it up.

Eight

The sunlight bathed Jed's eyes and he woke. Saturday.

The first thing Jed saw was the rose next to his bed, drinking from a recycled ketchup bottle, Daisy's pressed flower taking refuge under its shade. He pulled the rose out, twirled it in his hand, and then splayed the outer petals. Black words marked one petal. He pulled it free. Penned in perfect script were his mother's words: "I'm on your side." Mama'd been writing on flower petals ever since Jed turned five and ventured away from her to what she called "the wilds of kindergarten." Jed found petals in his backpack, hidden messages written on pink, lavender, pale yellow. She sometimes wrote petals to Sissy, but in all his memory, he couldn't remember her writing flower messages to Hap.

Once he asked Mama why she wrote notes on flowers.

"Nothing's permanent in this life," she'd said. "As much as I want flowers to stay pretty, I can't keep 'em that way. My writing on them is my way of keeping them alive, among other things." She'd smiled down at Jed. "Because words, they stay with a person long after a rose dies."

He thought maybe all mamas wrote messages on flowers until Timothy Taylor flat-out laughed at him when he asked which flowers his mom preferred to write on. "Don't be goofy, Jed. No one writes messages on flowers. No one. Your mama ain't normal."

Hearing those Daisy-words in his head made Jed all the more miserable. He smashed Mama's petal in his hands. The rose's crushed scent teased him, made fun of him. Told him he was a coward for leaving Daisy behind. He threw it in the wastebasket with a violence that startled him.

"Time for breakfast." Mama stood in the doorway. The morning sun dusted her in light. Angel Mama. If only she knew.

Daisy's book bore a rectangular hole into his chest. Before Jed sat up, he tucked it under the covers on his lap.

Mama brought a tray, set it at the end of his bed, and straightened his covers. Her face looked determined, the same as when she threaded a needle at dusk. Wrinkled forehead, fussy hands. She was trying to smooth over the past evening, he knew. But the twisted bedding didn't cooperate much.

He coughed. "I'm fourteen, Mama. I don't need breakfast—"

She handed him a glass of orange juice.

He took a long drink. He studied Mama's face, remembering Hap's the night before. "Do you love Hap?"

She smoothed Jed's bed covers over him, concentrating hard to remove every wrinkle. "Of course I love him. He's my husband. That's a strange question to ask."

"It's just …"

Her voice got quiet. "It's a long story. Not for today." Mama's eyes settled somewhere else. She wouldn't look at him, though Jed attempted several eye-darting gymnastics to catch even a hint of a glance. Whenever Mama went numb like that, Jed knew exactly where she was: the home she grew up in where her pearly past glimmered under an oak tree. She once told Jed she traveled there in her mind, sat in the tire swing hung from a scratchy rope, when Hap got in one of his moods. "Soothes me," she'd said.

How could Mama love someone who treated her that way?

Whose raised voice sent her to a swing under a childhood tree? The only thing he could reckon was that love was a mystery. After all, Daisy loved Miss Emory who didn't exactly treat her like a princess, who preferred drugs and men to her own daughter.

Mama shook her head, came back to Jed. She sighed. "Miss Emory's a mess, as you can imagine. I'm trying to be a good friend, but she's like a cactus—her stickers poking folks away." Mama touched Jed's forehead.

He jerked his head away. "I'm fine."

She looked out the still-open window. The sun splotched on and off her face. Peekaboo sun, Daisy called it when it played hide-and-seek behind clouds. "I'm sorry, Jed. All I can do is pray Daisy's okay."

He wanted to throw up. To spew everything terrible inside him onto his covers and then ball it up inside his sheets and incinerate it in the burn barrel.

"You hungry?" she asked.

"No."

"I made pancakes—your favorites. Shaped like the three bears."

"Mama, I don't need bears anymore."

She lifted the tray onto his thighs and set it just so. It clapped the book underneath. With a confused look, Mama moved the tray of three bears, pulled back the covers, and lifted Daisy's book from Jed's lap. "What's this?"

Jed's face grew hot—a bothersome thing his Grandma Pepper called "getting griddled."

"Is this Daisy's?"

Jed nodded.

"Why do you have it?"

"It's mine. She gave it to me."

"When?"

"For my birthday."

"Don't you think the police might need this?" Mama grabbed at her forehead. Jed could see the fight leave her.

"I don't know. Do you think so?"

Mama fluttered a hand in the air.

Jed held the book to his chest. "It's mine. Daisy said she had no money for a proper gift, so she wrapped it in funny papers and gave it to me. See here?" He covered Daisy's words with his dirty hand, his finger pointing only at his name. "It's for me."

Mama nodded. She placed the plated three bears, now cold, on Jed's lap. "Suit yourself," she said. "You need to clean your nails. A great deal of Defiance lives under there."

"I know, Mama. I will. I promise."

She stood, smoothed her pants, ran a hand through her hair. "Daisy'll be fine, Jed. I know it. I have a sense about these things." Her voice sounded far away, like a whistled wind on the outskirts of Defiance.

Jed didn't believe a word she said, but he needed her to be right. He cut off Papa Bear's head and ate it. He left Mama Bear untouched.

Nine

Mama placed bologna and cheese sandwiches on four paper plates around the kitchen table that Saturday. Hap breezed in late. He kissed Mama, patted Sissy's head, and nodded at Jed. From his briefcase, he pulled out a stack of paper.

"I've been talking to the police," he said.

"You mean Officer Spellman," Mama said.

"What's that supposed to mean?"

"Just that he's a deacon, Hap. And you shouldn't know all about a police investigation. If you ask me, he's brownnosing you."

"That's ridiculous, Ouisie. You're head is full of fluff. They're busy, as you can imagine. Interviewing folks. Creating perimeters. Organizing volunteers. Even called in the county sheriff's office." He took a bite of sandwich. "Of course I asked what I could do. Spellman gave me this." He handed a piece of paper to Jed.

On it was a smiling picture of Daisy with the word "MISSING" standing on her head like a crown. A queen's crown. He saw her again, the day they met, queenly and laughter filled.

"Jed!" Hap slammed his fist on the table.

Jed dropped the flyer.

Sissy scurried away, her sandwich untouched.

"Sorry." Jed reached to pick up the flyer, but Mama beat him to it.

"It's the sweetest picture of her, don't you think?" Mama said.

Jed nodded. Seeing Daisy's one-dimensional face plastered to paper sunk his heart. Where was she?

Hap grabbed his shoulder, held it tight. Mama put a light hand on top. Hap lifted it away, then angled a glare at Mama. She sat down and took a bite of sandwich, not saying a word. Hap looked at Jed. "You need to pay attention. These flyers are something you can do to help find Daisy, you understand? There are five hundred of them. I told Officer Spellman you'd put them up today."

"Yes, sir."

Hap stood. He shoved the last bite of sandwich in his mouth. Mayonnaise oozed out the right side. "I have to work on my sermon." He grabbed a paper napkin off the table and wiped his mouth. "You're the one who lost her; you may as well find her."

His leaving made Mama let out a breath. She cleared the table, then washed her hands. "I'm going to lay down," she told Jed.

"I hope you feel better."

Her response was a weak smile.

Sissy scooted back into the kitchen.

"I'm going with you," she said. "And I won't take no for an answer."

Much as he'd like the company, Jed had no choice but to say no.

"Yes."

"You aren't going with me."

"I am too."

"No, you're not. This is something I have to do alone. Hap even said so."

"And leave me here?" She jutted out her lower lip.

Girls. Jed pushed his finger on her lip. "A dog could step on that."

"If only," she said. Sissy was made for dogs, like God punched a dog-shaped hole right in the center of her heart.

"Listen, Sissy. I gotta do what I gotta do. You understand?"

She pulled away. "No, I don't."

"Well, you're going to have to trust me then. Can you do that?"

She turned away and stomped uncharacteristically toward the doorway. She turned back. "I'll never forgive you if you get taken, Jed Pepper. You hear me?"

Jed smiled. So that was it. All this fussing because she was scared. Truth was, she was right. He was scared out of his gourd. But if he let her know that, she'd grab onto both of his legs and never let him leave. He'd have to drag her clear across Defiance. "Yeah, I hear you. Now stay in your room and color or go outside and play in the backyard. Don't be talking to Ethrea Ree, okay?"

"But she's my friend."

Jed shook his head. "How could she be your friend? She's a mean old woman who only likes her roses and her nutty son Delmer."

"He's not nutty."

"Suit yourself. He talks to squirrels."

"So?"

"So, it's not right. Animals don't talk back."

"How do you know?"

Jed threw his arms in the air. "Sissy, listen. You remember the story, don't you? About Ethrea Ree poisoning me?"

She clapped her hands together and smiled. "Tell me again!"

"It wasn't funny."

"The way Mama tells it, it is."

Years later, Jed's children begged for the poison-berry story.
With each telling, it grew more dramatic, the stakes heightening into ridiculous hilarity.

Ethrea Ree'd sprayed bug killer all over her blackberry brambles, something he didn't realize. He ate a handful of berries.
She saw him and exploded from the house, shaking an angry fist
his way. "Jed Pepper, you're going to die," she shrieked. Mama
made him drink syrup of ipecac, causing a ruckus in his stomach
that led to throwing up purple from where he sat to kingdom
come.

"Satisfied, Sissy?"

Sissy nodded.

"I need to go. Mind your own business. Steer clear of
Hap—he's spitting angry today *and* he's finishing his sermon.
You promise me you'll keep away?"

"I'll stay away from him, sure. But I might go have me a
talk with Ethrea Ree." She darted out the door before Jed had
a chance to scold.

Sisters.

Hixon always sat around on Saturday afternoon. Always
said the church had the Sabbath wrong—that the real day
of rest was Saturday and that's what the Good Lord intended.
He kept his Saturdays sacred by reading a week's worth of papers, books from the library, and anything else he could get his
hands on, from sunup to sundown. Though reading was slow
going, Hixon read best when he said the words out loud. Today
being Hixon's Sabbath, Jed hoped to interrupt him, maybe ask
a few questions.

Running north and south through Defiance, the town council named the streets after trees or anything to do with trees:
Elm, Ash, Hemlock, Forest. Besides Main Street where the bulk

of New Defiance did business, the streets running east and west, just south of Main were holy words. Hap said the folks who rebuilt the town after the fire must've had the fear of God burned into them, naming the streets Love, Hope, and Faith. Jed wondered why such a name like Faith Road sidled up alongside Daisy's Haunted Forest. Explorer she was, he couldn't get over her insistence he stay away.

"Promise me you won't ever go in there," she warned Jed last winter.

"Why?"

"You know the woods are haunted, don't you?"

"Sure." Jed spat a long arch of spit so it hit the outskirts of the forest.

"You tempting fate?"

"Nah, just trying to get a rise out of you."

Daisy grabbed Jed's shoulders, her eyes as haunted as the woods were supposed to be. "My mama is scared to death of those woods, and she isn't scared of anything 'cept darkness at night. I'm guessing the two are connected, you hear me? Promise you'll never go in. Cross your heart."

He crossed his heart. Said, "Hope to die. Poke a needle in my eye."

Jed shrugged the memory away, but he stood a good long time on Faith, looking at those woods, wondering if he should break his pledge. He shook his head of the notion, then systematically canvassed every street, finally walking and sweating his way down Elm.

Right in the middle of the block was Hixon's house. An old washing machine sat sideways on what should've been a lawn but held more electronics than blades of grass. A squirrel, skinny as Hixon, sat on an old metal chair on the porch. He seemed to wink at Jed, begging him to come closer.

I don't care what Delmer thinks, Jed thought. Squirrels don't talk.

When Jed creaked the steps, he realized the squirrel was as still as stone. Taxidermied. Hixon had shown Jed the entire collection of snakes, squirrels, cats, armadillos, doves, and possums last winter. The menagerie lined an entire wall of Hixon's living room, on a makeshift shelf of cinder blocks and two-by-fours.

Jed remembered the willies he had when he first met Hixon's "friends."

"You have to let them dry-bake in the sun," Hixon had said. This poor squirrel, stiff and nearly saluting, was baking just right.

Jed knocked on the door. It bent inward, then outward as he knocked. "Hixon? You here?" No words came from the crooked house. Only silence, the squeak of the boards under Jed's feet. Jed sat on Hixon's porch, hearing his heartbeat in his head. Where was Hixon?

He pressed his hand against Daisy's diary, shoved down the front of his shirt. He stood, walked down Hixon's walkway, and headed back down the street. She was with him. He could nearly feel her. For her sake, and for the sake of his own investigation, he had to hide this piece of her — in their secret place.

A police car slowed beside him, then stopped. Officer Spellman got out. "Glad to see you're putting up posters. Every little bit helps." He patted Jed's shoulder, an I'm sorry in his eyes. But then his expression darkened. "Could be a kidnapper in this town. Be careful. And when you're done here, go back home."

Jed nodded.

The officer got back into his car and sped away, leaving Jed with a few flyers in one hand. What if someone had kidnapped Daisy? What if he was next? Or Sissy? Walking the streets of Defiance, ducking in and out of shade, Jed wondered what it would've been like to be the one kidnapped instead of Daisy. He turned left on Hemlock, then right on Love Street where Daisy's home stood.

Jed paced in front of her house a few times like he was picketing. The June sun beat down, piercing the air with the smell of heated animal carcasses. Why did Defiance need a rendering plant? He welcomed a warm breeze that blew the carcass smell away. He wanted to run around behind Daisy's house, pelt her window with pebbles, but the thought of doing that and not seeing her face or, worse yet, seeing Miss Emory's scowl made him turn away and head toward the woods.

Jed found their special clearing, though he could see people had trampled through. Boot prints traipsed here and there, no doubt policemen looking for Daisy. Tucked into the hollow cavity of an old log were their prizes. Jed pulled out a black trash bag, overturned it. Pieces of their friendship spilled out like tears.

Five marbles. One of them special. He didn't touch it, didn't dare. A transistor radio. A flashlight. Two plastic cups. A folded tablecloth decorated with ladybugs. Too many treasure rocks to count. A whittled stick. The last thing floated out like an autumn leaf—a picture. Daisy. Jed picked her up before she hit the dirt.

She smiled at him in fourth grade wonder. Crooked teeth. Freckles. A sideways grin—the one she wore when she dared Jed to do something that would no doubt get him in trouble. Hair not combed. Miss Emory'd never been up on grooming, at least that's what his mama had said. Told him once that she needed to go over there and teach Miss Emory a thing or two about hygiene and little girls. Maybe even give her some ribbons and spray-on No More Tangles.

Jed turned the picture over, hoping there'd be some message printed there, dotted with daisy i's and heart periods. Printed in Miss Emory's swirly print was the date 1974. Three years ago. When Daisy laughed in the forest and Jed knew where in the world she was.

He sat on a nearby log, the one they'd drug there, and looked up. They'd chosen this place because of what Daisy called "The

Cathedral of the Trees." They'd found it together a year into their friendship when Miss Emory stopped caring about where Daisy went after school and Hap gave Jed permission to play in the woods. They were nine and eight years old. When they came upon this place, Daisy said, "It's as if God wants to be worshiped here." She twirled herself on one foot, both arms wide like she was welcoming the sky to herself. "He made himself a circle of praying trees."

The circle of trees lifted their branches to the clouds. The round spot of sky looked down on Jed. The sun burned his nose.

He bent low and placed everything back in the bag, remembering the words of his father, something from Ecclesiastes about a time for scattering and a time for gathering. He'd scattered, only to gather and put away again. But not smiling Daisy. He couldn't place her back in a suffocating black plastic sack. He placed her in his shirt pocket, covering his heart with her freckles.

He opened the diary and started reading while the sun continued to singe his nose. She wrote of chores, homework, nature, and him. One entry caught his breath.

"I don't get boys. What's with them? Take Jed, for instance. He always has to win. We'll be running down a dirt road. He'll pull ahead of me and laugh. If I catch up, he gets cross. So I keep losing, even though I really want to win and rub his nose in it. That boy will be the death of me."

Jed looked behind, wondering if someone had stooped over his shoulder and read Daisy's damning words. Not a soul around. Only the short breaths of wind moving the leaves above.

Oh God. Even missing, Daisy accused. He should've stayed behind.

Oh God. Oh God.

He nearly shut the diary, but something compelled him to keep reading. Maybe it was the sunshine warming his nose.

Maybe it was the need to know more. Maybe he liked having Daisy for his very own conscience, liked her voice.

"If I could have one wish, it'd be to know my dad. To touch his face. To know his name. I want to see where I get my eyes from, because Lord knows I didn't get these peepers from my mom. Jed has his dad. Sure, he's loud and all, but at least Jed has him. Me? I'd give anything, even my arrowhead collection, to at least know my dad. God, if my dad is out there, lead me to him. I'd do anything to find him. Go anywhere. I'd even hop on a plane. I need to find him."

Jed reread the entry, his heart quickening. Daisy's desire to know her father came out now and again, but reading her words heightened Daisy's desperation. Her dad. She wanted to find her dad.

An idea fiddled with his mind. Maybe her going missing was something she planned. And Daisy's warning to Jed about leaving her behind was to cover up her dad-finding adventure. For the first time, Jed grabbed a piece of hope. Maybe Daisy wasn't missing. Maybe she was finding. Looking. Seeking. All Jed had to do was find Daisy's father and there she'd be.

He placed the diary inside the bag, rolled the plastic around itself to keep everything inside dry, and carefully put the whole package back into the log. Way back, so no one would find it. Jed ran full throttle toward town, his chest burning while he imagined Daisy's picture watching the scenery go by from his pocket. He skidded to a stop in front of her house. He no longer cared if Miss Emory would be bothered or look at him crossways. He ran up and knocked on the door. Hard.

Miss Emory appeared, eyes swollen, shoulders bent forward. "I am not taking visitors."

Jed stepped around her and walked straight into the house.

"I said, I'm not—"

"You want to find your girl or not?" Jed sat himself on the couch, a sorry-looking thing Daisy hated. The faded paisley made her angry, so she'd taken to covering it with an old quilt. Every time someone sat on it, the quilt would shift, revealing paisley all over again. Jed couldn't count how many times Daisy scolded him for pulling away the quilt.

Miss Emory shut the door and sat opposite Jed in her rocker. "Of course." Her words sounded like anger and sadness mixed, like one of Mama's Joni Mitchell records.

"Where's her dad?" Jed asked.

"What?"

"Her dad. Where is he?"

"I don't concern myself with him. Daisy doesn't even know who he is." She lit a cigarette, blew smoke toward the ceiling. "That's not your business, anyway."

"What if she's trying to find him?"

Miss Emory leaned forward. She took another long breath of the cigarette and blew it out in a steady stream, this time straight in front of her.

Jed coughed.

"I've already talked to the police, Jed. They know all about him and are following up, I'm sure. But I'll tell you this: he's not the issue. I don't even know where he lives."

"But …"

She smashed the cigarette butt into the already full ashtray and rocked, not saying a word. "Sometimes folks go missing," she said.

Jed stood, rage filling his frame. "Folks go missing? It's only been a day. Daisy's out there, somewhere. We have to find her."

"The police are doing their best."

"Are *you*?" Jed walked past her. She kept rocking.

"I'm not the one who lost her," she said, her voice dull.

Miss Emory's words attacked him, slicing his heart clear through.

First Hap, then Daisy, now Miss Emory. Sweaty fist on the

doorknob, Jed cleared his throat. "I will find her, Miss Emory. Don't you worry."

But he doubted she worried in her empty house. Not one little bit.

Ten

Once, just once, Jed had interrupted Hap's preaching practice.

Because Mama needed milk, she'd asked him to ride his bike to the church to deliver a grocery list to Hap. Jed stood behind the double doors to the sanctuary, a frightened witness to the pastor calling curses down on sinners, yelling the hell out of them, though the pews sat empty. Back and forth Hap paced, whispering, hollering, intoning Jesus' name as if he sung it. Sweat misted his forehead, but he didn't wipe it away. When Jed stepped into the center aisle, he jarred Hap's rant in mid-air—arms raised to the rafters, mouth in a perfect O. Hap lowered his hands, slapped them on his thighs. His mouth closed, lips pressed into a frown. Hap silent, Jed figured he'd sucked all the anger out of his father in that holy moment, simply by interruption.

"Oh, it's you," Hap had said. "Only you."

The screen door squeaked on its hinges, then slapped closed. Jed jumped. Was it punishment time? Surely passing out flyers wasn't it.

"I've got a job for you, son," Hap said.

Jed stiffened. "Don't you need to finish your sermon?"

"Thanks to a quiet house, it's done."

Jed wondered how his father could write a sermon when Jed's

best friend had gone missing. He must've had supernatural concentration or complete disregard. It was hard to say.

"I did what you asked. The flyers are all gone." Maybe that was enough.

"Good. Come with me out back."

Jed took a deep breath. He followed Hap, his thin-boned footprints fitting uncomfortably inside Hap's in the red sand. How many times had he walked that side path to the shed? How many beatings? Jed watched his father's broad shoulders, strong enough to carry the spiritual weight of a congregation. The world could live on those shoulders, he thought. The whole wide world. But as his father opened the shed's crooked mouth, Jed detected a slight hunch, a weariness that hadn't been there even last night.

"Time to fix a few things," he said. He pulled the long white string in the center of the shed. A bare bulb clicked on, throwing hazy light that barely reached the shed's corners.

"Like what?" Jed had prepared himself for the inevitable punishment and actually was quite relieved to know it was happening now. At least he could get it over with.

But Hap didn't pull at his belt. Instead, he grabbed something off a top shelf. "This birdhouse," he said.

"What?"

"It's Miss Emory's. I promised I'd fix it months ago."

Jed squeezed his eyes shut to adjust better to the dim light. He opened his eyes again, then touched the broken little house, felt its rough-sanded roof. And missed Daisy all over again. The Daisy who loved birds.

Loves birds. *Loves.* She *loves* birds.

Hap pulled some tools from his workbench drawer and lined them up like tick marks. Awl. Hammer. Planer. Screwdriver. Chisel. "Miss Emory, she ..."

He looked away, gripped his chin in his square right hand. He pulled fingers over the stubble; the shed being so hushed, Jed could hear the sandpaper sound. Hap's arm muscles twitched even at this small gesture, so much so that Jed despaired he'd ever be able to stand up to Hap. He'd never be stronger than Hap. Didn't know if he wanted to be.

Jed picked up the birdhouse. He could smell the cedar even though it'd been whitewashed. He turned it over. HP was carved into the bottom, his father's woodworking signature. Between the H and the P, above them, a cross stood like a steepled church. Yep, that's how Hap would do things. When Jed set it down, half the roof fell off. He winced, waiting for his father's tirade.

It never came.

Instead, Hap picked up the decapitated house and peered inside, like he half expected Daisy to be there. The man who lined up tools, who insisted on shoes off in the house, who ordered his day like he lived in the Army, the stiff must-stay-on-task-at-any-cost man slowed. And said not one word.

Jed wondered why Hap had called him in there if not to punish him. The air felt awkward; the silence, painful. "Why don't you build her a new one? This one's shot." Jed glanced at the pile of fresh wood. Surely starting something new would take less time.

"No!" Hap hammered his fist on the workbench. Dust leaped upward, easily disturbed. "No," he said again, but the room swallowed most of his voice.

"Why not?"

"Because sometimes you can't give up on things no matter how broken they are." He caressed the roof, pulled a piece of sandpaper from a shelf above him, and sanded it like it was mahogany or oak. He loved that piece of wood, loved it to death.

Jed stepped back. He'd known his father in many ways, but as the man who *gently* fixed broken things? Because they needed a chance? He was a man who beat perfection into Jed, never gently. Jed often thought his father wished him gone so he could have a new son, a better son, one who didn't make him cross or violent or loud. That's what Jed learned so long ago in the church, when he interrupted Hap's practice preaching.

Hap sanded, paying no mind to Jed, who backed toward the door. Jed inched away. Hap sanded. Once in the doorway, he debated whether he should say good-bye.

"Fixing is hard, Jed," Hap said to the birdhouse roof. "It takes more effort to fix than to make. A lot more. Mind what I say." He looked at Jed, blue eyes to blue eyes. "Someday you'll understand."

When the sunshine blinded Jed, he wondered if he'd been punished or kissed.

Eleven

Jed invited Daisy to church seemed like a hundred times, but she didn't see the need, really. "I can talk to God wherever I please," she'd said at seven. It wasn't until Miss Emory flat-out told her she couldn't go that she gave it a second thought and snuck out while her mama slept away a late night. She'd worn striped Wicked Witch of the East socks—the kind that curled underneath Dorothy's house—a jean skirt with patches, a knitted rainbow shawl from Goodwill (she told Jed which rack she found the poncho on and how much it cost), and a tie-dyed T-shirt. And cowboy boots. And gum. That girl smacked gum something fierce. Pew sitting, she didn't seem to care what God thought of her. Or others, either.

Jed wished some of Daisy had worn off on Hap, who seemed to think people's opinions of their family were as important as God's.

The first Sunday after Daisy's disappearance, the Pepper family rode in silence to church. Jed closed his eyes, sitting in the backseat, knowing every turn. Out the driveway, right on Dyer, right on Forest, left on Love near Daisy's house where they used to pick her up, left on Hemlock, right on Faith. Defiance Community Church was seven minutes away, door to door. Eight minutes if they got behind Gladys Haymaker, who drove with her eyes just above the steering wheel, slower than a meandering longhorn.

Hap shut the door to the Chevy. He straightened his shoulders, pasted on his smile, a kindly pastor who loved his family. On Sunday, Jed could count on Hap's attentiveness and patience. Hap held Mama's hand as they mounted the steps of the steepled church. Once inside, Hap picked up a stray piece of paper marring the perfectly vacuumed carpet and placed it in a waste can nearby. The family walked the quiet, empty aisle down the center of church, doing their Sunday routine. Mama picked up the bulletins on the front pew and brought them to the back to hand to the ushers who weren't yet there. Hap fussed with his Bible and notes. Sissy and Jed scanned the red velvet pews for old bulletins. Hap changed the hymn numbers on the sign to the left of the pulpit. He pulled out a hankie and dusted the organ.

Church that Sunday was a particularly solemn affair. Even Sly Owen played the organ like he performed a funeral. Mama was thankful they sang "It Is Well," though Jed didn't understand how Daisy being gone could make anyone well with their soul. The only thing that'd settle his soul was Daisy singing that song to him right now, in the flesh. Alive and loud and laughing.

Hap's fiery preaching fell flat. Jed felt it, as though God Almighty poured lukewarm invisible water on the preacher as he preached. He spoke of hope, how important it was not to lose it. He pounded the pulpit once, and even then, it didn't raise the rafters like normal. Officer Spellman, in the second pew, right-hand side, said his amens particularly loud. Mama smugged a look Hap's way. Jed knew what she thought of the officer who seemed eager to win Hap's approval.

Jed, sitting in his assigned spot, pew one, left side, fourth from the right, wanted to leave now that Hap had said his last amen and stood outside shaking folks' hands. Every Sunday morning, Hap warned him and Sissy to stay in their spots until he'd shook everyone's hand in the congregation. They couldn't even draw. "You can read the pew Bible or memorize a hymn" was Hap's Sunday lecture. So Jed and Sissy stayed put, taking turns pointing to words in the Bible, one at a time, writing their own silent stories. Today's story started, "Balaam wore a multi-colored adultery to the Temple."

Sissy giggled. Hap cleared his throat from the back of the church. She stiffened. Jed grabbed at his collar. He hated these stupid church clothes. Wished them burned. Or at least worn by Balaam.

Someone tapped Jed's shoulder. He shivered, then turned around.

Hixon. "Your daddy spoke up a storm about hope," he said.

Sissy smiled at Hixon. "Not sure if it was a storm, Mr. Hixon."

"True enough. He seemed a little sad today. Like me. I feel the mood of a place."

"You're a prophet," Sissy said.

Hixon laughed.

Jed eyed his father's place at the back of the church. Hap must've slipped away. Mama was no doubt attending to the last nursery stragglers. She could only hold babies for so long without boo-hooing about not having more, so she took to relief duty, letting the workers go home while she rocked the remainders.

"It's true. He's a prophet, Jed. Everyone says so," Sissy said.

Jed turned full around now, catching Hixon's gaze.

"*Some* say so," Hixon said, laughing.

"Hixon—he's like Jesus." Sissy looked skyward, as if Jesus would smile on an upturned face.

Hixon looked away. "I'm no Jesus. Far from it. But I do know a thing or two about hope. Your daddy talked about hope like it was all about grabbing at sand through your fingers. Maybe. But I think the problem isn't with losing hope. It's with grabbing it in the first place."

"Like with Daisy?" Jed couldn't help bringing Daisy into

their pew circle. And he couldn't help but feel a little smug about the hope he'd stashed away like treasure in his heart. Daisy had ventured on a trek to find her dad, Jed would find her, and he'd be a hero. His father would turn the corner from wishing Jed holy to knowing he was. All because of hope as real as the pew beneath him.

"I don't know," Hixon said. "Daisy's cloudy to me."

"You think she's gone forever?" Sissy's voice sounded small.

Hixon turned his hands over, palms up. Scars lined themselves up across his wrists, like Hot Wheels cars with razor tires had skidded back and forth in a ferocious race.

Sissy touched the lines, petted them. "What happened?"

"Just a time when I didn't get myself some hope," he said. "A time … a time … long ago." Hixon's eyes grazed above Jed's and settled onto the cross behind Hap's podium.

Sissy took Hixon's right hand and kissed the wrist. "I'm sorry you were hurt." She said it like a girl who knew all about hurt.

"Thanks." Hixon wiped away a tear with his left hand, while Sissy seemed to hold his soul in her small hands. To Jed, her hands seemed too trusting.

Jed couldn't look at the scars without feeling queasy inside. Hap called Hixon crazy, a bit whacked in the head, but suicide? Even allowing the word a mention in his mind terrified him. Besides, where was Hixon when Daisy went missing? Was he really fixing a roof like he said? Jed shook his head, willed some hope in himself once again. "We'll find Daisy," Jed said. "She's always playing games like this."

Hixon looked at his fingers, splayed out like starfish. "Like I said, Daisy is cloudy to me."

Because you already know what happened to her? Jed wanted to yell his thoughts, but the warmth in Hixon's eyes changed his tactic. "Where were you?"

"I told you. Helping a lady with her roof. But first I was up a tree." Hixon laughed. "Why?"

"Because . . . what? Up a tree?"

"Sometimes I can't rest proper in my house, so I climb a tree. I have a particular one, with a low-slung branch. It's out in the middle of a yellow field. The branches, they're bare naked, not a leaf at all, and the trunk is black. I reckon it was torched once, or maybe it died being left out there all alone to fend for itself."

Hixon eased his hand away from Sissy's grip.

"I have hope." Jed looked down at Hixon's hands, clasped on his lap. "Mama, she has a sixth sense. And she thinks Daisy's fine." Jed wanted his mama to be right on this one. Maybe if Mama wrote "Daisy is alive" one hundred times on one hundred rose petals, Daisy would reappear, happy, holding the hand of her father.

Hixon stretched his arms wide and rested them on the back of the pew. "Sometimes this world isn't worthy of good folks."

"What does that mean?" Jed felt panic rise in his voice. He hated when that happened. Lately, his voice teetered between a girl's squeal and a man's roar. Why'd it have to squeal right now? Jed looked up just then to see Hap standing over the trio. Hap always seemed taller when Jed sat in a pew.

"Hixon, you keeping my kids entertained while they're supposed to be reading the Good Word or memorizing hymns?" He said it with a laugh, but Jed knew better. Sounded more like a well-placed slap. Still, Jed was glad for his father right then. Hixon was a crazy, unstable loon, sure as day, and Hap had rescued him and Sissy both.

Hixon stood. He shook Hap's hand. Jed noticed, as he extended his hand, his cuff pulled away, revealing the scars.

Hap had said his own father died that way when Hap was fourteen, Jed's age. Suicide. Except with Hap's father, it was a gun. Left Hap, who everyone called Happy growing up, without a father. Hap's only reminder of his father was his '52 Chevy, bought three months before he shoved the barrel of his gun in his mouth and pulled the trigger.

Of all the ill thoughts Jed had toward Hap, he couldn't wish him dead, not for a million years. He loved his father, needed him. Even Mama loved him. He held them all together, kept them safe. Sure, he lost his temper now and again, but didn't everyone? At least Hap didn't leave for them to fend for themselves. Jed wondered what happened to Hixon to make him want to leave this earth.

Or maybe he didn't.

Maybe Hixon was crazy. Maybe he had Daisy. Crazy Daisy. Fear teased Jed's brain. Did he really know Hixon? Could he trust him? Did God really tell him to look for Daisy—or was he already in the woods when Jed saw him?

"Sorry, Pastor. Just making conversation," Hixon said.

Hap nodded. "Thank you kindly, Hixon. Now, kids, let's get on with our Sabbath."

Jed knew Hap said this to shovel a little holiness dirt onto Hixon's Saturday Sabbath belief. If there was one true thing Jed could stake a claim to in this world, it was this: Hap Pepper's view of things was spot on, never wrong, always perfect. Hixon should've kept his Sabbath to himself, that's for sure. Jed smiled at Hixon.

Hixon smiled back, but his smile looked weak and his eyes reminded Jed of a scolded dog that retrieved a faraway stick only to have the owner take the stick, drop it, and walk away.

"What was that all about?" Hap asked.

Sissy enfolded her small hand in Hap's. "Talking, that's all. Hixon gave me hope. A little bit of hope."

"You be careful of that man. He's not to be trusted."

Sissy took her hand away. She stopped and looked up at Hap. "Why not, Daddy?"

"I just know. He's a wolf, little one. Wearing sheep's clothes. You understand?"

Sissy's head nodded, but her eyes didn't seem to understand.

"You and Jed go ahead and walk on home. Your mother took the car so she could start supper. I'll follow behind in a bit."

Jed took Sissy's hand—the hand that touched Hixon's scars and held Hap's strong hands—and walked her out of the church, leaving Hap and Hixon to have their words. The preacher and the prophet.

He looked back at Hixon, knowing who would win the battle. Sometimes Hap was straight-on right. Hixon didn't know everything, did he? Daisy was fine. She was fine. And Jed aimed to find her. But when the sun sweltered Sissy's hand and they parted grip, he felt dread ice its way up his neck. Not about Hap giving Hixon a talking to, but about his friend Daisy—where she was, what she was doing, how she was doing. He hoped his hope stayed. Hoped it wouldn't erase itself from his heart like chalkboard blanked. What if he couldn't find her? What if she—

"Jed, Daisy's going to be all right, isn't she?" Sissy asked.

"Of course she is." Jed parroted Mama's words. The sun cast short shadows on Sissy and Jed as they ambled home, past peeling white picket fences, manicured lawns, old rockers on porches—the hodgepodge of Defiance, Texas. "She has to be."

Twelve

It'd taken Jed two years to get up the gumption to swim all the way out to the floating swim platform at Lake Pisgah's center. Used to be he'd get halfway and chicken out, visions of drowning and gulping too much lake or meeting slithery water moccasins turned him back every time. Sissy used to laugh at him. "Ah, c'mon, Jed," she'd say. "You made it halfway there and back. That makes the whole way. Stop chickening out!" Her fish-swimming way was the only thing she had on Jed, and she took every opportunity to taunt him about it.

Last year, he made it. Even though three-quarters of the way there, he swore a snake slimed past his leg. When he opened his eyes in the water, all he could see was dark green haze. Lord knew what lived down there ready to eat him up. "Don't turn back!" Sissy screamed. Jed pulled himself up to a breaststroke. Seeing her jump up and down like a Defiance cheerleader gave him the guts to keep at it. Plus, he wanted to finally show her.

And once he made it there, he swam to the raft every time they'd go to the lake.

Monday, in the bright morning light of the kitchen, Mama said, "We're going to the lake." She poured milk on cornflakes. "Everyone knows a body of water brings healing." Mama set her spoon down.

Jed remembered Mama's long haunts at Lake Pisgah after

her own mama died. Seemed she spent a year on Lake Pisgah's shore, never swimming, just looking. Try as he could, Jed could not imagine the muddy waters of Lake Pisgah healing anything. Cause a rash? Sure.

Even so, it didn't make sense to Jed they'd traipse to the lake when Jed knew folks had spent their Sunday afternoon hollering and hooting Daisy's name through the woods, then into the open fields beyond the outskirts of town where longhorns lazily grazed. Jed wore a hole in his already messed-up sneakers walking until his voice cracked. He'd croaked "Daisy" a hundred times. Maybe even a thousand.

"We need ourselves some peace, Jed, and I can't seem to find peace between the four walls of this house. I'll go crazy if I stay here one more minute."

Sissy came in, rubbing her eyes, hair askew. "What're we doing?"

"We're going to Lake Pisgah." Mama took a bite of cornflakes.

"Do we have to?" Sissy sat at the table. She stared at her empty bowl like she hoped it'd spontaneously erupt cereal.

Mama poured flakes into Sissy's bowl, fulfilling her wish. "Yes, we have to. I'm near sick with worry for Daisy, but if I stay here thinking about it, I'll go berserk. You don't want me crazy, do you?"

Sissy shook her head no.

Jed swallowed a bite of cereal. What if Daisy stared up blank-eyed from the bottom of Lake Pisgah? What if he brushed her cold fingers when he swam on by? He remembered her one shoe. Huffing it to the lake in one shoe didn't make sense. Course, what made sense these days? Though he'd try to convince himself Daisy was hamming it up with Pops, he couldn't help letting his mind think her a victim of terrible catastrophe: hit by a train, drowned in the lake, stolen by a madman, eaten by a crazed pack of girl-eating coyotes.

Mama lifted her cereal bowl and drank the last bits of milky flakes. She washed the bowl, set it on the dish rack to dry, and faced both of them. "So get yourselves ready, okay? We're leaving in ten minutes."

Jed grabbed his threadbare towel. Every time he fingered one of their towels, he seethed. Hap wouldn't let them buy new ones even though these barely dried off the bathwater anymore. "Thrift," Hap would say, "makes God smile." Well, God might be smiling, but if He jumped into Lake Pisgah and tried to dry off using one of the Pepper towels, He'd be drippy wet. And none too pleased.

Sissy bounced into the backseat of their brown Pinto, a funny little car compared to Hap's '52 Chevy. Jed rode in front. Mama looked over at him. "I've got a notion. You think we could kidnap Emory, help her take her mind off it?"

Jed's eyes widened at the word *kidnap*. Sometimes Mama used the wrong word. One time she went on and on about how fake people were who wore movie star sunglasses right in front of Maybelle Stuart, who wore a big honkin' pair. Maybelle never spoke to her again. Jed looked over at his mama. "I don't know."

"But the lake might help her, don't you think?"

Jed said nothing. When Mama didn't have a headache, he tried to indulge her, whatever it was she wanted. Make five dozen oatmeal cookies no one liked? Sure. Rip out all the shrubs along the west wall of the house and replant them on the east? Why not? Go to the lake when Daisy'd gone missing—take her sour-faced mother?

"Okay, Mama." But he wasn't okay.

On their quick trip to Miss Emory's they passed Crete's Car Wash, an oddly placed establishment smack dab in the middle of Forest Lane, which truly lived up to its name. There the car wash stood, forest on either side, a mishmash of cement-divided stalls, each painted a different color of the rainbow. A blue pickup faced away in the yellow stall, its bed open. A mangy brown dog sat on the opening while a cowboy-hatted man wearing too-tight jeans sprayed the dog and the truck.

Mama laughed. "I suppose that's one way to clean two dirty things with one soap wand."

"I want a dog, Mama," Sissy said. "Her greatest sorrow"—a phrase she used often after Daisy read her those girly Anne with an E books—was not owning a dog or, as she put it, a dog owning her. "Please?"

"Your father won't have it." Mama winked at Sissy through her rearview mirror.

"You winked! Now we'll get one!"

"Maybe someday."

Jed knew Sissy took those two words, *maybe someday*, right to heart, cataloging them like a librarian in the card file under dog. She would bring Mama's words back to her. No doubt about it. As sure as Dewey decimal.

Mama stopped in front of Miss Emory's house. Jed wished upon a thousand trees that Daisy'd hop-skip down those stairs. But no one came out. Mama laid on her horn, but the front door didn't move. Jed wanted to die.

"Don't you think you ought to go invite her yourself?" Jed asked. "She's your friend, after all."

"You know this car, Jed. Once it's started, it's started. If I stop it, it'll stop a good hour or so before it catches its breath. You go."

Jed hopped out and started up Daisy's stairs, dreading each step closer to Miss Emory's blank face. He knocked. He turned around. Mama motioned with her hand for him to continue. He knocked again.

Nothing. He turned toward the Pinto, relieved. But the front door creaked. He looked back.

Miss Emory stood in the doorway, her feet stuffed into pink fuzzy slippers. She wore a thin bathrobe that she pulled around herself. It hurt too much to catch Miss Emory's eyes, so he stared at the welcome mat. "Miss Emory, we were wondering—"

"She isn't here. I told the police she's not here and they keep bothering me. Reporters too."

"No, it's not that. It's—"

"And they go on and on about her living conditions. And my background. Stuff about poverty breeding this injustice. Or that we live near a rendering plant, as if where a person lives determines whether their kid is taken."

"I'm sorry, Miss Emory."

"Sure you're sorry. It's you they should be calling on. You. Not me."

Jed felt the guilt close around him like a suffocating hug by an overzealous auntie. Miss Emory continued in Jed's silence. "I did nothing wrong but love that little girl, probably too much."

Like you did when you left her alone at night?

Why was it that the one time he didn't walk Daisy home, something horrible happened, but Miss Emory'd left Daisy countless times, and nothing ever happened?

"You have something to say to me?" Miss Emory looked at Jed.

Jed knew Mama would ask whether he invited Miss Emory, so he mustered up what little courage he had left and blurted, "Would you like to come to the lake with us? Mama wanted to know."

She shook her head. "Ouisie?" She looked around Jed, looked at the car, nodded at Mama. Mama waved back.

"To get your mind off things a while," Jed said. "Mama says it's peaceful there."

"At the lake?" Miss Emory looked around Jed again. Mama beckoned. Jed backed away. He'd done his duty. Time to go.

She called behind him, "I'd like that. Let me get my towel."

Mama turned the Pinto left, now lurching and knocking, onto Hemlock, which veered onto Faith Drive, leading them out of town. From the backseat, Jed saw Miss Emory stiffen.

Mama looked in her direction. "Is this where it happened?"

Miss Emory nodded. Haunted Forest on her left, she looked out her window toward downtown Defiance.

Mama patted her leg. "I'm sorry," she said.

"Sorry, sorry ... there are never enough." Miss Emory put a quick hand on top of Mama's, then pulled it away. "Looks like it's going to be a choker today."

And that's the last anyone said until Mama pulled into Lake Pisgah's gravel parking lot. Great weeping willows arched over twenty or so parking spots. The Pinto spat each person out, one by one. Then Sissy escaped because she saw a dog, followed by Jed, who was thankful he could flee all the women.

Jed ran to the water and stopped right at the edge. In class, he'd heard there was only one real-live lake in Texas—all the others were dug, Lake Pisgah no exception. When the backhoes dug this one out, they left a few straggling trees toward the northwestern side of the lake, their stark black branches like gnarled hands ready to grab. Daisy, when she was going through her poetry phase at eight, said the limbs looked like "reminders from the grave."

"Why'd they leave the trees in?" he'd asked Hap that same year.

"Sometimes while they're digging, the lake'll fill up before they have a chance to bulldoze the trees. Like way up north near Dallas. They dug themselves a huge lake, but the spring had so much rain, the lake filled up. I hear there are a few bulldozers resting at the bottom of that lake."

Back then, when he heard the story, Jed wondered what it would be like to scuba dive there and find a bulldozer. A strange treasure indeed. "But mainly," Hap continued, "they leave a few trees in for a reason. The fish." He explained that fish like to hide themselves around tree trunks and branches and that the fishermen who helped dig the lake demanded a few trees be left behind. For habitat's sake.

Jed was glad for the fish, but it sure made for a haunted-looking lake. He took a deep breath of humidity, could nearly taste the air that smelled of honeysuckle and grease and horse poop. How could this be Mama's special healing place?

A voice sung something to his left. He spun toward the noise. "Daisy? That you?"

Only singing answered back. He trotted toward the voice, through waist-high grass that bent low near the lake. Stick-a-burs bit his legs, but still he ran. The voice didn't grow louder—or softer either. It stayed the same. "Hello? Anyone there?"

"La-la-la-la-la. Sing a song. Sing out loud. Sing out strong."

Jed spun again.

"Don't worry if it's not good enough." More singing.

"This isn't funny. Who's singing?"

"No one," came a voice.

Jed searched the grass. A head popped up. An older head. A woman, not a girl. She held a transistor radio, then clicked it off. "Got you," she said.

Got me? Jed felt like belting the lady.

Her hair was redder than a Red Delicious, more like crayon red. She walked slowly, picking over the tall grass. "I'm Muriel." She extended her hand straight in front of her, a sorry mess of a hand, crooked and bent like a bois d'arc tree at the end of its days.

Jed took her hand. Muriel. At least he could be polite. "I'm Jed."

She pumped his hand like she was thrilled to meet him, then dropped it. She smiled. "I believe you know my friend Hixon."

"I know Hixon, but he hasn't mentioned you."

"Well, he's mentioned you. Favorably, I might add." Without

moving her head, she gazed skyward. "I don't have hair any-more." She reached up, pulling at her red mop. Whisking it off, she revealed a mayonnaise white head.

Jed gasped.

"I know. It's scary."

Jed looked for Mama and Miss Emory, but a rise in the hill between the field and the lake's shore prevented him from spy-ing them. Though he hoped Daisy was safe with her daddy, truth was, everyone was a suspect. Maybe this bald woman took Daisy. If that was the case, Jed wanted to make sure Mama was nearby. "You from around here?"

"Nearly. Up the road a piece past the city limits. County Road 458. You know it?"

"No." Was Daisy there? He made himself remember the number, 458. He swallowed. They walked toward the lake.

"Is that your mama over there?"

He let out a breath. "Yep."

"You have her look." Jed thanked God for those words. All of Defiance had called him Hap's twin. But favoring mama? This woman was the first to make the connection, bless her. Bald Muriel reached down and grabbed a blanket in her wig hand. The transistor radio swung in her other hand. "I could use some company. Mind if I walk with you over there?"

"Not at all." But he did mind, a little. Okay, a lot.

But Muriel proved to be all right. She kept Mama and Miss Emory in stitches. Jed could hear laughter the whole time he and Sissy swam. Under the blazing Texas sun, Jed and Sissy laid themselves on the floating swim platform in the center of the lake.

"What're they laughing about, Jed?"

"Beats me."

"How can they laugh ... now?"

"What do you mean?"

"It doesn't make sense. Daisy's missing. How can anyone laugh?"

"Maybe folks need it." Jed could feel the sun burning his chest already. He rolled onto his belly.

"She's my friend too. She used to stand up for me at school. When I was teased. She hooked Brad Peterson's eye once. Told him not to ever call me Thithy again. I miss her." Sissy's voice sounded small, reminded Jed of when he used to give her piggybacks when she was learning to talk. "More. More. More," she used to whisper, never yell.

"I know." Jed sat up. He could see Muriel between Miss Emory and Mama. Her wig was back on and she gestured wildly.

"You going to find her?"

"I hope so," he said. He didn't want to say anything about Daisy's search for her dad. He remembered Hixon in the woods the night Daisy went missing. "Maybe Hixon took her."

"Ah, come on, Jed. Hixon? He wouldn't kick an armadillo. You know that." Sissy rolled to her side and rested her head on her hand. "He's practically Jesus."

Jed scooted to the end of the dock and dunked his feet in the water. He was hoping for a little relief, like a cool waterfall on a hot day—the kind you see on those soap commercials—but the lake water felt bathtub warm. He slipped all the way in, his elbows resting on the dock. "A good detective explores all the possibilities," he said.

"A good detective has his head on his shoulders and knows when Jesus isn't a suspect."

Jed wanted to swear. Just to shock her. But he held his tongue. "Shoot, Daisy—"

"I'm not—"

"Shut up. I know." Jed turned away as a tear slammed his cheek. Daisy had a way of leaking out of him.

"I'm sorry," Sissy said.

Jed dove, snakes be damned, and pulled himself through the water as far as he could without taking a breath. When he surfaced, he gulped air. But he wasn't halfway to the shore. He was halfway beyond the raft, almost near the haunted tree branches. How'd he get all turned around? Jed treaded water a minute, telling himself not to panic. He could swim to the branches, but the thought of fish slithering by his legs gave him the willies.

Something brushed by his left calf.

He remembered Daisy then. Maybe she'd walked to Lake Pisgah, one shoed and sweaty, and dove in. Maybe a snake did nip at her feet and bite her ankle. Maybe the poison sunk her way deep down so she couldn't breathe her way out. Maybe she laid to rest right below his kicks. Jed hollered. As loud as he could.

Sissy saw him. "What're you doing way over there?"

He felt a brush of something against his thigh. He pictured Daisy's fingernails clawing at him. Jed went under, opened his eyes, but he could see only murk. He kicked his feet, clawing his arms at the surface of the water. Head barely above, he sucked air. Panic, or was it Daisy's grasp, slipped silently around his neck, choking his breath. He wanted to yell again, but couldn't. He swallowed green. He heard Mama hollering.

Jed gargled more lake and kicked his head out of the water again. He prayed God would save him. The lake pulled him down, down, down. Closer to Daisy. The world above looked green and blurry, and for a moment, Jed wondered what dying would be like. He tried to remember everything he knew about swimming—arms across the water, head low, but it all jumbled with panic. All he could do was thrash. And pray.

But the water was winning.

Thirteen

Strong arms grabbed him from behind, lifting, lifting, lifting. He raked in another breath while the sun stole his vision. How did Sissy get so strong? And why was he so weak? An arm held him across his chest while legs beneath him kicked them both toward shore. He snorted like he was dying, stealing breaths overfast.

"Slow down your breathing, son."

Muriel?

"I got you. We're almost there."

Thank God. In the shallows, she pulled him to his feet. He gasped, spat lake water, coughed some more.

"You're fine, young man. Looks like you got in over your head." Muriel, bald and beautiful, smiled. Mama shrieked. She ran at Jed, nearly tackling him with oozing love. She fussed over him, kissed his cheeks. Sissy hugged him too, her spindly arms around his middle. Jed pushed Mama away.

"Quit messing with me."

"Jed, how will you ever forgive me?" Mama cried again, her hands blessedly away from stroking his hair to holding her face.

"Forgive you? Whatever for?"

"For never learning to swim."

Jed put a shaky hand on her shoulder. He cleared his throat.

"It all turned out fine. Don't you be worrying yourself sick. I'm fine." Jed coughed.

Miss Emory sat erect on a chair a stone's throw away. She neither smiled nor frowned—didn't seem ruffled a bit by the commotion. He wondered if she wished him drowned.

"You saved his life," Mama said to Muriel.

"He would've made it," Muriel said. "He needed a little help is all. I could see his sister diving in after him, and I knew she wasn't big enough to pull him above the water. So I did what needed to be done."

Mama stared at Muriel like she'd never met a hero. Lord knows Hap never rescued a soul, unless you counted all the sinners who walked the aisle at church. Jed coughed. Wiped his eyes. Sucked in life through his nose. In and out. Air—he would never take it for granted.

Mama nudged him. He knew that nudge. "Thanks, Miss Muriel."

"It wasn't anything, really. That's what the Good Lord put us on earth for—to help others, right? I was doing my job. Now, if you don't mind, I need to put my wig back on. I can feel the burn on my poor head already."

She walked back to Miss Emory's spot and plopped the wig on like a floppy hat. Sissy looked in her direction, eyes shaded by her hand. "Mama, what's the wig for?"

"I'm guessing it's cancer, baby."

The word stabbed Jed. It felt like Daisy's disappearance—something or someone out there that couldn't be controlled or understood or solved.

"I don't feel like swimming anymore," Sissy said. She walked toward the play area, head down. Mama looped her arm around Jed's shoulders. Jed coughed again, lake still caught in his throat. He studied Muriel under her stuck-on hair.

"Does she have long?" It was a question Jed wanted the answer to, but didn't—like wanting to know if he was going to get the racetrack he wanted for Christmas when he was eight but secretly hoping his parents wouldn't give any more clues.

Mama turned her back and pulled Jed closer. "I'm just guessing she has it. So I don't know, really."

"Why d'you suppose we've never met her before this? It's not like Defiance is a big town."

"My husband was afraid of the government," Muriel said.

Jed jumped. How'd she get here so fast?

"Mind if we sit a while? This is a long story, and ever since I got out of the hospital, I'm bone tired."

Mama gave Jed the look that said several things at once: one, do what the lady says and sit down, and two, be nice to the unstable lady. Jed sat on his threadbare towel. Mama offered Muriel their crooked lawn chair, which she took. Mama sat beside Jed. Mama looked over at Miss Emory. "Care to join us?"

"No, thanks. I'm going to take a walk." Miss Emory headed toward the trail that snaked around the lake. So much like Mama that way, haunting the lake.

Mama looked at Muriel. "Please don't feel obligated to tell your story."

"I don't feel obligated. Just liberated. I spent so many years without a voice that now that I've found mine, I can't help but prattle on and on. You tell me when I get to be too much. I tend to overwhelm people."

"I'm sure you won't. Besides, I like people telling their stories."

"Mine's complicated. I spent years hiding out in our home—no electricity, no Social Security card, no driver's license." She pointed to the parking lot. "See that little car? It's mine. I drive with a license now."

"Why didn't you have a license?" Jed asked.

"My late husband, Chuck, put the fear of Armageddon in me. Said the president was the Antichrist and that any sort of card having to do with the government would damn me to hell.

He was so afraid of unwittingly getting the mark of the beast that he grew his hair long over his forehead and got tattoos on both wrists, just in case."

"How long were you married?" Mama's face worried Jed. She looked frightened and eager at the same time.

"Twenty years. We had a little church in our house with folks living just like us, in shacks and homes on far-off-the-road properties. A tight group, that's for sure. We sang military hymns together, which felt entirely ironic considering the leader's angst toward anything governmental."

"Twenty years," Mama said.

"Those twenty sometimes felt like fifty."

Mama nodded.

"But now that I look back on them, they seem like a terrible dream that lasted a few days. That's what happens when you become free. Your old life gets farther and farther away."

"How'd you break free?" Jed asked. Mama elbowed him.

"It's okay. I don't mind talking about it." Muriel coughed. "It ended the day I found Chuck dead. You would've thought our church community would rally around me, bringing me casseroles and condolences. But you know what happened?"

Jed shook his head. "What?"

"Those folks must've been just as afraid of him as I was. Soon as he passed, they dispersed. And I was left completely alone. Without skills, electricity, identification. Sometimes without food."

"That's terrible," Mama said.

"That's reality. Church people, they're a fickle bunch if you ask me. They'll shower you with love one minute and turn their backs the next."

"So you were alone." Jed wanted to hear the rest of the story. All this rambling about church folks made him uncomfortable. After all, the Peppers were church folks.

"Completely. But you know what? That's when I started living. And I reacquainted myself with Jesus again. Chuck, bless his soul, did introduce me to Him, but Jesus had been veiled behind Chuck's doom and gloom so long, I forgot how amazing He is. So me and Jesus, we had a hoedown. Particularly after discovering Chuck's cache of cash, which helped when I needed to buy groceries."

"How'd you get to town?" Mama asked.

"Well, I drove. We had a car, just no licenses."

A dove shot through underbrush toward the sky, startling Jed. He wondered what it would be like to live with such a man, to be imprisoned like that. But more than that, what would it feel like to be suddenly free?

"I'll get the obvious question out in the open. Why am I bald?"

Mama shook her head. "We've just met you."

"I told you I can talk folks' ears off. Well, cancer, it talked my hair off."

"I hate cancer," Mama said.

"I do too. Especially after I felt free of so much, only to discover that terrible lump. That was a few months ago. The doctors have kept me stabbed like the pincushion of an overzealous seamstress. Funny how Chuck hated technology, and here I was hooked up to every gizmo modern medicine invented. Talk about irony."

"I'm so sorry." Mama looked at the lake, her place of peace, but her face looked like sorrow.

"It's all right," Muriel said. "I intend to leave my mark on this world. No amount of chemotherapy or radiation can take that from me. I've got a plan."

"A plan?" Jed noticed Muriel's hands. They shimmied and trembled.

"In due time, all will be revealed." Muriel coughed again, but this time her cough sounded empty and dark, like death itself.

Death stood once again, tall and proud, like a vampire between Mama, Muriel, and Jed. First Grandpa Pepper with the gun, then almost Hixon with knives or blades, then Jed's battle in the water, now Bald Muriel, a woman he barely just met, who dove in after him. Was death going to call Daisy's name? Had he already?

Jed spent a few Sissy-indulged minutes pushing her on the swing on the playground within running distance of Lake Pisgah. She'd pester him to death if he didn't give in, so instead of listening to her whining, he pushed her until she laughed and couldn't stop. "Higher! higher!" she cried.

He ran underneath her, aiming her feet at the clouds. He wanted to think he'd pushed her higher than he'd ever pushed, that his long, thin muscles were growing thick with strength, that one day all the push-ups would pay off and he could stand up to Hap, never let him touch Sissy or Mama again. But then today he nearly let water beat him, only to be saved by a bald woman with cancer.

"I'm done," Sissy said finally. "My turn to push you."

"Nah, that's okay."

"Get on and don't bellyache," she said.

So Jed did. When was the last time he'd swung? Or was it swang? He could never get that word right. Too much like swim, swam, swum. Sissy pushed him a foot or so. Jed drug his feet.

"That's not fair. You have to try."

"Do an underdog, Sissy."

"You know I can't do that."

"You can do anything you set your mind to."

"Quit Happing me." Sissy pushed Jed a few more times. He helped her a bit by pumping with his legs. She sucked in a breath, growled, and then hefted herself forward until she ran clear underneath Jed. She hollered a victory, jumping up and down. Then she ran toward Mama, who beckoned with snacks.

Jed hated to admit it, but swinging felt good. He pumped and pumped until, like Daisy, his toes touched heaven. He leaned back in the swing, watching the clouds race back and forth. He closed his eyes and let the swing rock him like a baby. He was a kid again, carefree. As the wind whooshed his face, he smiled. Maybe he should swing more often.

But as all good things were apt to do in Jed's life, the swinging motion slowed, then stopped, leaving Jed with a hollow ache. Standing up from the rubber-bottomed swing, he remembered the last time he was here.

"Swinging's God's business," Daisy'd said.

"That doesn't make a lick of sense," he'd told her.

"Of course it does." She pumped her skinny, tanned legs back and forth to the rhythm of her laughter. "When else can you touch heaven with your toes?"

Jed smiled. She had him there. He'd thrust his feet skyward, his toes practically licking the clouds.

"Bet you can't stand on it and get so high you're horizontal," Daisy dared.

"Bet I can." Jed pumped higher, longer, stronger, dwarfing Daisy's swing.

"Now stand up!"

He felt the gravity of the swing give way when he reached the top of each pump, a hiccup when he was nearly even with the top of the swing set. Swallowing, Jed let the swing continue its momentum while he crouched, then stood in the swing.

Daisy dragged her feet in the sand below, stirring up a dust cloud. She ran in front of Jed, hollering and clapping. "Now jump! Jump, Jed!"

"Are you crazy?" he asked.

"Yep. Jump!"

He wouldn't jump for Mama, not even for Sissy. He sure as heck wouldn't jump for Hap. But he would do it for Daisy—that's just how it was between them. Halfway between earth and sky, he released his grip on the chains, thrusting his feet from the swing, and hurtled through the air. Toward Daisy. Who didn't move. They collided, the two of them, in a laughing, hollering tangle, Daisy's elbow meeting Jed's left eye socket. It was the first black eye Hap didn't give him, and Jed wore it like a sacred badge.

God, how he missed Daisy, his heart black-eyed by her disappearance.

Daisy, please. Please come home.

Muriel walked Jed back to the Pinto.

"Thanks," Jed said. "You saved my life."

"On the contrary, young man. You saved mine." She laughed then. Her Ronald McDonald wig rattled on her head with each laugh.

"How so?"

"Gave me something to think on other than my sorry self. Saving folks saves folks, you know that?"

Jed nodded, but he didn't quite understand what she meant—this bald lady who had cancer. She stopped at the car and turned. Jed did too. He looked at the dead trees in the lake.

"Shorelines end," she said.

Jed thought of the lake, how its shoreline went clear around, never ending but going on forever in a circle. He hated science class when the teacher talked about eternity or math class when they discussed lines going on forever. Or that infinity sign. "This one goes clear around. It doesn't end." He didn't mean any disrespect, but what she said didn't make sense.

"That's true. But I didn't mean it that way. I meant that as you walk toward the shoreline, eventually you cross over from the shore into the water. The line between the two ends." She coughed. "And I'm afraid I'm about to step myself over the line."

He looked at her. When she told her story earlier, he thought her strong and brave. But now she seemed unsure and tired. Jed fidgeted with his hands. He turned to the car. Mama came just in time. "You ready?"

Jed nodded. He sat in the car while Muriel continued to look at the lake. He watched as Mama put an arm around her, no doubt thanking her again for rescuing him. Miss Emory stood far away, a towel dangling from her hand, her eyes scanning the field. Was she looking for Daisy?

Watching the three women, remembering the feeling of death creep up his throat, feeling the wind on the swing, Jed missed Daisy something terrible—maybe even more than Miss Emory did. He'd have shared all these things, including Bald Muriel, with Daisy at the day's end. They'd meet up at Crooked Creek Church, tell about their day, make a contest of jumping over the pews. Daisy was his best friend in the whole wide world, something the guys at school razzed him about. But he didn't care. It was true.

Sitting in a hot car, with no one but Sissy to talk to, Jed felt completely alone.

I have to find you, Daisy. Stay put, will you?

Fourteen

Truth was, without Daisy to occupy his summer days, he had nowhere to go. Hap had lined up chores a mile long. Jed mowed the grass, edged, trimmed the trees in the backyard, mopped the floor when Mama had a headache, cleaned his room, did more and more push-ups, cleaned under his bed, and once made the ultimate sacrifice of helping to fix dinner. What more? All this he did without a word about Daisy. The police were treating it like a kidnapping gone wrong. He hoped it wasn't true, hoped Daisy was having herself a tea party with her dad somewhere.

When Hap heard Mama talk about Muriel, he slammed the Bible on the kitchen table. "Ouisie, for crying out loud!"

She crossed her arms, a bit of fight still left. "No need to slam the Word."

Jed ducked into the hallway. He told himself he was being wise in doing so, but his stupid conscience just threw the word *coward* his way.

"She's a Catholic, Ouisie."

"And I'm a Protestant."

"She's not the proper friend to have." Hap's voice lowered, cringing Jed's insides. You'd think things would be worse with a loud voice, but Jed knew Hap's quiet voice meant violence.

"Since when is befriending a woman dying of cancer improper? Isn't that what Jesus would do?"

Jed peeked around the corner in time to see Hap step closer to Mama.

"Jesus kept his doctrine pure." He grabbed both of Mama's wrists.

Jed took a step toward Hap. "Stop it," he said. But his voice sounded terribly small.

Hap laughed. "What's this? A boy trying to be a man? Don't make me die laughing." He turned back to Mama. "I expect you to keep your doctrine pure too. Stay away from Muriel."

Mama shook herself free. She ran around Jed, down the hallway, and out the front door, slamming it. She jerked open the door again. "I will choose my own friends," she cried, then slammed the door. Jed heard the Pinto start. Mama peeled out of the driveway like a newly licensed teenager.

Hap looked at Jed, the whites of his eyes red. It was a curious thing Jed noticed every time his father got in a fit—like he got so mad the blood vessels in his eyes burst along with his temper.

"Unsubmissive wife."

He picked up the Bible, smoothing the pages. "They even have a different Bible."

"What?"

"Those Catholics. Apostates!" he said in his sermon voice. "And they worship idols, Jed. Like Hindus. You steer clear of anything smacking of Catholics, you hear me? You keep out of Muriel's hair."

"That should be pretty easy. She has none." Jed let the words free before he evaluated them.

Hap clenched his fists. "You're a sorry excuse for a son." Hap opened his fist, then squeezed it tight. "You're not even worth the fight." He walked out the front door.

Jed looked at his hands, forced into two fists. *Coward.*

Last year Jed read all the tracts Hap had given him; actually he was forced to memorize some of them. "The Roman

Road." "The Four Spiritual Laws." Thankfully, he didn't have to memorize the Catholic tract. He could barely remember what it said other than no one should be called father and that's what the Pope was called. Holy Father, or something like that. He didn't know what all the fuss was about, even dared to say so once—words that sent Hap into a fury. What was it about Catholics that bugged Hap so much? Jed left the living room, hoping Sissy hadn't heard all the commotion.

A week went by, but no Daisy. Officer Spellman came to the house twice, asking Jed more and more questions—most of which he couldn't answer. The officer seemed to have aged a year for every day Daisy'd gone missing. On his second visit, Officer Spellman pulled Hap aside on the porch while Jed listened, crouched under the front room window.

"Other than the shoe and sock and what your son saw, we've got nothing." The officer let out a long breath.

"Fingerprints?"

"You know I can't disclose that."

"It seems like you're asking my advice," Hap said. "How can I give it if you keep me in the dark?"

Officer Spellman must've stood because Jed heard the porch boards creak. "We're looking for her father," he said. "That's our best lead, and so far, we've got nothing."

Hap always said, "If it's almost wrong, it's wrong." Jed was about to do an almost wrong. And he couldn't tell a soul. He would've told Daisy, of course, but she wasn't here, and anyway, she was the reason for all the secrecy.

After overhearing Officer Spellman, Jed spent the rest of the day in the woods reading Daisy's journal, taking notes about her father. Name? David. Last name? Unknown. Daisy was born in Tyler, Texas. She'd looked for her birth certificate but couldn't find it.

"David's out there," she wrote, "and I'm guessing Tyler holds the answer. Maybe the hospital has a record of him. I have to get there, but how? My mama hates Tyler, says it's too far away and very expensive. It's where the richies go. I'm saving my pennies and nickels. Maybe I'll con Jed into going with me."

Well, she did con him. Only not the way she thought.

This morning, on a honeysuckle leaf, Mama wrote, "This is your day," real small. He hoped Mama was right. His day. His day to find David and Daisy. Jed felt his pocket. Inside was a wad of dollars he'd saved up.

Part of him wondered if taking this into his own hands was the right thing to do. He promised himself this one shot — if it didn't work out, he'd give up and let the police know everything. It was his fault Daisy was gone, his fault he didn't walk her home, so it was up to him to fix it. If he could.

Jed tiptoed through the house, hoping not to rouse a soul. He shut the back screen door carefully, wanting to skedaddle without an adult's voice hammering after him. 'Specially not Hap's.

"Jed? That you?"

Hap. Jed turned. He pasted a smile on his face. His innocent face.

"Hold on a minute, son. I'll be right back."

Jed had hoped if he had to say the lie out loud, it'd be Mama he'd breathe it to, not Hap. He sucked in a breath. Hap returned. He stood tall in the doorway behind the screen door.

"Where're you going?"

Jed looked away, toward Defiance's center. "I figured I could ask Miss Emory if she needed things done. I already did my chores, sir."

"Why don't you take her the birdhouse?"

Jed had nothing to do but to nod. Though his day of lies was jam-packed, he figured he could cram in delivering the birdhouse. "Sure," he breezed, as if it'd be no big earwig — a phrase he learned from Grandma Pepper.

"Great. Here you go." Hap snuck around the screen, not letting bugs into the house, and handed Jed a whitewashed birdhouse.

"You re-painted it."

"It deserved some paint," Hap said. He slipped back indoors. Jed could hear Hap's footsteps pound the house. He turned the birdhouse in his hands, marveling at what his father had done. He'd taken a broken, shoddy house—a lean-to in the bird world—and made it a mansion, the kind that welcomed company. Important company, like the bird mayor.

Jed came to himself, realized he hadn't much time. He tucked the white house under his arm and ran clear to Miss Emory's. Breathless, he knocked on the door. He set the birdhouse down and ran away. He heard the door open but didn't bother to turn back. He had more important things to do.

He caught his breath at the town's edge. He knew his armpits smelled to high heaven, but what could he do? He had to wear his shirt; it was part of the plan. A shirtless boy could go nowhere important. Like on Sundays when the boys had to wear long pants, even in summertime. When the potluck ladies milled around under a shade tree, the boys raced under the Defiance sun, ending up with a severe case of "swamp bottom." With all this running, Jed had swamp bottom, swamp belly, swamp knees, swamp head.

Defiance, according to Mayor Haskell, defied all the other Texas towns. Where they had squares and centers and big, fat courthouses, Defiance had one road where shops and banks lined up next to each other like the Lego cities Jed made—smacked up against each other, each touching the sidewalk at the same place. Those city planners in the fifties must've liked straight lines, hated squares.

It was hard to say what the center of the street was, though Pete's Gas seemed to be smack dab in the middle, its old-fashioned pumps set a ways back from the road, breaking up the same-fronted stores.

The sidewalks buckled a bit. Weeds grew through the seams. Jed picked his way down Main Street. Every time he heard a car, he ducked into a doorway. Hap seemed to know every-thing—like God. What was that word Hap used? Omniscient? Or was it omnipresent? Hap'd quizzed him on both last March, but he couldn't remember. Why was it he could remember all the books of the Bible and not those two words? Didn't mat-ter what he remembered anyway. Hap only seemed concerned about what he didn't know.

When Jed reached Pete's Gas, he fished in his pocket and pulled out his wad of dollars. A woman he didn't know manned the cash register. A hot fan blew greasy air all around her, while her black hair stayed plastered to her head. How did that work?

"I'd like a bus ticket, please."

The glue-haired lady smacked her gum. "Where?"

"Tyler."

She looked at Jed, a mean streak behind her eyes. "Why there? It's pretty far."

Jed hadn't counted on questions. Everything depended on his carefully plotted plan. What was it she asked?

"Boy, what're you doing going to Tyler?" Her voice boomed.

Jed looked around, his heart beating faster. "To buy a gift for my dad."

She rolled her eyes. "It's not fair." She picked something on her chin. "I never get to go anywhere, let alone the big city. You going to Penney's?"

"No, to a hardware store." Jed worried two things: one—why was it becoming so easy to lie; two—would he miss the bus?

The lady fished through her drawer. "One dollar fifty," she

said. She handed him a ticket. "Wait for it out by the pumps. If Garland doesn't see someone out there, he drives on by."

Jed nodded and took the ticket. He didn't want to wait out by the road where all of Defiance would see him. How could he look invisible next to the regular gasoline pump? Someone would see him. The pavement radiated heat, and Jed started sweating all over again.

He prayed.

I gotta find Daisy and this is the only way I know how, God. I know you're on Hap's side, listening to his prayers, him being a preacher. I don't quite know how this works. What if I pray something different from Hap? How do You answer both prayers at once? Do You play favorites? Well, I'll give You my list. Please don't let anyone see me leave town. Have Miss Emory keep her mouth shut. And in Tyler, help me to find Daisy and her dad. I need Your help.

For the next five minutes, Jed's heart beat rock and roll in his chest. No one walked by. No cars passed either. Jed had read about all the miracles in the Bible, even reenacted the falling walls of Jericho with cardboard boxes, but when God so quickly and miraculously answered his prayer, he thought maybe there was something to this God.

That is, until he saw the '52 Chevy at the end of Main, plodding its way toward him.

Fifteen

Where could he go? The bus was right behind the Chevy. If he ran back inside, he'd waste all that money and risk never finding Daisy, but he'd be saved from his father. If he stayed by the pump, he'd have to face Hap.

Heart catapulting in his chest, he stood. Strong. Afraid.

But as the car neared, he chickened out. Ran into the station, back to the black-haired clerk.

"What're you doing back here?"

Jed shushed her.

She made a face.

The car stopped at the gas station, right at the pump where Jed had stood.

Hap got out.

Jed looked around wildly. Only one door. Would the woman take pity on him? Shelter him behind her desk? Jed backed himself against the wall, now barely visible to the street.

The bus bellowed by.

"What's gotten into you? Your bus just went by." Smack, smack, smack echoed her gum.

"That's my—"

Hap opened the door.

"Your what? That's your what?" The woman smiled at Jed, nodded at Hap.

Hap looked to his left, leveling surprised, then angry eyes on Jed.

"This isn't Miss Emory's now, is it?"

He turned to the clerk who, by some small miracle, stopped smacking her gum. "This here is my son. Care to tell me what you're doing here with him?"

Jed's chest hurt from holding his breath prisoner so long. How long had he held it? He felt the same as when he nearly drowned in Lake Pisgah — panicked, dying, grabbing for air. He sensed the tiniest bit of alarm in his father's voice. Maybe he thought this woman was a kidnapper.

Oh, please, let him think that, Jed prayed. God, if You're there, make him think that.

"Nothing, sir. Nothing at all. He came in here and bought a bus ticket to Tyler."

His life was over.

Hap threw a five on the counter. "For my gas," he said.

He stepped calmly toward Jed, reached out a large hand. Jed expected him to pinch the flesh between his neck and shoulder blade, but instead Hap put his arm around him. Hap led him to the car that way, pretending to be a loving father.

Hap opened the passenger door. In a flourish, he gestured Jed inside. He smiled.

He pumped regular gasoline into the Chevy — how he hated full service, said they were out to cheat you — while Jed watched the numbers flip by. Hap missed five dollars, bringing the total to $5.03. He left Jed to pay his three cents. Sweltering in the car, Jed wanted to open the door but didn't dare. Hap washed the windshield painfully slowly even though Jed couldn't see a spot on its gleaming glass.

On the way home, past graceful trees and painted houses, Hap didn't say a word. He didn't have to.

Sixteen

Mama was right when she wrote "This is your day" on the honeysuckle leaf. His day to pay the penalty for lying, stealing, and cheating under the watchful eye of the shed out back.

"Lying, son. You lied to me."

Jed nodded. Hap was right. But he didn't like it.

"Stealing too."

But the money was his, what he earned. How it could be stealing, he didn't know, but what Hap said was gospel.

"Cheating."

Did he cheat? Maybe Hap had to write so many three-point sermons he'd locked himself into threes. Cheating seemed to rhyme with the other two; either that, or it sounded like a country song about a no-good husband.

A house-shaped cloud, dull and gray, erased the sun while Hap's belt bit into Jed's backside to the rhythm of a hummed song Jed didn't recognize. A hymn, maybe?

Sissy came in his room, a plastic cup of water in her hand. "Where were you going?" She closed the door behind her.

"Tyler, like Hap said."

"Why? Were you running away?" Sissy held that frightened look in her eyes. She handed the water to Jed.

"Heck no, just investigating."

"Hixon?"

"No, not Hixon."

"Then who?"

"I can't say."

Sissy sat on the bed. Tears wet her eyes and rolled down her freckled cheeks. She sucked the tears up her nose. "You better not leave me." Her voice was a breath, a whispery breath.

Jed sat up. Yowled. He stood instead. "I won't ever leave you, Sissy. It's my job to protect you."

"Your job? I don't understand, Jed."

"You wouldn't understand."

Sissy huffed in a whisper of impatience. "If it's your job to protect, Mr. Superman, then why'd you leave today?"

"I was coming back before sundown." Jed paced his room, careful to place his feet so he wouldn't make the old house's joists creak. No need to rouse Hap again. The old house protested with every footstep, so Jed had learned which joists kept quiet.

Sissy let out a sigh. She wiped her face with the back of her bony hand. "I think Daisy's gone, Jed."

Jed wheeled around, then thought the better of raising his voice. "She's not gone," he whispered. "She's fine. I know it. Mama said so last week, anyways."

"Mama's not always right about things." Sissy folded her hands between her knees.

Maybe Mama didn't always have the best judgment. "Daisy has to be okay."

"I know, but what if she's not?" Sissy startled at a branch scratching against Jed's windowpane. She settled herself. "It's just the wind," she said.

He could hear the tears in her voice. Jed reached over and put his hand on top of hers. It felt cold, small. "I don't know. I just don't know."

Footsteps rocked the hallway. Hap's.

Sissy shot a frightened look Jed's way. She stood.

The door opened. Hap filled the space. "Sissy, get out of here. Jed's on restriction."

"I just—" She lowered her eyes, then pointed to the cup of water, now on Jed's nightstand. "I thought he might be thirsty." Her voice melted away.

"Leave." Hap stepped into the room. He pointed to the doorway.

The floor squeaked under his weight. Jed winced at the noise and stood still. Hap shoved Sissy halfway across the room. She thudded headfirst into the doorjamb. The branch clacked the window again in the terrible silence. Crumpled Sissy. His sister. Lying there. Not saying a word.

Jed ran to her, tried to gather her up, but Hap stepped between them. "She'll be fine, won't you, Sissy?"

But Sissy didn't move.

Jed melted away, all the while yelling at his cowardly self in his head, as insistent as the scraping branch.

Mama's footsteps, tight-sounding on the kitchen, then hallway floor, stopped above Sissy. "Hapland James!" she shrieked. "What in God's name have you done this time?"

She bent low to Sissy. "Oh God. Oh God. She's bleeding, Hap. Bleeding!"

Sissy stirred. Flutter-opened her sky blue eyes.

"Sissy! Are you okay?" Mama cradled her, rocked her back and forth.

"Yeah, Mama. I'm okay." She looked at Hap. Fear danced in her eyes. "I just fell. Running in the house again. You know me. Silly me."

Jed tried to will Mama a backbone. Force his resolve into her by thinking, Stand up, stand up, stand up. Stand up to him. But she stayed crouched, hovering over Sissy, while her apron soaked up Sissy's blood. It all made him sick. He should be the one to stand up to Hap, not her. But he was weak, so weak. It was Jed's job to protect Sissy. Would he ever be strong enough? Or have the gumption to wear the pants in the family?

Jed couldn't see Hap's face. Was he sad that he had thrown his daughter? Angry? Lost? Hap turned on a dime, faced Jed. Then Jed knew. Anger. Nothing more. Just pure red anger.

"If I've told you once, I've told you a thousand times. Don't chase your sister!"

Blame. Jed looked south of Hap's eyes, focusing on his open mouth, the pink of his tongue, the glimmer of his gums, the silver of his fillings.

"You have nothing to say for yourself?" He shut his mouth, cutting off Jed's view of Hap's white teeth. Hap pointed to Sissy, his index finger shaking. "Now look what you've done!" He drew that same hand high above his head and swooped it down, flat palmed, onto Jed's face.

Jed reeled back, his back glancing off the corner of his bed frame. He let out a cry. He hadn't even stopped Hap's hand. If he couldn't defend himself, how could he defend the rest of the family?

"Maybe that'll teach you."

Jed pulled a hand across his mouth. Blood smeared a red line on its back. He sucked it clean until what remained was a pink haze—perfect evidence of his weakness. He looked northward, above Hap's red mouth cavity to his awful eyes.

It was then, he would say later, he finally understood his father, though he wouldn't articulate it quite that way until he'd left adolescence in the dust. Under the narrowed gaze of his father's eyes, Jed felt Hap's anger and kept it for himself. The rage that thrust Sissy into an unforgiving doorjamb took up residence behind his own eyes then. He hated his father with every string of muscle he had fought to build. Hated him.

"What do you have to say for yourself?" Hap crossed arms over his chest, like he waited for a fight.

Jed nearly spit. Nearly. He could haul off and hit Hap right now and not feel a hint of sadness about it. Hap might be the Protector of the People, but Jed could become the Defender of the Family. Should be.

But his body disobeyed. And gumption spilled out. What would it really matter if he hauled off and hit Hap? He'd just get the life beat out of him.

The room, charged with anger a minute ago, quieted itself except for the sound of a lone branch scraping against Jed's window.

Jed looked full into Hap's eyes and whispered, "Nothing."

Seventeen

Worrying about Sissy was part of Jed's penance, he knew. But it wasn't the only part. Every day he'd have to look in Miss Emory's eyes, thanks to Hap's plan for Jed. "You lied about helping Miss Emory," he said. "Well, guess what? You're fixing to turn that lie into truth. She's expecting you tomorrow. And she has a lot for you to do." Every day he'd have to hear how he'd ruined the woman's life, how he was responsible for Daisy's disappearance.

She hadn't liked him when Daisy was around, something Daisy said had to do with men. But Jed suspected it was something else—something like how he felt when his friend Timmy started spending more time with Jake Drogan. It wasn't that Jed was particularly fond of spending time with Timmy, but when Jake suddenly had Timmy's attention, Jed wanted it back for himself. That's how it was with Miss Emory. She didn't seem to want Daisy around half the time. She treated her like a nuisance, like a cricket problem in springtime. But when Daisy switched her attention to Jed, Miss Emory got that green look in her eye. She'd had green eyes ever since.

Walking up the steps to Miss Emory's home, he calmed himself with one thing: he might be able to tease out Daisy's father's full name. That thought alone delivered him to Miss Emory's front door. He knocked.

The door opened. "There you are. Your father told me you'd be here."

She handed Jed a paintbrush. "The whole house," she said. "White." She pointed to a can on the porch.

The door slammed shut. So much for conversation.

Jed grabbed the paint can and headed to the back of the house. No use starting in the front where all of Defiance could walk by and watch the poor boy doing penance by painting Miss Emory's house from gray to white. Jed hated pity.

Almost as much as he hated painting.

The next morning, Sissy pled with her eyes, then her voice while Jed was pulling on his socks to go to Miss Emory's. "Please, Jed. Please stay home. Summer's no fun without you." She rubbed her head the way Mama did when she got a headache, only this time Sissy had a reason to. The lump from Hap's flinging had turned a purpled brown.

"Stay out of Hap's way."

"How am I supposed to do that?" Sissy sat on the chair next to his desk.

Jed put his growing feet into too-small sneakers. "Play outside if he's in, but steer clear of that Ethrea Ree lady."

"Why don't you like her? On days you're not around, she's pretty friendly. Besides, she lets me weed."

"Exactly. She's after your work."

"It's better than staying here," Sissy said. "Besides, she's a widow. Doesn't the Bible say we need to help widows?"

"I don't like her."

"That's not holy, Jed Pepper. You're supposed to like widows. Even love them."

Jed ignored her. "And Delmer, well, he's—"

"He's what?"

"Unexplainable. Listen, Sissy. If Hap's outside, read a book in your room." Jed left his room, Sissy trailing behind him.

"What if I want to make cookies?"

Jed turned. "Only bake if he's at the church." Hap hated a messy kitchen.

Sissy nodded, her big watery eyes pleading *stay*.

"You'll be fine. I'll be home late afternoon. Call today cookie day, all right? I think Hap'll be gone at church most of the day." He opened the back door. "You be good, Sissy."

"I will," she said, waving a small hand.

Jed had to admit he was pretty good at painting—or at least preparing for painting. He initially figured he could pull the paint over the crackling gray. But then he remembered Hap, the way he drilled into Jed how to "do a thing." Jed found a scraper in Miss Emory's garage. For hours that morning, he scraped off paint as high as he could reach along the back of the house. With each scrape, paint floated like gray snow to the brown dirt below until the ground beneath him looked like soot. Jed said prayer after prayer for Daisy. When his arms felt shaky and hot from so much reaching, he prayed they'd grow a will, enough to stand up to Hap someday.

Jed pulled himself up on a rickety ladder braced against the house and scraped more. With each push of the metal, his prayers weakened. With each gray snowfall, he despaired even more.

Where was Daisy?

Why wouldn't she come home?

Peeling the paint suddenly became useless. He made himself finish the upper eave, then backed his way down the ladder. A rush of wind unsteadied him. He scrambled down as the ladder tumbled. It thudded on the ground, bouncing once, then settled into the ashen dust.

Miss Emory flew out the back door. "What happened?" She spoke motherly words, then threw a hand to her mouth as if she could stop her mothering from spilling out.

"I fell is all." Jed stood and dusted the paint from his pants. "I'm fine."

Miss Emory's face instantly went blank—like when Jed turned off the black and white TV before bed. From something alive to a black, dead screen—a tiny white dot the only evidence it'd been alive once. But Miss Emory didn't even have a dot. "Best get back at it, then," she said. Enough mothering.

Jed righted the ladder.

Miss Emory stepped down the stairs. She turned to examine the back of the house. "I told you to paint. Not scrape."

"I have to do a thing right." Jed smoothed his hand over the now-clean clapboards.

Miss Emory leveled her eyes at Jed. "What did you say?"

Jed squirmed. "Just that I should do this right—by scraping and priming, *then* painting."

"Do a thing." She looked at her house slippers.

Jed thought she'd stare at the ugly pink house shoes forever. She did it as if they were telling her a clue about Daisy, like she had to concentrate real hard to see it. She lifted her head, finally, and placed hands on slim hips. She looked straight at Jed. Not a blank stare this time, but a tired, helpless look. "You have your father's eyes," she said. "You're his spitting image."

Jed felt her words tear into him. Of anything someone could say to mess with him, this was the kicker. He wanted to yell at Miss Emory, tell her she was wrong, tell her it was none of her stinkin' business who he looked like or sounded like or acted like. He wanted to hurt her. Wanted it like nothing else in life. "And Daisy doesn't have your eyes. Or how would you know?" he spat.

Miss Emory gasped, clutching a pale hand to her throat. For a moment she looked stricken. She blinked away whatever emotion she felt at Jed's words and plastered on a cold, hard smile. "Yes, just like him." She turned and walked back into her gray home.

Jed grabbed the scraper and flung it to the clouds—as high as he could. It hit the apex of the garage and skidded down the tar roof, clanking onto the pavement below. He thought the flinging would stop the anger, like he could throw it clear away. But it boomeranged back at him, this time larger.

He waited for Miss Emory to come out. To yell at him. Anything. He stood there a good three minutes, but the door stayed shut. Jed's hands tingled, his insides shaking.

"Looks like you could use some help."

Jed spun around. Hixon. Dressed in ragtag overalls and a stupid smile.

Jed looked at his hands, hoping to steady them. "No. This is my job. I aim to do it."

"By throwing tools at the Good Lord in heaven?" Hixon laughed.

Jed tensed his hands into fists. Said nothing.

"God's got it all, Jeddy. He doesn't have a need for your scraper."

Jed ran at Hixon, tears stinging his eyes. Rammed right into Hixon's midsection, but Hixon held firm. Jed flailed angry arms this way and that, but Hixon stood, accepting each blow, waiting without words.

Jed kept at it. He willed his arms to work, to use the strength they'd gained from ten thousand push-ups.

Hixon stood his ground.

The sun poked its head out, warming Jed to a sweat.

"You done?"

Jed wasn't sure what he was. Done? Would he ever be done? Jed threw another punch.

Hixon caught it midair. Held his hand firm—a brown hand hugging a tight white fist. "You done?"

Jed let him have it with his left, but Hixon caught that one too. Both pathetic hands trapped, all he had left was his words. "What right do you have messing in my business, anyway?"

"You a believer?" Hixon's eyes smiled on Jed. Kept his hands for ransom.

Jed spat. "Yeah. So?"

"That's where my rights come in. We're a body, you and I. I'd say you're the fists right now, but a body has to take care of itself. I'm being your head 'cause you seem to have lost yours."

Jed struggled. But Hixon held on.

"My mama wasn't fixin' to have a baby. But I came anyways. So she rhymed me with my will: Hixon, fixin'. The Good Lord, He put me here on the earth to fix things. Fixin' Hixon. He told me to hurry myself up this morning. Told me to find Jed 'cause he sure needs some fixin'." Hixon let go of Jed's hands.

"I don't need fixin'." Jed examined the ground. Paint flecks covered a heap of scraggly flowers. He hadn't intended to dirty the flowers, but it happened anyway. Shoot. He kicked at the dust, letting the flowers shed their paint coat and their petals besides.

"We all need fixin'. I do."

"You're a grown-up. You don't need fixin'."

Hixon laughed. "Don't tell me you don't know any screwed-up grown-ups. We're all a sorry mess, one way or another."

Revelation. Jed knew prophets were all about it. Heck, there was even the whole last book of the Bible with multiheaded monsters and blood and meteors and holy-holy-holies dedicated to it. But hearing that grown-ups were a sorry mess like Jed sounded like revelation. Or confusion. If everyone was screwed up, then what was the point?

"The point is ... Jesus."

Jed shook his head. Had he said his thoughts out loud? "Jesus?"

"Jesus. He's the point. We can't do this crazy thing called life ... not without Him."

Yeah, well, Jed had himself a plan. He didn't need Jesus. He needed strength.

"You need more than strength, Jed."

Jed shook his head. "How'd you know what I was thinking?"

"I didn't. But sometimes Jesus whispers words to me."

"That's what Hap says. Says Jesus tells him things." Jed kicked at the ground. "Doesn't seem to make much difference if you ask me." But a swift punch to Hap's solar plexus would. Boy, it would.

"That's his stuff, Jed. You only need to worry about yours." Hixon stepped over to the back porch and sat down. He patted the stair next to him—an invitation.

Jed stayed where he was.

Hixon smiled. No teeth—not his laughing smile. Only a thin line turning upward toward dancing eyes. "It's like neighbors, Jed."

"Neighbors?" Suddenly Jed felt very tired. The empty space next to Hixon looked good, but pride kept him swaying on weary feet.

"Take your neighborhood, for instance. Tell me about the yards."

"Some are good. Some aren't."

"What about yours?"

Jed pictured their yard on Dyer Street—much like Miss Emory's smile. Lifeless in terms of flowers—flowers being an "idol of indulgence"—but perfectly taken care of. Usually by him. "It's fine."

Hixon nodded. "It's a fine yard. You're right. But what about next door?"

Jed remembered Ethrea Ree's yard—definitely full of life, but completely messy. Tangles of roses and flowers and grass—you couldn't see where one shrub began and another one ended. "It's crazy."

"True. Funny how both yards have the same dirt, the same grass, the same potential, but they look so different, isn't it?"

"I guess."

"God gives you your own yard, Jed. You're responsible for it. Not anyone else's. God's the gardener. He tills your soil. He plants the seeds. Waters them. But if you run around throwing weed seeds in the air, or you don't take care of what God put there, it will end up being a mess."

"I hate pulling weeds." It was the truth. Especially dandelion weeds with their long tap root and the soured milk that spilled on his hands when he broke them off at the quick.

"Me too, but it's a thing worth doing. My aunt Nellie always said, 'Never walk past a weed.'"

"Why?" Jed sat himself on the ground, cross-legged.

"Because when you walk past it, you're not pulling it. It's easier to pull little bits at a time—much harder to weed an entire yard."

"What's this have to do with Hap?"

"He has his own yard, Jed. You have yours. You don't have to have the same yard. You have a choice to let Jesus in your yard or not."

Jed sat there. He picked at the dirt, not saying a word. One thing he knew: He didn't want to become Hap. Not ever.

Hixon stood. Rubbed his head back and forth with his hands. "It sure is hot."

"Yep." Jed wondered if Miss Emory was watching or listening. He worried that she'd tell Hap how little he worked. He stood too, picked up the paint can and brush.

"I'll help," Hixon said.

"Thanks, but I only have one brush."

"Brought my own." Hixon reached into a pocket on the side of his pant leg and pulled out a brush. "Be prepared, I always say."

They dipped brushes into white paint. Jed grimaced when the paint didn't cover well. "Should be priming it," he mumbled.

The back door opened. Miss Emory stood there, hair wild as

a hay roll after a windstorm. "You better get to work, Jed Pepper." She angled a look at Hixon. "You need something?"

"Thought the boy could use some help."

"You did, did you?" Miss Emory stepped out onto the porch. Arms crossed across her chest, she sighed. "I made you lunch."

"Me?" Hixon smiled.

"Yes, you. I saw you two out here blabbering on and on. Made some egg salad sandwiches. I'm not completely uncivilized."

"No one ever said that, Miss Emory." Hixon bowed.

Miss Emory rolled her eyes. "I'll set it out here." She turned to leave.

"Miss Emory?" Jed placed his paintbrush in the can.

She turned back. "What is it?"

"Primer, ma'am. If you want this house done right, you'll need some primer first."

She stepped farther out on the porch, her feet still encased by slippers. "Do I look like I'm made of money?"

"No, ma'am, but we have some leftover primer. I can see if my father will let me use it."

Miss Emory smiled. But she didn't look in Jed's eyes. More like the top of his head or the horizon beyond. "Good luck asking for that," she said as she went inside.

Eighteen

Jed had taken to painting barefooted. In the Defiance heat, shoelessness didn't really make sense, but neither did Daisy not calling or letting Jed know she was fine, hanging out with David the Dad, eating snow cones, red licorice, and Cracker Jacks as they caught up on old times. How dare Daisy not let him—her best friend and apparently her groom-to-be—know where she was and how she was doing. It made Jed want to spit. He took off his shoes the day after he started on Miss Emory's house, his way of protesting Daisy's selfishness.

"Why're you barefooted?" Hixon asked.

The sun broiled Jed's head. It baked the dirt around the house and the scrub of grass here and there, making Jed's feet smart. Bare feet kept him moving, that was for sure. Moving and priming. Someone watching from the road might think Jed a dancer-painter, hopping and leaping from clapboard to clapboard in a frenzy. Jed noticed Hixon's scrappy overalls and nodded. "Same reason you wear those same overalls every day."

"Point taken." Hixon laughed.

That's what the summer days were like. Stolen (borrowed, Jed liked to say to himself) primer. Jed shoeless. Hixon wearing those same smelly overalls. With each brushstroke, Miss Emory seemed to grow better and worse. Better in that the more the house looked white and happy, the more she combed her hair.

One day she even wore a Sunday dress, complete with those fancy high-heel things Daisy swore she'd never wear. And perfume that smelled like roses.

But as the house "prettified," as Miss Emory called it, her smile pressed in on itself, like it was collapsing under the weight of too much happiness. She looked beautiful, but sad. Like a mannequin in the Penney's window, holding a tragic story hidden behind plaster eyes.

"I'm off to the store, boys," she said one day. "You want anything?"

Jed shook his head. He wiped sweat from his drippy hair. He looked at his hands—speckled white. Under the splatter, his arms looked bulkier. At least that's what he prayed.

Hixon bowed his head like he was acknowledging the queen. "No, ma'am. I'm fine."

"All right then," she said. "I'll be home in a few." Purse in hand, heels clacking the sweltering sidewalk, Miss Emory toted herself down the block in the direction of the grocery, her head held high, but her eyes a million miles away—probably in a place where daughters don't go missing.

Jed and Hixon made a contest of priming the last side of the house, at least the lower part, while Miss Emory was away buying peaches and whatnot. Hixon, armed with two paintbrushes, painted two clapboards together, doubling his coverage. Jed, to keep up, painted faster. When they reached the last corner, the sun burned a square of earth where Jed needed to stand to paint. No matter how much he leaped and tiptoed his way through and around the square, his feet smarted so much he had to get his shoes.

He dropped the paintbrush in the can and took off running through cooler grass. His feet'd holler "thank you kindly" if they could. He'd put his shoes at the base of an old live oak, a tree that shaded workers as they made their dreary way to the rendering plant down yonder. Miss Emory had hung the birdhouse Hap fixed a few feet above where Jed put his shoes. Jed wondered briefly if that meant he'd get bird presents or seeds in his shoes, but he stuck 'em there anyway.

"Where're you going, Jeddy?" Hixon raised both brushes toward the sky. He looked like a *W*.

Jed looked back. "My shoes. The dirt's too hot."

The tree, only a few strides away, smacked Jed upside the head.

Hixon laughed. "You okay?"

Jed shook his head. "Barely." He rubbed his ear. It smarted. "I think the tree moved."

"It's *you* that did the moving. That tree's been there a long, long time."

Jed turned back toward the tree trunk and looked down. In front of his dirt-crusted feet sat one shoe. Just one.

"Very funny."

"Funny what?"

"Taking my shoe. Very funny."

"I didn't take your shoe."

Jed ran around the tree. He stubbed his toe on a rock. He yelped. And then sat, holding the throbbing, blood-gushing thing.

Hixon came over. "You okay?"

Jed pointed to his toe—blood as red as Miss Emory's lips on a good day seeped out of a dirt-colored toenail. He nearly yelped the word that popped into his head, but Hixon being practically Jesus and all, Jed held his tongue. Actually bit it to keep the word from running out.

Hixon knelt on the dirt under the live oak. He pulled out a hankie the color of Miss Emory's old paint and pressed it to the toe.

"Ouch!"

"Quit your bellyaching, son."

"Don't call me that." Jed shut his eyes, then opened them.

"It's an expression. Like darling or ma'am or sir." Hixon twisted the hankie around Jed's toe, then tied it in a knot. "There, you should be fine. Maybe it's time to take a rest."

"But Miss Emory's east side—we were going to finish the bottom half before she got back."

"Some things are fine to be left undone. And what's this business about the shoe?"

Jed retraced his circle around the tree in his mind. Had he seen the other shoe before he stubbed his toe? No. A queer feeling settled into him—the kind he got when he watched a scary movie and the music started getting fast and loud and ... "My other shoe. It's gone."

"Gone? What do you mean?"

"It's not here." Jed scanned the yard again. He even gazed up through the branches thinking maybe some passerby threw his shoe up there. No luck.

Hixon stood. He seemed taller with his dark skin against a darkening sky. He poked around the tree, picked up the shoe—a raggedy tennis shoe, once white, now red-stained from Defiance dirt—looked underneath it as if there were clues living there. "You sure you put them *both* here?"

"Sure as 100 degrees in July."

"Well, I'll be fooled. Where do you suppose it's gotten to?"

Jed swallowed. "I don't know." He remembered Daisy's shoe. Her left shoe. Left behind. He grabbed the shoe from Hixon—his *left* shoe. Also left behind.

The clouds rolled dark and blue gray in the hazy sky. A drop of thick rain plopped on Jed's shoe, like a terrible joke, as if the sky pointed out the obvious. It's not just Daisy. It's Jed too. Maybe it's kids in Defiance. Or anyone connected with Daisy. Whoever has her wants Jed. Is after him.

Another raindrop hit Jed's toe. Then his elbow. His head.

"Storm's a brewing." Hixon said. "We need to take shelter."

Jed looked at his shoe while drippy rain turned into curtains of water sloshing over him. He felt its wetness on his tongue, a gritty taste of leaves and dirt. He spat. Hixon ran toward the house, grabbing the cans of primer and the brushes. "Come on, Jed."

Jed looked at his bandaged toe and examined his shoe again. He half expected a message to be written on it, but none was scribbled. Only a smelly, wet shoe without a mate.

He looked up and down Miss Emory's street.

Questions pelted him faster than the rain that drenched his clothes. He stood there, rooted to the perimeter of the live oak, unable to move. Fear had that way about it.

Hixon ran to meet him.

"We need to get inside. C'mon."

Jed stayed put, holding on to that stupid, scary shoe. He dropped it.

Hixon yelled, "Lord Jesus!" He scooped Jed up like he was a bag of horse feed and carried him toward Miss Emory's front door. He could hear and feel Hixon's panting. Jed couldn't remember the last time he'd been carried like that. Like that picture in Sunday school where Jesus carries the lost lamb. Thunder growled the heavens. Lightning snapped a picture of Miss Emory's front gate.

Jed wrestled himself free. He didn't need to be carried. He found his voice. "We can't go in there. It's private."

Hixon swung the screen door open, then pulled the door in a rush. "We can today." He motioned for Jed to sit. "I'll be back. She might be out in this." Hixon snagged the quilt on the paisley couch and sprinted out the door. It slammed shut.

Thunder shivered the house as Jed rocked himself in Miss Emory's chair, his hands clenched.

He looked up. On the mantel, smiling as big as all get out, sat Daisy—framed in gold. Her same fourth grade picture, only larger. Next to her, a picture of Miss Emory in earlier days. No worries creased her eyes. She wore a white dress that dusted her ankles and a necklace made of shells. Her blonde hair hung straight on both sides and touched the end of her fingertips. Jed could see Daisy in Miss Emory's smile. A bit crooked. A hint of mischief. Alive. So alive.

He wondered how long it would take until Hixon and Miss Emory returned. Jed limp-hopped over to a small desk behind the couch. Miss Emory's desk. He wiped his hands on his shorts and fished through papers. A phone bill. A past-due electric bill. A scrawled note with a phone number for Elmer Truitt, Painter. *Well, at least I'm saving her some money.*

A crack of lightning spotlighted Jed through the window next to the desk. Jed let out a holler. Was it God's way of telling him to quit snooping? He sucked in a breath. Let it out. And kept shuffling. Nothing looked important. A grocery receipt. A business card for Haley's Hair House. A ripped-up phone book with Daisy's doodles inked on the cover. Horses. Unicorns. Rainbows. Angels with halos.

He'd give anything for a fresh drawing by Daisy.

He glanced around.

He ripped off the phone book cover, folded it, and shoved it into his wet pocket.

Thunder shook the house. Jed always wondered if that's what folks felt when an earthquake rumbled a house. And did earthquakes make noise? He remembered hearing Hap say it was a strange summer indeed, with thunder coming past its May prime. It was nearly July and the dark clouds kept coming, the thunder kept rock and rolling.

A tornado siren sounded. Reeeeeaaaar. Reeeeeaaaar.

Where were Hixon and Miss Emory?

Jed looked back at Daisy's picture. He remembered her diary. And then her room.

He had to risk it.

Jed ran into Daisy's room, stopped in the center, and turned himself around. He could smell her. Tears prickled his eyes. He squinted them away. Her stuffed animal collection sat like soft-bodied soldiers along a white shelf above her bed. "My zoo," she'd said. From tallest (Gerry Giraffe) to smallest (Merry Mouse), they looked at him with button eyes. Lonely eyes. Those same eyes he'd seen when she commanded him to off their heads. He remembered what came next as he lifted a fake knife in the air, a crooked crown on his head. He was eight.

"Stop!" Daisy hollered. "I was only kidding. Spare them! Spare them all!"

For a moment, Jed couldn't move. Daisy's animals, her flowered bedspread, the yellow curtains pulled back in bows — all of this halted him. Stuck him to the floor. Her floor.

Lightning threw buckets of light onto Daisy's desk. Jed took it as a sign, remembering Hixon's words that everything in life could be a kiss from God, or a piece of direction, or ... he couldn't remember the other thing. But the lightning flashed again — a second time, spotlighted her desk again. "If the Good Lord shows you a thing three times, it's Him pointing His finger, giving directions. Boy, is it Him," Hixon told him yesterday. Jed waited for the third flash. It came brilliantly, sucking Jed's breath away. "All right, Hixon. You win."

So Jed limped barefooted to Daisy's desk. He rummaged through each drawer, like an archaeologist on an important dig, searching for Daisy's whereabouts. Each small thing he touched tensed his shoulders.

A yellow long-handled comb. Her favorite one. "If I ever die," she told him under a canopy of stars three Fourth of Julys ago, "I want to be buried with my yellow comb. A girl never knows when she'll need to primp — even in the afterlife." Jed ran his fingers along the comb's teeth. He pulled away the hair, looked at it. Touching something that had once been alive on Daisy flustered him.

A photo of the two of them when they first met. Daisy had

that mischievous smile, smeared with chocolate pudding lips. Jed's face was relatively clean, but his hair spiked straight up, Daisy's pudding hands making use of his hair as if it were her mud pie.

An extra large paper clip, nearly a foot long—something Jed won for Daisy at the local fair last summer. He had to bust three balloons to win that stupid thing. "Thank you," Daisy said, capping off her thanks with an embarrassing hug.

School papers, old stubby crayons, a Snickers wrapper, four broken light blue robin's eggs, a rainbow sun visor, a thing of ChapStick, a folded piece of notebook paper.

Jed unfolded the paper whose creases seemed to have been folded and unfolded a hundred times, like if he kept at it a few more times, the paper'd fall apart in four rectangles, cut by years of creasing. His fourth-grade handwriting stared back at him.

"Daisy, This is Jed. Kwit your folowing me. I do not want to be your pal. I do not like you becuz you are a pest. Leeve me alone, K? Jed."

Jed let the letter flutter to the floor. What a fink he'd been.

Thunder shook the floorboards. Lightning flashed his feet, pulling him from regret to reality: his dirty, shoeless feet. How would he explain his lost shoe? Jed couldn't plod through summer without shoes. Sure, Mama wasn't the most observant woman in the world, but she'd surely notice one shoe. Hap would blame the lost shoe on Jed's "debauchery" and try to smack it clear out of him.

He remembered the two Daisys right then, almost as if Daisy was in the room, reminding him. Sure, she loved bows and combs and prissy things. But deep down, Daisy lived and breathed all things tomboy—something that preserved their friendship in spite of her pestering. Daisy climbed trees, ate oversour plums not yet ripe, tried to catch possums, ran almost as fast as Jed on a straightaway (though Jed pulverized her on hills), baited her own hook, and told Jed someday she'd chew and spit tobacco.

Jed opened Daisy's closet where her two halves lived. Frilly dresses and shiny shoes butted up against raincoats and hiking boots. He looked through Daisy's pile of shoes, finally locating her favorites—a worn pair of sneakers. Boy sneakers. She'd triumphed over him when she proved her feet to be bigger than his. Jed hated it then. But now he thanked God as he slipped his feet inside Daisy's shoes, wishing it was her doing the slipping. He was Cinderella in reverse—Cinderfella—putting on a girl's shoes that fit him nearly right. Though his toe smarted inside, he was glad to at least have a bit of wiggle room. He'd give the shoes back to Daisy as soon as she showed up. Or when he rescued her.

Miss Emory's front door yowled open. Jed sucked in a breath. What would Miss Emory do if she found him snooping? He tiptoed back to the hallway, then into the kitchen. He'd appear like he came from there.

"Jed, where are you?" Hixon.

Jed ran through the kitchen doorway. "Just getting a drink of water."

Miss Emory, drenched like a pathetic dog left out in a storm, quilt pulled around her shoulders, eyed him. But the fight had drained from her. She looked plain tired. "Can you get me some?"

Jed nodded.

The three of them sat on towels laid across furniture while the storm howled, flashed, and rocked. Mama phoned, asking if Jed was okay and did he remember to take shelter. "Yes, Mama," he'd said.

Hixon cleared his throat. Jed had never seen the man act uncomfortable. He'd always been so easy, so sure. But Hixon fidgeted on the couch. "Miss Emory?" His voice didn't boom. More like leaked.

"Yes?" Hers sounded waterlogged.

"You might want to think about making plans."

What's he up to now? Jed looked at Daisy's shoes, hoping Miss Emory wouldn't notice.

"Plans?" Soggy voice.

"Have you figured out what to do if Daisy doesn't turn up?"

"What to do?" Miss Emory stood. She looked like a willow tree bending backwards to the wind. "What to do? What is there to do but wait?"

"What I'm saying is—"

"Don't say it."

Hixon wrung out his hands.

She spun around, angling at Hixon. "My baby is fine, you hear me? Just fine. In times like these, a woman needs folks to prop her up, to help her through a day. Empathy. You know what that means?"

Jed squirmed.

Hixon sat there, touching the fingers of his right hand with the index finger of his left hand, like he was counting to five to make sure they were all there.

The room got real quiet. The thunderstorm disappeared in that instant, replaced by a blazing blue sky and windows full of sunlight. Jed would call it a picture of peace had he not heard Miss Emory's words a moment ago.

"I think it's time you went home." Miss Emory sat in her rocker. She pulled Daisy down from the mantel and looked full at her.

Hixon stood. So did Jed.

Hixon dipped his head Miss Emory's way on his way out, but she made no gesture back.

Jed closed the door. He noticed his soggy shoe under the live oak tree.

Hixon looked at Jed's feet. "You got another pair?"

"I always leave a pair at Daisy's in case we want to go exploring and I'd brought flip-flops," he lied.

Jed walked slowly down the porch steps, careful not to re-stub his toe, now sheltered by Daisy's shoe. The world smelled new. The grass sparkled in the sunlight; the trees stood erect and proud like they'd made it through another storm trial and passed with flying colors. The sky looked bluer, the white of Miss Emory's house seemed starched and bleached—like Mama's whites on the clothesline.

Hixon waved good-bye, not saying a word.

Jed didn't wave back.

Instead he looked at Daisy's sneakers hugging his feet while a single tear forced its way down his cheek.

He grabbed his shoe from under the tree and walked away.

Nineteen

Jed sat at their small dinette, remembering the last time Hap slammed Jed's fingers in the doorway on purpose. He and Sissy had been laughing and chasing while Hap was trying to share the gospel with not-yet-brother Bob Laughlin. Though Bob said the sinner's prayer that evening and was ushered into glory while angels sang, Hap was none too pleased. He told Sissy she couldn't leave her room for a day except to take care of business, and he forced Jed's hand against the doorjamb.

"You're lucky Brother Bob met Jesus tonight." He'd held Jed's hand in the jamb while Jed twisted and squirmed. "Because if he hadn't, you'd be guilty of sending his sorry soul to hell. How would that make you feel? How do you think that makes God feel?" He slammed the door with a vengeance even the Devil didn't seem to have.

Jed let out a scream.

"That's how God feels about you, Jed. He's angry. He's punishing you for being ridiculous. You're the oldest. You set the example for Sissy. You led her astray tonight, so your punishment's worse, you hear me?"

Jed nodded.

A slap clapped the side of his head. "What do you say?"

"Yes, sir."

Funny thing about Hap. On days when he was feeling

charitable, as he called it, Hap would apologize, but never in person, never in words. After the door finger-slamming, he'd given Jed a dollar. Set the crisp thing on his desk for Jed to find in the morning. When Jed asked about it, his father's face looked like Mount Rushmore—a stone, neither sorry nor angry. Just silent. Jed's fingers had throbbed and his face wore a red handprint.

Jed touched his cheek, rattled back to today by Mama's whiz-bang of the back screen door. She flustered through the room, opened the fridge. She pulled the waxed paper from a potato salad, plunged a wooden spoon inside, and went back outside. Whizbang.

Hap called for Jed and Sissy from the living room. They sat next to each other on Mama's floral couch while Hap stood, finger raised to the ceiling. Jed and Sissy got the familiar elder-deacon-pastor barbecue instructions before folks arrived.

"No doubt the deacons will arrive first," Hap said.

Jed looked at his shoes, thankful Hap hadn't noticed they weren't his.

"What do you say to the adults?" Hap asked.

"Yes, ma'am, and yes, sir," Sissy said.

"Good girl." Hap patted her on the back. "But do your best not to lisp."

Sissy hung her head.

"Do my children argue when the deacons and elders are over?"

"No, sir." Jed noticed Hap's square chin. How his cheek muscles tensed when he spoke instructions.

"And what about serving?"

"We always ask if we can get drinks," Jed said.

"Right. And what about food?"

"We eat last," Sissy said. "Grown-ups first. And if there isn't any food left, we smile and keep serving." Sissy looked over at Jed. Her grin looked like she'd crayoned it on herself, but with permanent marker instead. A stuck-on smile, for Hap's sake.

"That's my girl." Hap smiled down at both of them. "A preacher's kid has to represent Jesus every minute, you hear me? We don't want the elders and deacons to get any sly ideas about us, now do we?"

Hap left to tend to the burgers. Sissy scurried to her room to put on her Sunday best even though it was Friday. She knew the routine.

The doorbell rang. Sissy beat Jed to the front door. "Glad to have you here, Officer Spellman."

The policeman nodded at Sissy. "Where's your father?" he asked. Jed pointed out back.

Mr. and Mrs. Mohler came on the policeman's heels. Sissy nodded at Jeremiah Mohler, the couple's eight-year-old son who was known for eating anything on a dare: sticks, snot, dog food, horsetail hair, orange juice concentrate—anything, really.

Jed shook everyone's hand, including Jeremiah's. He ran through a list of things in the backyard he could dare Jeremiah to eat. A worm, maybe?

Right on the Mohlers' heels were the Dicksons. Mrs. Dickson, a frowny mouse-haired lady who always wore plain denim dresses and cloddy shoes, had perfect teeth—something Mr. Dickson gloated about forever and a year. "Never been to a dentist and looky here," he'd say, pointing to her teeth like she was a horse and he a proud horse trader. Mrs. Dickson, Mama had whispered once, was "barren," which meant she couldn't have kids. Which explained her love for stray cats. Fourteen of them. All named with the letter F. Frisky, Fiona, Fiasco, Fatty—names like that. Each with its own bowl, box, and bed. Mr. Dickson, a terribly allergic man, banished the cats to the garage, which Mama said smelled like one giant litter box.

Jed opened the door for the elders: Mack Slocum and his wife, Betty Sue, who wore matching yellow shirts. Harold Homer and his wife, Sally, and their twin five-year-old girls, Holly and Molly. Bob Patterson, by himself since his wife, Louise, died last Valentine's Day. If ever there could be a face that screamed "widower," it was his—drawn up tight, eyes one million miles away.

The house was always spic and span on picnic nights. Hap insisted and Mama made it so, even dusting the never-used china inside the china cabinet. Jed thought it a waste. He and Sissy took purses and directed traffic through the house to the backyard—about as far away as someone could get from the shiny china.

Holly and Molly obviously didn't have a father like Hap to scare the squirms out of them. They ran through the backyard like angry roosters, toppling over a side table with lemonade atop it and not even looking back.

Hap laughed. *Laughed*. Turning to Harold, he said, "Those girls of yours sure are pistols."

Harold nodded, beaming a bit.

Jed watched as Hap carefully righted the table. He went into the kitchen and returned with a sponge. He smiled as he wiped the sticky lemonade from the card table. He even ruffled Holly's and Molly's hair as they ran by again.

Mama looked at him in shock. Jed knew she'd seldom seen Hap holding a sponge.

Sissy stopped and watched as Hap picked up the paper cups, stacked them neatly, and brought them back into the kitchen.

Memories flashed through Jed's mind like a helter-skelter movie. Spilled milk. Hap's yell. Jed, holding a sponge, on his hands and knees. Sissy dropping the Pink Cloud, their name for this Jell-O-y pink fluff with pineapples and marshmallows, and running away from Hap's hand. How many times had they spilled? Hundreds? And every single time, Hap made them pay.

While the twins ran and shouted and thought Hap the nicest daddy in Defiance.

"You're so patient, Pastor," Mack Slocum gushed. "Tell us your secret to parenting." Mack took a bite of his hamburger at the long, long table Mama had set out—two sawhorses, a long piece of plywood covered in three red-checkered tablecloths.

Jed and Sissy sat on a large quilt spread on the ground, beside Jeremiah, who was indeed slurping up the worm Jed dared him to eat, and Holly and Molly, who pulled each other's hair.

"Ah, that's easy," Hap said. "You get into the Word, brother, and let the Word get into you."

Officer Spellman nodded solemnly.

"Maybe that explains," Mrs. Dickson frowned, "why that Daisy girl's gone missing. Maybe Miss Emory didn't get herself into the Word. I hear she has a past."

Jed felt his face warm. How dare folks talk about Miss Emory that way! The Cat Woman never even had kids. How could she criticize? Jed willed his father to step up. After all, he fixed Miss Emory's birdhouse, right?

"That she does," Hap said. "It goes to show"—he took a bite of potato salad and twirled his fork in the air like he was sermonizing—"that a loose life will have loose ends."

Jed stood. Hap's cold stare shot through Jed, and he sat, hands trembling.

Hap smiled. "My son here is Daisy's friend. You can imagine how hard it's been for him."

Adults around the table who knew nothing of Daisy nodded their heads.

"He's the last one who saw her alive."

Alive? Did Hap know something he didn't know?

"I don't let my girls outside anymore," Sally Homer said. "I'm afraid. Who d'you suppose took the girl?"

"Beats me," Mr. Mohler said. "I've heard it could be her father. Might've taken what was his."

Could it be true? Could he turn out to be a kidnapper? And all along Jed'd thought Daisy happy and safe with her father. Jed watched as Jeremiah grabbed a handful of grass and shoved it into his mouth. The twins hollered, but their parents didn't stir.

"That's why it's important to live right," Hap said, fastening on his preaching voice. The elders and deacons and their wives leaned forward, nearly at the same time, straining to hear the truth Hap proclaimed. "Why church is so important. Miss Emory, she hasn't come in a long, long time. She's walked down roads the Devil has paved for her. Poor thing is scared at night. Ever wonder why she keeps her lights on? It's the Devil. He's after her soul. And she keeps letting him picnic on her doorstep."

Ethrea Ree, their rose-loving next-door busybody, poked her head over the fence. Jed often marveled at the short woman's timing. "Quit your hollering, Happy Pepper. The whole neighborhood'll hear you."

Hap seemed to wither at her words. "Sorry, ma'am."

"Sorry sometimes isn't enough, you hear me?" She pointed a bony finger his way. "My Delmer doesn't like you, you know that? Says you preach too loud."

Poor Delmer, Jed thought. Her son didn't have a chance.

"It's always nice to see you," Mama cheered.

Ethrea Ree humphed and walked away.

Mama looked at the crowd, sadness in her eyes. "She's never been the same since—"

Mrs. Mohler raised a hand, shushing Mama. "We all know the sorry story, Ouisie. Must we dredge up Vietnam and Slim's death? I'm not sure it's much of an excuse anymore for that woman's strange actions."

Several heads nodded.

"Do continue, Pastor. You were talking about Miss Emory."

You could always count on Mrs. Mohler to keep the gossip flowing, using church words to make it okay.

Hap looked over Ethrea Ree's way. He cleared his throat. "The Lord chastises sinners. He watches. He catches. He allows terrible things to happen because of our wrong choices. Miss Emory is reaping what she's sowed."

Mama mumbled something, but Jed couldn't make it out.

"What did you say?" Hap smiled, but Jed heard him hiss through his teeth.

"Nothing." Mama winced.

Sissy placed a hand on Jed's arm. Jed let it stay there. He held his breath. Would this be the day Hap blew up in front of the church folk? What would they think then?

"Now come on, Ouisie. You said something, sure as day. I think the good folks want to hear what the pastor's wife has to say."

Jed noticed Mama holding her temples. Another headache.

"She gets headaches." Hap patted her shoulder. "Now tell us what you said."

For being outside in the summer, it sure was quiet. Not even a cricket dared to speak. Even Jeremiah kept his trap shut.

"I said," Mama whispered, "nothing." She looked at Hap, then cleared her throat.

Hap smiled. "That's the beauty right there of a submissive, quiet wife. Ouisie, you're an example to us all."

Mama's strawberry pies lightened the mood some. Raves and mmmm's buzzed through the yard. Something about strawberries, vanilla cream, candy-red glaze, and a dollop of whipped cream put the evening to rest in a proper way. Maybe, just maybe, Hap's satisfied strawberry pie face would forget that Mama muttered something. Strawberry pie had a way about it, Jed was sure.

Sissy picked up paper plates, depositing them into the burn barrel at the back fence line, while Jed helped get more tea for the guests. All at once, black, oily smoke rushed into their yard. Mrs. Mohler shrieked. Hap grabbed the tablecloths and started fanning the smoke away.

For all her rose-loving, Ethrea Ree sure knew how to poop a party. The Pepper family had endured her rug burnings for several years now, most every time they had a crowd over. Ethrea Ree would cackle over the fence, then huff back into her home. Mama joked once that Ethrea Ree'd be a fine weatherwoman because she always burned rugs when the wind carried itself west, right to the Pepper backyard. Jed swore she had a pile of rubber-backed carpet remnants she'd found at the county dump sitting by the fireplace ready to burn. He pictured her smiling as she shoved papers underneath a particularly rancid rug and lit it, the smoke billowing to the high heavens, spitting soot on Jed's family and their guests.

Mama ushered the church folk inside. Jeremiah lingered, opening his mouth to catch a few rug snowflakes. When one singed his tongue, he made a face, said a choice word, and opened his mouth again. His mama finally pulled him inside.

Jed's mouth no longer tasted like strawberries and cream. Nope. Inside the bustle of their spotless home, his tongue felt like sandpaper, his taste buds licking oily smoke.

"I could give her a code violation, Pastor," Officer Spellman said.

"That won't be necessary. Sometimes it's good to offer grace." Even with all the commotion and Ethrea Ree's successful attempt to bother yet another Pepper picnic, Hap smiled. Seemed unfazed. "We need to pray for that woman's soul. Need to pray her out of the fires of hell."

A few snickers popcorned throughout the living room. Hap could be funny, at least around strangers. Jed only wished he'd be the same when the last guest left and he locked the door behind them. No, he wouldn't be full of jokes tonight. No doubt about that.

Twenty

Jed couldn't let Hap's words die in his head. He'd learned that ability over the years in order to control his own anger. If Hap said something jarring or uttered a lie, Jed told himself to forget it. He'd seen Mama do it a thousand times. But this was one thousand and one, and he couldn't, *wouldn't*, let it die. Besides, if he took away some of Hap's rage, maybe he wouldn't throw it Mama's way.

He found Hap sitting on the front porch, next to Mama's rocking chair. He was looking off into the night like it held a clue to a mystery — so much concentration.

"Sir?" Jed remained standing, didn't sit in Mama's chair.

"What is it?"

"You said something." Jed looked away, couldn't meet Hap's eyes.

"I say a lot of things. I'm a preacher."

Jed put his hands in his pockets. "You said I was the last one who saw Daisy alive."

"Yeah, so?"

Jed took one step back and cleared his throat. "It's just that … do you know something you're not telling me? Did they find Daisy? Is she — "

"Don't be ridiculous." Hap measured out his words. Kept his voice calm, using his children's sermon voice.

"Because if you know something, I'm man enough to—"

Hap let out a booming laugh. "Man enough? Oh, that's a good one, Jed. Man enough? All of thirteen years?"

"Fourteen." Jed looked at his feet. He waited for the tornado of words.

"Fourteen. That's right. By your age, I was man enough. I had to be, with my father dead. But you? You run around Defiance with that girlfriend of yours like you don't have a care in the world. Meanwhile, I'm working myself to death to keep food on the table. Man enough? Try being me for a while."

Not on your life, he wished he could say, but he knew how well that would go over. "When was the last time you saw Daisy?" Jed crossed his arms across his chest.

"How should I know? I saw her when you saw her, when you hauled her over here."

"I hardly ever did that."

"Are you defying me?"

"No, sir. I was just wondering."

"I saw her in town, on occasion. And if she looked hungry, I'd buy her some ice cream." Hap turned away, looking out at the night once again. "That Miss Emory just didn't know how to raise a child."

"Didn't? Please tell me what you know. If Daisy is gone, I have a right to know."

"Kids don't have rights." He directed dark eyes Jed's way. "And that's the end of the conversation."

In the sticky wet of that night, Sissy twiddled her thumbs, something she often did when she sat on Jed's bed and worried about Hap. "I'm going to the closet."

"No, you aren't."

"Yes, I am." She stood.

Jed yanked her upper arm. "Listen to me."

Sissy pulled away. She had that same look as when Hap grabbed her.

Jed swallowed. Calmed himself down. He never wanted Sissy to fear him, never wanted to be the cause of *that* look. "I'm sorry. I don't want you to go, is all. He's in a mood. He's in *that* mood."

Sissy put her hands on her hips, like Mama scolding. "They've never caught me before. Besides, you said that Daddy knows more about Daisy's kidnapping than he's letting on, right?"

"I don't care."

"Don't lie to me, Jed. You do too care."

"It's not up to you to go around listening. I already tried to get something from Hap, and he didn't say anything. I've done my job."

"Since when does talking to Daddy ever help? But snooping works. I've done it a hundred times. I only have a few more minutes before they go in. I need to go."

Jed stood. "Sissy. No. You can't." He took a deep breath. "Not with how Hap is tonight. If he finds you—"

"You care about finding Daisy, right?"

Jed nodded. But he hated to.

"And so do I. Which means I need to hightail it right now if I'm going to find anything out."

Before Jed could catch her, Sissy ran out of his room.

He sank into his bed. First Daisy, now Sissy. He couldn't protect either of them. Shoot, he couldn't even protect himself. Jed got down on his knees—the only way to pray, the kinds of prayers God answered, at least according to Hap.

Jed crawled into bed. He strained to hear Mama's and Hap's murmurs. Soon they came—mostly Hap's voice. He could make out his mama's name. Ouisie this. Ouisie that. Twenty minutes passed, mostly Hap's voice. Louder. Then louder.

Jed clapped his hands over his ears, then took them away. Then put them back again. A crash. Glass breaking. Jed jumped up, ready to rescue. Then he remembered the last time he tried that and slipped back onto the floor. Prayed.

Clunk.

More prayers.

Thud. Mama's scream. Mama's no. Jed flexed his arms, praying they'd answer Mama's distress call, but he stayed stuck to the floor. Footsteps drummed the hallway. Pound. Pound. Pound. The front door opened. Then shut. Then opened again.

"Ouisie, I can't even look at you," Hap belted. "You've made me do this. It's all your doing. I'm going to sleep at the church. Where I'm respected."

Mama didn't answer back.

"You can sleep in your bed of lies, you hear me?"

The front door slammed shut, shaking the house. Jed heard the Chevy grunt to life. Tires churned the gravel in reverse, making the driveway crackle. Tires screeched against the street. Then silence. Blessed silence.

Jed had never quite figured out how to protect Mama. Last time he did, Hap stepped on both of his bare feet with steel-toed boots. Instead he bore the guilt of staying in his room. He heard Mama crying, knew he had to go to her—if only to distract her while Sissy slipped away undetected.

Mama sat on the corner of her bed, the very corner, head bowed in her hands, her body hiccuping.

"Mama?"

She looked up. Tired eyes peered right into Jed's soul, a look that nearly made him run all the way to church and give his father a piece of his mind. But Mama motioned for him to sit beside her.

From behind the lamp on her end table, she retrieved a glass full of clear liquid. She swigged the rest of it. She smiled, wiped her lips with the sleeve of her robe.

On the floor in front of them both lay Mama's only vase, shattered. Flowers—products of one of Mama's meadow hunts—crisscrossed over the shards like fragrant pick-up-sticks. Jed stepped around the mess, careful to sit nearer to the window than the closet to keep Mama's eyes away from Sissy's hiding place. He looked at Mama's feet—her left big toe was bleeding.

"Your toe."

"Stepped on the vase after—" She stopped.

Mama kept her secrets, though Jed had already filled in Mama's last words ... after Hap sent it crashing to the floor. "It'll be okay, Mama." Jed turned slightly, enough to see Sissy peeking around the closet door behind him. He gave her a yes-it's-okay-to-leave look. Sissy obeyed and slipped quietly down the hall, Mama unaware.

Jed stepped around the glass and ventured into the bathroom. He grabbed the first aid kit. "Let me clean that up, Mama."

"No, I can do it." She cleaned her toe with Bactine, then dried it off with a cotton ball. Blood soaked three cotton balls before she could stretch a bandage around it. "At least I can put on my own bandage."

Jed liked that hint of fight in her voice. It came and went so little these days. When he was younger, Mama threw pans at Hap. She didn't do that anymore, but from time to time, she sassed. With every word, she seemed to pay more and more.

Mama looked around the room as if for the first time, like she'd just woken up. "My flowers. My mama's vase—the only thing left of hers."

"I'm sorry, Mama."

"Tissue?" She sniffed her cry way inside.

Jed fetched a box and set it beside her.

She pulled paper hankies, as she called them, one by one, blowing her nose with each piece. "He's a good man, your father." Jed said nothing. "But I'm not a good wife." She breathed in a breath the size of a horse and let it out slow.

When Mama drained the rest of her glass, she started spilling everything in her heart. It made Jed queasy. All at once, he wanted to leave, but her neediness held him there. She needed him. And somehow, her needing him meant he needed her.

"I can't submit. I've got a stubborn streak a mile long." She got on the floor, on hands and knees, and pulled a long narrow tube from underneath the headboard. "I'll prove it to you." She handed the tube to Jed.

"What's this?"

She smiled. "Something your father doesn't know about. A little bit of me held back."

Jed opened the end of the tube.

Mama took it from him. "You need to be careful." She pulled out rolled pieces of paper. They curled upon themselves on Mama's bed, looking like a handful of drinking straws, only bigger. She uncurled one.

A painting of a single pink rose startled Jed. "Where'd you get that?"

"I painted it."

"You painted that?" When had he seen Mama paint?

"I paint when he's gone. It's the one thing I do for myself. You'll keep this between us, won't you? Our little secret?"

Jed nodded. He put his arm around Mama's shoulders. It felt awkward there, like the Scarecrow walking the yellow-brick road with Dorothy beneath a gangly arm. But it felt right, almost like he was protecting her. "You're a good mama."

She slurred something, but Jed couldn't make it out. "What?"

"I said, if only you and Sissy were the ones needing convincing."

Jed shushed her. "Don't worry, Mama. I'll take care of you. And you don't have to convince me of anything. Truth is, you're a good mama, and that's that."

She patted his head.

"And besides, you're the only mama who writes notes on flowers. The only one."

Mama smiled. "Really?"

"Yeah."

She looked away. "But your father gets so angry at me."

Jed nodded. "He's the one with the temper. Not you."

"It *is* my fault. He said so. He says so. He's the preacher, so it must be so. I can't get it right, that's all. Can't fix supper right. Can't iron shirts right. Can't sweep the floors right. Can't buy enough groceries for the amount of allowance he gives me. Nothing's right. If only I could get things right."

What could Jed do? What *could* he do?

What any self-respecting boy would do at a time like this. "I'll be right back, Mama. You stay put."

She made a slight motion to get up, to protest, but Jed shushed her back. "Don't you worry. Wait here. I won't be long."

Jed grabbed a pair of scissors from the junk drawer. He stole out the back door as quiet as he could. Hunched low along Ethrea Ree's fence, he reached her front yard. There, in all its glory stood Mama's favorite rosebush—all abloom in purple roses that smelled like heaven, at least according to Mama. She'd purloin—a word Jed learned from Daisy—roses from the side of the bush so Ethrea Ree wouldn't notice. The rug smoke lingered in the night air, stinging his nose. Jed stood in front and started clipping. Hacking, really. He cut away every bloom, even tight buds, until the bush resembled a horrid haircut.

The porch light behind the bush flashed on.

Jed's heart threatened to leap out from behind his rib cage.

The door squeaked open.

Delmer, Ethrea Ree's not-so-there son, stood dumbly. "Whatcha doin'?"

Jed saw no anger in Delmer's eyes. He saw nothing there. Just emptiness. "Pruning," Jed said. "Your mama asked me to."

"She did?"

Jed swallowed, then looked at the roses in one hand, the scissors in another. "It's a secret, you hear me? She told me roses can only get pruned at night, or they'll die. And if anyone sees them getting pruned, they'll get a fungus that'll infect an entire yard." Jed sucked in another breath, willing his heart to stop its ferocious beating. A squirrel scampered up a nearby tree. "And that's why you can't say a word of this to your mama. She wants the pruning done, but she told me she can't know when it happens. Or bad things will surely come."

"Bad things?" Delmer wiped a thick hand across his mouth.

"Death, Delmer. Death will happen. To squirrels. So keep your mouth shut."

"Squirrels? Die?"

Jed nodded.

Delmer put a finger to his lips, his shushing look. "Folks think my daddy's dead, but he's not. He's alive."

Now Jed knew Delmer was crazy. He'd seen the town parade honoring Mr. Ree, banners flying, firecrackers popping. Slim'd been killed by Vietcong, hunched low in a jungle. It made Jed shiver to think of it. Though he wanted to be brave and strong, he didn't think he had the chops for war, especially not in a sweaty jungle halfway around the world.

"Well, where is your daddy then?"

Delmer pointed toward Jed's house, a frightened look in his once-dull eyes, like he'd just seen a horror movie. He turned around and thudded through the open door. From the front window, Delmer waved, happy again.

But Jed didn't wave back. He ran like the dickens to his home, knowing Daisy would've given him a talking to for messing with Delmer like that.

A man's gotta do what a man's gotta do.

J ed placed the roses in the oversized mason jar Mama used for
sweet tea, filled it with water, and walked to Mama's room,
roses smelling up the hallway.

He knew Mama could say nothing about his purloining. If
she did, she'd admit to stealing herself, and Jed knew she didn't
have the gumption to do that. Mama's flower stealing was another one of her little secrets, so he imagined she held it to her
heart. Only for her. Jed understood. Just like his need to keep
the investigation silent.

So when Jed handed the makeshift vase to Mama, she smiled
a real smile, with all her teeth showing. "Thanks," she said.
"They're beautiful."

"You're welcome." Jed kicked at the carpet and begged with
his eyes to be allowed to leave.

She granted his request with a nod.

He went into Sissy's room and shut the door behind him.

Sissy, who'd been pretend-sleeping, sat right up.

"Shh," Jed said.

"Don't you think I know I'm supposed to whisper?"

Jed sat on the end of her bed, then scooted himself against
the wall so he could relax a bit. Truth be told, he was tired-er
than a wild hog in hunting season. He'd spent his days dodg-
ing bullets—Miss Emory's eyes, Ethrea Ree's rugs, Hap's hand,
Mama's tears. With Daisy gone missing, it was too much. "Did
you learn anything about Daisy?"

"Nah, Daddy went on and on about some man named
David."

Jed sat up. "What?"

"David. I'd never heard them argue about someone else before—usually it's all about Mama not doing enough or acting
right. But this time it was David this, David that."

"What did he say?"

"Daddy accused Mama of pining after a man named David. Said he knew she was. Had his proof, he said."

"What proof?"

"Mama calls his name at night, when she's dreaming."

"She does?" Jed picked at a scab on his knuckle, trying to act like this piece of information was no big deal.

"Well, not according to Mama. She said, 'There's more than one David in the world.' "

"What did she mean by that?"

"Her stepdad—you remember her talking about him?"

"Yeah." Jed picked the knuckle scab clean off. Blood bubbled there. He licked it.

"Ew, Jed. Get a napkin or something."

"No need."

Sissy rolled her eyes. "Anyway, Mama said something about how she has nightmares about David her stepdad and that's why she hollered his name at night."

"Did Hap believe her?"

"Nope. Said he knew it was the other David."

Jed couldn't imagine his Mama pining after another man. "Did he say David's last name?"

"Why would he do that?"

"Oh, nothing. I was curious, is all."

"Hap said he found David's letters in a shoe box, and why was Mama holding on to them. Actually, he yelled all that." Sissy made a church, then a steeple with her hands.

"What did Mama say?"

"Not much. She cried. Said it'd been over before they met. Said she kept the letters because they reminded her of high school and happy times." Sissy opened the doors to her finger church and wiggled the people.

"What else did they say?"

"Mama didn't say anything. But Daddy said a lot. About Mama being rigid in bed and that she's a terrible housekeeper.

And that she doesn't listen well. And that she's not submissive. And that God's probably sorry He made her." Sissy'd been saying all the words, the terrible words, without emotion, but when she said the last bit, Jed heard her catch her breath.

She let out a wail, then threw her hands to her mouth.

Jed scooted next to her, his lanky arm around her thin shoulder blades.

"How could he say that, Jed? Doesn't he love Mama anymore?"

"I don't know, Sissy."

"Does she love him?"

"She told me as much, yes."

She sucked in a few tears, then wiped her face with her bedspread.

"Did he say anything else about this David person?"

"Just told Mama to burn the letters. Or he would." Sissy straightened, her frightened face taking on a hint of a sly grin.

"What?"

"I figured if those letters made Mama remember happy times, I'd best keep 'em for her. They're under the bed."

Jed nearly kissed his sister. Nearly.

"You better let me hide them, okay?"

"Sure thing. Only—"

"Only what?" Jed held the box to himself.

"Keep 'em safe."

"You know I will. It'll be our little secret." Jed said good night to Sissy and slunk down the hallway. The door to Mama's and Hap's room sat ajar. Though he knew he should get to his room, he couldn't help but notice his mama, back turned, her face poked right in the middle of the purple roses.

Don't you worry, Mama, I'll take care of you.

Twenty-One

Y ou're my hero." Mama's inked words on a purple rose had teased Jed's nose.

He remembered how the flower shifted in his hand. How a thorn pricked his pointer finger, drawing dark red blood. He sucked it dry then, hoping again for hero's strength.

But none came. Would it ever? Even now? Though he'd stopped sucking his blood after high school, the longing for the heroic never left him. And the desire to find a simple solution to his cowardice pulsed through him, particularly when Jed revisited that year when he was fourteen. Sucking blood didn't bring it. Willing strength into himself failed too. Heroism—all too elusive.

The shower sizzled at the back of the house. Jed knew Hap was back, cleaning up before getting back to God's work—even on Saturday. It happened that way. Hap hollering at Mama, leaving her behind to listen to his voice over and over again in her head, then coming back in the morning, whistling and happy.

As if he'd never made his wife cry, or his daughter snoop, or his son hate him.

If all went according to pattern, clean-shaven Hap would gulp down a few eggs, ruffle Jed's hair with a laugh, tell Sissy she was the prettiest girl in Defiance, and make a nice comment about Mama's coffee. Mama would smile thinly and say nothing—her way of punishing, he guessed. Sometimes Jed thanked the Lord for Hap's yelling—at least it led to a peaceful home for a good three days. Did Hap feel guilty? All Jed knew was that if he ever wanted anything—a fixed bike tire, a day off from Miss Emory, a trip to the lake on the weekend, this was the time to do it, while Hap was happy.

Jed took a long shower right after Hap. As the water dripped over him, tears formed in the corners of his eyes. He hated that about himself, hated that he cried like a stupid baby, but he couldn't stop. The flyers he'd posted around town curled at the edges. The searches turned up nothing.

Only Daisy knew about his real family—not the one everyone saw all shiny and bright on Sundays—the real one. That was why she said, "Your family ain't normal" on the night she went missing. He'd hated her words but liked them too, because it meant that one other person in the world *knew*. And maybe understood a bit. Daisy knew Jed stole a Snickers bar from the grocery store in town. She cried when he got stitches from falling into a ditch where a broken bottle sliced open his calf. Even though she blabbed a lot, she knew how to listen. Now Jed had words he needed to say, but not a soul to hear them.

He dried himself off. Naked in the bathroom, he worried about becoming a man. When his back grew strong like Hap's, would he turn into his father? Would this transformation mean he'd not become a man with a deep voice, but a man who used that voice to yell and scream? Or would it mean he could finally stand up for what was right—put Hap in his proper place, even though it meant not respecting him. Pulling up his shorts, Jed said a prayer.

Lord, I know I'm supposed to respect Hap. I know it's a commandment and all. So I hope You understand when I ask that You please help me turn into a kind man, that I won't turn into Hap. Please. Please. Please. Amen. Oh, and one more thing. If You could, make me strong enough to stand up to him just once.

He opened his eyes before the mirror, saw eyes the same color as his father's. Anger stared back at him. Hard anger. He'd prayed the prayer, but he wasn't sure if God heard him. Or if he really wanted to be kind after all.

Jed sat at the breakfast table. Morning sun spotlighted purple roses in a mason jar—smack dab in the middle of the table. He wondered if Ethrea Ree would notice the empty spot he made in getting them for Mama. He watched Mama cook eggs sunny-side up in the pan. Jed hated sunny-side up. Sissy did too. But that was the only way Hap wanted them to be cooked, so that's what she did.

Until she flipped them over. Jed smiled. Sissy slipped into her chair. Dark circles haunted the skin under her eyes. Mama didn't look up, didn't say a word. Hap hummed his way into the room. Jed saw his mama's shoulders pull up toward her ears.

Hap ruffled Jed's squeaky-clean hair. Jed ducked his head, trying to avoid Hap's touch, but was too late. Hap sat down. Jed twirled the fork in his hand. He knew now was the time to ask. "Miss Emory, she said she didn't need me today. Said she was meeting all day with the police, organizing another search party. Can I have the day off?"

"Of course," Hap said, his voice cheerful. Mama clanked a plate in front of Hap. Two eggs, like cartoon eyes with yellow pupils, stared back at him, only the eyes had brown lace over them because they'd been flipped.

Jed expected a protest, but none came. Hap broke both yolks, then cut the eggs together. With a piece of white toast, he mopped up the eggs and shoved it in his mouth. He took a drink of coffee, then grimaced. Jed waited.

"Ouisie, you still make the best coffee there is." He took a drink of orange juice.

155

Mama said nothing. A dove called from outside, over and over again.

"What's with all the quiet?" Hap shoved another mopped-up egg into his mouth, followed by a swig of orange juice. "Sissy," he said, "you're the prettiest gal this side of Defiance. You know that?"

Tired-eyed Sissy mumbled thanks. Hap stood. "Well, I can see y'all got up on the wrong side of the bed. Too bad. It's a beautiful day." He hummed a line of "Amazing Grace." "Well, I'm off to church. Got a few things to rustle up before the sermon tomorrow. Ouisie?"

Mama turned. She hadn't sat down yet. Still scrubbing the stuck-on eggs off the old pan that Hap wouldn't let her replace. She nodded.

"Tomorrow's sermon will be one of my best. Just you wait." He winked at her. She didn't wink back. He crossed the floor, put his arm around her. "I love you, Ouisie," he said.

The dove called again. Sissy looked at Jed, tears in her eyes. Jed looked away, through the window in their back door, hoping to see the gray dove in the yard, anything to keep him from watching this. Sissy's tears. Mama's silence. Hap's cheer.

Mama said nothing. Jed heard Hap kiss Mama, heard him say good-bye, heard his footsteps pad down the hallway and out the front door that he shut kindly. So different from last night. Mama opened the back door. She left it open, a no-no Hap would've hollered at her for. She sat down on the cement stoop and cried.

Sissy pushed her eggs away. She walked over to Mama, put her hand on top of Mama's head. Jed watched them, the doorjamb like the lopsided perimeter of a television screen framing Sissy and Mama. Mama cried everything out while Sissy kept touching Mama's head like she was trying to stop the tears from flowing out the top. Mama said no words. She didn't need to. The way her body heaved in and out said it all—so loud Jed was tempted to cover his ears. His eyes held him there, kept him watching the show.

His two women. His responsibility. And yet they cried and consoled like actresses in an after-school special about a family breaking apart. A single dove flew in front of the two, perched on a chair in the distant yard. Both heads looked up at the bird, startled. The dove sang, "It's sa-ad, sa-ad, sa-ad," then ruffled his gray feathers and looked right at Jed behind them in the doorway. The peculiar way it looked at him brought him back to a forest path two years ago, where Daisy had stooped to the dirt, tears wetting the still-alive fluttering of a baby dove.

"It's hurt," was all she'd said.

Jed couldn't stand to see Daisy cry. And seeing that bird so helpless made him sick inside. He bent near the dove, scooped it and a bit of Defiance dirt carefully in his hand, and brought it home to Mama.

Mama cried too. "God's given you the gift of empathy, sure as pie." She looked at Daisy and the bird when she said it.

"What does that mean?" Daisy asked.

"It means Jed here has a heart for folks. And critters."

Jed felt his face and insides warm all at once. To hear her say this gave Jed hope. If Mama felt God gave Jed empathy, maybe it was true. The three of them took turns feeding the dove eyedroppers of water. Even though worms gave her the willies, Sissy joined in the crusade by digging them up for the poor bird. Daisy cooed over the little bird, gently petting its head. But nothing could prevent the dove's heart from beating wildly, then going still.

Jed could do nothing about everyone's sudden grief when the dove died, other than pet Mama's and Daisy's and Sissy's heads and feel completely helpless.

He felt that way now. Daisy was missing. Daisy. He prayed her heart was beating—somewhere.

Twenty-Two

After one hundred weak-armed push-ups, Jed spent his Saturday morning reading through love letters. His face burned red. He knew Mama's David's last name now: Carter. And he couldn't help but wonder if Daisy Marie Chance, whose daddy's name was David, was actually Daisy Marie Carter.

Mama had loved David Carter, but he'd barely been a man when Mama knew him. High school sweethearts, all four years, which meant they'd started "sweethearting" when they were Jed's age. Mama thought she'd marry him. Thought he'd take her away from the other David, her stepdad. Jed opened another letter.

"It kills me to see him treat you that way. Don't you understand? You're like a bunch of wildflowers—the kind to be appreciated, cherished, enjoyed. I pray to God you see I'm not like him, Ouisie. I think you're holding yourself back from me because you think he and I are kin somehow. We're not. I love you. He doesn't. I hold you. He hits you. When will you understand? All I want to do is take you away from Defiance, away from David. We could start a new life, a perfect life. I'd plant a thousand rosebushes to see you smile."

When he first learned of David, Jed wondered how his mama could love someone else, being entirely dedicated to Hap. But reading this letter, Jed got angry. Angry that Mama hadn't listened to this David fellow. That she stuck around Defiance long enough to meet Hap.

But then, if she hadn't, Jed wouldn't be here, right now, reading these letters. But then if he wasn't here, maybe Daisy would still be around. The letters tangled Jed's insides like a no-see-um bug caught in a spiderweb with no hope of escape.

The afternoon sun felt hot on Jed's face. Sissy's too. She said so. He'd promised her they'd put up more signs, so they walked together through Defiance streets, this time stapling Daisy any which where—picket fences, mailbox posts, telephone poles. Jed even rolled some into chain-link fences while Sissy taped a few to windshields. "You never can be too thorough," she said.

"Where'd you learn the word *thorough*?"

"From Daisy."

Jed looked at the last flyer. Daisy's whole face smiled in the picture: dancing eyes, animated cheeks, a dimple just left of her upturned lips. Oh, how he missed her—so much he thought the missing would kill him. He handed the flyer to Sissy. "It's our last one. You choose where we put it."

"Hixon's house."

Jed's face was nearly as wet as his underarms. "Why? It's a good five blocks from here."

"He's magic, Jed."

Jed leaned on a chain-link fence, then pulled his hand away. Too hot. "He's not magic. He'd tell you that himself. It's Jesus telling him stuff, he'd say."

"Isn't Jesus magic?" Sissy started walking in Hixon's direction. Her flip-flops slapped the dirt-stained pavement.

Jed caught up. "No. Magic's evil. Haven't you listened to Hap's sermons? Shoot, even card tricks are the Devil's playground."

Sissy walked faster, like her life depended on posting Daisy at Hixon's gate. "Jesus *is too* magic. You can't tell me different."

"I can tell you what I want," Jed panted, "because I'm older than you."

"Nope. Besides, I know your secret."

"Secret?" Jed searched his mind. What secret? He jogged a bit to catch up with Sissy. He wiped sweat off his face with his shirtsleeve.

"Those aren't your shoes, are they?"

"Yes, they are."

"Are not."

Jed swatted a lazy mosquito.

"I swear, Jed Pepper, you're as easy to figure out as algebra." Sissy kept walking.

"Algebra? Since when is algebra easy?"

"Since I stole your book and figured it out."

Why did girls have to be so unpredictable? "Listen, Sissy. Keep your trap shut about my shoes."

"You mean *Daisy's* shoes?" Sissy started skipping the sidewalk.

Jed picked up his pace. "Sissy, please!"

She skipped a circle, then stopped in front of him. "I won't tell. I promise. You wearing 'em for good luck?"

"No." Jed rubbed sweaty hands on his shorts.

"Then why?"

"I got my reasons."

"Like—"

"Like I have reasons and they're mine. Quit it, Sissy."

"You lost your shoes, didn't you?"

Jed wondered if she knew the whole sorry story. If she did, she sure didn't act scared, skipping the streets of Defiance without a care. He wouldn't dare shatter her joy and tell her someone took his shoe, like someone took Daisy's. He had to protect Sissy. It was his job. "Nah, I remembered Daisy had these. They're in better shape. With all the painting I'm doing, I couldn't have shoes with holes in them, now could I?"

"I guess not." She winked at Jed.

What did that mean? Sissy skipped far ahead of Jed. He grudged his way down the hot sidewalk, miffed at her energy in this weather. It wasn't fair. Why'd God make him be born in Texas? He needed California's mild weather. Every time he spent too much time in the sun, he got a terrible headache, wet clothes from too much sweat, and a foul temper to boot.

Let Sissy skip. I'm walking.

A gray car pulled up alongside Sissy. Jed flat-out ran to catch up, but he was two blocks away. Sissy bent toward the car's window. Laughed.

Sissy, no!

The door opened out.

"Sissy!" One block away.

Sissy looked up.

"Don't!" Jed sprinted toward her, now a half block away.

The car inched forward.

Sissy walked around the door and stepped off the curb.

"I said don't!" Jed crashed himself into Sissy, pushing her into the opened door. He grabbed her shoulders. Shook them. "What are you thinking?"

"What?" Sissy looked around him to the car's driver. "What's gotten into you, Jed?"

Panic stole his voice.

"It's just Muriel. She's on her way to Hixon's." Sissy pointed inside the car.

Jed wrenched his neck to the left. Sure enough, bald Muriel sat smiling behind the wheel.

Jed swallowed and took a breath.

"I didn't mean harm, Jed, really I didn't. I saw your sister and thought I'd chat."

"Why'd you open the door?" Jed shaded his eyes from the

afternoon sun. He squinted, then shut his eyes and opened them so he could see Muriel better in the car's dark interior.

"This old car is a fiasco. Wouldn't that be a great name for a Ford? Ford Fiasco? Well, my Ford Fiasco's automatic windows only work when they feel like it, and they didn't feel like it now. So I opened the door. I must've looked like a stalker. Forgive me."

Her face radiated *I'm sorry*, so Jed let most of his anger slip out the back door of his temper. If only Hap would do that, but he seemed to have locked that escape door with twenty locks like the New York apartment Jed saw on a TV show.

"Jed?" Sissy tugged at his wet sleeve.

"What?"

"She's going to Hixon's. Said she'd drive us there if we want. I'm hot."

"Me too." Though Jed knew it wasn't proper to hitch a ride, he figured a woman messed up with cancer could be trusted. He hoped. Maybe. Besides, he was tired of walking. It's one thing he couldn't seem to tame in himself, his laziness when it got hot. Heck, he'd probably hitch a ride with Hitler on a day like today.

They slid across the front seat, Sissy first, then Jed. The vinyl burned Jed's legs, so he pulled at the bottom of his shorts to make them longer. Muriel put the car into gear and pulled away from the curb.

"How do you know Hixon?" Jed asked.

"He helped me when I became a widow. When Chuck died, I had no real friends of my own, with the church dispersing like it did. One day Hixon showed up at my door with a bowl of greens, a slew of corn bread, and a plate of honey ham. Even brought me a cherry pie he'd made himself. We've been friends ever since."

"That sounds like Hixon," Sissy said.

"It is. That man is a fine person. The finest." Muriel slowed the car to a stop right in front of Hixon's place. Like she said she would.

Hixon poured lemonade. Not the kind you get from the freezer in a can, not even the powdered variety, but real honest-to-goodness lemonade. Squeezed lemons, ice cubes, sugar, and cold water. Jed realized he'd never again enjoy lemonade done any different. From now on, it would be Hixon's way or no way at all.

"You like it?" Hixon poured more into Jed's glass. The ice tinkled against the glass.

"Yes, sir." A ceiling fan blew warm air around the porch, much to Jed's joy. It was hot, but at least the air moved and the shade of the porch chased away the sun's scorch. He could smell his armpits, though. This getting to be a man thing had its drawbacks. He took a long drink and considered the two Hixons: there was Sissy's Hixon, who could do no wrong, and there was Jed's Hixon, who seemed all right on the outside but too good to be true. Jed wanted to settle into Sissy's Hixon, especially as lemonade cooled his throat, but a small niggle of fear kept its place in Jed's mind.

Hixon set the pitcher on a small table topped with a tablecloth full of roses and leaves.

Kind of girly, Jed thought.

"You like my tablecloth?"

"It's kind of girly."

Sissy laughed. "I love it."

"You would," Jed said.

"My mama gave it to me." Hixon looked away.

"Really?" Muriel sat on a wicker chair, the only one on Hixon's porch with a cushion.

"Well, actually, no." Hixon fussed with his shoes. Tied the laces in double knots. "I got it from her estate."

"Why?" Sissy asked.

"My mama and me, well it was just the two of us." Hixon sat back on his old rocker, his hands behind his head. "And we didn't get along so well."

Muriel took a long drink of lemonade, topping it off with a long aaaaaah. "You've never told me this."

"It wasn't ripe for the telling until now." Hixon bent forward.

"Sounds like it'll be a sad story," Sissy said.

"It *was* sad. Mama was into Mama and no one else. Maybe she figured she'd been dealt a bad lot when I came into the picture. Mama never did like surprises. Had her whole life figured out, and then I came along, messing with everything."

Jed looked at Hixon, wondering if Hap'd ever felt that way about him—an interruption. Up 'til now, he'd believed he was wanted.

Muriel took another long drink of lemonade. "Why didn't she put you up for adoption? Or—"

"Thank God she didn't do the 'or.'" Hixon sat back in his chair, his face glistening brown. "Or I wouldn't be here chatting with you folks."

"Why?" Sissy asked.

"It wasn't legal back then, killing your baby, but that doesn't mean it wasn't tempting. My mama told me once that she entertained the idea, even if it meant breaking the law."

Sissy's eyes grew wide. "Oh, my." Jed had heard the word *abortion* before, but talking to someone so alive as Hixon, thinking his Mama might've made that choice, made him uncomfortable. He took a shoe off, then his sock, and scratched a mosquito bite, all at once remembering how Hap scolded him for lacking self-control when it came to bites. He put his sock back on. "Well, if she didn't want you, why'd she keep you?"

Hixon looked injured, like those bad guys on TV who've been shot in the chest and stagger backwards. "It's a mystery."

He pressed his hands to his knees. "One that'll never be solved, I reckon. My guess is that her mama and papa said she couldn't keep the baby. I can say this about Mama: she was stubborn and had a will of her own. If someone told her to do one thing, she'd do the other, and *boy* would she do the other."

"Did she ever tell you she didn't want you?" Jed asked. He swatted away a mosquito.

"Not in so many words. She didn't hit me or anything. But sometimes you just know you're not wanted. She didn't have to say it out loud. I knew."

"What about your daddy?" Sissy threw a glance Jed's way.

"Don't know who he is, child. Only that he's black."

"Black?" Jed asked. Wasn't that a given?

"Mama told me that much. That certainly didn't narrow down my search. No matter how much I tried to find out who my father was, I could never find one clue."

Like Daisy. Her face flew into Jed's mind all of a sudden. But instead of the happy face Jed posted all over town, this Daisy looked tired. And worried. And alone. Was she searching for her daddy?

"I'm sorry," Sissy said. A tear dripped down her face.

"Not half as sorry as I am, Sissy." He took a long breath, let it out. "So Mama, she seemed mad at me since before I can remember. Had her own life, her own plans, and I didn't fit. In any way. Whenever I needed something, like shoes for school, she'd bark at me about how much I was costing her, how ungrateful I was." He took a long drink of lemonade.

Jed put his shoe back on, though his foot still itched. He remembered school starting last year, how Hap told him to wear his old shoes. When Mama protested that Jed's feet were far too big for them now, Hap roared on and on about how much his kids cost him. He threw a wad of money Mama's way, told her to buy a pair at the thrift store if she was so bent on spending his hard-earned money. Jed looked at Hixon with new eyes. Understood him.

Hixon looked small. He searched the sky for words, it seemed. Like the right words were scattered in the clouds, but they weren't in any particular order and it was up to him to piece them together proper. He sighed. "After her pregnancy scandalized her parents, I came howling into the world. They refused to see me. When I was five days old, they both died in a car crash — drunk driver. They'd left all their fortune to Mama, which was a funny thing, given their distaste for me. Probably never got around to changing their will fast enough. Mama said they'd be hollering in their graves because they ended up paying for us after all." Hixon touched his chin with his right hand. "Though Mama still made me feel bad when I cost her money."

"That's awful," Muriel said.

Sissy looked at Jed. He nodded. They both knew that feeling.

"I agree," Hixon said. "My mama loved no one. Only herself. Spent her life rolling around in her money. Bought herself a nice house, a shiny new Cadillac, vacations everywhere. Met lots of men who loved her for her money, but not for her heart. As the money died down, the men stopped knocking. I left home for good. When I did, I could just imagine her sigh of relief. When I heard she died, you know what I did?"

"What?" Sissy asked.

"I cried like a baby. My mama never knew me. Never bothered to find out who I was. So what did I do? I ran around life with a mama-shaped emptiness, trying desperately to fill it with a fast lifestyle." Hixon stopped, his eyes wet.

Would that be Jed's life? Part of that wandering and rebelling appealed to Jed, if he was really honest. Stick it to Preacher Hap Pepper — the failed father of the prodigal son. But then he thought of Mama's tired face, what all that rebelling would do to her. How angry it would make Hap. How he'd take it out on Sissy too. No, he wouldn't be as weak as Hixon. He'd keep on the straight and narrow — for the sake of Mama and Sissy.

"When my mama died, I wept crocodile tears, not because she was dead but because when she was alive, she never lived. Never really loved." He took a drink of lemonade, then raised his glass as if in a toast. "So I drove clear to Sulfur Springs. I went to her funeral, saw her lifeless in the coffin. Maybe fifty folks were there and none of them knew who I was. Not one. The funeral director, he tried to shoo me away until I told him. I had to show him a picture of me and Mama out in front of the State Fair of Texas to prove it. Even then, he eyed me when I paid my respects."

"That's strange." Muriel folded her hands on her lap. Jed thought her eyes seemed far away, like they were imagining heaven.

"I didn't cry when I saw Mama there. I held myself together. Something about grieving in front of folks who didn't even know who I was. So I looked at Mama, touched her cold, hard hand — the hand that seldom held mine unless she was pulling me down the street — and said good-bye. I left the funeral home, got in my car, and let the waterworks flow."

"How'd you get the tablecloth?" Sissy perched her chin on her hands, looking into Hixon's chocolate-chip eyes.

"Her estate had a sale — everything she owned. I slipped in to the house I'd never grown up in — she bought that house in celebration after I left home. Funny thing, the house smelled like Mama, like her flowery perfume. By now I knew she'd left nothing to me. Her will said she'd given everything to the sorority she'd joined in college, which, according to her, were her glory years, when she had a life before she had me. So I walked inside. First thing I saw was this tablecloth. Mama always did like pretty things. I paid five dollars and fifty cents for it and left. I haven't been back to Sulfur Springs since."

Sissy touched the cloth. "It's old."

"Yep, like my heart feels sometimes. I've tried to convince myself I never really needed a mama. But you know what? I did. I do. And I'll never really get over that. It's one thing to get over a daddy you've never met. But it's quite another to get over a mama who never really loved you."

Hixon turned away.

Jed could see Hixon's shoulders shake a bit, so he steeled himself. The only thing that mattered in life was self-control. Responsibility.

Muriel stood. She walked over to Hixon and placed a pale hand on his shoulder. "If you were my son," she said, "I'd holler praises to God every single day of my life. I'd be so proud of you. Let me say it now, Mr. Hixon Jones."

Hixon turned toward her, eyes wet.

"I am proud of you. I love you. You have been the delight of my widowhood. You are the best son I never had. And if you'll have me, I'd like to be your mama from now on. As long as I have breath."

Sissy hiccuped a cry. Jed's eyes remained dry. Hixon hugged Muriel, hugged her tight, so tight Jed hoped he'd squeeze the cancer clear out of her.

Muriel laughed and pulled away. "Well, I don't much look like your mama, I'm sure. Me being pasty white and all."

Hixon pulled out his wallet. He opened the black leather and fetched a raggedy picture. "My mama and me," he said. "In front of the State Fair of Texas." He turned it toward Jed, Sissy, and Muriel.

"She's white," Sissy said.

"White as a cloud in a blue sky." Hixon handed it to Muriel.

Muriel smiled. "Well, isn't that like the Lord?" She stepped away from Hixon, her chalky head shiny with sweat. Muriel opened her arms wide, like she'd welcome the world in her embrace. She spun a full circle on the porch. "I can almost taste the grace."

Jed took another drink of lemonade. Grace? He'd always thought it something you said before a meal. Or something God offered sinners. Could it be that real grace had a taste? And would it taste a lot like lemonade on this porch with these folks? Jed knew he'd experienced something he'd longed for but didn't know existed in the world: family, without yelling, sprinkled with kindness.

Jed remembered Hap's promises that he wouldn't lose his temper again. That he'd be a good father. A good husband. And he would be, for a brief snatch of time. "It won't last," Jed said in a hushed tone. "It never does."

"What did you say, Jed?" Hixon leaned closer.

"Nothing," he mumbled. "It was nothing."

"He said it won't last." Sissy's mouth stretched into a lower-lip pout.

Jed shot her a look.

She wilted.

"It's okay," Muriel said. "Your brother has a right to his opinion. And I have a right to my own. And here's mine." She looked at Hixon. "If only I could be your mama a long, long time. Then I'd be happy." Muriel looked at a bird cawing on a telephone wire. "But I'm afraid my crowing is nearly up."

"You'll beat cancer. I know it." Hixon's voice sported tremors. He didn't sound so much like a prophet. More like a scared boy.

"That's something I don't know. But I have a plan to keep me alive." Muriel rubbed her bald head.

"How?" Jed asked.

"In due time, child. When the fullness comes."

Twenty-Three

In the hallway before church started, Hixon pulled Jed aside. "Muriel's agreed to come to church with me."

"So?"

"So, she said if I went to Mass with her Saturday nights, she'd come along to church with me. You don't think it'll be a problem, bringing her along, do you?"

Jed looked through the open double doors leading into the sanctuary. Hap did his usual Sunday rushing around up and down the aisles, straightening things. "No, I'm sure it'll be fine."

Hixon and Muriel sat in pew three, left side, something that caused quite a stir. Jed didn't doubt the elders' and deacons' wives would be chatting about this for years to come. Not only because a black man sat holding a white bald woman's hand but even more because Muriel was Catholic, something Hap had been sure to preach about ever since he knew Mama befriended Muriel. Last week it was "The Seven Deadly Sins of the Catholic Church."

Funny thing was, if Hixon was Jesus with a Hixon suit on, like Sissy said, to Jed, Muriel was Jesus as a bald woman. Kind. Forgiving. Dancing eyes. Full of love and compassion. How could Hap's words be true? And didn't they all worship the same God anyway? The God of the Bible? The One who made the world? Who sent His Son?

He craned his neck to look back again at Muriel and Hixon, both singing "Amazing Grace." The congregation sang in whispers, so it was a welcome change whenever he heard Hixon's voice above all the hushed voices. Joined with Muriel's, the church nearly sounded alive.

They all finished with grace leading them "home."

Hap rose. He paced the stage around the pulpit, not saying a thing. Jed's skin prickled, then burst into sweat. When Hap paced, they were in for a long, long sermon. Hap stood at the pulpit, both hands clenching the wooden sides with white knuckles. His Bible sat open to the Old Testament.

Yep, this was going to be a long morning. Jed slouched in the pew.

Mama whispered, "Sit up." He did. Hap stiffened as if he obeyed Mama's command too. He looked like a rocket on a launchpad, ready for countdown. Three. He looked above everyone's heads. Two. He breathed in really deep. One.

"I've come before you today." Hap spoke in his happy-friendly voice. Jed knew it would only be a matter of time. "To walk us through the Ten Commandments. Now don't you worry. We'll not cover all of them this week. Just one. An important one. Adultery." Mama stiffened next to Jed while Sissy colored ponies on the back of the bulletin.

"I am going to tell you a story. A parable, if you will. The beauty of telling stories is that folks can find themselves written into a story better than they can see themselves in sermons."

Jed noticed the congregation to his right, all smiling and nodding in agreement. Hap had them right where he wanted them. "There once lived a poor man who worked his fingers to the bone. His only solace in life was his dear, sweet bride. Every day, after working in the fields, cutting his fingers on thorns and feeling the heat beat down on his head, he refreshed himself by sitting down to a delicious dinner made by his wife. Even if they had no money, his wife made suppers you wouldn't believe. Honey ham. Black-eyed peas. Corn bread so light the heavens sang its praises. Having dinner became the poor man's only joy."

Jed remembered their dinner last night, how Hap licked the ham juice that dripped from the corner of his lips, how he forked his black-eyed peas and shoved them hungrily into his mouth, how he praised Mama for the best corn bread this side of East Texas.

Hap looked at Mama. But he didn't have the same look of corn bread glee this time. Mama pretended not to notice. She put her hand on Jed's shoulder, pretending to whisper something to him. She'd been the object of sermons before. She seemed not to notice, but for days and days after, she'd take to her room, battling headache upon headache.

"But one sorry day, the man came home. His dear wife had neglected her appearance. Instead of her usual neat clothes, she wore rags. Instead of smelling like roses, she reeked of sweat and toil. And what did she have to show for it? Gruel. The man ate the tasteless paste, then spat it out on the table. 'What's gotten into you?' the man asked his wife. 'I'm busy,' she said. She didn't meet his eyes."

Sissy wrote, "Draw me a kitten," on her bulletin. Mama drew a kitten with its stomach exposed, a ball of string tangled in its paws.

"The poor man didn't know what to do," Hap said in his storytelling voice. "His wife had never acted this way. 'You were never busy before,' he said to her. 'I have my reasons,' she said. 'I'm tired of you, always coming home every single day, expecting me to feed you, all with very little food. It's a miracle I've lasted this long.' That's when a man stepped out from the shadows of their home. 'She's mine now,' he said. 'It's as it should be.'"

Hap shook his head. A tear leaked down his cheek. "That poor man didn't know what hit him. Here he'd been toiling long hours, believing his wife loved him, when really she was sneaking around. The woman in that story? She's the face of adultery. Unsatisfied with her lot in life, she went looking for more. She didn't cherish her husband's love. Didn't appreciate his hard work. All she could do was complain inside herself until who she thought was someone better came along."

As Hap strung words together, Jed tried to settle his mind. Tried to convince himself that Mama was innocent and didn't deserve this backhanded talking to. Sissy patted Jed's leg.

"I'm scared," she whispered.

Jed put his arm around her. She trembled beneath it.

"The human heart has a terrible capacity for treachery. Folks who look moral on the outside can be like tombs of death on the inside, full of lies and deceit. Lies and deceit are terrible twins. Terrible. Left unchecked in the human heart, those twins will wreak havoc on families. Will even destroy them."

Mama picked at her fingernails.

"The Bible says, 'Do not commit adultery.' No truer words were ever written. Why? Because adultery is the deepest of betrayals. The worst of all sins." He settled his gaze on Mama once again, but Mama kept her head down, supposedly taking notes.

An amen echoed from the back of the church.

Jed looked at Mama's drawings. Roses, daisies, tulips. Hap's words had that way about them with Mama, made her go away to a different place, a better place, a happy place, a garden of flowers.

Jed felt hot. Really hot. Outside-in-July hot. He wiped his forehead with his church shirt, but it was no use. More sweat came, replacing what he took away. That's how life felt. Just when he grabbed a bit of relief, another problem came along, making things the same or worse than they'd been before. Murphy's Law, Hap had called it. If something was bound to go wrong, it would. Jed lived his own Murphy's Law as Hap pounded the pulpit like a judge would bang a gavel.

"I'm just going to say it, folks: adultery is wrong!"

Bam, bam, bam. A spattering of amens.

"We should not tolerate it!" Bam, bam, bam, bam, bam, bam, bam. A whoop from the back. "Sin will find you out!" Bam, bam, bam, bam, bam.

"Preach it," came Officer Spellman's voice.

Mama doodled. Sissy colored. Jed peeled away his thumbnail. Hap hollered, then got quiet.

"Mark my words, fellow pilgrims. God is aware. He sees. He's like Santa, always knowing when you've been bad or good." He looked at Mama again. "So be good, for goodness sake," he sang.

Laughter stuttered throughout the church. Hap wiped his forehead and smiled. Mama colored all her flowers in black and then scratched them out altogether. Sissy's ponies took on wings and flew in a cloudless sky. The kitten remained colorless. Jed did tic-tac-toe with himself. Cat game every time.

And Hap preached. Spoke of stoning, Old Testament laws, and the word *submission*. He told compelling stories about wandering wives that made the women in the congregation cry. Jed tried to block it all out, crammed his mind with tic-tac-toes. Without a pew in front of him, he had no way to hide his wandering mind. He distracted himself with Mama's "note-taking." She'd turned her bulletin over. A picture of a cross on a hill stood in front of a blazing sunset. Or was it a sunrise? Mama wrote the name "Jesus" in large letters. She pressed her black ballpoint into each letter. J-E-S-U-S. She pressed and pressed until the pen poked clear through, then she started again. Jesus. Jesus. Jesus.

It was Jed's prayer too. Jesus. Jesus. Jesus. Was it right to ask Jesus to deliver him from his own father? He repeated Jesus in his mind while Hap worked himself up into a man who resembled a windmill—arms flying in various circles while folks behind Jed shouted and hollered amens and hallelujahs.

"We have a missing girl, folks."

Jed flushed.

"Daisy, one of my Jed's friends. Folks have prayed. Searched. Put out flyers. I know I have. But let me let you in on a little secret. That child's missing because of her mother's sin. And not a pretty sin, I'm telling you. God has his ways of punishing folks who run headlong into sexual sin."

Jed fumed. He wished he had the gumption to stand up and scream his own words. Words about how Hap treated his own family. How it was all a big, fat lie. How Daisy didn't deserve any of this. Miss Emory either, no matter how cold her stare. How his mama didn't betray anyone. If anything, she held the whole family together somehow, paying for her miraculous work with headaches and crying spells. How Sissy ducked when Hap walked by. How Jed's backside had been crisscrossed with belts and tree branches.

But he sat there. Stewing in his anger. Flexing his arms. Willing them strength.

"Pastor?" Hixon's voice. Right in the middle of the sermon. Jed turned around. So did everyone else. Hixon stood all alone, Bald Muriel holding his hand from her seat. In the other hand he held a beat-up Bible.

Jed snapped his head back to Hap. "Hixon, I am preaching a sermon. You mind?" When Hap's eyes revealed anger's fire, he measured his words.

"The Good Lord, He told me to read us a Scripture, that's all. Would you mind if I did that?"

Jed heard a catch in Hixon's voice—not something regular folks would've noticed, but a close friend would. Hixon, nervous. Jed too.

"Well, then, by all means. For our edification, Hixon, read the congregation your Scripture. I was wrapping up anyway."

Anyone who didn't know Hap would think him kind, one of those flexible pastors who welcomed the Holy Spirit at a moment's notice. Jed knew better. Someday, maybe even today, Hixon would pay. Jed squirmed. He begged Hixon with his eyes to please stop, but Hixon kept his eyes on the page of his Bible.

"Jesus went unto the mount of Olives," Hixon read, his voice still hitched. "And early in the morning he came again into the temple, and all the people came unto him; and he sat down, and taught them."

Jed let out the breath he'd been holding. Something about Jesus.

"And the scribes and Pharisees brought unto him a woman taken in adultery; and when they had set her in the midst, They say unto him, Master, this woman was taken in adultery, in the very act. Now Moses in the law commanded us, that such should be stoned: but what sayest thou?" Hixon's voice lost its waver.

Jed knew the punch line to this Bible story; he'd never understood it because it meant sinners got off scot-free. No, God wasn't like that. God punished—the Bible was full of God's wrath against sinners. Made the earth open up and swallow an entire tribe. And yet Jesus seemed to turn God into a nice guy, a favorite uncle who pardoned everything.

"This they said, tempting him, that they might have to accuse him. But Jesus stooped down, and with his finger wrote on the ground, as though he heard them not. So when they continued asking him, he lifted up himself, and said unto them, He that is without sin among you, let him cast a stone at her." Hixon looked around at the congregation. Met Jed's eyes.

Jed turned and looked at Hap. His face appeared blank, a sure sign of doom. Jed could handle hot anger, but Hap's cold silence he could not bear.

Hixon cleared his throat, spoke a little louder. He got through the part where everyone from old to young left the woman alone. "Woman, where are those thine accusers? hath no man condemned thee? She said, No man, Lord. And Jesus said unto her, Neither do I condemn thee; go, and sin no more."

Hixon sat. Jed could feel the electricity in the room—an uncomfortable feeling, like when a scrawny kid stands up to a bully and you don't know what will happen next but you're pretty sure the scrawny kid's gonna get a walloping.

Hap nodded to Hixon. "Brother Jones served us a good reminder about grace today. That no sin is unforgivable, 'cept of course the blasphemy of the Holy Spirit. Thank you kindly for that reminder. And it's a reminder we all need to heed. Some of you out there are walking the Devil's path right now. You're that woman. You're caught. It's time you took yourself to Jesus, to let Him know how wretched you are." He angled a look at Mama, but Mama didn't return the favor.

"Because you never know when your last breath might come. Or whether your sins will be upon the heads of your children. Come." The organ struck up a melancholy tune. Hap spread his arms wide to the congregation.

Jed remembered when Bald Muriel did that on Hixon's porch, how she seemed to embrace the world to herself. Hap's open arms felt more like the doors of a jail cell to Jed. He knew Hap had expectations. He'd instructed him and Sissy—and Mama too—close to a hundred times. "Whenever there's an altar call, even if you don't feel like repenting, you need to come forward. To set an example," he'd told them. "Sometimes folks need others to prime the pump. And you're the prime, you hear me?"

Sissy looked at Jed, eyes sad. Yes, she'd heard.

Together they stood. Like robots, they marched the three or four steps from the front pew to the stairs before the pulpit and knelt. Others came too. Heck, most of the church came, kneeling before Hap, who whispered, "Praise Jesus," like a skipping record.

Jed craned his neck around.

Mama sat on the pew, pressing her pen into Jesus. Jed felt green. Mama defying Hap by not repenting would make this day one of the worst days of his life, he knew.

Hixon and Bald Muriel were nowhere.

Jed prayed.

Jesus, take me. I'm a sinner. Take me. Let Hap mess with me. Not Sissy. Not Mama. Not Hixon. Not even Bald Muriel. Let me take it. Please. Let me take it like a man.

When Jed stood, he felt taller, even as the shadow of his father fell across him.

Twenty-Four

When they veered slowly into the driveway, a dog wagged a happy tail at them. It sat on the front porch like he owned the place, barking when Hap stopped the car.

Sissy tore out first. "A dog! A dog! A dog!" she kept hollering.

"What in tarnation is this?" Hap said.

"Be careful," Mama said. "You never know about dogs. Sissy? I said be careful!"

But Sissy paid no mind. She flung herself at the golden retriever with a red bow around its neck. He or she licked Sissy square in the face with a red velvet tongue. Jed petted the dog's head. Hap did too. "It's probably a stray," he said.

"No, Daddy. Look! A ribbon! He's a gift!"

"From who?" Mama asked. She unlocked the front door.

"Don't know." Sissy hugged the unnamed dog. "But I aim to keep him."

"Could be a her." Jed squatted on his haunches and looked into the dog's brown brown eyes.

"I'm not checking," she said. "You check."

"We'll do that later." Hap put a strong hand around the dog's bow. "Let's take it to the backyard and see what we can figure out."

Jed worried all through lunch and dinner that Hap would

remember Mama's doodling, her non-repenting. He fretted about Hap calling Hixon and giving him a piece of his mind (which usually took an hour or so of loud talking). Instead, Hap played catch with the dog. Jed had always wondered about circuses and how all those lions got tamed, but maybe it was the other way around. Maybe a golden retriever with a red bow tamed Hap.

After Hap determined the dog was female, Sissy named her Clementine, as in "Oh my darling, Clementine."

The family sat at the picnic table eating hamburgers, potato salad, watermelon, and sweet tea while Clementine tried to hop on the tire swing. She nipped at the rubber, then yelped when it swung away.

"Clementine?" Jed took another bite of burger. "That's a weird name."

Sissy hummed the tune.

"And what a strange song to name a dog after. It's a sad song."

"It isn't sad," Sissy said. "Clementine'd been lost and gone forever, then we found her!"

"More like she was a gift from someone," Mama said. "With that bow and all. Who d'you suppose did that?"

"Beats me." Hap shoved down some potato salad. "Probably a loyal church member."

"Aren't you going to try to find out who sent her?" Mama wiped ketchup from the corner of her mouth.

"We'll find out in due time, no doubt in my mind." Hap finished his potato salad. Clementine ran to him, put her golden head on his leg. He stroked her head and looked at Mama. "That's a good girl. A good, obedient girl."

Hap started Ouisie-ing right after Sissy and Jed went to bed. "Ouisie, you're not telling me the truth. Ouisie, how long will you taunt me like this?"

When Hap turned up his volume, Jed thanked the Lord for Clementine, who would distract Sissy from shaking at Hap's voice. Clementine followed that girl around like it was the dog's job to fulfill every dog wish Sissy'd ever had. Even went to bed with her. Knowing Sissy, Clementine would sleep next to her, dog-snoring with that big golden head on Sissy's flower pillow.

With no dog to keep his mind elsewhere, Jed heard every last bit of Hap's yelling, but he couldn't hear Mama's voice. On a rare occasion, she yelled back, but usually, like tonight, she'd be like Quiet Jesus, mouth shut before His accusers.

Thick footsteps pounded the floor beneath Jed. More Ouisies. A crash.

Jed sat up. Then stood. Then listened at his doorway.

"Just admit it!" Hap screamed.

A clicking echoed down the hallway into his parents' bedroom. Then a bark. And another. And another. Jed ran to the room, wondering if Clementine had found Mama bloodied this time. He ran into Sissy, who stood in the doorway, a hand to her mouth.

In utter silence stood Hap, his hand on Clementine's head, who had no more barks. "You're a good girl," he said. Mama pulled the covers to her chin and seemed to aim a thank-you the dog's way.

Jed opened his window to let in the night. In his nightshirt, lying flat on his bed, he gazed out the window. Stars seemed brighter tonight. Crickets sang. The air moved slightly, enough to breeze a bit of relief on Jed's warm face.

Clementine clicked once again down the hallway and entered Jed's room. She carried Jed's shoe. Actually Daisy's.

Jed sprang from bed. "No, Clementine. No!" He pulled the mangled shoe from Clementine's wet mouth. Daisy's left shoe, or what had been. The dog had chewed the sole clear off. The laces were gone. The top? Mangled. Jed moaned.

Twenty-Five

Jed painted with one shoe of Daisy's and one shoe of his own all that next week. When Miss Emory allowed, he left early. He'd spend an hour or two at the old hideout, re-reading Daisy's diary, wishing her home. But as the weeks wore on, Miss Emory kept him close by. Day after day without a peep from Daisy made Miss Emory clingy and Jed more desperate.

Hixon helped him finish up Miss Emory's house. They painted it white with green trim. "Miss Emory lives in Anne of Green Gables' house," Sissy'd said to Jed yesterday.

Jed and Hixon knocked on Miss Emory's front door the day they finished the job.

She came out, pitcher of tea in hand. "Sit on the porch," she told them.

"We finished," Jed said. Every time he put the brush to one of the house's clapboards, he hoped to cover his guilt. But when the whole house shined, he didn't feel any better. One look into Miss Emory's pale eyes and the guilt backed up like a stopped-up toilet, forcing him to wish he could rewind the clock and walk Daisy home, for crying out loud. If Jed had a stick big enough, he'd beat some sense into himself.

Miss Emory walked from her porch steps all the way down the path that cut her front lawn precisely in half. She stopped at the front gate and turned around. She smiled. Really smiled. "It's beautiful, boys. I feel like a princess."

Jed let out his breath. He actually believed she'd snarl and point out flaws, demanding they do the whole thing again. Not smile.

She walked up the steps again, poured them all tea, and lifted her glass. "To the house," she said.

Hixon lifted his glass. Jed did too.

She sat on the porch swing and raised her glass once more. Her smile vanished quickly as the sun when a thunderstorm banged through. "And to finding my little girl," she choked.

Hixon didn't lift his glass. Instead, he rose from the chair and walked over to Miss Emory. He placed his right hand on her shoulder, then knelt before her.

Jed stayed put while his heart motored fast in his chest.

"Dear, sweet Jesus," Hixon prayed. "This child of Yours, she needs You. Comfort Miss Emory right now. Give her peace. She's in anguish. We all are. But no one has anguish like the mama of a girl gone missing. Oh, Jesus. Please, please help us find Daisy. You know where she is. You know. Give us clues. Help us. Give us hope. And touch Miss Emory with Your kindness now. Please, Lord. Amen."

Miss Emory's eyes brightened. She grabbed Hixon's hand and squeezed it. "Thank you."

"My pleasure." He sat down.

She looked Jed's way, but he looked beyond her to the tree where his shoe'd been stolen. He looked down at his mismatched shoes. Wondered if she knew he'd borrowed Daisy's pair.

"I heard what your daddy said in church."

Jed didn't meet her eyes. Couldn't.

"How he said this was all my fault. That my sins caused Daisy to go missing."

Jed swallowed. "I'm—"

"Don't say you're sorry. Don't." An edge crept into her voice. "Your daddy is wacko. I don't care a hind leg what he says. Besides, he's not God, and it's God I'm mad at."

Jed wondered why Miss Emory seemed touched by Hixon's prayer a minute ago and now growled about God. Maybe it was like Hap said: "Son, you'll never ever understand women. Accept it. Trying to understand 'em will make you crazy."

Hixon didn't say a word. Neither did Jed.

"What kind of God—" Tears slipped down her face, letting her question hang quiet in the porch air.

Hixon handed Miss Emory a hankie. She bowed forward, the white cloth smothering her face, and wept.

"You keep that hankie, Miss Emory. You might be needing it."

She sat up. "Don't you say those faithless words, Hixon. You hear me? Daisy is coming home. She's coming home to stay. She's away, that's all."

"That's not what I meant. I'm sorry, Miss Emory. I'm sure she's away, just like you said." Hixon stepped back.

Jed drew circles on the outside of his tea glass. He knew now was the time to ask Miss Emory about Daisy's dad again. His thoughts kept coming back to David Carter, Mama's first love. Was he the same David? After all, Miss Emory and Mama both grew up in Defiance. May as well have liked the same fellow. "Miss Emory?"

"What."

Jed stiffened. Her *what* was not a question, just an angry statement. "I was wondering ..." Jed looked at his mismatched shoes, like they'd give him strength. "Have you had any contact with Daisy's dad?"

She sat back, her eyes smaller. She looked none too pleased. "I believe that's my business."

Jed fidgeted. He tried to swallow his fear, but it stayed like a wad of too much bubble gum in his throat. "Do you think he might be behind Daisy gone missing?" There, he asked it. He let out his breath.

"Do you think," she mimicked, "that I'm a fool? An idiot?

Folks think that just 'cause I'm poor, I don't have sense, an education. I am an intelligent woman."

Hixon looked her way. "We all know you're smart. What Jed's asking is—"

"I heard what he said. I'm not deaf." She looked at Jed. "Of course I thought of that. Who do you think I called first, but David Carter?"

Jed's heart quickened.

"And?" Hixon turned in his chair to see Miss Emory, who now stood at the opposite end of the green-trimmed porch.

Her shoulders slumped. "He didn't take her."

Jed let out a breath. But something bothered him. He remembered Miss Emory doing nothing the day after Daisy's disappearance, like she was too paralyzed to search. Had she let this detail slip away too? Asked one question and let it rest? Jed owed it to Daisy to risk Miss Emory's wrath. "How can you be so sure?"

"Well, after what your daddy said about me, I'm sure everyone has their doubts about my judgment. But I can tell you this: David keeps to himself. He's private. He's never wanted anything to do with Daisy anyway, so I pretty much figured he'd have nothing to do with Daisy going missing."

"Really?" Jed's heart pounded.

To Jed's surprise, Miss Emory didn't look angry, only tired. "I'm absolutely sure. One hundred percent."

"Then who?" Jed didn't ask the question to anyone in particular, just to the wind, or maybe God.

Hixon raised a hand, as if he sat in sixth grade and wanted to answer properly. "A dark world causes bad stuff. Used to be I was shocked by this sort of thing. No longer. This world we live in ... well, it's the Devil's playground."

Miss Emory ran her hand along the pure white clapboard to the left of her living room window. "That it is. I've seen both sides of life. The so-beautiful-it-takes-your-breath-away side and the deepest darkest pit you can ever imagine. I wish I could always live in the beauty."

Hixon stood. "Me too. I get it when Jesus comes near, like a rush of cold wind through a Texas summer. Those are the times I sing to the heavens. Real loud. Because I know the wind will pass, and it'll be sorry old me, sweating and sweltering under the frying pan sun. Those beautiful moments are what save me when the dark comes crawling along."

Miss Emory's eyes leaked again, but this time quiet tears moistened her cheek. "How do you know?"

"What's that?" Hixon sat on the porch ledge across from her, his long legs like whittled-smooth sticks stained brown.

She leaned against the wall so that she faced him.

Jed's face felt hot, like he was spying on a kissing movie, though the two of them said nothing mushy to each other. He wondered if he should excuse himself to go home.

"How do you know? How do you really know Jesus is real? You speak as if He's your best friend, that He's as near as your breath. I don't understand."

Jed said a silent prayer. Hap had lectured Jed's Sunday school class about fruit and picking and souls, how when the Holy Spirit draws a person, they start asking important questions. Miss Emory, well, she seemed at the ripe stage all of a sudden. You knew it, Hap said, when folks asked the same questions they used to, but this time they asked them without anger, without a fist toward God. Hap was right. Seeing the lines on Miss Emory's face—usually scratched deep into her skin—smooth out like a new peach started Jed on a new journey, a journey where he realized that not everything Hap said was a lie.

Hixon let the question float through the Defiance air. Let it take on wings and fly clear away. He rubbed his chin with his hand. Shook his head.

Jed almost started in, but then stopped. What could he say? When had Jesus come near? When had he sung to Jesus, all loud and strong under the sky? Sure, he could give Miss Emory a few facts about sin separating her from God, there being a chasm between her and him. He could share about Jesus bridging the chasm by being a perfect sacrifice. But what did that all mean? What kind of Jesus helped Hixon stand in church and say a Scripture that knocked Hap off his high horse? Or gave Bald Muriel that angel face when she had cancer? Truth was, Jed didn't know either. Didn't know a thing about Jesus, really. Only some facts typed neatly onto tracts. Now those words seemed lifeless.

Hixon crossed one leg over the other. He looked at Miss Emory, who promptly looked away. "The way I see it, you're either full of yourself, or you're full of nothing, or you're full of others' expectations, or you're full of Jesus. My guess is that right now you're full of nothing, Miss Emory ... you're at the end of your rope."

Jed thought about this. Was he full of himself? He sure felt empty, so that could be it. Others' expectations? One thing he did know: He constantly made his dad angry. He'd never meet with Hap's approval. Or at least he hadn't yet.

Hixon pushed himself away from the ledge, then turned around. He put two large hands on the ledge, looked at the front yard. Maybe he thought it was easier talking to Miss Emory if he didn't have to look in her eyes. Or maybe it was respect. Jed didn't know for sure. But the silence felt terribly awkward.

"Miss Emory?" Jed asked, filling the silence.

"Yes?"

"I wish I could take it all away from you."

Miss Emory sucked in a breath.

"Why would you wish that?"

"Just do, that's all."

"Because you understand?" She pushed a strand of blonde hair from her face. Jed nodded. Oh, how he understood. Hixon whistled a dove's call.

Miss Emory picked at her fingernail, something Jed saw Mama do nearly every morning during breakfast. "Funny thing? I live on Love Street, but I've never understood the word. 'Specially not referring to God. Hearing about God's love, it didn't make any sense is all. Why would someone so big think kindly on someone so small like me?"

Hixon placed a warm hand on Jed's shoulder. His way of taking over the conversation. He faced Miss Emory. "Do you love Daisy?"

Miss Emory looked at the old tree where Jed'd lost his shoe. "What kind of a question is that? Of course I love her."

"What makes you think you're any better than God? If you love Daisy, why wouldn't He love you? He's your daddy. He made you. Of course He loves you."

She shook her head. More tears. Jed looked away.

"Listen, I didn't mean to upset you. I think you're on a long journey with Daisy and all. I'd hate for you to walk it alone, without holding God's hand."

Miss Emory's lines came back. Sharp, like they'd been drawn with a ballpoint pen. "Hixon. You listen to me. Daisy's fine. She's alive."

"That's not what I meant." Hixon shook his head like he was scolding himself.

"I don't want to hear another one of your doom-and-gloom predictions about her. She's fine. She's lost is all. If your God, all high and mighty, can't take care of one little girl, then what's to say He'll take care of me?" She stood to her full height. "I'll be much obliged if you'd leave right now. And, please, don't come back."

Jed's eyes widened. Hixon looked injured. He appeared like he was about to say something—a good two or three times—but he shut his mouth each time. A silent prophet. Slow feet marched down Miss Emory's front porch steps. Head down, he said nothing. One foot, then the next, he plodded to the gate. He didn't turn when he unlatched it. Didn't nod. Didn't cock his head. He turned right and stepped like a man walking into prison. One step at a time.

Jed felt sick. He set down his tea glass. "I best be going."

Miss Emory shooed him away with her pale hand, her eyes once again blank, her frown lines more visible than they'd ever been. Her peachy skin scarred by lines and welts.

He walked down the pathway, past the big tree.

"You look like your father," she called.

Jed turned. He almost said, "And you and my mama loved the same man," but he didn't.

Twenty-Six

Clementine slobbered all over Jed when he came home. Jumped on him. Begged with those big brown eyes for him to play fetch. So Jed threw sticks and prayed. Each stick he threw, he said another prayer.

Lord, find Daisy.

Help me find out about David Carter.

Teach Miss Emory how to be filled with You.

Heck, teach me how to be filled with You.

Protect Sissy from Hap.

Protect Mama from Hap.

Protect us all from Hap.

Help me protect us all from Hap.

Help Hap to be filled with Jesus in a different way than he already is.

Please let us keep Clementine. For Sissy's sake.

Oh, and Sissy's lisp. Make it so no one hears it, Jesus.

Cure Bald Muriel.

Jed's arm hurt a little because he threw the Bald Muriel stick as far as he could. *Wimp!* Maybe if God saw how much he meant that prayer, He'd answer him. But he wasn't sure. God didn't seem to listen to him much, at least not lately. Used to be he'd said silly prayers at night, the easy kind God would always answer: help me to be good at school, bless everyone in the

193

whole wide world except Satan, bring world peace, and thanks for the food all day long. Those He could answer. It was when Jed started praying hard prayers that God seemed silent. Maybe he'd ask Bald Muriel what she thought. Maybe those Catholics had prayer nailed down.

Funny thing about the Bald Muriel prayer—God seemed to answer it right away. Not in the way Jed thought, but pretty immediate. She drove up in the driveway in her gray car. A coincidence? Maybe. He wasn't so sure anymore. Hixon said everything in the whole world was ordered by God. But did that mean Daisy's disappearance too?

Muriel, wig off-kilter, stepped out of her car and slammed the door hard.

"The door doesn't shut so well. Sorry about that." She walked right up to the front porch like she owned the place and plopped herself down.

Jed dropped the stick and joined her.

"What're you doing on this side of Defiance?" Jed called Clementine by slapping his knees.

Bald Muriel didn't answer. Clementine sat between them, placing her head on Muriel's lap. If a dog could purr, Jed was sure Clementine would. "Nice dog." She petted Clementine's head, looked into those dark eyes. When she pulled her hand away, Jed noticed it trembled. She covered it with her other hand and looked back at her car like there was something important there she forgot.

"She showed up one Sunday after church," Jed said.

"Well, imagine that." Her voice shook too, with the same rhythm as her hand.

"Are you all right?" The question popped out before Jed had time to think about it. Mama was right about God giving him empathy. He couldn't help but care about folks, ask about them, worry about them. One time Hixon said that meant God was calling him to be a shepherd of people. A pastor. Like Hap. But Jed would never be like Hap.

"Well," she said, "I am. I'm always all right. Long as I have the Lord holding my hand."

But Jed wasn't convinced. Her words were pure Muriel, but her voice sounded spooked. Jed looked down at her hands, still trembling. They were pale, with ropes of veins like earthworms crossing over each other in a sickly dance.

She must've noticed his gawking. "Don't mind them, Jed. It's what tired hands look like. They're not pretty, but they've sure done a lot of loving." She interlaced her fingers. "At least since Jesus got a hold of me."

"You didn't always know Him?"

"No, sir. Not even close. Of course, folks would blame my wayward ways before Jesus on me being Catholic. But it's not so. Once I met Jesus, I longed to go back to the Catholic Church, to discover what I'd missed. Only then, I couldn't go."

"Why not?"

"Chuck."

She looked at her hands. "I shudder to think of what things my hands did before I met Chuck."

"But I thought—"

"Well, he was a hard man. That's to be said. But Chuck, in his own Chuck way, introduced me to Jesus. When things were really hard, I talked myself back into loving him. Because who could hate the man that gave you Jesus?" Clementine licked Muriel's hand, but Muriel didn't wipe the slobber away. "I only wish I'd met Jesus sooner."

"Why?"

"So I would've been spared a heap of regret."

"I can't imagine you doing something you regret." Jed couldn't see it. Not when he looked in those kind Jesus eyes. He looked at his own hands. What had he done that he wished he hadn't? Oh, loads of stuff. And he was only fourteen. In a way, it felt good to know someone as holy as Bald Muriel did bad things too. Made him feel less alone.

Bald Muriel didn't say a word for a good minute or two. She shaded her eyes from the downing sun. Tears swept down her face, but she didn't wipe them. "I'm not proud of it, Jed. Not proud at all of my life before Jesus. Someday I'll tell you the whole terrible story, but today I don't have the strength for it. Suffice to say," she turned to Jed, "sometimes folks are just plain mean."

Jed didn't know if she meant she had been mean or someone else was mean. And he wasn't sure he wanted to know. It was easier for him to believe Bald Muriel was like a singing angel—all white and pure with a halo over her head.

"Do you ever wonder why folks are mean?"

Jed nodded.

"Me too. Given the chance, people will turn on you like an angry dog to its victim, baring teeth, ready to bite. They'll say all sorts of lies, or they'll easily believe other people's untruths about you. That's the way of the world, if you ask me. It bothers me that someone's unkindness surprises me … every time. I guess that's the penalty you pay for being an optimist."

Clementine cocked her large head, as if listening to Bald Muriel's sad speech, and slobbered another lick onto her shaking hands. "This dog, she seems to know, doesn't she?"

"Yeah, she does."

"What's her name?"

"Clementine."

"As in 'Oh my darlin'?"

"The same. Sissy named her. She's calling Clementine a miracle. An answer to prayer." Answer to prayer was something Hap said, particularly from the pulpit. Hearing Hap's words come out of his mouth pulled Jed from his talk with Muriel to worrying about whether Hap was fixing to come out the front door, spoil the moment. He often interrupted Jed when he was good and happy. But the front door stayed wonderfully shut.

"Maybe it is. I've seen stranger answers to prayer."

"You have?"

Muriel looked at Jed, seemed to look right through his heart. He wasn't sure what to do with his eyes when she did that, so he looked straight ahead, avoiding her gaze.

Jed remembered the prayers he threw like sticks moments ago. He wondered whether God heard them, though he knew inside that God could hear anything and everything. He wasn't quite sure if God tuned into his prayers, or whether He had so much to do that He didn't have time to listen to a fourteen-year-old boy prattle on and on. When he'd asked Hap about prayer, Hap said God answered three ways: yes, no, or wait. Then he started picking apart Jed's prayers, telling him which ones God preferred to answer quickly, like "help me sit still in church," and which ones He shoved aside, like "please bring me a new bike."

"Now it's my turn to ask," Bald Muriel said. "Are you all right?"

Jed scratched both ankles, the victims of chiggers and no self-control. He desperately wanted to ask her about prayer but worried she wouldn't have the answer either. And he didn't want to upset her. Still, he needed to know. And asking her seemed easier than pestering Hap again. "Yeah, I'm fine. It's that … well, what *do* you pray for?"

"Lots of things." She fidgeted with her wig, fussed with it, but it wouldn't sit right on her head, preferring to lean off-kilter. "Oh, snap!" She grabbed the wig and flung it across the yard toward Ethrea Ree's home. Clementine jumped up and chased after the wild hair, bringing it back to Muriel in her slobbery mouth.

Jed couldn't help but laugh.

Muriel belly laughed too. "Oh, goodness. Thank You, Jesus!"

She turned her face toward the upper branches of the oak tree out front. She clapped her hands together like folks did in church when someone sang special music. "You knew it, didn't You? Knew I needed a good laugh. Especially today." She took the wig from Clementine. Held it in her hands. Petted it like a cat.

She sat there, cradling the wig, for a long time. Not saying a word.

Normally Jed didn't like silence, but the quiet between them wasn't that anxious quiet he'd grown accustomed to in his house. No, it was more like a peaceful silence.

She looked at Jed, eyes wet. "I hate cancer," she whispered.

"I know."

Bald Muriel shook her head so furiously, Jed thought she was shaking the cancer clear out. "Well, if you can't do a thing about it, you may as well shake hands with it," she said in a loud voice.

Jed looked behind him. It was just a matter of time before Hap came pounding out the front door.

She flung the wig into the sky. Clementine brought it back, breathless. She dropped it at Bald Muriel's feet.

"Think I should put it on?" She winked at Jed. "Naah, this is far too much fun." She threw it again, toward the street. In a wink, Clementine returned, tail beating the air. "Now where were we?"

"Prayer."

"Yes, prayer. I pray for everything."

"Even your, um, your cancer?"

"Heck yeah, I pray it'll fly away, kind of like this wig. Problem is, it's staying put, unlike the wig." She catapulted the wig again, but it didn't go very far.

"Why doesn't God answer prayer?" Jed swallowed. What he really meant was why didn't God answer *his* prayers, but it would've been wrong to say that out loud.

"I don't know. It's a mystery."

That answer didn't satisfy. "A mystery? That's all you can say? I thought you were close to God." He regretted his words the moment they crackled out. Like lightning, they zapped Bald Muriel, knocked her joy clear away. Jed read it on her lifeless face.

"I've had moments when I feel very close to God, but sometimes those stagger between long stretches of desert. I've learned to relish it when He comes near to me because I know what a privilege His presence is."

"He seems far away." Jed scratched his ankles. Again.

"I know. And I'm sorry about that."

"No need to be sorry," Jed said. "God must be busy, that's all. Bothered by more important things."

Muriel sighed. "Used to be I thought God was simple to understand. That you said prayer a certain way, a certain number of times—you know, I'm Catholic, so I know all about saying the same thing over and over—and God was obligated to send a few miracles my way. The older I get, the more I realize how small I am and how silly my belief in the formula is." Clementine returned the wig again. Bald Muriel held it, examined the sloppy mess. "It's funny, you know. Funny." She stuck her white legs in front of her. "Just look at my legs."

Jed looked.

"What do you see?"

"Um. Legs?"

"Fat legs?"

Jed shook his head no. White and skinny as could be.

"There's a strange prayer God answered. They used to be fat lady legs. When my husband was alive, he'd poke fun at them. Called me his elephant woman. So I prayed. For skinny legs. Now I got 'em. Along with cancer."

"That's not fair." Jed watched as the sun lowered. In its light, the front yard looked like a photo on the cover of *Life* magazine.

Mama called it the best light of the day for taking pictures. Jed saw why. Muriel looked downright rosy.

She looked toward the trees. "No, it's not."

"So why pray?"

"Just to talk. God wants us to spend time with Him, and prayer's a great way to do that. Besides, like I said a minute ago, I'm small, Jed. Terribly small. Who am I to tell God anything?"

"It's confusing, that's all." Jed felt tired. He'd said far too many words just now—more than even Sissy would string together. Maybe even more than Daisy.

Muriel seemed to understand. She kept to herself while the sky kissed her face.

Jed could smell Mama's macaroni casserole and biscuits. He expected Hap any moment now.

"I need your help, Jed." Muriel said it so softly Jed had to bend near.

"What's that?"

"Painting."

Jed leaned back on his arms. He'd rather work for Bald Muriel than Miss Emory any day. And now that he was done ... "What are you painting? Your house?"

Muriel laughed. "Heavens no. It won't last much longer than I will. I was thinking of something more artistic. Something that'll outlast me."

"I'm no good at art." Jed remembered Hap's sermon about Jesus drawing in the sand, how it meant that He was some sort of amazing artist. Jed couldn't even draw a dog right.

"Don't have to be." She stood, holding the wig like a purse. "It's nearly supper time, isn't it?"

Jed nodded.

She walked to her car and opened the door. She turned. "I need to paint the wall by the rendering plant."

"What color?" The wall had been a hotbed for graffiti and

Tammy loves Chris and swear words; it could use a good covering over. Jed stood. He heard commotion in the house.

"Every color. A mural. With posies and green grass and animals and sunshine. That place could use a little cheer, don't you think?"

The front door opened, startling Jed. Muriel plopped the dog-slobber wig on top of her head. "Good evening, Preacher."

Hap put a strong hand on Jed's shoulder. "Evening."

"Have a wonderful supper." She sat in the car, slammed the door, and rolled down the window.

"I aim to." His words were straight, no highs, no lows.

"See you then. Bye, Jed." She waved.

Jed waved back as Hap tightened his grip on Jed's neck.

So much for prayer.

Twenty-Seven

Hap shoved a forkful of greens in his mouth, his macaroni and cheese untouched. "How do you know that Muriel woman didn't take Daisy?" Hap ate like a blind person, always clockwise from the top of his plate all around. Greens were at twelve midnight, or noon, whichever way you looked at it.

"That's crazy," Jed said. He knew Hap said preposterous things from time to time, something he normally chalked up to him being the kid and Hap being the dad, but in this instance, Hap made no sense at all. How could Bald Muriel possibly take Daisy? Jed dug into his mac and cheese. Mama made it better than anyone anywhere. All the ladies at church said so. She always topped hers with bread crumbs and baked it until the crust turned a warm brown. Pure heaven.

"The police found something." Hap shoved more greens in his mouth.

"I don't think discussing this at the dinner table—"

Hap threw a fist on the table, rattling the plates. "For crying out loud, Ouisie!"

Mama turned away. "You're not supposed to know what the police found," she whispered.

"I'm the chaplain," he spat.

She faced him. "You're not a policeman. Last I heard, investigations are private."

Hap pushed away from the table.

Mama wilted, backed away. "I'm sorry."

"Let's hope you're sorry. I trust you to keep your mouth shut, like a submissive wife, when I'm talking to our son. Besides, if you'd ever watch TV or read a paper now and again, you'd see this is common knowledge."

"You're scaring me," she said.

"Enough!" He strode toward Mama.

Sissy howled. Put her hands on her ears and slammed her eyes shut—her usual stance when words and arms starting flying.

Jed crashed between Mama and Hap.

"Oh, so you're a man now, I see." Hap's stare into Jed's soul was colder than winter. Jed backpedaled. He sat down.

"I've got a headache," Mama said. She left the kitchen.

Sissy whimpered at her plate. She pushed around her macaroni.

Hap sat down. "Now I can eat in peace. Eat, son."

Jed's nerves fired through him like electricity. He wondered about Mama, whether she'd sleep the night away. Or take drinks from hidden bottles. He stayed in the kitchen for Sissy's sake, he told himself. But really, he wanted to know what the police found.

Hap took a bite of macaroni. "They think they found her other shoe."

"Where?" Jed tasted bile. Felt hot and sweaty and cold at the same time.

"Found it out by Muriel's place. Just a stone's throw away. The reason she's been in town today is for questioning. My guess is she returned from there. Did she act strange?"

Jed remembered Muriel's shaking hands and voice, how sad she seemed until Clementine fetched her wig. She did act different. But then, he'd only known her a short while. How could he really know? "No, sir," he answered, but he didn't give Hap his eyes.

Hap attacked his macaroni, plopped on his plate between three and six o'clock. Sissy picked at her food, barely eating. Mama reappeared in the doorway.

Hap cleared his throat, took a long drink of sweet tea. "It makes perfect sense, if you ask me. She was an unsubmissive wife back in the day before her husband died. No doubt there's other sin lurking below the surface. That's the way of things, you know. I can't remember how many times I've preached that sermon—how one sin on the outside means bigger sins on the inside."

"She is a sweet woman dying of cancer, Hap." Mama wrung her hands.

Jed scarcely heard her voice, but it was apparently loud enough for Hap to hear.

"Watch out!" he hollered. "The sin that entangled that Muriel character is becoming your sin—one of many, I might add. Submissiveness is next to godliness." Hap placed a forkful of corn bread, seated at nine o'clock, into his mouth.

"I thought it was cleanliness," Sissy said.

Hap narrowed his eyes. "My women," he hissed, "need to remember who is boss in this house."

Mama cleared each plate, slowly scraping leftovers into the trash. Jed wanted to hug her, but he stayed put. Hap took another drink of tea. His plate was perfectly clean, not a spot of food left. Mama scraped it into the trash anyway.

"Officer Spellman needs you to come down to the station." Hap lowered his eyes to meet Jed's.

"Why?" Jed wondered if he was in trouble. The way Hap said *station* made him think so. Would they arrest him for keeping Daisy's diary? If they accused Bald Muriel of kidnapping, would they do the same to him?

Hap cleared his throat. "You're the one who found the first shoe."

Worry ignited his heartbeat. He absolutely did not want to

go to the station. He couldn't even really say why, just that he didn't want to. "What about Miss Emory? She'd know Daisy's shoe."

"They tried that. Went over there with the evidence, but they didn't even get a chance to show her. She started throwing things around and screaming. Officer Spellman said he could hear her hollering as he drove away. They don't want to traumatize her. Do you blame them?"

Mama stopped her scraping. "I really don't think you're supposed to be privy to—"

"I'm privy to what I need to be privy to, Ouisie. It's none of your business, anyways."

She walked out the back door.

Jed tried to find other reasons why he didn't need to go. "Wait," he said. "They have the other shoe, remember? Why can't they compare the two?"

"Because the man who handled the shoe sent it off to Tyler. And he's gone right now. You're all they've got. I'm sensing you don't want to help. Is there something you're not telling me?"

Jed swallowed. "No, sir."

"That's my boy. Now let's drive to town. I know Officer Spellman's working tonight. I'll call ahead and let him know we're coming."

Jed got in the Chevy. The car's stale air choked him, making his body one mass of sweat. When Hap got in, Jed's chigger-bitten ankles screamed at him in the heat, begged him to scratch.

But he wouldn't. Couldn't. The engine turned over, then roared under Hap's foot. The itch above Jed's feet hollered for relief. He rubbed them together, hoping Hap wouldn't notice, but that just made him itch all the more.

Hap backed out of the driveway. Jed reached down to scratch

just a little. But once he started, he couldn't stop. He scratched so much, he felt sure he drew blood.

"Jed, you want to know something?"

Jed stopped scratching.

"Want to know what life is really all about? Can you tell me?"

Jed knew enough not to say a thing. He could say "Jesus" and still be wrong.

"It's a little thing called self-control."

Jed knew this lecture. Could almost repeat it word for word. But he kept quiet.

"The apostle Paul wrote it down as one of the fruits of the Spirit. It's the last one, if you need to know." He turned right on Forest. "And the last one means it's the most important." He turned left on Love. They passed Miss Emory's house on the right. For a moment, Hap was silent.

Hap turned right on Hemlock, heading toward downtown Defiance. "I have it, Jed."

"Have what?" Jed swallowed.

Hap looked over at Jed, fire in his eyes. "Follow along. I swear you're more flighty than your mother. I have self-control, but so many people don't. You don't. You can't even tolerate a few chigger bites. For crying out loud, you've lived here fourteen years, and you still can't stop yourself from scratching a stupid bite?"

Jed scratched one last time as Defiance rolled by.

Twenty-Eight

Miss Emory'd purchased the ice crusher at a garage sale for fifty cents five summers ago—one of those summers where a hundred days hit a hundred degrees and everyone sweltered like a swamp. She brought the contraption home, put it on the counter, plugged it in, all while Jed and Daisy watched. And sweated.

"What is it?" Daisy asked.

"Go get me some ice." Miss Emory motioned to the freezer.

Daisy handed her a blue plastic tray. In one smooth motion, Miss Emory twisted and released the ice onto the counter with a clatter. She pointed at the cupboard, motioning for Jed to get cups. He did, placing three side by side next to the ice.

"It won't exactly be snow cones, but you never know." She opened the white mouth of the machine. A grinding, yowling sound pierced the hot air.

Jed and Daisy both jumped back.

She shoved ice, piece by piece, into the machine until it ate its fill of the entire tray.

"Where'd it go?" Daisy asked.

"Here." She pulled out a plastic drawer underneath. She tipped the drawer gently into each cup, mounding crushed ice in each. She glided to the fridge, pulled out a jar of strawberry syrup, the kind you put on pancakes at pancake houses, and poured a little on each mound of snow, like blood on a polar bear's belly, all the while humming some sort of folk tune. "Try it," she said.

So they did.

And they did again.

Nearly every day they were together, Jed and Daisy crushed their ice—put it in Cokes, ate it straight, shoved it down the back of each other's tank tops. Miss Emory's fifty-cent treasure kept them cool, providing a ritual to their friendship Jed could never quite shake.

Thirty years later, an ice crusher, much like Miss Emory's, sat on Jed's counter between cookie jar and blender, though he owned a side-by-side fridge with its own ice maker. His tribute to friendship.

At the police station, Officer Spellman met Jed and Hap at the door and escorted them in. He thrust a thick hand Hap's way. "Good to see you as always, Pastor." He looked at Jed. "Mind if we go to the back room?"

Mind? Of course he minded. Jed's head filled with black and white police movies where angry policemen shouted at potential suspects. Or when one prettied up to a suspect, coaxing him with pretend friendship. Good cop, bad cop. Jed's heart rumbled. The officer led them both to a white-walled room. A long table sat in the middle with four folding chairs, two on one side, two on the other.

"Pastor, I'd like to talk to Jed alone, if you don't mind."

Alone?

"Of course, I understand." Hap nodded to Jed.

Though there were times Jed wished Hap would leave him be, this was not one of them. He looked at Hap, begged him with his eyes to stay.

"Tell the truth, son, you hear me?"

The door clicked shut. Jed started sweating again.

"You want some water?" Officer Spellman smiled. His silver white hair unkempt, dark straight eyebrows, and a mustache licking the top of his mouth reminded Jed of someone. The name teased him like a fly needing swatting, but he couldn't remember.

"Sure."

When the officer left, Jed noticed the dangling light above him, like one of those rooms in the movies. He worried. It wasn't like he was hiding anything, other than Daisy's diary. He wondered what Muriel felt when she was here. He thought about the water Officer Spellman would bring. Would it be tainted with truth serum? Would he spill out things he didn't even know? What was that word? Incriminate? Would he incriminate himself? Would Officer Spellman find out the truth? That he was a no-good kid?

Mama tried to soothe his no-goods away, but it never worked. Hap, well, he was perfect, or near perfect. Jed? Not at all. Nothing he did ever measured up. Even when he tried to do something right, it got messed up somehow.

The door opened.

The policeman paced across the floor, click-click-click-click. He placed a Dixie cup in front of Jed. It sure looked like water.

Jed didn't want to drink it. But crushed ice danced in that water. Truth serum or not, he took a swig of the crushed-ice water until it all drained cool down his throat but somehow left him feeling thirstier.

Officer Spellman sat opposite him.

Jed searched his brain. Who did Officer Spellman remind him of? His eyes were kind. So kind. He'd seen the officer on many occasions, especially at church, but never this close, shut alone in a room with just him.

The officer reached down.

Jed winced. When Hap reached down, it was always to grab something—a stick, a whip, a bucketful of anger.

"I know this must be bothersome for you. Don't worry. I just have a few questions."

"Okay." Jed breathed in and out, in and out, trying to steady himself. The water sloshed inside him.

"I wish I could remember Daisy's shoe exactly, Jed. But I can't. And the other officer's away. His grandmama died, and I can't seem to get a hold of him. You know how funerals are."

Jed really didn't, but he nodded anyway. He looked into the policeman's eyes, then darted his gaze away. That's it, he thought. Captain Kangaroo! Officer Spellman looked like him—kind eyes, soothing voice, a laugh behind his words. Jed relaxed his hands, unballing his fists.

Captain Kangaroo placed two rubber gloves on the table, then a bag.

"The shoe's in here." He stretched the gloves on, then opened the bag. He placed the shoe on the table.

Jed lurched backward, sending his chair to the floor in a crash. He stood quickly and righted the chair.

"What's wrong?" Captain Kangaroo stood, his eyes calm as Lake Pisgah at five a.m. "Isn't this her shoe?"

"No, sir." Jed pointed to his foot. "It's mine."

Twenty-Nine

Y*our* shoe?" Captain Kangaroo looked at Jed with one of those Hap looks that bled blame. "Where's the other one?"

Jed lifted his foot. "Right here."

"What's on your other foot?"

"Daisy's shoe. I borrowed it."

Captain Kangaroo stood, looming over Jed with a snarl. "Do I need to remind you to tell the truth?"

Jed quickly realized he'd made a mistake. "Oh, no. Not that shoe. A different one. I borrowed it when my other shoe went missing." His voice shook like bluebonnets in a thunderstorm, but he couldn't calm it down.

"You borrowed one shoe?"

"No, sir, two. I wore Daisy's pair until our dog chewed on one. Then I combined the two." Jed wished for some gum, anything to keep his tongue and teeth busy.

"You're telling me Daisy wore men's shoes?"

"Daisy was—" Jed bit his lower lip, punishing it for saying another "was." "Is a tomboy, sir. She might've worn ribbons and all, but she could sure climb a tree. These were her playing shoes."

"I know all that." Officer Spellman's voice softened. "It's my job to know everything about her. That she likes Cheerios only, hates the color pink, has a particular fondness for jackrabbits, and sings loud when she thinks she's alone."

Jed looked away. More times than he could count, he'd found Daisy singing love songs to the trees. When he caught her out there, she jumped a mile high, saying, "You startled me near to Hades and back, Pepper Boy." What he wouldn't give to hear one more song, even a stupid love song.

Officer Spellman paced the room. "You said your shoe was taken. When?"

Jed took a deep breath. He tried to convince himself that it wasn't a crime to have a shoe taken. He'd done nothing wrong, right? "A week or so back—"

"Jed, look at me."

Jed did. He couldn't tell whether Captain Kangaroo was about to bark something angry or cry.

The officer didn't say a thing. He didn't tell Jed that Skeeter James had his shoe taken five days prior while he was swimming at Lake Pisgah. Just one shoe. His right. He didn't tell Jed that just yesterday Ella Mae Planter lost her right shoe while she was swinging at Bryant Park.

Jed looked at his two shoed feet. A sudden dread crept up his spine and wrapped its icy fingers around his neck. Breathe, he told himself. Daisy was with her father, he knew it. She had to be. But the more Captain Kangaroo paced the room, the more he thought maybe Hixon was right. Maybe something was terribly wrong. And it was all his fault.

The officer tangled his fingers in his whitish hair, then shook his head. "I need precise details, Jed. Can you do that for me?"

Officer Spellman sat down. He placed a tape recorder between them and clicked it on. He wrote notes on a yellow notepad. He asked Jed every question that could be asked, in painstaking order: Where were you standing when you realized the shoe was missing? Describe the shoe. Who could have had access to the shoe? Where precisely was the other shoe? Had it been moved? Did you touch it? Where is it now? Question after question came out of Officer Spellman's mouth.

Jed spilled everything he could remember. The time of day he was painting, where he'd put his shoes, when he noticed one missing. The storm. When he borrowed Daisy's shoes from her closet.

It was strange to see Captain Kangaroo take notes. "You saw no one near the house?"

"No, Captain—"

Officer Spellman laughed. "I'm no captain, Jed." He looked away. "Maybe someday."

Jed said a "phew" in his head. It wouldn't be wise to call the officer Captain Kangaroo even if he was the spitting image of him. "Sir, it was me and Hixon outside painting Miss Emory's house. Miss Emory was inside. She left before the storm to buy groceries."

"Would Miss Emory have been able to take the shoe without you noticing?"

Jed remembered Daisy's eyes then, full of art she'd create, full of possibilities. He likened those eyes to sky, not the deeper blue of an August day but the pale blue of a November morning after fog. Miss Emory had those eyes, only no fire there. Not anymore. "I don't think she took my shoe," he said.

"Did you ask her?"

"No. Besides, I figured she had enough on her mind. Or if she did take the shoe, it was to punish me. So I kept my mouth shut."

"Why?"

Why didn't Captain Kangaroo, of all folks, know this? Wasn't it obvious? By the looks of his puzzled eyebrows, Jed realized the officer plain didn't know. "Um, because I was the last one to see Daisy alive? Because it's my fault she's missing?"

Officer Spellman put up his hands like he was trying to push back Jed's words. "Hold on a minute. You really believe that? That it's your fault?"

Any fool would believe that. Jed nodded.

Captain Kangaroo stood up, perched on the edge of the table. "Jed, it's not your fault."

Why did tears come at the dumbest moments? One fell out of Jed's left eye. He turned from the officer, pretending to stare at the wall behind him. Quick as he could, he wiped the tear away, sniffing in the rest. Mama would've scolded him for that. She said sniffing up tears and holding them back was dangerous business. Jed didn't care. He sniffed again.

"I mean it, Jed. It's not your fault."

Was this the officer's way of killing him with kindness? He wanted to tell Captain Kangaroo he could believe what he wanted, but that wouldn't change the truth. Didn't Hap preach a sermon about that recently? "I didn't take care of her. Didn't walk her home." More tears threatened to escape the jailhouse of his eyes, so he chained the gate by closing them clear shut.

"How about looking at it another way? You'd be missing too. Whoever it was who took Daisy would've taken you both, I reckon."

"So?"

"So? Don't you care for your own life?"

"If I was with Daisy, I would've protected her."

"Son, let me tell you something about crime. You can stick yourself back there, right next to Daisy, and things would be crazy. You could've been taken alongside her. Or beaten. Or any number of things. I have no doubt you would've *tried* to protect her. But only God can protect. Only Him."

"Then why didn't He?" He shot fire at Captain Kangaroo through hot eyes.

The officer sighed, letting out enough breath to fill a giant beach ball. "Some things can't be explained."

The light in the room buzzed a little, like a slow-flying fly.

Jed wanted to go home, even if that meant riding there with Hap. Strangest thing about Hap. Jed was afraid of him most of the time, but when things weren't right, he loved the sight of him. Like when Sissy landed in the hospital with pneumonia a few years back, Jed ran to Hap. Though an awkward embrace, Jed felt Hap's strength, his control through the fabric of his white shirt. And Jed loved his words about God's reliability, His steadfast love, His care for lost sheep while Sissy's bluish face pinked.

"Your shoe. We found it by Muriel's place. When did you last visit her?"

Jed felt sure his brain burst inside his skull. Was this what it felt like when Mama got one of her headaches? Mama usually had gumption until about ten in the morning. After that, she'd phantom her way through the day, losing opinions, pasting on smiles, saying "Mercy" when things didn't go her way. The headaches did that to her. He squished his head together at his temples, like Mama did, an automatic reaction.

"You okay?"

"Headache," he mumbled.

"Just a few more questions and I'll let you go back with your father."

Jed remembered the good cop, bad cop thought he had when he first walked into this room. Well, Captain Kangaroo sure wasn't bullying him. No, more like coaxing him with Three Musketeers up a pathway to a candy house. Jed burped, his stomach sending acid up his throat. He covered his mouth. Had he said too much?

The Captain cleared his throat. "Jed. Have you been to Muriel's recently?"

Jed put his face in his hands, blocking out the buzzing light. "I've never been to her place. I don't even know exactly where she lives!"

"What do you know about her?"

Jed wanted to scream, "Just that she's the nicest woman ever," but he kept those words to himself for once. "She's got cancer. I think she's dying."

"That's what she says." Captain Kangaroo's eyes narrowed. Looked downright mean.

"What?" Jed pulled his fingers from around his eyes and leaned forward. He could smell his breath. "She's got no hair!"

"Anyone can shave a head."

"You're telling me she doesn't have cancer?" His head pounded. Throb, throb, throb.

"I'm not telling you anything. Only that you can't trust everything folks tell you. Even those with cancer."

Jed sat back. The metal chair bit his shoulder blades. Captain Kangaroo sent him end over teakettle with all those words about Muriel. It couldn't be. She saved his life! "Muriel is sweet and kind." He meant to holler the words, but they flew from his mouth in a whisper.

"You know her story, right?"

"Just that she had a mean husband and now she's happier."

"Ever wonder how her husband died?"

Jed shook his head no.

"We wondered. It's our job. Did ourselves an investigation too. Heart attack, it seems. But I always wondered if she had something to do with it. We're out at her place right now, gathering evidence. We talked with her today. You understand we have to follow every lead, right? A shoe—your shoe—near her property. It might add up, don't you think?"

Jed wrestled in his head. He could trust Captain Kangaroo, right? But he liked Muriel. And he didn't think she'd do anything like kidnap … or worse. Something wasn't right. How could he make it right? How could he protect Muriel? He'd felt a long time ago that God reached down to earth and pinned a badge on Jed's heart—Protector of the Innocent, it read. That was Jed's mission. He'd heard all those missionaries talking about packing up their lives and learning to speak another language so they could reach natives and the like. Nothing about that stirred him, though from obedience he made his way forward in church when Hap made the missionary altar call. No, he camped on the word *mission*. It sounded nobler. Mission. His mission was to protect people needing help. He'd known it since he was four years old, practically. He'd kept that badge all these years until he stopped deserving it the day Daisy disappeared. He'd never forgive himself. Never. And now he'd do anything to protect Muriel. "Officer Spellman?"

"Yes."

"I have Daisy's diary. It doesn't mention a thing about Muriel. I know Daisy didn't know her because if she did, she'd love her. I know it."

"You need to give me that diary. Why didn't you give it to me earlier?"

Jed picked at a scratch on the table. "I thought I'd do a little investigating myself."

The door opened.

Hap walked in.

Jed's throat felt dry. So dry.

"Well? Anything of import?" Hap put a warm hand on Jed's shoulder.

"Yes, Pastor." Captain Kangaroo's voice changed right then. From syrupy children's television host to Rod Serling. The creepy music played in Jed's head. He'd been had. By Captain Kangaroo.

"Seems the shoe we found is your son's. And he's been holding back some evidence from us."

"Is that so?" Hap removed his hand, but it left a stain of his warmth on Jed's shoulder.

Jed shivered. "Yes, sir, but it's only her diary." He hated that he mumbled the jumble of words under his breath like fear itself, if fear had the lungs of a fourteen-year-old boy.

Hap looked at him square in the eyes. "Do you want her blood on your head, son?"

Blood?

No longer the kindly Captain Kangaroo, Officer Spellman put up a hand. "Not blood, Jed. Remember, Pastor, we still don't know where Daisy is. For all we know, she could be fine." His words sounded like a doctor's—antiseptic.

"Cut the fineries, Jacob. We all know what happened to Daisy. Every last one of us. It's lying to say any different."

Jed thought he'd throw up right there on the table under the constantly buzzing light. How could Hap give up on hope so easily? Did he know something the officer didn't know? He'd always thought Hap to be all-knowing—like Hixon but scarier. If that was the truth, then why didn't Hap come out and say where Daisy was and spare them all the investigation?

Hap grabbed Jed by the scruff of his neck. "Where's the diary?"

"In the woods where Daisy and I used to hang out."

He nodded to Officer Spellman. "We'll have it to you within the hour."

Thirty

Jed and dread rhymed. It was Daisy who told him that. When was it? Two months ago? He didn't pay any mind when she said what she called "things of import." But now he wished he had. Jed and dread. She'd rhymed Pepper with leper too, making his name Dread Leper ... a scaredy-cat boy who no one wanted to be near. Seemed to fit.

Hap made him sit in the backseat of the Chevy. Like a white-skinned leper. He wished Jesus would fly on in through the window and touch him, heal his heart. Isn't that what Jesus did to lepers? Touched them? The only way Hap'd touch him now was not exactly the calming Jesus touch. Nope. Not that kind of touch at all.

"Your friend Muriel." Hap roared the Chevy to life. "She danced at the funeral. Did you know that?"

Jed couldn't picture it. Couldn't see Muriel dancing at any-one's funeral. Under the stars, maybe, but when someone died? "I don't believe it."

"Did you know she lost a little girl once? She'd been fat as a bus, that woman. Always pined for kids, apparently. One day she was in awful pain. Her husband didn't believe in hospitals or doctors, so he gave her a stick to bite on while he convened folks from his church to pray for deliverance. Well, they prayed all right while she screamed. They prayed all the louder, trying to cast out Satan, apparently. Turned out she was delivered—of a baby. She'd been pregnant and didn't know it. A little girl. But she didn't live. Cried for five minutes, then died."

Jed's head stopped its drumming. Bald Muriel? Pregnant and not knowing it? Her little baby dying? "I don't understand."

"The thing to understand about Daisy gone missing is motive. And Muriel's got it. Her baby died and she wants her back. That baby's the only thing she ever loved. It's hard to know with crazy people."

Jed shook his head back and forth, hoping, if he did, he'd erase Hap's words. "She's different, but she's not crazy." Jed's voice broke to his high voice. He cleared his throat. "She's not," he said in his low voice.

Jed watched the back of Hap's neck redden. Could hear him breathe real loud, trying to capture and lock up his anger. Sometimes the breathing helped, but Jed didn't think any breath would help him this time. The breathing was an overflow for Hap, he knew. Like a well dug too shallow, spilling water over the top after a gully-washing rain. Once Hap let his anger bubble to the surface, it had to geyser out. Like a word-belching Old Faithful.

Hap stopped the car at the road's end that led into the woods. He pulled up the hand brake. He placed both white-knuckled hands on the steering wheel, not moving his body, not saying a word.

Should Jed get out? Wait for Hap to give instructions? Jed sat quietly. He picked at the dirt under his nails. He put his watch to his ear. It tick-tick-ticked the time away.

Hap turned. Caught him red-handed with the watch to his ear. Jed winced, waiting for the wheelbarrow of words to dump out. But none came. Hap's eyes, usually full of fire, had been washed cool with tears. "I know what it's like to lose someone you love."

Jed thought of the grandfather he never knew, thought of the gun going off in his hands. Jed wished Hap would yell, scream, holler, scowl, throw a punch. Anything but this. Hap's words held Jed's tongue hostage. He was a dumb mute leper full of dread. The rainy eyes blinked. Peered into Jed's mind like he was an attic, pushing boxes around, crashing through all the things Jed wanted secret. Was he stealing his thoughts? Could he?

"Cat got your tongue?"

Jed shook his head.

Hap smiled, showing every one of his perfectly white teeth. "The true mark of a man is how he manages life's storms. I have a feeling tornadoes are coming our way, Jed. Question is, will you fly around in circles and tumble to the earth, or will you be wise and find the root cellar? You know what the root cellar is?"

"No." Jed swallowed. He knew he was about to find out.

"It's the church, Jed. You find yourself shelter there. Protection. Problem is, the church is a fickle thing." Hap looked forward a moment, then turned on the Chevy's round headlights. He stepped out.

Jed did too. "Why are you keeping the lights on?"

"Because. It's getting dark."

"What about the battery?"

"This car's battery will last a nighttime." He touched the hood, noticing a small scratch.

Hap motioned Jed to follow him. "This way, right?"

"Yes, sir."

"Thing is," Hap said, "the church needs you to play by its rules to be protected. Don't expect its love and care if you step outside the boundaries."

Jed stepped behind Hap's large footprints.

"Do you understand?" Hap faced Jed. "You gotta play by the rules. Gotta follow the holy highway. Gotta earn your keep in the church. This world's a fading away, Jed. Things fall apart, sure enough. And if you behave, make me proud to be your father, well, the church will protect you. It always does."

"I don't need protecting." Why did his words take a life of their own? He'd meant to keep them in his head, safe and sound, but just like Jed, they didn't obey.

"What's that?"

"What's what?"

"You say you don't need protection?"

Jed wished he was one of those kinds of folks who said the right words at the right time, but he wasn't. "Yes. I said that."

"You need the covering of church, son, or you'll be a perfect heathen. You understand? Folks look to you to set a good example, being the pastor's son and all. It's a two-way street. You obey. We protect."

Jed nearly said, "You mean, like the mafia?" but didn't. Thankfully.

Hap stopped in the center of Daisy's sky chapel. "This is the place, isn't it?"

It was. How did Hap know the way?

Jed felt Daisy there. Like a scary ghost movie where a girl appears, then disappears, singing nursery rhymes. This was their place. Was. But now Hap knew. Or had he always known? Him knowing screwed up everything in Jed's mind. Bumbled his thoughts.

"Get the diary. It's getting dark."

Jed fished through the log, pulling out the black trash bag. A noise behind him like the snapping of a branch startled him. He turned. Hap stood there, arms crossed over his chest, his head turned toward the sound of the woods.

"What was that?"

"A possum, probably." But Hap's eyes held fear.

Jed pulled the bag out. Opened it. Pulled everything out. Every single treasure they'd stored splayed across the forest floor making Jed miss Daisy all the more. Everything, except the diary. Jed emptied the empty bag, hoping he'd missed it. Only air fell out.

Another branch snapped.

A rush of something through underbrush.

Five more twigs breaking under someone's feet.

Jed froze.

Hap didn't move either. Jed's eyes widened. Why didn't Hap lunge toward him? Do the fatherly thing and rescue him from the sound in the woods?

Jed heard out-of-breath breathing. It sounded familiar. The Daisy-shaped hole in his heart grew larger with hope. Was it Daisy's breathing?

"Anyone here? Clementine?" It was Sissy. Jed let out his breath.

She burst through the darkness, her feet naked, eyes wide open. "Thank God," she said, "you're here."

Hap ran toward her, whisking her into his arms in a way that made Jed ache inside. He'd settle for a roughing of his hair or a kind word, but Sissy got a full-on hug. Girls got all the breaks, he thought, but then he remembered Daisy, that she'd gotten no breaks the past several weeks.

"Where's Mama?" Jed asked.

"Headache," Sissy said.

"What are you doing out tonight?" Hap said as he set her down. Her naked feet touched the dry ground. "And where are your shoes?"

She looked at Jed. "Clementine took off after a rabbit." Sissy coughed, then hollered, "Clementine! Clementine!"

Jed smiled. Sissy was the one girl he knew who thought rabbits could talk. Ever since reading *The Velveteen Rabbit*, she'd taken to talking to the rabbits that scurried across the yard, asking them questions like, "What's your name? Do you have a family? How can I help you find your boy?" When she found Jed's lucky rabbit's foot, she inquired about purple rabbits. "What kind of purple rabbit would donate his foot?" she asked. When she learned the truth, she made it her life's ambition to reattach rabbits' feet to what must've been a million-strong population of three-footed rabbits in the world.

Hap bent low on his haunches, like a giant jackrabbit. "She's not here. Haven't seen her. Now where, young lady, are your shoes?"

Sissy looked down. "I lost them."

"Lost your shoes?"

"Just one."

Jed's knees felt like Jell-O. Hap stood. He placed a strong hand around his jaw. His worrying look. Dusk settled into night. A star poked through the sky. The moon kept Hap's head flash-lighted, like God was shining a dim beam onto Hap's brain. "Well, well. Maybe we need to get home."

Jed wanted to ask Sissy the shoe story, but he didn't. Didn't dare in Hap's presence. His father's voice sounded different, like he choked his words, strangled them before letting them release from his mouth. Something was wrong. Jed felt it in the voice of his father who always, always ruled their worlds with control. He swore he heard a hint of panic. And this unsettled Jed more than Daisy's missing diary and Sissy's missing shoe.

Wind picked up leaves from the underbrush and whirled them in their faces. Jed looked skyward only to find the moon being eaten by a charcoal cloud. Rain splatted his head, fat drop by fat drop. Through the trees he could barely see a hint of the Chevy's headlights. Or was he seeing things? Like a light mirage?

"Storm's brewing. Hurry!" Hap swooped up Sissy like she was nothing while Jed dashed hither and yon, picking up Daisy's things and stuffing them back into the slick trash bag. He threw it over his shoulder like a hobo and ran to keep up. Rain burst from everywhere, crying tears the size of superballs onto them. Raindrops jumped from the ground, muddied Jed's steps.

Hap shouted to the heavens. "Yea, though I walk through the valley of the shadow of death."

Jed tripped over a branch and fell face-first into a puddle. He tasted mud, spat it out. Flat on the ground, he felt his weakness again, felt all the strength drain away from him like rain from a roof to a downspout. He tried to stand, but couldn't. His ankle didn't work right. Didn't feel right. He reached for the bag that, miraculously, hadn't spilled its contents.

"I will fear no evil: for thou art with me." Hap's words sounded far away.

"Help!" Jed yelled, but thunder slapped his voice.

"Thy rod and thy staff they comfort me."

"Help!" Jed twisted to his feet, cursing the pain. He hopped forward, then fell again. Fear took root way down deep. He screamed, "Dad!"

But Hap kept on walking, trailing King James English behind him, "... dwell in the house of the Lord for ever."

Thirty-One

Jed felt mud in between his fingers. A crack of lightning flash-bulbed the sky, followed by rumbling thunder Jed felt underneath him. Transfixed, Jed said a prayer. Warm, wet wind brushed his face.

While the lightning flickered, Jed watched the Defiance night as if it were an old movie. The rain blew sideways and showered him from the north. Though he shielded his eyes from the pelting rain, something held him there on that spot of forest earth. Something besides a painful ankle. With a half-wet face, he hugged himself and begged God to turn Hap around, though he hated needing Hap so.

Until the barefooted man appeared in the clearing.

Jed blinked. The lightning flashed behind a figure twenty paces away. Rain jumped up from the ground where he stood as if the thirsty earth had drunk enough and was sending it back to the heavens.

Another lightning strike. In that moment, Jed saw bare feet and nothing more.

He wanted to run or scream, but fear kept him lame and mute—a dread-filled leper. Like him, the man remained motionless, letting the rain pelt him, letting it muddy his shoeless feet.

Jed pinched his eyes together, but he saw only a faceless form.

When he pressed his eyes together and opened them again, the figure was gone, disappeared like a fickle shadow on a cloudy day. Jed felt his pulse pound his eardrums in a steady, frightened beat. When the trees moaned from the wind, he gasped. Lightning zigzagged the sky, highlighting the place the person had stood.

Had he just seen Daisy's kidnapper?

Jed knew one thing: he wasn't going to stick around these parts and find out. He army crawled through the forest, lugging the trash bag, inch by inch. He spat. Dirt from his first fall gritted between his teeth. Rain slapped his forehead in regular splats—a real frog choker. He pulled his body through the Crooked Creek gully, now waterlogged, where the rain covered his backside, sending shivers up and down his spine. Every snapping branch sent Jed's heart so far up into his throat he thought he'd choke on it. At the top of the ridge beyond the gully-turned-stream, Jed called "Help!" again, but only thunder replied. How he'd give anything, even barter a thousand days working for sour Miss Emory, to hear Hap's voice. He didn't even care if Hap hollered at him or said I told you so. His voice would put Jed's heart back into its proper place. If Hap came, everything would be okay. No bogeyman could stand up to Hap, Jed knew.

Jed put his head down in his arms. His nose touched the wet ground. Something jostled his right foot. Panic ripped through him.

He turned.

Clementine licked his face, then barked. Her howl sounded like worship in Jed's soggy ears. Clementine nudged Jed, tried to push him over. He winced. The dog looked into Jed's eyes and seemed to know he was injured—like good ol' Lassie.

And like Lassie, Clementine bounded away, barking through the wet night.

All Jed could do was wait. And say a few meaningless prayers. He was beginning to think the God thing was all a made-up story, like the one about the Velveteen Rabbit. A story to make folks happy that a God in heaven created them. If Hixon read Jed's thoughts right now, he'd surely call him a heathen, but Jed didn't care. While rain sogged through him, he shivered under what used to be a moonlit sky. Jed wondered if God was there. Or here. Or anywhere. Where was He when Daisy stepped out of her shoe? Or when Hap screamed and yelled? Or when Mama had headaches and snuck sips from the vanilla bottle or the Nyquil? Or when Sissy lisped and got teased so much Jed'd become sore from beating up her tormenters? Or when Bald Muriel got cancer? Where was He?

Jed sat up. The rain changed from sheets to drip-drip-drips falling from wet tree branches. The sky lightened as the moon winked at him once again. Defiance weather was like that—wild as hell one minute, calm as heaven the next. In that moment from wild rain to calm night, Jed went from saying prayers to God, using words like you and yours, to thinking things about God—him and he. And they weren't pretty thoughts.

Branches snapped again, but this time Jed flat-out didn't care.

Come and take me, bogeyman. What does it matter? Nothing will change. Prayers don't get answered. Bad stuff still happens whether a person calls on God or walks the other way.

Looming above him stood Hap, a worried look on his face. Clementine panted next to him, Hap's hand on her head like praise. "Let me help you up." Hap reached down and lifted Jed to his feet. He put a strong arm around Jed, his bad foot between them, and helped him limp through the woods.

Jed clutched the trash bag to his chest. He looked around for Sissy.

"You left Sissy?"

"The doors are locked."

Jed swallowed. Hap seemed to be bothered by the thought too. He picked Jed clear up, cradled him in his arms like Jesus held the lost-then-found sheep. Jed's legs dangled from Hap's side. In all his life, he'd never felt more loved, more cared for. Even Mama's thousand rose-petal messages didn't hold up to snuff when compared to his father carrying him through the woods on a muggy, soggy night.

Jed let his head rest against Hap's shoulder. Hap's powerful heart beat lub-dup, lub-dup, lub-dup. Jed could live here, he thought. Live against the beat of his father's steady heart. The moment he settled into it, Hap dropped him to the gravel. A gasp left Hap's mouth.

The headlights were off.

The back door gaped open.

No Sissy.

Thirty-Two

Clementine yelped as Hap tried to start the Chevy. He turned the motor over. Nothing came but a sputter and a grunt. On the tenth time—Jed was counting—it growled to life. As they sped through Defiance, Clementine rode shotgun, her head hollering out the front window while Jed sat in the back, worrying. First Daisy. Now Sissy.

Through the wet bag, Jed felt something familiar. He pulled it out: a stick. He and Daisy'd whittled away the bark and carved DC+JP=BF on the smooth pine. Daisy Chance and Jed Pepper equals Best Friends.

Jed ran his fingers over the thick stick, remembering the day they carved it, remembering how hard it was to carve their names with a knife so dull it couldn't rip through flesh.

It was just two years ago when Daisy'd brought the terribly dull kitchen knife to their hideout. The afternoon shivered golden under the trees, the sun shot light at crazy angles. "I hate this knife," she'd said.

"Because it's so dull?"

"No, because of what it's seen."

"Knives can't see."

"Sure as heck they can. Don't be fussing with me." Daisy used the knife to clean the garden from underneath her nails. "You wouldn't be messing if you knew what I was gonna say."

"Well then, say it." Jed smirked.

"My mama, well, she's not very happy."

"Miss Emory?"

"Um, yeah. Who else would be my mama?"

"Sorry. Go ahead. Why don't you like the knife?"

"Mama tried to slice her wrists again with it last week, but the thing was so dull, she couldn't do it."

Jed remembered looking at Daisy, wondering if she was pulling his leg, but the look on her face told him she was serious. Dead serious.

"I caught her with it. She was using words from the rendering plant wall, potty-mouthed as could be, trying to stab her wrists, but the knife wouldn't break the skin. She sure did yowl when I grabbed the knife away from her."

Daisy'd told him how she'd taken every knife, except the dull one in her hand, out of the house and buried them in the backyard.

Jed remembered that it took him a mighty long time to carve their initials in the stick, but stubborn as he was, he did it. When he finished, Daisy told him it was a magic stick because it was so hard to carve. "Magic comes from folks who put their hearts into things," she'd said.

Problem was, she didn't have the magic stick when Jed left her alone in the church. No magic words of friendship to comfort her. No piece of Jed she could hold near when her shoe went missing, when she went missing. Jed's heart felt stabbed by a dull knife, pummeled black and blue. Could a heart be black and blue? He wondered if this was what a broken heart felt like. He was pretty sure it was.

Hap turned toward the police station only to crank the wheel sharply to the left to head back home. He didn't say a word. Neither did Jed. Clementine said all there was to say—a long doggy wail into the Defiance night.

Hap stopped the car in the driveway, threw open the door,

took the porch steps two at a time. Clementine streaked after him. Jed shoved the stick back into the garbage bag and lugged the Daisy memories toward the house, hopping as fast as he could to the stairs. He half crawled up the stairs, slapping the porch with the wet bag.

Jed heard cries of "Ouisie! Ouisie!" coming from the house—a panicked father's voice blaming his wife.

A noise bustled from Ethrea Ree's rosebush.

Jed turned, unable to move.

Sissy emerged from behind the roses, her face as white as Miss Emory's clapboards. When she saw Jed, she didn't run to him. Didn't even walk. She stood there, not a word on her tongue.

"Hap! Hap! She's here!" he yelled.

Hap scooped Sissy up like homemade peach ice cream and held her to himself. Jed wondered if she felt his heart beating. Wondered if she relished it.

Mama came out, wet-eyed and empty looking. "Oh dear God," she said over and over, fawning over Sissy under the moon. Petting her hair. Touching her cheek.

Ethrea Ree slammed her screen door. She wagged a bony finger their way. "So much commotion," she said. "How's a woman to sleep around here?"

No one answered.

Her face colored itself red as her backyard roses. "You hear me?"

"Sorry, Mrs. Ree," Jed said. "We thought Sissy'd gone missing."

"Missing, schmissing," she hissed. "This town's gone and got themselves spooked. Everyone knows that Daisy waif ran far, far away. A wayward girl, she was. With a wayward mama."

Jed limped toward Ethrea Ree, anger behind his tongue begging to escape. His ankle shot arrows through him, but he ignored the pain.

Hap stood, his hand on Sissy's head. "Jed, don't pay her no mind."

Jed didn't listen. He lunged at Ethrea Ree, but in an easy movement, she stepped to the side, letting Jed hit air, then the ground. He groaned when his ankle bent again under his weight. Wanting to save face, he tried to stand, but couldn't.

"You're a wild one, boy. Get the wilds out. It's okay." Ethrea Ree stood above him, a smile on her wrinkled face.

Jed stopped. He huffed in a few humiliated breaths.

Ethrea Ree lifted him to his feet, her grip surprisingly strong. It wasn't Hap who paid any mind. Not even Mama. Just the bony-fingered neighbor lady. She hobbled him back to the porch, her shoulder blade under Jed's armpit, while Mama and Hap hovered over Sissy.

On the first step, she whispered close to his ear. "I understand, Jed," then disappeared into her roses. No one thanked her, not even Jed.

He crawled up the stairs. He pulled Daisy's bag through the entryway. Mama and Hap brought Sissy inside. Sat her down on the threadbare divan. "Where were you?" Hap asked.

Silence. Sissy looked at Jed, her mouth muted.

"Why'd you leave the car?" Hap asked it loud, then took a breath, as if to calm himself. Hap brushed away a strand of hair that covered Sissy's left eye.

"What happened?" Mama twisted her hands.

"Why would you care?" Hap stood. He threw his arms in the air. "For crying out loud, Ouisie, what gives you the right to worry? When you get your headaches, you're a zombie. A tornado could take the house clear away to Oz, and you'd be laying in bed none the wiser."

Mama said nothing. Tears wet her eyes.

Sissy kept her eyes on Jed, but they were somewhere else.

Jed wanted to talk to Sissy alone. He knew she'd talk with only him around. Maybe she was afraid she'd lisp. Or maybe she had secrets only Jed would understand. But how would he get her by herself? With his stupid ankle, he could barely get himself anywhere.

Hap sat, looked at Sissy. "What happened to your shoe?"

Nothing.

"Leave her alone," Mama said. "Can't you see she's traumatized?"

Jed wanted out of the room. He could see where this was going. So he stood. "I'm going to bed." Neither Mama nor Hap said a word. He hopped halfway down the hall, memories of Daisy in hand. He dropped the bag, still wet, on his bed, then returned to the hallway to spy. To make sure Sissy was okay.

"I know your secrets, Ouisie. Know them as well as I know Paul's letter to the Galatians. You're caught in a vice that nullifies your motherhood, you hear me?"

Jed wondered if Ethrea Ree heard all their secrets, with Hap's voice booming like that. And he worried how Sissy was doing. Was she scared?

"I don't have secrets," Mama said in a plain, undecorated voice.

A slap sliced through the air.

Mama hollered.

Jed hopped back to the living room. Though no match for Hap, he had to do something. If God called Hap one of His own special servants, then God wouldn't stop His running of the universe to help Jed or Mama or Sissy. No. God favored Hap. Every sinner knew that. God liked preachers better than parishioners.

"You knock that off, Hap," Jed said.

Hap's eyes flashed wild. Nearly as wild as when he preached hell from the pulpit. A scary, angry, wild-dog look that sent dread right back into Jed. "What did you say?"

"Stop it." Jed swallowed.

Hap's eyes narrowed.

Clementine burst into the room, jumped on Hap, nearly tackling him to the couch. He steadied himself. Clementine didn't growl or bark. She licked. Killed him with spit and kindness. "Down, Clementine," Hap said, but his voice had lost its edge. He stood, his hand on Clementine's soft head.

Sissy shook her head, ridding her zombie trance. "I'm tired," she said. She padded to her room, barefooted.

Mama wiped the tears from her face with her apron, still on, even after she'd gone to bed earlier. She sighed and left the front room to sit on the porch. Hap patted Clementine's back.

Jed hobbled to Sissy's room. With each lurch, he marveled that a dog could save a family, not with straight-shouldered defiance like Jed but with wet kisses and humor. Was that the secret to managing his temper? Humor? He remembered Daisy's terrible temper; then he remembered her jokes and laughter. "I want to be like that," he whispered to the hallway.

Sissy lay in bed, her back turned to him. She still wore her play clothes.

"Sissy?"

She stirred, then faced him, her head propped on her hand. "What?"

"You okay?" Jed hopped to her bed and planted himself on the edge.

"Not really."

"What happened?"

"I lost my shoe."

"When?"

"Today."

"And?"

She sighed.

With each little word Sissy spoke, life trickled from her eyes. Jed worried that if he asked too much, she'd grow sick and die.

He petted her head. Worried over her. Beat himself up inside for not protecting her once again. "You don't have to say anything right now. Get yourself some rest. Sleep as long you want. I'll bring a bowl of cereal."

"Okay."

"Sissy?"

"Yeah."

"I'm sorry."

"Why? You didn't do anything."

"I know."

Jed waited for Sissy to release him from guilt, to stand up tall with fire in her eyes and give him a talking to about his stupidity for thinking such thoughts. He'd hoped that saying his crime out loud would make him feel better and that somehow God would hear it all and swoop to earth to tussle his hair and say, "It's all right, Jed." But nothing of the sort happened.

Instead, Sissy rolled away from him and faced the wall without a word.

Jed watched her there, shoulders turned, failure sickening him. He wanted to call her back to him, to see her hopeful eyes, to take care of any worries that lived beneath. He lifted a hand to touch the back of her head but let it slip quietly back to his side. Jed limped away, feeling older than fourteen, but not wiser.

In his room, Jed pulled out Daisy's remainders from the trash bag, all wet. The stick. Some marbles. A dead flashlight. Their waterlogged transistor radio. Two plastic cups. A ladybug table-cloth—the one used when they picnicked. A handful of special rocks collected from the forest around them.

He switched on the radio. Hissing answered back. He turned it off.

He took out the rusted batteries of the flashlight. He stuck his tongue on one, remembering Hap's instructions not to. Acid burned his tongue. Maybe Hap was right about some things. Not always, but sometimes.

He picked through the marbles and rocks, rolling each in his hand. Something about them stirred up hope in the bowl of his chest. Why? What was it? He picked up their favorite marble, the one they fought over. No swirls inside, only light blue all the way through.

They'd found it four Octobers ago during the time the pecan trees were releasing their nuts, blessing squirrels—and the natives of Defiance—with treasures. Jed's sneakers crunched nuts underfoot, a hollow crackling sound. Daisy spied something, then bent low on her haunches. "Look," she said. She didn't touch the blue marble. She pointed.

Jed bent to pick it up.

Daisy slapped his hand away. "Don't! This is something special." She cleared away the pecans from around the blue marble, isolating it in the middle of a pecan audience. She blew away the leaves next to it. Only then did she pick it up. She stood toe to toe with Jed. "This is God's eye, sure enough."

"God's eye? It's a marble."

"Shush, Jed. Don't make fun." She looked through the marble to the sky, her smile as wide as Texas. "God has blue eyes, Jed. Everyone knows that. Blue as the sky. This marble is the precise blue."

"You're telling me God's eye is rolling here and there on the trails of Defiance, Texas?"

She nodded.

"He must be awful dizzy," Jed said.

Daisy rolled her eyes and pocketed God's.

In the emptiness of his room, Jed looked through God's eye as Daisy did that day in October. In a sickening rush, he remembered Daisy standing in the old church the last time he saw her. He boasted about it, didn't he? God's eye. Daisy didn't have it that night; it was far away in the woods. Jed watched himself from above, replaying the scene on the movie screen of his mind. She hadn't answered when he told her about God's eye protecting her. She stared. He looked in his mind at her. Her round mouth said three words: "You'll regret it."

Boy did he. He wished at once he could rewind the terrible movie and jump back in today. He'd walk her home. He'd carry Hap's gun with him too, cocked and ready to kill any bogeyman who dared put a hand on Daisy Marie Chance. They'd find God's eye, maybe dig a few worms for fishing the next day, and have a good old laugh.

He rolled God's eye like clay between his palms, felt the smooth coldness of the marble on his skin. Wouldn't it be something if he could control God so easily? He'd tell Him to shape up, get on the ball, and find Daisy. He'd make God give Hap the gift of apology or strip his anger clean free. God would be forced to give Mama ten thousand smiles, one million songs of laughter, and no need for stashed bottles. He'd have to touch Sissy's tongue, stealing all the *th*'s from her *s*'s. And, to make things perfect, He'd give Bald Muriel hair and give Jed a brand-new bike.

But God was not One to be told what to do. So much like Hap.

Jed pinched God's eye between thumb and finger and examined his room through it. It looked dreary through the cold, blue glass—like his life. He threw the marble across the room with a superhuman thrust that shocked him. God's eye headed to Jed's framed picture of Jesus, the one where a pasty Jesus looked to one side. God's eye cracked the glass in front of Jesus' left eye, then thudded to the floor.

Jed shook, wondering two things: Would Jesus be mad at him? Would Hap come in and punish him?

But the heavens didn't roar. The floor outside his door didn't creak. Jed ran over to the picture, took it off the wall. The glass stayed in the frame, but its crack covered Jesus' face like a thickly spun spiderweb. He'd never noticed before how sad Jesus looked.

He shoved Jesus into the bottom drawer of his desk.

On hands and knees, he felt for God's eye. He found it under his bed, surrounded by dust balls and old candy wrappers. He lifted God's eye to his own. Now cracked, the eye made his room look like modern art, the kind of stuff in the books Mama checked out from the library. What did it mean that God's eye was cracked? Hixon would assign something important to it, something about God being sorrowful about the world. But Jed knew better. It meant that God didn't see anymore. Mama'd written "God sees" on too many petals to count, but Jed knew now that Mama lied because *she* needed to believe God saw.

And even if He did see, Jed would put a blindfold on Him, ensuring God's blindness. He dropped the marble into his pocket.

God's eye felt heavy there, weightier than he remembered. Jed thought of Sissy, how her closed eyelids faced the wall. He retrieved God's eye and placed it on the table next to his bed. For Sissy's sake.

Thirty-Three

Come morning, Jed pulled to a sit, then rubbed the sleep from his eyes. Sucking in a yawn, Jed dangled his feet over the edge of his bed. Someday his tall bed, purchased cheap from a garage sale, wouldn't be so tall. Someday his feet would hit the floor in man triumph instead of dangle like a boy's.

Jed tested his ankle as he stood. Must've been a little sprain because today it felt almost like new. How could something so busted be happy and new in the morning? Didn't Hap say God's mercies came up with the sun? Jed hated that Hap's words were true sometimes. It made for a lot of confusion. If Hap was wrong all the time, that would be one thing, but from time to time? As a kid of seven, Jed and his world were ruled by Hap. And Jed served the king proudly. Folks in Defiance tipped their heads to Hap when he walked by. When they did, Jed stood taller.

But turning eight changed everything. Until then, Hap and Mama seemed happy. Those were the days Hap built houses and cabinetry, was known as Defiance's best carpenter. He took Mama on dates, sang songs on the radio when he drove through Defiance, the Chevy's windows rolled clear down. He laughed freely.

When Jed moved from second grade to third—the year he met Daisy and Hap finally finished restoring the Chevy—something snapped inside Hap, like a brittle twig bent over a strongman's knee. Mama sang to him on his birthday, thirty-three candles ablaze on a chocolate-frosted cake. Sissy, then four, sang the birthday song over and over.

Hap shushed her. He sat, placed a checkered napkin on his lap, and cleared his throat. "I have an announcement," he said.

Jed inched to the edge of his chair. Usually an announcement by Daddy meant a special trip to the zoo or a chance to ride in the Chevy to the park.

Mama smiled, but something about her grin unsettled Jed, even then.

"I'm thirty-three now. The age of Jesus when He died on the cross for our sins—when He fulfilled His mission." He winked at Jed. "So that means, I'm following in His footsteps. Gonna go to Bible school and become a pastor."

That year became the Year of the Ketchup in Jed's mind. His father blamed Bible school when he hollered at Mama, said the stress of driving and worrying about money was getting to be too much. With a fury Jed hadn't seen before, Hap threw a ketchup bottle right near Mama's head. She ducked just as it smashed into the kitchen clock, stopping time and bloodying the walls with red goop.

"Hap!" Jed yelled then.

Hap had spun around, wild-eyed. He took several breaths, shoved big hands into his hair at his temples and let out a long stream of air. "What did you call me?"

"Hap," Jed said, simply.

Hap looked at Jed a long, long time, steel blue to watery blue eyes. And then he turned his back on Jed. "Ouisie," he'd said, "best get to cleaning this mess up." Hap left the room, his footsteps loud on the hallway floor.

On Jed's nightstand were three roses, yellow ones, sharing the secret of their scent. Mama had been in his room.

Jed pulled the petals apart. No messages on the first two.

The third one held four words. "I am sorry. Mama." How many times had she written those words to him? Mama apologized in other ways too, with words spoken in whispers, in pancake breakfasts with sausage and eggs, all served with painted-on cheerfulness. In a good week, Jed could count on her being the most attentive mother ever. You'd think he'd love that. But he hated it. He knew when her love came from being sorry. It didn't feel anything like love. It felt like a had-to.

Jed dropped the rose. God's eye stared at him. He pulled on shorts and a T-shirt and crammed God's eye back into his pocket. Feeling it there sparked an odd hope, but he couldn't figure out how or why.

He sat on the floor, the pile of rocks and marbles before him. He spread them out, searching, thinking. A soggy Cheerio peeked out from underneath a small marble, a remnant of one of Daisy's Hansel and Gretel trails. He squished the spent Cheerio in his hand. Maybe Daisy left more clues. He'd found a shoe, a sock. Was there more?

Jed yelled at himself in his head. Scolded himself for not thinking through things, for not looking for more. For all he knew, Daisy was fuming somewhere, angered at his knock-headed self for not following the trail. By now it could be gone, and it would be all Jed's fault. Stupid, stupid.

Jed snuck to Sissy's room. He stood in the doorway, his ankle raised up like a lame horse. Though much better, it did smart a little if he kept his full weight on it. He watched Sissy sleep, but it made him nearly cry. Something about watching someone like her, so innocent, breathe unconsciously in and out stirred hunger in Jed. Not the hunger for s'mores in summer, but a deeper hunger. He was like God there, looking over His creation, loving that Sissy girl with everything in him. Did Hap ever watch him sleep? Did he feel this way about Jed?

He tiptoed to her bed, afraid to touch her.

She sighed.

He inched backwards.

"Sissy," he whispered.

She rolled toward him. Opened one eye like a pirate. "What?" she whispered.

"The car," he said, hushed. "Why'd you leave?"

Sissy sat up, rubbed her eyes. She shook her head, as if shaking the sleep away. "The car?"

"Last night, you were in the car, and then you weren't."

"The car?"

Jed took a breath, tried to steady his voice. He tried to remind himself that it took a good fifteen minutes for Sissy to wake to the land of the living. "Last night, remember?"

She shook her head no, then slunk back under the covers and closed her eyes.

Jed rustled her.

"I'm asleep!" she whined.

"Just tell me how you got home, and I'll leave you alone. I'm going to look for clues today."

Sissy sat up again. "Don't."

"Don't what?"

"Just don't go looking for clues."

"I have to."

She put her pale hand on his shoulder. "No, you don't. Please don't go sticking your nose into trouble."

"Listen, Sissy." He held her shoulders. "Look at me."

She did. Those big, big eyes looked right into Jed's heart.

"I have to find Daisy's kill—kidnapper."

"Don't be meddling. Please."

"I owe it to Daisy. Just like I'd owe it to you to find you if you went missing." He regretted saying it the moment it flew from his mouth.

"I nearly did go missing," she whispered.

"Sissy, what happened?"

Sissy shook her head no. Her eyes looked like she'd seen a monster. Not the ridiculous kind you saw on Monster Theater on channel 8 but the evil kind that looks like your next-door neighbor.

"Sissy, please. You're safe here in our home. Stay here all day. The walls will protect you, you hear?"

"Don't tell lies, Jed. If evil's coming to get you, it'll find you — even in your bedroom."

Jed didn't like such words coming from his innocent sister. She'd become wise about evil overnight, kind of like Adam and Eve after their meeting with the serpent. What happened last night? Why wouldn't Sissy tell him? He realized Daisy was probably facing this evil right now, unless he could put an end to it. The police were doing their duty, but she still wasn't found, and Miss Emory didn't seem to bother with it. "I need to find Daisy. Have to find who did this. You can help me. Tell me what happened."

She shook her head again. "I can't," she whispered.

"Please. Something. Anything. Like why were you in Ethrea Ree's rosebush?"

"I don't know." Sissy started to cry.

Jed shook his head. What did this mean? "Can you tell me how your shoe went missing?"

"I was in our backyard." She wiped her eyes with her fingers.

"Did you see anyone?"

"Nope. I was swinging in the tire, hurly twirly, round and round. I thought I saw Clementine streak by, but it's hard to say. I was whirring in circles, dizzy as a bee. When I hopped off the swing, I dashed this way and that. Then I stood. Wobbled a bit. I tripped again, into Mama's basil patch. That's when I saw them."

"Who?"

"Not who. What. Armyworms. Slimy green things crawling and chomping all over Mama's herb garden. It grossed me out. I ran inside to tell her."

"Wait. So you didn't know your shoe was gone?"

"Not yet. I got Mama."

"How long did that take?"

"How would I know? I didn't have my watch on."

Jed shook his head, slapped his knee. "Sissy, guess, okay?"

"Five minutes."

"So whoever it was could've taken the shoe when you were inside."

"I guess so."

"Then you came out?"

"Yep. I'd set my shoes on the picnic table, on the corner near the swing. When I ran to pick them up, I noticed one was gone."

"Your right shoe."

"Yeah. I looked underneath the table, but it wasn't there. Mama freaked out when I told her. Started hollering about Daisy's shoe and looking over the fence."

"I don't understand. If your shoe went missing, how in the world did Mama let you leave the house last night? Especially since she was so panicky."

"Headache, Jed. I told you that. You were gone. Daddy too. Clementine barked at the front door something fierce, so I let her out so she wouldn't wake up Mama. She bolted like she'd seen a ghost. That's when I saw the Velveteen Rabbit scat away, Clementine after it. I called her and called her, but she didn't come back. So I chased after her. By then, Mama must've been asleep. I didn't dare wake her."

"Weren't you scared?"

"More scared than ever. I thought I'd lost Clementine!"

Jed sighed. "Not scared about Clementine. About going out alone."

"It didn't seem that big a deal."

Jed asked more questions, but when he got to Sissy being locked inside the car, she froze. Her words stumbled over themselves. The more words she bumbled, the sicker he felt.

He patted her head. "Maybe you should sleep some more, okay?"

Sissy nodded. "Thanks, Jed. I'm awfully sleepy."

He tucked her in, smoothing the covers over her stick legs. "You get better, you hear? I'll be back soon."

She turned to him, her face still like death. "You keep yourself safe."

"I will."

"Promise?"

"Yep. I promise."

Thirty-Four

Jed walked toward the field behind his house, his shortcut to Crooked Creek Church. He'd scampered that path a million times but not since Daisy'd disappeared. It boiled his insides to do it, made him near starved for Daisy. Every rock, every scrub tree, every bend in the path made him think of her. Her smooth face. Bright eyes. Freckles dotted along the top of her nose like the Milky Way. Most folks wouldn't look at Daisy and say she's striking, but Jed knew the truth: Daisy was beautiful, in a soap-washed sort of way.

Clementine barked at Jed, bounding to his side. She'd become an escape artist in the past week, so much so that he'd taken to calling her Houdini. Normally Jed would welcome Clementine's wet nose and happy tail wagging, but today he had business to do and he didn't need a dog around messing things up.

"Go home, Clementine. Now!"

Clementine stood her ground, tail wagging.

"Git!" Jed threw a red rock her way.

Clementine ducked, then smiled, saliva dripping from her open mouth.

Jed tossed a branch, but she caught it in her teeth and brought it safely back to him.

"I said *git*!" Jed ran at Clementine with Hap's rage, nearly growling.

The dog slunk away like a scolded child, leaving Jed alone. He nearly chased after the dog, begging doggy forgiveness, but knew her absence was the right punishment. Even so, he longed for Clementine to bound back on her own accord, to be as forgiving as Sissy the morning after Hap screamed. Head down, timid as could be, Sissy'd hand Hap a pencil drawing of the two of them smiling in a field. But Clementine couldn't draw. And Jed had been far too mean, especially considering Clementine saved his hide last night.

Behind Ethrea Ree's home, he noticed something different—a white head jutting above the rosebushes. He picked his way through a few cacti, careful not to get poked, and leaned over the falling-down pickets. Craning his neck to the side, on his tiptoes, he spied the head again, attached to a white body. A statue of Jesus. A crown of thorns rested on top of the head, but not a marble crown—a real one, twisted around and around itself. Blood'd been painted on Jesus' paste white forehead, as if bursting forth from the rose thorns. Bleeding Jesus held His hands together in prayer, like He was praying for the roses. Maybe He was praying for Ethrea Ree's soul. Jed hoped so.

Seeing Jesus all red and white, brown thorns poking His head, made Jed wonder about addressing God as only he or him. Should he pray? To God? Again? What good would it do? Would God even hear such a prayer from someone who yelled at dogs? Hap said prayer didn't change God so much as it changed you. Well, if that was true, and Hap was a praying man like he said he was, God hadn't seemed to keep up his end of the bargain. Hadn't changed Hap ... for the better ... as far as Jed could see, that is.

But he couldn't keep from looking at the Jesus statue. Couldn't help but feel tears in his eyes for the poor guy who'd suffered so much, even now at the hands of Ethrea Ree. For a moment longer, he watched Jesus, who stared downward on roses while sun warmed the top of His head like heaven smiling.

Jed shielded his eyes from the sun. He squinted. A black form appeared in the sky, slow flying, like a St. Bernard with wings. A vulture. The bird circled directly above Jed, circles getting smaller and smaller like he'd been the victim of shrinking radiuses in geometry—the math subject Jed sneaked to read when Hap wasn't looking. So what if he wasn't supposed to know it yet—Hap had the book, so Jed read it, enjoying its simplicity. Smaller radius. Smaller circle.

The vulture dove lazily out of the sky, heading toward Jed. It occurred to Jed that not only dread rhymed with his name, but dead did too. Was the vulture a sign that he was next? The bird swooped lower, so close to Jed that he ducked. When he stood, the bird flapped away in another circle.

Jed looked at his hodgepodge shoes. One Daisy's. One his. The vulture, black and dull, swooped again overhead, then the black bird, dark as pitch, perched proud on Jesus' pure white head, his gangly wings covering Ethrea Ree's blood painting. He stared at Jed with death eyes. Though it was nearly a hundred and five degrees and his armpits dripped stink, Jed shivered.

He ran away to the field as fast as he could, trying not to holler when he pounded his tender ankle. An abandoned house made of craggy red rock reminded Jed of the grave, its windows like empty eyes. He and Daisy played in there on occasion, but Jed couldn't bring himself to explore it. From behind him, a rush of wings pursued him. The vulture dipped low above his head and swooped to the sky, its wings black against the blue sky.

Like that, it disappeared.

Jed stopped. Tried to steady his heart that pounded Satan's beat. Hap always told him any song with a fast beat was all a part of Satan's plan to overtake the earth. "The beat will woo you to sin, Jed. Mind you, don't listen, or you'll endanger your soul."

A field of wildflowers interrupted only by a narrow, red-dirt path waved hello. Indian paintbrush and black-eyed Susans, names Mama schooled him about, didn't seem to mind that the world was ending for Jed. They hadn't paid attention to vultures or snakes or folks snatching Daisy and right shoes. They just were. Jed wished he could just *be*. But deep inside he knew. Life would never be the same.

He scampered over a wooden fence into the next pasture. Rusted barbed wire snagged his shorts. He carefully pulled them free. Only one more pasture until he'd made it through the "hidden path" he and Daisy had used so often. Remembering his quest for clues, he ducked into the old tractor tire in the field's middle. It'd once welcomed guests to the Weldon Ranch. If he looked real close, he could make out WELDON painted a faint white on one side of the tire, half buried in the earth. He and Daisy spent time inside that gigantic tire, he on one side, she on the other. A terrific place for hiding from the rain, it was there she'd triple-dog-dared him to touch his tongue to hers this last March. He said no.

She said yes.

He said no way.

She said yes way. "Just get it over with, or you'll forever kick yourself for wimping out on a dare."

"No," Jed had said, but he'd felt himself wavering. "Why should I?"

"Because Sally Cumberland did it with Timothy Taylor and she said it was cool, so there."

"If Sally jumped off a bridge, would you?"

"Stop Happing me, Jed."

That did it. "Why do you always bring up Hap when you're trying to mess with me?"

"Scolding is unbecoming," Daisy said. "I do it because it gets your goat. Don't you want to kiss me?"

"Whoever said anything about kissing, Daisy? You said touch tongues."

"Well, it's *like* kissing."

Sweltering in the tire, no Daisy across from him, Jed felt the moment again. How he threw up his hands in defeat, closed his eyes, and stuck out his tongue. He leaned forward. She must've too because he could smell her. She smelled like cherries and wet earth. He felt her breath, how it warmed his face. Then her wet tongue. He reeled away in disgust. It'd felt like tasting a snail, only worse: a snail connected to a girl. Daisy huffed away. No doubt she'd thought the moment would be like the movies. It hadn't been.

But as Jed sat there alone while Daisy ranted under the sky, he wanted more than anything to try it again. Just once. Just one kiss. But he never got up the nerve.

And now he'd never have the chance.

Thirty-Five

At field's end, Jed wiped sweat from his forehead. He hadn't been back to Crooked Creek Church since the night of Daisy's disappearance. Why? He'd tell others he was staying away from the crime scene. But if Bald Muriel asked him, he'd be forced to tell her the truth, because everyone knew someone dying of cancer only had time for truth. Besides, she of all people deserved it. And the truth was? He was scared silly. All that boasting about how he would've protected her was hogwash, he knew.

Hap was right about this: Jed wasn't perfect. By any stretch. He'd taken to reminding Jed more and more the past few weeks, heaps of words that squished together with his guilt like mashed potatoes under a fork. With each step closer to the church, the words mashed him.

"Why don't you say thank you, Jed? You're ungrateful."

"For a smart kid, you sure are stupid."

"I love you, sure, but right now I don't like you."

"I only smacked you because you made me do it—by your insolence!"

"It's terribly hard being your father."

"God as my witness, you're the fool, Jed. Like Proverbs says."

"Someday you'll understand theology. Or maybe not."

"You're messing with my ministry. If George Abbot doesn't come to faith, it'll be because you interrupted me while I was on the phone."

"I can only hope you'll learn to work with your hands. College seems farther and farther away from you."

"You should quit your moping and accept it. Daisy's gone. Take it like a man."

The quit-your-moping words walloped Jed. Hap had caught him close to tears, but instead of pulling Jed close, he said those words, his forearm muscles twitching as he crossed them in front of himself. He left the room, his sentences like stingray tails snapping behind him.

Take it like a man. Take it like a man. Jed marched to the words. Take it. Step. Like a. Step. Man. Step.

But his heart didn't feel brave or manlike.

He pushed through the grasses, a dove seeming to call his name. Used to be he'd locate the bird on a branch and cock an air gun to pow it. Not today.

He stopped before the church. He hadn't noticed it before, but the woods formed a distant semicircle around the front side of the church and the pasture it set itself in, like the trees were a reluctant congregation to an angry preacher on the church steps. Thinking of the forest that way, like the trees were people, he wished they'd talk. If the trees had eyes to see and mouths to tell secrets, Jed would know where Daisy was.

Jed ran to the church like someone was chasing him. And maybe someone was. He swore he heard branches or twigs or footsteps. He looked behind him. Nothing. Just the wide field and a semicircle of too-still trees to his left. At the church's steps, he pulled up like a horse ready to stop. Voices?

Yes, voices. A man's. A woman's.

Jed snuck around to the side of the church near the broken windows. He was a sissy again. His eyes stung with tears. He should've swallowed his stupid fear and walked Daisy home.

But he didn't. He'd feared Hap more than he cared for Daisy's safety; this was true. He'd let one man's opinion strip away his responsibility.

The voices grew louder.

Who could be in the church?

Jed inched closer to the windows, crouched low to the ground. He made no noise. His heart beat wildly in his neck. More murmurings. He didn't dare look through the window. His ears would have to be his eyes.

"I need to get Jed to help me."

"There's no hurry."

"The end's coming," Muriel said.

"God's ways aren't ours," Hixon said.

"All I'm saying is, time is short."

Jed wondered if helping Muriel finish her mural would speed the end of her life. He wanted to hop out and give them both a fright, but he stayed crouched beneath the broken window, bees buzzing around his head. He took out God's eye and held it high enough for it to see inside—broken eye to busted window.

"I'm resigned and resolute." Hixon's voice.

"Sometimes we mistake God's voice for our own desires, you know." Muriel's again.

Jed stayed low. He felt like Sissy must've, holed up in Hap's and Mama's closet that night. A strange deliciousness stirred in him. Maybe it was his way-down-deep desire to be a spy for the CIA, or maybe it was pure curiosity, or maybe good old common sense.

"The Good Lord told me to do it." Hixon coughed.

"Well, if that's the case, you better hurry."

"Muriel, you of all people should know you can't rush God."

Jed's skin prickled. He wondered what strange thing God told Hixon to do—all this prophet stuff shivered his insides. Didn't God tell Abraham to stab his kid? And didn't Abraham

259

raise the knife? Jed's pushed-down worry about Hixon came to the front of his mind, like a kid cutting in line at the movies. Could he trust Hixon? What if God told Hixon to take Daisy and hide her away? Wouldn't he flat-out do it, being so obedient and all?

Did God really know what Hixon was about to do? Jed lowered God's eye and stuck it back in his dark pocket. No, God didn't see.

Jed heard no more voices, only shoes against the church's wooden floor. The door creaked open. Jed crept to the church's corner where he could see better. A scraggly crape myrtle with flowers the color of grape Kool-Aid kept him mostly hidden. He saw Hixon standing tall at the church's entrance, holding Muriel's hand. She looked pasty white. She shielded her eyes from the sun.

"It won't be much longer."

Hixon nodded.

"Quit your somber face. You should be rejoicing."

Hixon put both hands to his eyes, breathed a long breath through his palms.

Muriel placed a white hand on his shoulder. "Come on now. We've got much to do. You even said so yourself. Now be a gentleman and help me down these stairs."

Jed watched them make their way across the field—a sad brown-skinned man and a strangely happy whitewashed woman. They looked like friendship walking in such a way that made Jed miss Daisy even more.

As if that were even possible.

Thirty-Six

Jed crept into the church.

Quiet footsteps.

Slowly. Slowly.

With ears pricked to any noise, he swallowed.

He walked down the church's center aisle like the father of the bride, each footstep bringing him closer to his Daisy place. When he stood even with their pew, he stopped. And breathed. And swallowed a cry.

He slid down their pew, running his fingers along the smooth wood. Dust came off in his hands. He blew it away. The sunlight narrowing in through several windows caught the dust in a dance. Jed sat back in the pew, watching it swirl in front of him.

He pulled out a hymnal, then opened it.

He'd played this game before, but with the Bible. Hap called it biblical Russian roulette, opening the book and pressing a finger down on a passage that was surely meant to be a sign from God. Jed's pointer finger came down on the words "though the darkness hide Thee" from "Holy, Holy, Holy," his favorite hymn. He read, "Though the eye of sinful man, Thy glory may not see."

Well, it was true. This world was chock-full of sinful folks, Jed knew that. Especially him. But what did holy mean? And glory? Would Bald Muriel see glory? What about Daisy? Did she see glory right now?

Jed remembered the last time he'd played roulette with Daisy in church, the day before she disappeared. Her finger fell on "love," of course, and she took it as another sign from God that she'd marry Jed, sure as the freckles on her face.

Daisy took everything as a sign. Once, while they were on the playground, she said to her friends, "The fifth boy who walks out from around that corner will be my husband." And who would it be but Mr. Simpson—a man who wore thick glasses and smelled like corn chips. She said he didn't count, being a man and all. When Jed walked around the corner, a group of giggling girls shrieked, something that made his face terribly red. Only later did Daisy tell him what it all meant. "God's giving me signs, Jed Pepper. You're to be my hero. And then my husband."

Hero?

How could he be her hero? He sat in the pew doing nothing at all but pointing a dirty finger into a hymnal, desperate for clues, but scared out of his wits. He shut the book, put it back in its proper place.

He crouched low to the ground and peered under the pews. Nothing but dust.

He walked up and down the center aisle, paying particular attention to the place he found her shoe. Nothing.

On hands and knees, Jed crawled back and forth, hoping he'd missed something. But he hadn't. The place was empty. Terribly so.

He left. In the field, the sun winked at him from behind a fluffy cloud. Though it was morning, Jed knew it must be at least ninety degrees with just as much humidity. His shirt felt instantly wet. He pulled out God's eye. "Well, God, if You see like You say You do, show me where a clue is."

A hot breath of strong wind surprised Jed. He let go of God's eye.

Looking down, he couldn't see the blue eye through the brown, swaying grass. Knowing Daisy would kill him if he lost their treasure, he crept along the ground, looking for the blue marble. The fear of chigger bites pestered him, but he kept at his search. He found nothing.

Jed wanted to scream. Was this how God did things?

He clawed at the ground, pushing over longer and longer stalks of grass, hoping to find the eye. It couldn't have rolled away on the flat field, could it?

Something sparkled a yard away. Jed stood and walked over to it.

God's eye.

And Daisy's hair clip.

He left God's eye to rot under the sky.

And picked up the hair clip.

"Show me where you are, Daisy," he said to the wind.

Thirty-Seven

It was hers all right. Light yellow, faded by the sun, with a metal daisy smiling at him. Daisy had always been very particular about her clips, something Jed didn't quite get, though maybe Sissy understood. "They have to match your outfit, silly," she'd told Jed too many times. She'd used two flower clips to pull away her crooked bangs from her face the day she disappeared. That, he knew.

Jed's thoughts flew around in circles like that vulture, around and around, never landing on anything. Should he find Officer Spellman? Tell Hap? Run and find Miss Emory? Figure this out himself? Share it with Sissy? He turned the clip over in his hand. Rust gripped its back where it had rested on the grass. The smiling daisy teased him. He opened the clip. Then closed it. All the while thinking, thinking, thinking.

Jed looked behind him. He remembered where the shoe was inside the church. Where he stood was smack dab in the middle between the shoe and the sock he found. An exact line, Jed being the midpoint. He walked slowly, one foot in front of the other, toward the place where Daisy's sock had been. Perhaps if he kept to this straight and narrow path, he'd find her.

Jed veered right into the woods and walked as straight of a line as he could. The day he lost Daisy played like a movie in his head. All the smells, the sights, the sounds came back to him as if he were walking through the woods that very evening. Though the sun climbed higher in the sky, he felt the moon overhead, heard the birds call their night sounds.

It was Daisy's shoe that crunched the gravel underfoot first. Jed's shoe followed. Both walked slowly over the rocky street toward the place where he found her sock. Fifteen steps later, he was there.

Jed thought maybe there'd be a giant arrow pointing to the exact spot where he'd found the sock with daisies chained around it. But no arrow existed. Only a terribly eerie feeling he couldn't shake.

In the distance, a red car spun its tires. Jed jumped. A headache threatened. Then Jed did something Daisy would surely laugh at. He sat. Right there in the middle of the gravel roadway. Sharp rocks threatened to cut into him while the sun shone from the top of the sky. He pulled out Daisy's clip, held it high so the sun would see it. Though Hap would've given him a terrible talking to, involving a switch for sure, Jed couldn't help but believe in the power of this clip to find Daisy.

Looking behind him, remembering the angle he'd walked from the church to the clip to here, where he'd found the sock, he stared forward. If he launched a water balloon from a trebuchet in the proper direction, he would hit more woods, not the road. This startled him. Sure, he knew anyone who took Daisy probably was a crazy person, not taking into account a straight line. Wouldn't crazy people dart here and there? Still, Jed couldn't shake the fact that he'd missed this obvious clue. Daisy hadn't been on the road for long, which would make sense. She'd be taken where folks wouldn't see her — into the Haunted Forest.

Jed's heart sped up the closer he got to those woods. He remembered Miss Emory's stiff form in the Pinto, heard Daisy's warnings in his head. "Promise you'll never go in. Cross your heart," she'd said. Jed almost did as the woods loomed tall. Even folks who lived in Old Defiance spread their rumors about these woods. Ethrea Ree said the ghost of her ex-husband, Slim Ree—she never called him her husband now deceased, just her ex, like she'd been divorced—prowled around those woods. "Those trees are his," she told Jed over their back fence last winter, "and they do his bidding."

As the trees extended piney branches, sending their scent Jed's way, he remembered a particular camping trip he'd had up north. Hap hauled the family to Colorado in the Chevy "to see the glory of God's majesty" and to preach a revival outside Colorado Springs for a dying church that promised a hefty love offering.

Jed couldn't believe mountains could be so tall. The highest place he'd been besides a few rolling hills in Defiance was on an overpass in Dallas, and even then it gave him the willies to be so high. He didn't like how the mountains carved away the sky. But Hap was determined to reach the clouds, so he drove them all the way up what Sissy called a perilous road that dropped off to the right and hugged the mountain to the left. Once on top of Pike's Peak, Jed felt woozy. They ate doughnuts and drank lukewarm hot chocolate. Though he saw the wide sky again, it didn't make Jed feel better. It made him want to get off the mountain.

As Jed stepped farther into the forest, another memory, small at first, then bigger than a fair's Ferris wheel, grew in his mind. After their trip to Pike's Peak, they pulled off the main highway to a mountain road. Trees taller than roller coasters swooped branches around them. Hap scared him and Sissy both saying, "Stay put in the car tonight and pray we don't get tangled in by the trees."

"What does that mean?" Jed asked.

"Stop it, Hap," Mama said.

With a smile, Hap replied, "Don't you know? At night the trees curl their limbs around cars that aren't supposed to be there. They lock them in a death grip so tight they can't get out.

No one can open a door. After a while, folks get so thirsty they go crazy."

Jed shivered. He remembered fighting to keep his eyes pasted open the entire night. At every noise, he convinced himself a tree was drawing itself near, scraping its way to the car. When he did drift to sleep, nightmares assaulted him. Trees chased him through darkness, branches strangled his breath. And a terrible tree ate Sissy right up, belching pine needles afterwards.

Standing stock-still, his shoe and Daisy's barely inside the haunted woods, Jed looked around. No trees swooped their branches at him. If anything, they were quiet as stone statues, not a breeze ruffled their needles. Jed picked his way through the forest, trying as hard as he could to walk a straight line. Of course, it would've been easier in a Colorado forest full of tall, pencil-trunked aspens. But East Texas forests were different—shorter trees, for one, and prickly vines that felt it was their God-ordained right to scamper over everything, claiming even old tires as their own. Truth was, Jed would've renamed Defiance's forests. Called them jungles instead.

A sticker bit his calf. He let out a yelp, but nothing answered back.

Every ten steps or so, he stopped and listened. He would've welcomed a chatty bird, but the silence coming back from the trees spooked him. No rustling. No birds. No skittering. Only hot, wet air without a breeze and a heartbeat throbbing his ears. Jed tugged at the neck of his T-shirt, trying to get a bit of relief. For a moment he thought of taking it off altogether, but decided not to bother.

Jed walked through the Haunted Forest for what seemed like miles. He remembered Hap saying their trek up a mountain once was one mile long. Four hours later, Jed questioned whether it wasn't one mile, but ten. Hap pointed Jed to the trailhead where "one mile" was etched into a wooden sign to prove his point. This walk felt like that mountain hike, like he was walking on one of those fat-lady treadmills he saw on TV, getting nowhere. Eventually, light angled in the woods directly in front of him. A clearing.

He broke into a sloppy run, if there ever could be such a thing, and loped to the clearing. Open sky greeted him. "Thank God," he said to the opening.

The sun throbbed the late morning sky, throwing heat like arrows right onto the top of Jed's head. He shielded his eyes from the sun and counted clouds—something he and Sissy did when Hap went on a rampage and they were outside. They'd made it to forty-nine once until Hap kicked the side of the house and boards fell off under his boot. Jed wiped his face in his T-shirt, scolding himself for not bringing water. He looked down at his Daisy-Jed shoes, nearly asking them to find Daisy. Magic shoes—that's what he needed. Jed looked straight ahead.

A crooked black tree stood alone in the open field.

Hixon's tree. What was it Hixon said in church? Jed ran to the tree, several hundred yards off. He circled it, heart pounding.

"Daisy!" The heat swallowed up his voice. "Daisy!"

Jed looked up. Charred branches angled themselves to the sky like thirty broken arms asking for help. Directly behind the branches, circling mid-sky, soared another vulture. Or was it the same one? Jed felt sick. Hixon was practically Jesus—isn't that what Sissy said? Hixon wouldn't hurt a June bug. Besides, walk a straight line and find Daisy? What was he thinking?

Vultures were everywhere in Defiance. Usually fat too. Critters died here all the time.

But this was Hixon's tree. And Hixon wouldn't kidnap.

Stop it, Jed. Stop it. Go home. She's not here. She's not anywhere. You made all this stuff up in your head.

But what if she is here? And I can help her?

"Daisy! Daisy!"

Jed walked away from the bent tree toward a gravel road that snaked away from the wide, flat meadow. He wondered about chiggers biting him to kingdom come, but told himself to be a man. What's a few chigger bites, anyway? When gravel crunched under his feet, his midsection tightened. He looked to the sky. The vulture swooped beyond where he stood.

"Daisy!"

Something glinted in the path ahead. He didn't run to meet it. Slow footsteps brought him closer to the small object that seemed to capture the sun from below and shoot its brilliance back to the sky. A yardstick away from the shiny object, Jed stopped.

Daisy's other flower clip winked back at him. His feet, glued to the earth, wouldn't move. A curdled cry from deep inside growled through his lungs, lighting fire to his voice. "Oh God!" That was all he could say. "Oh God! Oh God! Oh God!"

A noise rustled behind him. He reeled around, unsticking his feet. Clementine rushed at him, not barking, not smiling. But she was there. Jed crouched down. Clementine rested her head on Jed's knees and looked at him with sad eyes.

"I'm sorry, Clementine. I shouldn't have yelled at you before. Forgive me?" He needed her forgiveness right now like nothing else, except maybe Daisy's. Clementine seemed to nod. She licked Jed's hands—a bath of drooling forgiveness that never felt so good. Jed wrapped lanky arms around the furry dog. Clementine seemed to hug him back, nuzzling his neck with her large head.

Jed stood. Clementine sat nearly on his feet—as close as a dog could get, Jed thought. They walked together toward Daisy's clip. Jed picked it up. Turned it over and over. Clementine stiffened next to him, her muscles clenched. The dog barked something fierce, so loud Jed nearly shushed her.

Clementine bolted forward. Jed followed, calling after her. At the top of a hill, Clementine stopped. You could see all of Defiance from this hill. If Jed jumped, he could see his house over to the south—the view of it all made him feel like God.

Clementine circled back and nudged Jed farther beyond the hill, over its weedy rise.

A blazing wind blew Jed's face. He sucked in a hot breath. The smell of sulfur stung his nose. Jed looked up.

A vulture stood on a ragtag mound of underbrush just ahead of him, its leathery wings outstretched to the sky. He looked right at Jed, burning a hole into him with dead eyes. He tucked dark wings around him, then stood still as Ethrea Ree's Jesus statue.

Clementine barked it away. But the bird circled, circled, circled above. Jed wrapped arms around himself. From the side of the mound, Jed saw something. He looked closer. A hand, shrunken and bony, nails painted a pale orange. Circling loosely on the ring finger was Daisy's favorite sunshine ring—the one Jed got her in a bubble gum machine.

Jed dropped to his knees, then kissed the earth with his face and vomited. "Oh God," he said. "Oh God. It's Daisy. It's Daisy."

Clementine sat, ears drooped, eyes sad, staring at the hand, but she didn't lick it. Jed pounded the dirt. "No. No! It can't be her!"

But it was. He saw her clear as day, a blonde-headed girl shining in a dark church, following after him. "You going to leave me here alone? I traipsed all the way from town to come here." Her voice sounded hollow, a death of a voice, echoing through his head. He remembered how the light haloed her head, how she seemed to know this was her last conversation on earth, the glint of sun readying her to join the angel choir in heaven.

"It's not like we don't meet here every single day. You'll be fine. How many times have you walked home from here? A thousand? Two?" Jed shook his head. No, he couldn't have said that. Shouldn't have.

"It's a long walk." The words bounced off the church's walls, sounding more and more like the wail of a dove than the plea of his friend. He saw her shake her head, while watery tears streaked live cheeks.

"For crying out loud, Daisy, this is Defiance, Texas. There's nothing to be afraid of. Besides, you've got God's eye for protection." Jed heard his words in his head as a teasing voice, taunting to Daisy who would soon be taken by a stranger to this field. He covered his ears.

The vulture swooped near Daisy's hand. Jed chased it away, arms thrashing, voice moving between boy and man, high and low.

But even all that hollering couldn't stop Daisy's last words from stabbing through the hot Defiance day. "You'll regret it," he heard her say—a ghost of a voice, shrill, haunted. Jed forced himself to look at her shrunken hand, then reached out to touch it. He expected it to be heated by the sun, but it felt cold in his. So terribly cold.

"Daisy, I'm sorry. So, so sorry."

"I'm a good forgetter," she'd said. Her words stung. Would she forget his betrayal from heaven? Or would she yell at him the moment he passed to glory, scolding him for leaving her? One thing was for sure. He wouldn't leave her now. Wouldn't give her cause for more scolding.

Clementine stood, then barked ferociously toward the Haunted Forest. She grabbed Jed's shorts and tried to pull him away from Daisy, past the hill to the other side toward town. Jed cried no, but Clementine wouldn't let him go. As slow as the vulture in the sky, his hand slipped breath by breath away from hers.

"I need to stay here," he told Clementine. "Daisy, she needs me." He darted back to Daisy's hand, but Clementine would have none of Jed's promise, growling and pulling and keeping Daisy's dead hand from being held.

Jed crooked his neck behind him, looked at the woods. A single figure, too far away to make him out, stood outside thick trees. Jed's hands trembled. His arms shook. His torso shivered. Growling, Clementine pulled Jed away with a fierceness that startled him. Soon Jed's legs took hold and he found them running, keeping pace with Clementine while Daisy's solitary finger pointed to heaven.

He looked back once. Only the looming hill behind him. No man. He hoped he'd dreamed the bony hand, the clip, the vulture, but his instinct told him no. Daisy was gone. He couldn't even protect her grave from the bogeyman.

All these thoughts ping-ponged in his brain to the rhythm of his run. He didn't stop until he mounted his porch and crashed through the front door.

"What in the—" Hap rose from his chair, unsettling the morning paper.

Clementine answered with a bark.

Sissy peered around the hallway corner.

Mama hurried in, wiping her hands on her apron.

Jed retrieved his voice. "I found Daisy."

"What?" Hap look startled. "Is she okay?"

"No. She's dead. Near Hixon's old tree."

Then everything went black.

Thirty-Eight

As long as Jed knew Daisy, Miss Emory had turned on nearly every lamp in their home, even through the night, so Daisy took to sleeping under her covers. She told Jed she worried she'd die because she had to keep breathing recycled breath. Jed told her no, everything would be fine, but he stewed about her every night. Said a prayer before he'd shut his eyes that she wouldn't suffocate.

He said the prayer again, out of habit, until snapshots of Daisy's gnarled hand slapped him in the face, obliterating any hope. All those prayers. And she suffocated anyway under a blanket of dirt.

Darkness crushed him, pulling him deeper into nightmares. Halloween dreams haunted him. Ghouls chased him. He fell into pits of sulfur air—pits without bottom. Trees strangled him. A man with menacing eyes and bare feet stood nearby, never moving. The more Jed ran from him, the more the man stayed the same distance away. Jed said "Jesus" over and over again, finally making the barefoot man leave in a huff.

A bony hand clutched his throat and wouldn't let go. It had a voice. Daisy's.

"I miss you," it said.

"I'm sorry," he croaked back.

"Quit scratching those bites!" Hap's voice interrupted the dream. The bony hand became Hap's strong one.

"I can't help it," Jed choked.

The choking stopped. Flower petals floated from the sky with strange messages. Jed caught them in his hands and read a few.

The weak grow weaker, the strong, stronger.

Where is Daisy?

Who's afraid of the bogeyman?

Seven days without prayer makes one weak.

No use in crying over spilt milk.

There is a chasm of sin separating you from God.

You're afraid of the bogeyman.

Flower petals stopped their falling. Jed told himself to wake up, but his dreams snuffed out his voice, kept him to a raspy whisper. Something touched his forehead, something soft. More flower petals?

"Jed."

Jed shook his head, this time actually felt it moving. The paralyzing dreams stopped. He opened his eyes.

Sissy sat next to him on his bed. The curtains were closed. Her small hand rested on his forehead. She looked awfully small.

"Wake up. You've been in la-la land for fifteen hours."

"What?"

"I thought you were dying."

He removed her hand from his forehead. Looked into her eyes. Hoped to God she didn't see fear in his. Was he dying?

"Are you okay?" she asked.

"Was it Daisy?" Jed knew the answer, but he had to ask.

Sissy cried, then cried some more. "It was Daisy." She huffed in tears, then blew her nose. "Near Hixon's tree like you said. The police have been talking to Hixon about it. They said they need to talk to you."

"You think Hixon did it?" Jed pushed himself up.

"Nah, but it's near his tree, so they're asking."

"What about Muriel?"

"They're talking to her too."

Jed felt queasy inside, like all his organs had gotten together and decided to feel nauseous. The wooziness kept him nailed to the bed. "It's all wrong," he whispered, but the nausea attacked. "Sissy, I'm—" From somewhere down deep, Jed hurled what seemed like every food he'd ever eaten all over himself, parts of Sissy's hands, and his old bedspread.

Sissy reeled away. She looked at her hands.

Jed wasn't sad about soiling the bedspread. It was about time to put that thing to rest, but he hated throwing up on Sissy almost as much as he hated the vinegary taste of digested food over and under his tongue.

"I'll be right back," she said.

Jed looked over at his nightstand where an orange rose crooked toward him, petals wide open. He lifted it from the vase. Sure enough, one petal held words.

"I'm sorry" was all it said.

The words jarred Jed's mind like a skeleton dance, clacking against each other—hollow, lifeless words that Mama said over and over again until they became a clattering noise no one paid any mind to. Just once he'd like to read "I'm *not* sorry" on a flower petal. Or hear her say, "That's really not my fault." But Mama seemed to take on everyone's guilt, mistaking others' guilt for her own. In a rush, Jed remembered his words to Miss Emory on the porch, when she came close to understanding Jesus. Jed said he wished he could take away her pain. Because he understood. Jed felt the same about Mama. Oh, how he longed to suck all the sorry out of her because he knew what it felt like to feel sorry and not be able to shake yourself of it.

Moments later, Mama stood in the doorway, her eyes red-rimmed. She rushed to his side, clutching a handful of daisies. "Oh, my. Sit up. Let me get you out of these things." She laid the daisies in a heap on Jed's nightstand.

"I'm fine, Mama." Jed stood, while the mess of vomit ran down his nightshirt. "I'll go take a shower."

He may as well have slapped her, she looked as stricken.

"Let me help you," she said.

"I can take care of myself."

"I know. I'm sorry." She backed away, then rubbed her temples.

Jed reeled around. "Stop saying that, Mama. Just stop it, will you?"

She looked at him, red eyes now wet with tears. "Stop what?"

"Quit apologizing. If this is anyone's fault, it's mine. Not yours." Jed's high voice creaked through. He swallowed.

"Don't take that on. It's not your fault."

"Well, then, whose is it? I was the last one to see her alive."

Mama sat on Jed's bed, paying no mind to the vomit there. She fiddled with her hands on her lap, concentrating like they were a puzzle to be solved. "I'm sorry," she whispered.

Jed looked at Mama. He shook his head. Maybe Mama needed to be sorry. Maybe she didn't know any different. And maybe she'd born the weight of Hap's anger so long she'd become like Jesus taking on someone else's sin. Being sorry was her way. Jed crossed the room, touched Mama on the head, and said, "I'm sorry."

He met Sissy in the bathroom. She wiped her hands on one of their threadbare towels. She looked at him with sad eyes. "I'm sorry about Daisy." She brushed past him.

Jed locked the bathroom door. He'd never done that before but felt he must this time. A man needed his privacy.

He pulled off his soaked shirt and balled it on the floor, careful not to let the vomit out. He started the shower and jumped in without checking the water temperature.

Cold water flooded over him. It made him want to scream,

but he kept his voice inside, fearing if he let a little out, he'd never be able to block in the rest.

The water warmed, eventually. But his heart stayed cold. He should be crying. He should be. But Jed couldn't leak a single tear even as the water showered his face. Did he miss Daisy? Yes. Did he realize that the hand he saw poked toward the sky was hers? Yes.

But he didn't want it to be.

It couldn't be. Just couldn't be.

But it was.

Jed played that night again in his head. Daisy talking about marriage. The butterfly she was sure was a sign. Her eyes pleading for him to walk her home. He checking his watch, thinking of Hap, not her.

Jed turned in the shower, letting the warm water wash over his back. A conversation with Hixon jumped into his mind.

"Idolatry is when you place something above God and worship it." Hixon'd been sitting, back against Miss Emory's half-painted house. Only weeks ago.

Hixon had smiled. "Let me ask you this, do you care more about what your dad thinks about you on any given day than how God thinks of you?"

"I don't know," Jed had replied.

"That's a lot of power," Hixon said. "A lot of power you've given him."

Jed turned off the shower. He wrapped a towel around his midsection and sat on the closed toilet lid. For as long as he could remember, he'd lived for power — to be stronger than Hap so he could lick him once and for all, so he could protect Mama and Sissy. He clenched his fist. It felt strong.

Someday, Hap would pay.

Jed stood. He faced the sink and mirror and saw dead rage living behind his eyes. He made a fist again. A growl from deep inside roared through him, leaving his throat in a rush. His fist left its place and shot through the bathroom air, square into the mirror, shattering it with a crash. Jed cried out.

Sissy screamed his name from outside the door, but she sounded far away, so very far away.

Thirty-Nine

Jed sat on his mattress where Mama had already stripped and re-sheeted the bed. Nothing around him felt familiar other than the song playing in his head. "Cat's in the Cradle" haunted him—a song Daisy'd shared with him on the transistor radio. She'd been allowed to listen to Satan's music by the degenerate Miss Emory, according to Hap. "It's like you and Hap, only I'm hoping you'll make it untrue," she'd said last spring. "Promise me something, okay?" She looked at him with thirteen-year-old eyes that seemed like ancient pools of wisdom.

"Anything," Jed had replied. It'd been one of those rare Texas days—temperate, sunny, and not many bugs vying for bites. The field they walked through to get to Crooked Creek Church was crowned by a thousand bluebonnets.

"Don't get angry like Hap."

"Don't be ridiculous, Daisy. He's the last person I'll be like."

"Promise me?"

"Of course."

How could he make a promise like that? Jed looked at his bloody right hand. He clenched it even though it burned to do so.

Mama came in, gauze and medical tape in hand. "Here, let me help you."

Jed said, "Let it bleed."

Mama sat next to him. "Your father will fix the mirror. No need to worry."

"That's the least of my worries."

"I know." She sat on the end of his bed, smoothing the sheets over and over again like she was petting them into place. "But he's good at fixing things."

"Oh, really," Jed said.

"Yes, really. Don't be disrespectful."

"Is that why you married him? Because he could fix things?" Jed heard the sarcasm leave his mouth. He let it hang out there.

"When I first fell in love with your father, you know where I was?"

Jed shook his head.

"Stranded on the side of the road. My car was overheated, steam or smoke was blowing out of the engine. He stopped, told me not to worry. He jimmied and wrenched under the hood, slapped it shut, and drove me to the repair shop. He took care of me, Jed. And I needed to be taken care of. Or maybe it was I loved being looked after."

The funny thing was, Jed could picture the entire scene. Jed didn't want to think of Hap this way, didn't want to hear more about his fixing ways. He swallowed. "I read those letters from David."

"What?"

"Sissy found 'em. I hid them so Hap wouldn't burn them."

"Those are private, Jed." She looked at Jed with eyes nearly as cold as Hap's.

"I'm sorry. I can give them back if you have a good hiding place."

"No." She shook her head. "That was a lifetime ago. It's not my life anymore. Hap was right to want to burn them." She stood. "You sure you don't want me to take a look at your hand?"

"No, Mama. I'm fine."

Head down, she left his room without another word.

Jed heard Hap pulling down the mirror, shard by shard, unlatching it from its glue bed. Hap didn't yell. Didn't make one peep. Only the phone ringing apparently stopped his dogged pursuit of broken glass. When he came in Jed's room, his left index finger was bandaged, blood peeking through. "It's time. You're needed at the scene."

Hap drove Jed to the outskirts of town where Officer Spellman waited. He walked them up the back hill toward the mound of dirt. Jed stopped. "Is she still ... there?"

"No, the coroner's come and taken her to Tyler," Officer Spellman said. "I'll drive her mother there for identification." The life had drained out of Captain Kangaroo's eyes, replaced by what looked like dark sadness. He walked the last few feet with his head down.

Hap's was down too.

Seeing the hole where Daisy last rested ripped through Jed. She'd been there, reaching for him, and he didn't bother to unbury her. He'd let his fear get the best of him once again, let a stranger dig her up and take her to Tyler.

"Do you need a moment?" Hap's voice sounded small, smaller than it had ever sounded.

With that small-sounding voice, Jed thought he'd feel sorry for the old man, but all he could do was make a fist. He wished the wilderness had a wall he could punch, but all he could see were the lines of his father's face. He turned away. "Yes, a moment." Inside, he seethed.

He sat near the hole, wanting to say he was sorry to Daisy, but he couldn't bring himself to voice the words while Hap stood nearby and Officer Spellman's face grew more somber. So he sat. Shook his head. Bit his lip. Scratched his ankles.

"I'm really sorry, Jed, but I need to ask you a few things. It's customary procedure when someone discovers a body."

Hearing "body," Jed trembled. Daisy was no longer a person. She was a body.

Officer Spellman pelted Jed with a dizzying number of police questions. When did you see the hand? What time of day, exactly? Did you see the hand or the fingers? Who did you suspect it to be? Was there anyone else with you? How did Clementine react when she saw the mound of dirt? Were you standing to the south of the pile? The north? Describe the figure you saw. Did he or she say anything? Where were you standing when you saw the person? On and on it went while Texas Rangers combed a thousand-foot radius around the hole in the ground where Daisy had been. Hap stood, staring into the hole, his hands folded in front of him like he was praying. Maybe he was.

A small wooden casket took the place of Hap's podium. Draped across it was the quilt Daisy used to cover her hideous paisley couch; now it covered her decaying body—a blanket to warm her cold hands. It seemed fitting there, like a quilt placed by a loving mother on a bed. Mama put a loose arm around Jed. He shrugged her off.

Miss Emory sat three people down the row. Jed couldn't bear to look at her. He wondered what she saw when she identified Daisy. Did she cry? Holler? Swear? Curse Jed? Jed felt her grief almost so much he could taste it. Then regret. Then something else. A raging desire to never face someone's disappointment again. A need to protect anyone needing protecting.

The man behind the podium wasn't Hap. Jed looked over at his father, two places down the pew. His shoulders slumped slightly.

Hixon stood before them, even more slump-shouldered than Hap. Jed wondered why Miss Emory chose Hixon to remember

Daisy properly. She didn't exactly relish his company. But then, Miss Emory'd always made her own decisions, and there was no turning them back once they were made.

The police dismissed Hixon when his story proved he'd been fixing a roof of an elderly woman that evening Daisy went missing. She'd hobbled up the police station's stairs in a walker to clear his name. But Hixon didn't seem relieved up there looking out over the congregation. After Miss Emory asked Hixon to preach Daisy's funeral, Hap had ranted and stormed, then sulked.

"I'm here at the request of Miss Emory Chance," Hixon said. "But I wish to God I wasn't." He cleared his throat. He walked forward and placed his hand on Daisy's coffin. "I know I speak for all of us when I say Daisy Marie Chance will be missed."

Jed heard cries coming from the congregation. He didn't choke up. He didn't cry. Neither did Miss Emory, who wore all black except for a chain of daisies around her neck.

Mama cried. When she did, her breath smelled like Nyquil. Hap didn't. Sissy did. She huffed in and out, her stomach pushing out and in to the rhythm of her tears.

"Daisy burst into heaven, we know that. But there's a lot we don't know or understand." Hixon spoke about the mystery of God, how His ways are unfathomable, unknowable. Jed nearly hollered, "You got that right," but kept his tongue behind clenched teeth.

Eyes wet, Hixon asked if anyone would like to say a few words about Daisy. Miss Emory stood, clutching a piece of paper. She didn't move. Hixon walked over to her, then put a strong arm around her. Jed watched her red, red lips. She unfolded the paper.

"A mother lives with grief every day of her life," she said, her voice shaky. "Grief that her baby is growing up and won't need her anymore. Grief over mistakes. Grief that time can't be bought back." She sniffed in a tear.

Somehow, Jed understood.

"I'm going to miss my Daisy. Going to miss her smile. Her laughter. Her—" She sucked in grief, then let it out, Jed thought, because all at once she howled, Hixon the only thing holding her upright.

Hixon walked back to the coffin. Touched it. Nodded at Bald Muriel, who sat on the opposite side of the church. Then he said, "Though I didn't know her much in this life, I can assure you today that Daisy is smiling and laughing and playing on streets of glassy gold right now. She's with Jesus. Dear sweet Jesus. And He's making everything right up there. Everything. Down here we live in heartache and battle bewildering evil. Life doesn't make sense. I've tried to make sense of it all, but I can't. But I can say this. Jesus makes all the difference. Even today as you wipe tears that keep coming, Jesus understands. He bled. He wept. He let earth's dirt grit His toes. He faced death."

Hixon stood directly in front of Jed but didn't look at him. "And Jesus will help us all walk through this terrible, horrible journey together. Let's pray."

During the prayer, Jed looked over at Bald Muriel—a welcome distraction from Miss Emory's grief. He wondered if Bald Muriel bowed her head and closed her eyes. She didn't. She looked heavenward, like her chin was on tiptoes, her eyes seeing pearly gates no one else saw. She turned her head, looked square into Jed's eyes. Her upturned mouth caught a trail of tears that she didn't wipe away.

Jed looked away. Face still dry.

He tightened his fist while "Cat's in the Cradle" played in his head.

Forty

Daisy never did say why her mama wanted the lights on every night. When he asked for the hundredth time, she looked away, tears in her eyes. "I can't say."

"Why?"

"Because mama made me promise only one thing in this life and that was to keep this secret."

She did that all right. Took it to her grave.

"She'd tan my hide if I told you. Besides, it's not good in the telling. Not good at all."

Jed had wanted to put a lanky arm around her narrow shoulders right then, to ease her pain, but he didn't. He remembered feeling suddenly shy and awkward, and he'd worried Daisy'd slap him away. Now, standing at her grave site, he wished more than anything he had taken the risk. Never getting to comfort someone again was a pain he wouldn't get used to.

He gripped the plastic in his left unbandaged hand. Jed closed his eyes, wishing he didn't have to give up Daisy's long-handled comb. But a promise was a promise. "If I ever die, I want to be buried with my yellow comb. A girl never knows when she'll need to primp—even in the afterlife," she'd said. Her Fourth of July words. Three summers later, he'd have to make good on his promise, but it wasn't his turn.

Each person at Daisy's graveside held one daisy and threw

it on top of her lowering casket. One by one. Sissy'd woven a daisy chain for Miss Emory and Daisy. She'd pestered Hap, whose eyes seemed wet, to please ask if the mortician could put the daisy chain around Daisy's head like a halo, but Hap never did. When Sissy placed it, wilted, on the coffin's shiny top, Jed nearly choked. It ached him the way she laid it there, like a beloved hamster in a box being laid to rest. But when Miss Emory placed her own circle of daisies on top of everyone else's, Jed had to look away.

Jed gripped Daisy's yellow comb harder.

Sissy sidled up to him. She whispered, "You need to put the comb on top. It's what she wanted, wasn't it?"

"Hush." Jed fingered the comb's teeth.

A vulture looped through the air, figure-eighting the clouds above. The crowd of mourners spied the heavy-bodied bird all at once. People looked at each other like they knew it meant something obvious. Little children pointed to the sky. Jed wondered if this was the same bird that led him to Daisy's first resting place, if he was swooping to make his joke more cruel. He remembered how Daisy's finger pointed heavenward even then, as if she knew where she was going and couldn't quite get there for the weight of the earth keeping her down. The vulture's wing carried the bird away over the trees flanking the graveyard. In the silence, a dove cooed.

Sissy elbowed him. "Jed. The comb?"

As Hixon said a prayer, Jed slipped the comb into his pocket.

While dirt was shoveled onto a plain casket, Jed broke a promise, letting Daisy drop into the earth without so much as a good-bye.

Doing push-ups felt like the right thing to do even though his bandaged hand made things harder. At push-up thirty-two, Jed wondered about a God who didn't protect, who made it so humans had to fend for themselves. A complicated thought at his age, he knew, but one that wouldn't let him be. Besides, it wouldn't be long until he hit fifteen, practically old enough to drive.

Sissy interrupted him by opening his door. He shot to his feet. "What do you want?"

She backed away.

He softened. "I'm sorry. You startled me, is all."

"Muriel's on the porch, asking for you."

"Tell her I'm busy."

"Tell her yourself." Sissy left the room. Bald Muriel was the last person he wanted to see right now. Her heaven-looking eyes would remind him of death and Daisy. He wanted to forget about it all. But he couldn't leave her on the porch alone.

She sat on their wicker rocker, a red bandana tight around her scalp. Clementine's head rested on Muriel's lap like it belonged there.

"Hey, Jed."

"Hey," he said. He stood opposite her, leaning his backside against their porch railing.

"You ready?" she asked.

Clementine stirred and looked at Jed.

"Ready?"

"For our project."

"Project?" What was she talking about?

"It's time to paint."

Jed looked away from her otherworld eyes. "I already painted Daisy's—"

"Not that. Our mural. Creative painting."

Oh, great. "I'm not really interested."

Clementine barked.

Bald Muriel looked as if Jed had slapped her. "Jed, I can't do this alone. You know that. I need your help."

"I'm not artistic. You should ask my mother."

"She's not the one God told me to ask. It's you, He said."

Why would God ask such a thing and whisper His will into Muriel's ear?

She patted Clementine's head. "Think of it as a way to bless the rendering plant workers. They don't need to see all that filth. Besides, Miss Emory would be able to see the mural from her kitchen window. It'd bless her too, in a way."

Why would he want to "bless" her? She hated him. Jed looked at his bare feet. They looked bony, angular—more like Mama's than Hap's. He waited for a rush of words.

None came. It was like she knew silence would get to Jed.

Clementine did her own convincing by licking Jed's toes. He laughed.

"Then it's settled." Muriel smiled. "Go tell your mama and get some proper clothes on—the kind you can get paint on. Put on your painting shoes too. I'll be waiting right here."

Jed thought they'd drive there in Muriel's Ford Fiasco, but she said she wanted to walk, something Jed protested, but Muriel insisted. So they walked toward Defiance's rendering plant, neither speaking. Jed's mind filled with Daisy adventures—the very ones the rendering plant created. They'd explored Old Defiance's many hideouts trying to escape its misery. Once Daisy said, "It's a good thing the town fathers put the rendering plant nearby. It's given us an excuse to roam." Roam, they did. Jed ached, remembering.

Clementine followed, matching their steps. Muriel couldn't walk very fast, and Clementine seemed to understand. She slowed when the woman stopped to get her breath and picked up when she started walking again, all the while wagging her tail. Jed used the time to clear his head. Bald Muriel had a way of seeing in there, so he'd best stick to thinking about fishing or school next year (he couldn't believe he'd be a freshman) or the chores awaiting him at home.

"Beautiful day, isn't it?" She said it just as a mockingbird sang, precisely when Jed got a whiff of a fully blooming rosebush.

He nodded.

"It's okay. You don't need to talk." She tugged at the satchel on her shoulder like it bothered her. It was the first time Jed noticed it.

"Let me take that for you." Surprised at how heavy it was, Jed sighed. "You shouldn't be carrying things like this."

"Are you my daddy now?"

"Hardly. It's just, you know. In your condition."

Clementine butted between them, looked square at Jed.

"And what condition is that?"

Jed couldn't say the C word. Daisy dying was all he could tolerate, and he wasn't even doing that well.

"Cancer. Cancer. Cancer."

Jed winced. Muriel's words echoed in his head like an over-sung song, shivering his spine.

She stopped in front of a grand Victorian home, kitty-corner from Miss Emory's place. It was the house Mama always described as "once a lady, now a derelict." It'd been beautiful one day. Naked now from peeled paint, crooked from being blown slightly off pier and beam, the home, with its boarded windows, looked like death to Jed.

"It's better to name it out loud than avoid it forever. Say it, Jed."

Clementine barked.

"Cancer," he whispered.

"Good. It's not something to be afraid of." But she didn't sound too convincing.

And Jed was afraid. Ever since he read one of Mama's books about a lady named Starlight who, as a young mom, got cancer and died in her husband's arms, he'd hated it. And feared it. How could Muriel say such a thing? Jed stepped away from the haunted mansion, but Muriel stayed put. So did Clementine.

"Listen, Jed. It's the facts, is all. Everyone has cancer in their own way." She shielded her glassy eyes from the sun, then moved under the branch of a very large tree. "We all have the curse of death written on our hearts. Think about that. Even those folks Jesus raised from the dead eventually died. It's a cancer, sin. And no one is immune."

"I don't like it," Jed finally said.

"I don't either. Not on your life. But it's the facts. And from what I've learned from my husband who's there now, heaven is a real place."

Hearing about her husband, remembering what Officer Spellman thought, Jed felt queasy. Did she kill him? Could she? "I thought you didn't like him."

Muriel sighed. "I didn't really like him. You're right. But I did love him."

Why did women love men who hurt them?

Muriel walked away from the house toward the rendering plant. "And not everything he preached was worthy of the trash bin. Some of it was good. When he preached heaven, I took notes."

She didn't say much the rest of their walk, which was fine by Jed. All that talk about sin and cancer and heaven and Muriel's dead husband quivered his insides.

"You need to say your good-byes," Muriel said as they passed Miss Emory's house.

Jed grunted. Hap said that's what teenage boys did, anyway. Might as well oblige him. But he felt bad once he'd done it. Grunting at Bald Muriel seemed a sin.

"Son, I'm just saying ..." She slowed to a stop. Clementine did too, letting Muriel rest her veined hand on the dog's head like a crown. "It's part of life, saying good-bye. Lord knows I've done my share."

Jed looked at Miss Emory's stark white house and wondered

if she was scowling at him from a window. "I said my good-byes," he lied.

Muriel removed her hand from Clementine's head and placed it softly on Jed's shoulder. It nearly melted his insides. "It's okay to cry, Jed."

He wanted to scream, No-it's-not! but he held his tongue. Instead he stared at the dead-looking house and said nothing. All windows were curtained shut. Miss Emory, usually attentive to her lawn, hadn't mowed the gangly Bermuda grass, probably didn't have the heart. Jed remembered how the house seemed at night, how alive it looked with all those lights, and how lifeless it looked right now.

"I'm sorry," Muriel removed her hand.

"Sorry?" Jed started walking away. He kept his pace slow so Muriel could keep up. Truth was, he didn't really want to paint a dumb mural, but he was so close it would look bad to back out now. Besides, he worried she might fall.

"It hurts to lose your best friend."

"Yes" was all he could say.

The smell of rendered animals bothered Jed's nose. He never grew accustomed to the stench. Even Daisy hated the smell, calling her home the dead animal zone. It didn't help that Daisy loved all of God's creatures, even the water bugs and scorpions. To smell animal death every day of her life must've been excruciating. At least now she didn't smell it. Or did she? Could she see him? Could she smell earth? Did heaven have a smell? If it did, it sure didn't smell like this. "Best get to painting before the sun bakes us," he said.

Muriel followed behind, humming something majestic, something churchy Jed'd never heard. It made him want to cry and laugh at the same time, but he kept his mouth shut, his fists clenched. They neared the wall, but Muriel said nothing. It'd seemed an average length when he was walking by it, but now that they were fixing to paint it, it loomed long and tall. How could they possibly paint the length of a football field?

"Well, here we are." Muriel's voice sounded small.

"You really want to paint this whole wall?"

"God told me to, so I aim to."

Full of graffiti, red and black and blue swirled cuss words, several "I love somebodies" penned with spray paint, the wall had to first be painted over. Jed felt suddenly tired.

"Don't worry yourself," she said. "I invited Hixon too."

"I thought you said God told you to have me help you," Jed said.

"He did. And he said Hixon could come along too. He should be here any moment now."

Clementine barked.

Hixon appeared, as if on cue, from behind the cement wall. Where he stood, a smokestack seemed to emerge from the top of his head. "Hey, there!"

Jed wondered why his hand made a fist, why his shoulders tensed at the sight of Hixon. Maybe it was because Hixon had declared Daisy dead at her funeral, or maybe because he was the last person to watch Daisy's coffin as it was laid to rest. Muriel embraced Hixon like any mama would. Hixon nodded at Jed. "How you doing, Jed?"

Jed couldn't talk. He nodded instead.

"Sure got plenty to do, don't we?" Hixon laughed, then patted Muriel on the shoulder.

"Why didn't you know Daisy was there?" The question flew out of Jed before he knew it.

"What?" Hixon slid a hand up the wall and leaned his frame against it.

"Daisy was there all the time, right over the hill from your tree." Jed spat, but instead of flying through the air, it dribbled down his chin. He wiped it. "I thought you fancied yourself a prophet."

Hixon's eyes grew wide. And sad. Jed regretted his sharp words. Muriel seemed to shrink back into the wall. Under the sun-baked sky, they stood, an unlikely trio, none of them saying a thing.

Hixon coughed. "It's what other folks say, Jed. Not what I say. Other folks call me a prophet, but I've never called myself that. Prophet is a scary title, if you ask me. Just ask some of the wrong ones."

"But she was over the hill. Didn't you ever walk that way?"

"No. For whatever reason, and I can't really understand why the Good Lord would have it, He wanted you to discover Daisy." Hixon looked away, grabbed his chin.

Rage boiled inside Jed, bubbling like a witch's cauldron full of thick pea soup. "What kind of God —"

Muriel placed a hand on Jed. "It's time we got to painting." She looked at Hixon. "Did you bring the rollers?"

Hixon took a satchel off his shoulder and produced rollers. "Three rollers, Miss Muriel."

"Good. Now Jed, the first day won't be the easiest. We're here to cover up this mess. But tomorrow will be better, I promise. That's when we create."

Hixon poured white paint into flat pans, wide enough to hold a roller. The paint made a slapping sound as it glopped onto the metal. He wiped his head. "Tell you what. I'll start from one end, Muriel will start from the other side, and Jed, you paint the middle. We'll work toward you. That way it'll be a contest to see who can get to you first."

"Great idea," Muriel said. She grabbed her shallow pan and roller and walked to the far end. Hixon split to his end, leaving Jed alone with paint and a dirty wall. At first Jed cursed under his breath. Not bad words that would send him to the netherworld, but words like *dang* and *shoot*. But once he dipped the roller in the clean white paint and covered a swatch of much worse words, he felt better. Not a lot, but a little. He rolled the white paint over more words, more swirls, more crude sprayed-on drawings, and as he did, he found himself humming "Amazing Grace." Maybe that's what grace was when you peeled everything away. Covering over filth with clean white.

They painted, each alone, for several hours. Jed felt the sun bite his neck. He wanted to take off his T-shirt, but knew if he did, he'd have a scorching burn down his back. The neck was bad enough. At first he painted smack dab in the middle, reaching high to get the top of the wall. Then he moved to his left, toward Hixon. He figured, though, that Muriel would have a harder time beating Hixon, so he spent the bulk of his time moving toward her end of the wall.

Lunchtime came. Hixon whistled. Jed felt thirst sear his throat. His tongue scraped against itself like sandpaper. His shirt fit snug against his chest, all that sweat making it cling like Mama's dress on a static day.

Hixon motioned for Jed and Muriel to come sit under a tree with limbs that spread wider than two houses. Under the tree, he laid a blanket—one of those faded patchwork quilts Mama liked so much. From behind the tree, he pulled out a cooler.

"May as well eat a feast with all this hard work." He winked at Muriel.

"Hixon, you think of everything." She took a checkered napkin from Hixon and tucked it under her chin. Hixon poured three glasses of cold, cold lemonade. Jed downed a glass in one teenaged gulp.

Hixon laughed. "Heavens! Don't make yourself sick."

"Is there any more?" Jed wiped his face with the napkin.

"Sure." Hixon poured more.

They dined on bologna and American cheese sandwiches, saltine crackers, strawberries, and peanut butter cookies—a perfect feast. Jed was so enamored with the cookies (Mama rarely made them—said they cost too much), he didn't notice Hap approach until a shadow crept across his face.

"Son, what're you doing here? I don't recall you asking for permission to leave the house. Your mother is worried sick."

Jed swallowed his cookie, washed the rest of it down with the remaining lemonade, and stood toe to toe with Hap. "Sissy knew."

"Yes, but not before your mother panicked."

Muriel stood, extending her hand Hap's way. Hap didn't take it. She withdrew her hand quick as a whip, then smoothed the bandana over her head. Still, she talked. "It's my fault, Reverend Pepper. I needed help repainting this wall. We're going to paint a mural. A real pretty one so the workers have something beautiful to look at when they leave work. I hope you don't mind."

Hap looked over her, something he did to Jed so much that he rarely noticed it anymore. Funny how he remembered it now and felt plain terrible that Hap did it to Muriel. Made him feel bad that Hap did it to him all these years.

"It seems strange," Hap said, "that someone who is not yet cleared in Daisy's murder is out roaming the streets of Defiance, fully free."

Jed swallowed. He balled his right hand into a fist and held it with his left hand.

Hixon stood now. "Sir, I mean no disrespect—"

"Sure you do. It's your bent. You aim to disrespect everyone, particularly me. But that's beside the point."

Hixon inched forward. The wind rustled the leaves above him. "Sir, if you knew Muriel—"

Hap's face turned red—as red as Mama's blusher. "Knew her? What's there to know, Hixon? You tell me. Everyone knows the woman most likely killed her God-fearing husband. What's another to her?"

Jed watched Hixon's face muscles twitch. Muriel cleared her throat. She pulled off her scarf and looked Hap straight in the eyes, something Mama rarely did.

"Look at me, Reverend Pepper."

Hap did, his face red.

"All I have to say is this: Banana Pie Alibi." She smiled.

Jed wanted to warn her to stop the smiling, but he knew it would be no use. "Banana pie?" he said.

"Well, you know how it is. Folks call it banana pudding, but I see it more like a pie. When Daisy went missing, I was making banana pies with the Episcopalians for their cakewalk dessert social that night. It's all part of my one-woman effort to be ecumenical. Once I asked an Episcopalian lady to clear me, and she marched right up there and straightened them out on the facts, the police let me go and cleared me of all suspicion." She wiped her hands with her bandana, then sat down. "Now, if you don't mind, I'd like to get back to my lunch. You're welcome to join us, if you'd like. I promise not to bite."

Hap said nothing. He fidgeted instead. Another first for Jed: Hap speechless.

"I have another sandwich, if you'd like." Hixon reached into the cooler and handed it to Hap. Hap looked at it a good long time, then nodded at Muriel. Hap took the sandwich, then sat on the quilt.

Jed stared at him like he was seeing a ghost.

Clementine unfolded her body between Hap and Muriel while Jed and Hixon each ate another cookie. Hap chewed and said nothing. He didn't say sorry. Hap never did. But his sitting there said sorry in his own Hap way.

Jed'd been one to see the world in comic book contrasts. Bad folks and good folks. Villains and innocents. Heroes and killers. But sitting under the shade of a wide-reaching tree, eating peanut butter cookies and drinking Hixon's ice-cold lemonade, he wondered if life was really like that.

Forty-One

Jed let the night air, still warm and wet, blow through his open window. He closed his eyes as the breeze blew over his sweaty body. In a rush of memory, he watched as the sun spotted his young head, Hap tall and strong like a hero, twirling Jed in higher circles toward the blue, blue sky. They both laughed. Giggled, really. It'd been before. Before Bible school when Hap turned thirty-three. Before church work. Before Hap gripped the pastorate in a strong fist and didn't let go. When he thrust Jed skyward, he worked with his hands. Made rocking chairs, hutches, dressers. Built houses and barns. He smiled more. Laughed more. Hugged more. Relaxed more. Jed opened his eyes, half hoping the twirling movie would play over and over on his ceiling, a delicious reminder of what had been. He wanted his father back, the one that used to belly laugh. But that father was gone.

Sissy slipped into his room, boo-hooing. "Mama doesn't like me anymore," she said, sniffing her tears.

"Of course she does."

"Nope. I cuddled up next to her, like always. She elbowed me, Jed. Told me to leave her alone. She hates me." Sissy cried more tears than Jed could count.

But then she stopped, quite suddenly. "But you know what? I kept loving her. I'm proud of that. You know what I did?"

"What?"

"I grabbed her favorite quilt, the one she uses when she watches TV, and I pulled it over her. I tucked Mama in bed. I fetched her a glass of water and set it beside her. I pulled the curtains over the shades so the room would be extra dark when she woke up. And then I laid down next to her, not touching her. I reached my hand toward her and prayed, Jed. Prayed that Jesus would heal her."

"I hope it works," Jed said. "Your prayer, I mean."

Sissy nodded her tear-streaked face and left, quiet as a whisper.

Jed stirred in his bed, the kind of rolling over that he wanted to relish. Staying tangled in his sheets felt good, really good. He kept his eyes closed while he stretched, making a whining, yawning sound. Clementine ran down the hall. He could hear the click of her nails against the hardwood. She pounced on him, licking his face.

Jed opened his eyes.

Clementine licked his nose.

He shook the sleep from his head and rubbed his eyes. "Good morning, Clementine."

Clementine barked a howdy-do. Jed sat up. When he did, he felt the last two days of painting in his arms. How they ached. Yesterday, his right arm turned into jelly, so he took to painting with his left until it jiggled too. Now both felt as weak as Sissy's everyday arms. Clementine jumped off the bed, then looked at him square in the face. She wanted out. Jed unfolded his legs and dangled them over the edge of the bed.

To his right stood an overflowing jar full of crape myrtle blossoms. Cherry red, purple, and white. There was no way Mama could write him a note on these—the flowers were big if you looked at them from afar, fat upside-down ice-cream cones of color, but when you got up close, you realized each cone was made up of a million little flowers. Jed pulled one out anyway. Mama'd taken to spending most days since Daisy's funeral in her room, the shades pulled way down, despite Sissy's prayers. Her headache lasted a terrible long time, at least that was what Jed thought. He'd never known her to go this long.

He pulled another stem. No message. Clementine licked his toes. He pulled out a pink stem. Nothing. Jed stood. He placed the flowers back in the jar. Something white caught his attention. Tucked inside the tangle of stems was a small piece of paper.

He grabbed it, unfolded it, then sat down. Clementine rested her chin on Jed's knee. Normally Mama's handwriting was third grade perfect, with loops in all the right places. This note, well, it was scrawled and scratched. For a moment he wondered what stranger wrote it. But the "Mama" at the end was distinct enough. It was her.

"Jed, I see you getting angry. It's not worth it. Stay angry for a long time and you end up like me. Please, please, please let the anger go. Give it up. I don't know why Daisy had to die. It makes me sick. I'm so sorry you had to see her that way. It kills me to think of it. I'm praying for you. It may not seem like it with the shades drawn and all, but I am. When I sleep during the day, you and Sissy are in my dreams. When I can't shut my eyes at night, you are both in the prayers I pray. I love you. Be a good, sweet boy, you hear me? Don't let the anger take you away, Jed. Not how it's taken me and made me like this. Not how it's taken your father. Please, please find a way to let it go. Love, Mama."

Jed meant to crumple the paper and throw it at the wall. Instead he met Clementine's sweet eyes. Jed folded the paper how it'd been and tucked it in his golden-paged Bible.

Sissy burst through the doorway, breathless.

"She's here," she said.

"Who?"

"Miss Muriel, silly. She says it's time to paint."

Jed groaned. He looked at the clock. Nine in the morning. Why? Why? How could that woman be so chipper? Besides, it was Saturday, for crying out loud.

"She says it's important."

"She always says that, Sissy."

"No, really. She said it."

"I don't doubt that."

"Can I please come along? You know how I love to paint."

Jed wanted to say skedaddle, but her eyes looked like Clementine's—pleading and bothersome. "Suit yourself," he said. "Now let me get changed."

When Jed saw her, he caught his breath. Though her eyes danced, her face looked the color of Daisy's lifeless hand. She didn't insist on walking to the rendering plant. Instead she drove, parking under the shade of the old tree, where Hixon met them.

"Resurrection day," Bald Muriel sang in a weak voice as she looked at the white wall.

"What do you mean?" Sissy said. She held Bald Muriel's hand.

"I didn't know it would take two long days to cover this wall with white. But it did. And it's God's precious timing, if you ask me." She waved her free hand at the sun as if she were checking in on God, making sure he knew she saw him up there.

Could folks wave at God?

Muriel sure seemed to think so.

She lifted a paintbrush heavenward. "So here we are. Day three. Like Jesus in the tomb. Only today. Today! We see resurrection. And we paint hope." She dipped her brush into some blue paint and splashed an arc near the top of the white wall.

Jed shook his head. "Aren't you going to draw the mural first?"

"Nah." She dipped the blue-tipped brush into red, something Hap would've scolded Jed for. Hap hated when their watercolors mixed in their plastic sets. Muriel pulled a blue-red-purple brush vertically, forming a cross. "I want us to paint what we feel. Grab a brush and have at it." She wiped sweat from her forehead.

Jed looked at the long, white wall, then at the ten cans of old paint lined up in front of him.

Sissy grabbed a brush with an angled tip and dipped it into yellow. She painted a circle. "The mural needs some sunshine, don't you think?"

"Absolutely," Hixon said.

Jed hollered at Sissy as her yellow paintbrush wet Hixon's knee.

But Hixon laughed. "Looks like I need some sunshine anyhow." Though she was ten years old and getting lanky, Hixon lifted Sissy high in the air and twirled her around and around while her laughter echoed off the white wall.

Jed turned away as Sissy's giggles stabbed his ears.

"Well, let's get at it, then." Muriel put a thin arm around Jed's shoulders. He didn't shrug her away. "Just paint what you feel. Fill up the white."

So Jed did. He threw heaves of black at the wall, smearing globs with his brush in angry oblongs. He swirled in red and brown until a three-by-three spot of wall looked more like a churning mud pool than a painting. He stood back.

Muriel painted a waterfall. She'd combined different colors with blue to make the waterfall come alive, Jed thought. She came over to Jed's brown goo and smiled. "You know the secret of life, Jed. I can see that now."

"What do you mean?"

She dabbed her multicolored brush into white. "Do you mind if I add something?"

Jed shrugged.

In the lower right half of his painting, she made a small white circle, then stepped away. "What do you see?"

"A white dot."

Sissy came near and rested her head against Jed's arm. She seemed tired. Hixon took off his hat and wiped his forehead with his upper arm.

"Jed understands," Muriel said, "that white stands out on a dark canvas." She made another dot next to Jed's picture, but this time on the white wall. "Can you see that?"

"No, ma'am," Sissy said.

"That's right. Jed, he understands. Life is dark and hard and full of all sorts of thievery and mischief. It's the result of all our sinning, if you want my opinion. That's what makes God's redemption so startling. He shoots into this world like a white-hot light, shining His way through the dark, dark earth. That's why it makes darned good sense that He called himself the light of the world. It's true. And it's because this world is in darkness that His light shines all the brighter."

Jed looked at his brown swirl.

"You got all that from Jed's painting?" Hixon asked.

"You can see into a soul through their painting. At least that's what I think." Muriel dipped her paintbrush into purple and started in on a cluster of grapes.

Jed remembered his mama's paintings then. How startlingly beautiful they were. Did Hap know Mama's beauty like that?

Sissy painted five more sunshines.

Hixon created mountains and valleys.

Jed looked a long time at his "masterpiece." Without a word, he wiped his brush with a rag until it was nearly clean, then dipped it into the sunshine yellow. To the left of his blob and Muriel's white dot, he painted Daisy's hair—hair big enough to adorn a semi tire. But he couldn't see her face in his mind, so he stopped. Instead he painted the buildings of New Defiance, one by one, all the while trying to remember her face.

Forty-Two

Muriel drove home early, weary from the day. Hixon went with her, no doubt to keep an eye on her.

Jed's arms were speckled every rainbow color. After their day of painting, the dying sun angled pale light on his skin painting. Sissy trailed behind as they walked home, singing Olivia Newton John songs with great volume, so much so that Jed shushed her three times.

"I can't help it, Jed," she told him. Her nose, a bit upturned, sported paint dots too.

"You can *so* help it. Please don't sing."

"But Jesus put a song in my heart, and I aim to let it out."

"Jesus put Olivia Newton John's words in your head? Really?"

She ignored him. "Besides, who cares? All of Defiance is eating their suppers anyway. No one can hear."

Jed rolled his eyes.

"I bet you're rolling your eyes. You don't appreciate fine music." She skipped from behind him and gave his shoes flat tires.

"Knock it off!"

"Oh, p'shaw." She did it again. "You need to lighten up."

Jed whirled around. "Lighten up? Lighten up? My best friend's dead. Stop trying to pretend everything's going to be fine, because it's not." As the words flew out, Jed noticed that he'd hollered them right in front of Miss Emory's. And there she sat on her porch swing and heard them all.

This time Sissy shushed him. He wanted to die. Frozen to the sidewalk, Jed watched as Miss Emory stood and trudged down her stairs. One bare foot in front of the other. Down the cement walkway that must've been warm from the day. She placed both hands on her rickety gate and looked straight into Jed Pepper's soul.

"Jed Pepper," she whispered. She pulled out a cigarette, lit it, and blew smoke to the sky. Sissy stepped closer to Jed, like she was afraid of a monster lurking in the tree shadows. Jed stayed put.

"You kids think you have the whole world figured out, don't you?" She took another drag, blew it out the side of her mouth.

"No, ma'am."

"You know, it's easier, if you ask me, to blame a mama for everything rather than see the real truth."

"I'm not blaming you." Jed stepped back to avoid the rush of smoke she blew in his direction. "Far from it."

Miss Emory stepped closer. Sissy tugged at his shirt.

"Daisy did," Miss Emory slurred. "Said all sorts of things about me that weren't true. I'll prove it to you." She turned and mounted the steps, wobbling her way up. She killed her cigarette underfoot. The front door slammed shut and immediately opened again with a creak. Miss Emory took the stairs two at a time. "This is why I know," she said, breathless. "This." In her hand was Daisy's diary.

"Her diary? But—"

"Don't think I'm some clueless mother, Jed. Like I didn't know the two of you scoured Old Defiance until it was explored full out. Or that you had a hollow log in a clearing with treasures inside. A mama, she knows things." She leafed through the book. "Here. Daisy writes, 'I'm afraid when my mama leaves me alone.'" Miss Emory sucked in a cry. "You hear that? It's not true, Jed. You have to believe it's not true."

Jed took another step back. "Miss Emory, I—"

"You're what? Sorry? Sorry doesn't bring back a missing girl from the grave, now does it?" She let Daisy's diary drop at her feet. "Sorry doesn't change the truth of a matter. And sorry," she looked at Jed, "won't change the fact that you were the last one to see her alive."

Sissy put her hand in Jed's. He let it rest there.

Miss Emory picked up Daisy's diary, gathering it to her chest. Her eyes grew bigger than Jed had ever seen them—so hauntingly like Daisy's he could barely stand it. "I have one thing to say to you, Jed Pepper." She took in a deep breath, let it out. "You're not alone." Miss Emory turned on her bare heel and walked, head down, back to her porch and planted herself on the porch swing. She didn't look at Jed and Sissy. Her eyes settled above them, somewhere far away in the clouds above Defiance. Maybe she was dreaming of Daisy or wishing her home.

Jed swallowed. Maybe he knew Miss Emory better than he thought he did. Or maybe he didn't know her at all.

At fourteen, he wouldn't normally think it cool to walk hand in hand with his sister down Defiance's dusty streets, but this time he didn't care. Sissy seemed to be all he had left in this world. With mama's sleeping spells, with Hap boomeranging from eerie kindness to expected grouchiness, with the light leaving Bald Muriel's eyes, Sissy was the only one he could predict would be the same girl she was before. So he kept her small hand in his. With all the sorrow in the world, her hand in his helped him feel less lonely.

They walked farther down the block, then Sissy stopped. "I lost a friend too, you know."

"I know. I'm sorry. Daisy touched a lot of folks, didn't she?"

"Yeah ... Jed?"

"What?"

"I need to see where you found her."

Jed let go of her hand. "Why?"

"I need to see the place. For myself." She pointed toward the Haunted Forest.

Jed followed with his eyes. "I don't think it's wise."

"I need to see. Because of my dream."

"What dream?"

"The dream I had last night." She started toward the woods.

Jed ran after her. He grabbed her arm, made her face him. "I don't care what dream you had, we're not going in there."

"Just listen for a minute, will you?" She sat on the upward incline of a ditch. She patted the earth. Red dust swirled its presence to the sky like a smoke signal.

Jed sat. "Okay, but hurry up. We'll be late for supper."

"I was a missionary in Africa. You weren't there. You were a preacher in Daddy's church."

Jed threw up a hand. "Are you sure it wasn't a nightmare? You know I would never be a pastor."

"It's my dream. Just listen. Anyway, I was caring for these sick children, the kind with rocks in their bellies because they were so hungry they'd eat anything. I was teaching them how to garden, almost as good as Ethrea Ree too. One of the girls, her name was Tatty, told me about the most beautiful garden in the area, and that she'd take me there come nightfall. So I said, 'Sure thing, Tatty. You take me there.'"

"I don't see what this has to do with walking through the woods."

"Let me finish, and you can decide if you'll take me to where you found Daisy, okay?"

"Fair enough." But it wasn't fair. Jed didn't want to hear about this dream. He didn't want to walk near Hixon's black-trunked tree. Didn't want to remember Daisy's hand pointing at the sun from a pile of dirt.

"So Tatty took me to the garden. And it was lovely. Under the moonlight, the garden looked like stars in the sky because it'd all been planted with white flowers — all different kinds, but mostly daisies. There was one of those gazebos in the center, which surprised me, being as how we were in Africa and all. A girl twirled inside the gazebo, kind of like Liesl from *The Sound of Music*. I got closer and sure enough, it was Daisy. We hugged and hugged and hugged. I could smell her, Jed. It was her. She told me to take care of you, to not let you become angry like Hap, to love on you until you smiled. Her eyes looked happy and sad at the same time, like she loved her garden dearly but missed her friends. When she gave me a daisy to give to you, I woke up."

Jed wanted to believe the dream had been real. That Daisy reached beyond the grave to send him a message, though he wasn't particularly fond of what Daisy had said.

"Well, now you know why I have to see where you found her." Sissy stood facing him.

"No, I don't."

"Because I never saw her dead. You did. For all I know she really is in Africa planting white flowers."

Jed shook his head. "Take my word for it. She's dead."

"I can't. I have to see for myself. Please show me, Jed. Just real quick. I promise to look and then run right home. Before supper too."

"No. You know about these woods."

"If you don't show me, I'll run off by myself."

The knot in Jed's stomach grew into a tugboat-worthy knot, thick and hard to untie. He couldn't let Sissy wander around by herself. He was her protector. What was the point of all those push-ups if it wasn't to protect Sissy? If it'd been anyone else, he'd have walked away. But this was his baby sister. Her one request. The very one he didn't think he could do.

"Okay, but the sun's going down, so we have to make it quick."

Forty-Three

The sun pulled Jed and Sissy's shadows longlike, made them tall thin giants walking across the empty field behind them.

"It's like the angels are following us," she said, looking back. She shaded her eyes from the setting sun, low and orange against the bluest sky Jed could remember.

Jed kept to himself.

"This Hixon's tree?" she asked.

"Yep."

Sissy stood under the blackened tree, its arms bent backward and frontward like double-jointed fingers. "It looks spooky."

"I know."

She walked over to its trunk, touched it like it was silk, then clamored up it like a squirrel possessed.

"You be careful, Sissy."

"Shush yourself. You can see all of Defiance up here."

Something about that bothered Jed. If Hixon could see all of Defiance, could he have spied Daisy? "Wait!" Jed pulled himself up into the tree, making a contest of it to only use his arm strength to pull himself up.

He sat next to Sissy on a low limb. Even from there, she was right. They could see the whole town. If he stood, he could probably see his street. He looked toward the hill where he found

Daisy. Sure enough, he could see where she'd been, plain as day, even as dusk shadowed the hill. Did Hixon see her before Jed did?

"Come on, it's getting dark." Jed dropped to the ground, then wiped his hands on his shorts.

Sissy climbed down backwards. "I don't feel so good," she said.

Jed turned. "You wanna go home? You can see this any old time."

"No. Let's get this over with."

Jed didn't walk his usual brisk pace. He kept it slow. He told himself it was because Sissy didn't feel good, but he knew the real reason. Seeing that spot again would bring up the memory in vivid color. And he didn't want to remember Daisy's lifeless hand again. They climbed the hill together, neither speaking. If music played to their slow march, it'd be the kind Hap listened to on AM radio in the Chevy, one of those sad classical songs in a minor key.

Jed stopped when they reached the crest—the crest Hixon could see clear as day from his burned tree. Sissy grabbed his hand real hard, nearly squeezing tears out of him. Right before their feet was that same hole he saw with Officer Spellman, dug smooth in the red dirt. A hole with no one in it. A hole where Daisy went to sleep the last time.

"She was there?"

Jed nodded.

"In that hole?"

"She was buried under a pile of underbrush. Only her hand—" Jed's voice cracked. A flood of memories of Daisy's friendship tidal waved him. He missed her more than her laughter in a storm, more than them scurrying like spies through Old Defiance, more than her skinned knee sorrows, more than their shared worries. All at once, he knew it wasn't the memories he missed. He had those. It was her. He missed her. Her. Jed sucked in a breath. Then another. He told his lip not to stick out, his eyes not to sting.

"Oh, Jed, I'm so sorry." Sissy folded her skinny self around him and cried a creek, a river, and a pond right into Jed's belly. He patted her back and looked beyond Daisy's hole to Defiance. He tried not to cry. He had to be strong, for Sissy. So he hugged her tight. And let her cry the tears he wanted to let out.

Forty-Four

Hap waited for them on the porch. His shoes were off, and he wore shorts and an old T-shirt—hardly his normal attire. Mama sat on the other side of the porch in her old rocking chair, looking like someone had taken her mind away to Tahiti.

Hap stood when Jed and Sissy walked up the stairs. He grabbed them both, smelled Sissy's hair, and roughed up Jed's. He held them tight to his warm T-shirt. He smelled like Old Spice and sweat and wood shavings.

"Praise the Lord." He released Jed and Sissy from his hug and backed away. "I would've scolded you up one side and down the other for wandering off, but I heard the good news."

"What news?" Jed sat on the top step.

So did Sissy.

Hap joined them, then put his arm around Sissy like he could sense she'd been crying.

"They know who Daisy's killer is. No more worrying, okay? You're safe."

"Who?" Jed's voice cracked, low, then high.

"Her father. Apparently he's conveniently in Mexico. The FBI and the Mexican authorities are alerted, but Officer Spellman says it's him." Hap looked at Mama, who gave no response. "Seems he's been up to some shenanigans." He looked at Mama again, but she didn't return the favor.

Mama stood, a stalk of wheat, the wind bending her any way it wanted. She set a hand on the porch pillar. "You suit yourself, Mr. Pepper." Mama's voice started out soft, but it grabbed hold, like someone had turned her volume up. "I love you. Only you. Maybe once in your life you can let a thing go."

"Like pining after David?"

A few tears dribbled down Mama's cheek. She grabbed at the pillar like it was the only thing that could hold her up. She shook her head but didn't wipe the tears. "You believe what you want," she whispered. "You always do anyway. I know I'm clean, Hap. You've made up this entire thing in your head." Mama let go of the post and slipped into the house.

Jed swallowed. He wanted to follow Mama, make sure she was okay, but he also needed to know more about Daisy's killer. "How can they be so sure it's Daisy's father?"

"Take my word for it, son. They know it's him. They wouldn't go after him if it wasn't. They'll get him."

Jed heard relief in Hap's voice, something that surprised him more than snow on a Texas Christmas. Hap cared? He worried?

Sissy stirred under Hap's arm. She looked up into his eyes. "Why would a daddy kill his baby girl?"

Jed remembered times Hap's anger flung Sissy across rooms. He knew daddies did such things.

Hap cleared his throat. Kissed Sissy's head. "I don't know. Maybe Daisy's daddy is sick in the head."

"Or maybe he got angry one day," Jed mumbled. He stood, then looked down on Sissy cradled under Hap's strong arm. If the time ever came, he'd have to battle that arm and the man attached to it — anything, if it meant protecting Sissy. Jed let the screen door slap the doorjamb as he walked into the house.

Jed thought knowing who'd done that to Daisy would make him feel better. Or at least be thankful that justice was served, but he felt sick. Unsettled. Something just didn't add up. If Daisy had no relationship with her father in the first place, why would he up and take her? Then kill her? It didn't make sense. He walked past Mama's room—shades pulled, no light, the smell of her soap lingering in the air.

The thought occurred to him that if God did run the universe and all, why couldn't He make things right in Defiance, Texas? Or even his home? Or in Mama's head? What kind of God let mamas sleep away life, fathers kill their only daughters, bald women waste away from cancer?

Jed's stomach dizzied inside him. He threw a hand to his mouth and ran to the bathroom, filling the toilet bowl with the day's lunch. He cradled his head in his arms, his face above the urine-stained bowl. He heaved again. Then again. Nothing came out. Until one tear wiggled out of his right eye and dropped into the bowl. Then another dropped.

A third.

Jed flushed the toilet. He turned on the shower. Just the cold. He wiped away the tears and locked the door.

He stripped buck naked and let the cold water shock him, taking his breath away. He would master this. He would. He had to. But he couldn't. Maybe he was as powerless as God. While water ran down his face and chest, his eyes gave up their heroic battle and let the tears spill over lid ramparts. Jed sat on the tub's edge, his middle heaving in breaths. "Nooooooo," he cried. "No. No. No." He cried like Sissy—a creek, a river, a pond—while the cold water teased his legs and toes. But it didn't numb his heart. It was too broken for that.

Like Mama's, he thought.

Forty-Five

Jed fought to stay home from church, but nothing he said or did made Hap change his mind. When he looked at himself in the mirror before making the request, he was sure Hap would let him stay in bed, what with his face being nearly as green as Mama's leaves.

"My family goes to church every Sunday unless they're on their death bed." Hap slammed his fist on the breakfast table. Sissy withered. She poked at her oatmeal. Jed ate nothing. Couldn't, really. Mama slinked in beside Hap, then poured him some coffee.

"He's sick with grief, Hap. Isn't that enough to let him be? Look at him, will you?"

Jed expected Hap to explode like a newly opened can of biscuits. Hap stood. He placed a heavy hand on Jed's shoulder. Flesh between thumb and forefinger, Hap squeezed. Hard. Jed didn't holler. He wanted to.

"You will come to church." Hap left the room, his coffee steaming in a cracked mug.

Hixon and Bald Muriel must've known about the battle at Jed's home because they sat behind him at church, loving on him. Muriel gave him and Sissy LifeSavers, three each. Hixon squeezed Sissy's hand. He touched Jed's shoulder, lips whispering prayers, but Jed shied away. Maybe God was powerless, but having someone like Hixon pray, even to a powerless God, gave Jed a strange sense of peace. Maybe it was that Hixon had God's ear, that God heard him, but didn't hear Jed. But there was that problem of Hixon being able to see Daisy from that tree. Everything Jed thought about folks, especially Hixon, was getting mixed up, like Mama's beaters against pancake ingredients. And he didn't know which pancakes were safe to eat.

After several hymns that Jed mouthed and Sissy hummed, no doubt for worries that her lisp would come out, Hap gripped the pulpit with white knuckles. "The Word," he said. "Use it or lose it."

Jed stiffened. Every time Hap said "The Word," Jed knew it'd be a long, angry sermon. He looked over at Mama. She played the part of the smiling, supportive wife so well, sometimes Jed was fooled. While Hap's words hurled against the thin walls of the church, bouncing off the pews, Jed wondered if he'd be able to keep a Mama-like face or if he'd stand up and throw a hymnal right at Hap's head. Sissy seemed to know Jed's dilemma. In one smooth motion, she grasped the hymnal on his lap and put it back in its home.

While Hap threw twitching arms into the church air and hollered the words *sin* and *death* and *hell*, Jed watched him. What if God held Hap up like a trophy in heaven? What if God had a wallet, and Hap's picture was the first one displayed, God proudly announcing, "This is my very good child. Watch him, heaven. Just watch him." What if Hap was God's perfect example of godliness? Where did that leave Jed? He'd be a perfect heathen if he strayed from Hap's path. But if he walked that path ...

Jed snapped back to the sermon when he heard his name.

"My son, Jed, knows all this. Knows it, folks. But like Eve, he's easily swayed—by circumstances, by folks bent on evil, by whatever cockamamy thing gets into his head. Like this morning, for instance."

Jed looked at Mama.

"… said he was sick. Look at him, brothers. Look at him. Does he look sick to you?"

Jed shrunk lower in the pew. Sissy put a light hand on his knee.

"He needed the direction and firmness of a loving father to get him to church. And now, I bet, he's glad he's come. Because he's getting fed the Word of God, and that will never come back null and void." Hap laughed. "We're all like Jed, aren't we? We kick and scream to get our own way, all the while knowing our way is the path of destruction. But when a brother comes along and encourages us to go the proper way, we're grateful, eventually."

Was this Hap's apology?

Jed felt breakfast rocking and rolling inside. Hap sure wouldn't let rock and roll happen any other way. It made Jed smile, though he knew his moments with his breakfast intact were numbered.

"Doing right's like when you were a kid taking a bath. You need someone to run the water and force you to get in. Once you're in, you're glad, and you play for an hour there, glad someone put the bubbles in."

At the word *bubbles*, Jed felt the inevitable earthquake in his stomach. He stood, stole a quick look at Hap, whose face held anger with a hint of worry, and bolted from the sanctuary. He turned the corner, pushed through the bathroom door, and sank to the floor before a toilet. In that very moment, breakfast flew.

Jed stayed on the floor, breathing hard. He took some toilet paper from the roll and wiped his face. The bathroom door opened behind him. He wished he'd remembered to shut the stall.

In a moment, someone's hand was on his shoulder. "You okay?" came the voice. Muriel, in the men's bathroom. She smoothed his sweaty hair away from his face, something only a sissy boy would allow, but Jed felt so weak, he couldn't help but welcome her mothering ways.

Jed tried to stand, but felt dizzy. Muriel stood behind Jed and lifted him to his feet. How could a small woman do such a strong thing?

She helped him to the sink and splashed water on his face. She helped him settle into a chair nearby. Muriel bent low, a red bandana tied tight over her bald head. "You look at me, Jed Pepper."

He did.

"You're not going to become him. You hear me?"

Jed didn't believe her. How could anyone promise such a thing?

"I know you don't believe me, but it's true. I'm frightened out of my gourd to die, truth be told, but I have found some blessings in cancer. The best thing is that the closer I get to heaven, the easier I see into people's souls. I'm getting nearer to those pearly gates, son. Nearer by the minute. And God has shown me your heart, bright and clear. It's a good heart, Jed. A good heart."

Tears fought Jed's eyelids for escape. He was supposed to be a man—a strong, arm-flexing man—and here he was in the men's room with an old lady making him cry. Muriel helped Jed to his feet before he could say a word. "Now, you best be getting back. I'm sure your family's wondering where you are. No use making anyone mad, now, is there?"

"Muriel?" Jed steadied himself by holding the bathroom counter.

"Yes?"

"Thanks."

She nodded, pointed heavenward, and left the bathroom.

"You're an angel," Jed said to the space she left behind.

Forty-Six

Days passed in a haze of throwing up and washing up. Mama'd taken to putting a large plastic bowl by Jed's bed so he wouldn't have to crawl to the bathroom. She sponged him cool, read Jack London books, and sang a few songs. It almost made the sickness worth it to hear her sing again. Until he threw up again.

Sissy played dolls in his room to keep him company. She seemed fidgety, though, and she kept looking over her shoulder. She wouldn't let Jed open the curtains either.

Hap stopped in now and again quoting Scripture about sickness and saying things like, "This too shall pass."

Things passed, all right. So much so that Jed felt completely emptied, a Twinkie without the cream. The memory of the ipecac Mama gave him when he ate Ethrea Ree's poison berries came back to him as he spent far too much time emptying his stomach, napping, and emptying it again.

During one nap, Jed was in a remodeled Crooked Creek Church. Broken windows became stained glass wonders. Crickety pews sported new red velvet cushions. A suited Hixon preached from the pulpit, talking about Jesus being near. No-longer-bald Muriel sang hymns in a brand-new microphone. And Daisy, alive as alive could be, danced on the stage, trailing streamers back and forth, a rainbow of ribbons floating behind her. She smiled. Laughed. Jumped.

It was the kind of dream you didn't want to end; Jed certainly didn't. Though he knew it to be a shut-eyed fantasy, he willed himself to stay cradled there. Daisy stopped her dancing, the streamers giving up the chase as they floated like cottonwood blossoms to the red-carpeted floor.

She looked right at Jed with those blue eyes. "Jed Pepper," she said, "I was going to marry you in this here church."

"I know," he told her. He gazed at his feet, shoeless.

Daisy hollered at him, enough to make him look up. She had that look in her eyes that meant business, no fooling around. "Listen here. I'm lonely. You come back when you have the chance. Real soon. I promise you'll find what you're looking for."

What was he looking for? Daisy's killer? Freedom from Hap's tirades? A mama who didn't have headaches? What was it? Whatever it was, he had to go back to church, had to find what Daisy said he was looking for.

He tried to open his eyes, to will them alive, but, paralyzed, Jed stayed in that church, Daisy angling another feisty look his way. She pulled something from her pocket—God's eye—but this one wasn't cracked. She held it to the light of a gold chandelier. Light bounced from its electric candles to God's eye, shooting a rainbow of colors around the church. In a flash, she shoved God's eye back into her pocket. She looked at Jed. "You never did say good-bye, Jed Pepper," her voice haunted.

With that, he sat up in bed, his body wet with sweat, her face burned into his imagination forever.

Jed could see Daisy clear as a Texas summer day, even thirty years later, with a scold in her eyes, a wrinkle to her nose, and a sad smirk, if there ever was such a thing. It's how Daisy looked when she told the truth and meant it. Her command from the grave. And he intended to obey this time.

Jed heard Mama open the front door and welcome guests of some sort. Probably from the church, bringing casseroles —terrible concoctions he couldn't eat anyway.

"He's in here," he heard her say.

Muriel and Hixon stepped into his room.

Jed pulled the covers back up, covering his bare chest.

Hixon sat on the foot of his bed. Muriel sat on Jed's desk chair.

"You don't look so good," Hixon said.

"I'm fine." Jed noticed Muriel, how fragile she looked. He wondered if she should be near him, considering how weak she was.

"Well, we wanted to stop by to tell you we're praying," she said, a strange warble to her voice.

Jed nodded his thanks. Remembering Daisy's invitation to come back to the church, Jed hoped that while the world had stopped for him in a bout of sickness, the police hadn't stopped. He needed to know they found who they were looking for. He looked at Hixon. "Have the police found Daisy's killer yet?"

"No."

"Where is he?"

"No one knows. Not really, anyway. Rumors are flying, though." Hixon stood. "Best be going."

"Rumors? What rumors?" Jed sat up, swung his feet around so they dangled off his bed.

"Stay put," Muriel said. "You're sick."

"Stay put? How can I?" Jed's voice cracked. He cleared his throat, then grabbed Hixon's elbow. "What rumors?"

"Ethrea Ree said she thought she saw Daisy's father yesterday, out in the field near Crooked Creek Church."

Jed felt the air in his lungs constrict. "Is it true?"

"Hard to say. The police are looking. Shoot, practically all of Defiance is searching. Folks are panicked, as you can imagine." Hixon walked toward Muriel, still seated. "But I've said enough. You concentrate on getting well, you hear?" He lifted Muriel to her feet, helped her hobble to the door.

She waved good-bye, whispered, "It'll be okay," and left, Hixon supporting her.

Jed sat back on his bed, grateful for something solid beneath him. Suddenly his belief in a God far away who was powerless seemed dangerous. He needed God to be powerful. Needed Him to nab Daisy's father. Needed Him to point the police in the right direction. He nearly prayed.

But instead, he planned to leave the house the moment he was strong enough.

Forty-Seven

"Mama's real bad this time, Jed." Sissy pulled at Jed's night-shirt. "She's asking for you."

Jed shook himself awake. "Where's Hap?"

"On a church call. Someone's in the hospital, I'm guessing. Please hurry."

Jed rushed to Mama's bedside. Her moaning bounced off the walls, seemed to make them narrow in on him. Jed sat next to Mama. "What's wrong? Do you need something?"

"Aspirin. Please."

Jed looked at Sissy. She shook her head.

"We're out, Mama."

She moaned again. "Can you real quick run next door? Ethrea Ree will have some. And if not her, then try Emory."

Jed went back to his room, pulled on a pair of jeans and a T-shirt, and padded down the hallway. As he opened the back door, Sissy sidled up next to him. "I'm coming with."

"No, Sissy." He'd marveled at how easy it'd been to get out of the house. Hap gone. Mama telling him to go. But Sissy coming hadn't been part of his plan.

"I've been cooped up for a week, Jed, almost as if I was as sick as you. Please let me come. I won't be a pest."

"No."

"You know how Mama gets, how she hates loud noises. I can scream, you know."

"Shush, Sissy. It's dark out. You can't come."

She siphoned in a breath, readying a holler.

"No!" Jed whispered. "Come on."

Jed was careful to ease the screen door shut, though it took him a long time to do so, with all its creaks and squeaks. They walked out quietly, quietly, quietly while crickets sang tired songs.

Sissy ran to Ethrea Ree's porch and knocked on the door. Nothing. Jed joined her on the porch. He knocked, louder this time. Nothing. Jed smiled. Perfect. Now they'd have to go to Miss Emory's and he wouldn't have to lie to Mama about it either. They were simply following her instructions, right?

"Come on, Sissy." Standing behind Ethrea Ree's rickety back fence, where they could see the alabaster Jesus bowed to the ground, Sissy whispered, "Why are we going this way?"

"I need to stop by the Crooked Creek Church on our way. Need to find something."

"What?"

"God's eye."

It wasn't a lie, really. He did need to find it, particularly with ghost Daisy holding it up to the light like that in the dream.

"Why are you looking for it now?"

"It's just … I have this feeling that I missed something out there—something that will show who Daisy's killer really is."

"And God's eye's supposed to help you? You sure are superstitious."

"It's not just God's eye. I think I'm meant to find something else in the church."

"Can't you go there when it's not so dark outside?"

"No. Hap'd never allow it. But since he's away—"

"The flu's gotten to your brain, Jed Pepper. You really want to risk daddy finding out? Because he will tan your hide something fierce if he does."

"At least that's a known thing. It can't get much worse than it's been. You know that."

Sissy swallowed. "You sure you want to do this?"

"I need to put Daisy to rest, say good-bye."

"Didn't you say good-bye at the funeral?"

"Not really." Jed kept walking.

"You can do that any old time. There's no rule that says we can't turn around, you know."

Jed kneeled down, catching Sissy's eyes in the moonlight. "Be my guest."

Sissy humphed and followed behind. Jed kept walking. He didn't like having Sissy so near. He knew God placed him on this earth to take care of her, and he also knew he might be putting her in danger right this very minute. Why did she have to follow him? Sissy caught up and slipped her hand into his as they walked toward the pasture behind Ethrea Ree's. Sissy didn't say a word, but he could sense her trembling.

He flexed his other arm, made a fist. A low swooping bird circled nearby. A vulture?

He should turn back, he and Sissy. Should get the heck out of here. But they'd come this far, and Daisy's dream-promise lured him farther. Besides, he was stronger now. He could protect Sissy, he told himself. He plunged his hand into his left pocket, the one opposite her, and fingered his Swiss Army knife. They'd be fine. Just fine.

A rustling behind them stopped Jed's heart cold. Sissy froze.

"Where do you think you're going this time of night?"

Jed whirled around to see Ethrea Ree, hair like a mixture between Mark Twain and Einstein, shaking a stick at them both. "An errand. For Mama," Jed said.

"You ought to know better, Jed Pepper. My mama used to say, 'Nothing good ever happens after nightfall,' and I'm inclined to say she's dead-on. Now get back to your home. You near scared me to death."

He scared her?

"Ma'am. It'll be okay, I know it," Sissy said, her voice smaller than a cricket.

"I have half a mind to tell your pa about your wanderings. And your mama would be worried sick."

"She's the one who sent us. She's sick and needs some aspirin," Jed said.

"You wait right here. I've got some." She ran back to her house, leaving Jed and Sissy at the field's edge.

Sissy pointed to the sky. "It looks like rain." She hugged herself.

Jed looked at the sky, spied the moon, then watched chalk gray clouds threaten to overtake it. When Ethrea Ree came back, bottle in hand, he'd already made up his mind.

"Here." She gave Jed the bottle of aspirin. "Now turn around and get back home." She looked at Sissy, touched her face. "I seen the killer with my own eyes, right out here." She pointed to the field.

Sissy nodded.

"Thanks for the aspirin." Jed started back toward home.

"No problem," Ethrea Ree said. She stood there a long time, watching them, as Jed led Sissy back home, only to double back once they were out of Ethrea Ree's sight.

"Jed, we got what we wanted, right? You can go to the church any other time. Like tomorrow morning."

"This'll just take a moment. Feel free to run home and give this to Mama."

"No way," Sissy said. "I'm staying with you."

"Then keep up and stop talking so much."

The first plop of rain came as the old Crooked Creek Church stared them down. Unlike Miss Emory's house, which lit the neighborhood like the Hollywood sign, the church had dark eyes. They darted inside the church as the trees started swirling. Their dark branches reminded Jed of H.R. Pufnstuf, the show where the trees came alive and grabbed folks. He couldn't bring himself to watch it after that.

The church croaked while the wind blew through its jagged windows. Sissy grabbed Jed's hand. Jed held it and didn't let go. He wished he'd remembered a flashlight. In the creaking darkness, lightning provided the only light, only that wasn't entirely reliable, popping on and off like a kid reaching the light switch for the very first time.

"What're you looking for, Jed?"

"I don't know."

Lightning spotlighted the pulpit. Jed led Sissy there. He looked up. Sure enough, the roof had blown off right above the podium. Rain pelted them both. Lightning cracked again, this time illuminating from behind them, showing Jed a single book.

A Bible.

On a lower shelf below the angled desk of the pulpit.

He opened it.

Wet pages answered back while thunder barked outside and rumbled his insides. A piece of paper stuck out kitty-corner from the New Testament. Jed pulled on it.

"What is it?" Sissy asked.

"I don't know." He couldn't slide the piece of paper out; it was too wet. So he opened the Bible to where the note was: 1 Corinthians 13, the love chapter. He gently peeled the note away from the text, but some of the type clung to the note. "Let's go sit a minute." Jed brought Sissy to Daisy's pew and opened the note. He squinted his eyes to read it, but he couldn't. It would take him forever to wait for lightning to shine on it seconds at a time.

"Wait a minute. I've got something." Sissy stood and shoved

her hand into her front pocket. "Here." She handed Jed a lighter.

"What're you doing with that?"

"I found it."

"Where?"

"You know where Daddy sits in the backyard near the tire swing? In that old wooden chair?" She waited for Jed to nod. "I found it there, in the grass below the chair."

"Do you think it's his?"

"Of course not, silly. Daddy doesn't smoke. Cigarettes are the Devil's matchsticks. You know that."

Jed shook his head. He didn't know what he knew. For all he could muster, he lived in some sort of parallel universe where everything was normal, but if he stepped out of line in any way, he'd land in a place he couldn't figure out. Like where Hap smoked.

He clicked the lighter to life, then handed it to Sissy. "Just hold this part down and nothing more. Don't move. I don't want it burning you."

In the light of a small flame, Jed saw Daisy's words. Seeing her funny handwriting (she'd always hated that she smeared her words, being left-handed and all), made him ache inside.

"Well, read it!"

Jed took a deep breath. "It's from Daisy."

Sissy's eyes grew wide. "From beyond the grave?"

"Don't get so spooked. No, she must've written this months ago." Jed scanned the words, but didn't read them out loud.

"Jed, I put this note in here because I knew one day you'd find it and we'd have a good laugh. Because this is where we're supposed to be married, right in the front of this church. As I'm writing this, I'm imagining it all. You in a tux. Me in a white dress with daisies being tossed by a flower girl. Sissy'll be too old for that by then, but that's how I imagine it anyway."

"I can read, you know. I want to be a flower girl."

"Just shush, Sissy. Let me finish."

The lighter flickered off. "Shoot, Sissy, can't you do anything right?" He grabbed the lighter from her and ignited it again, but it died.

Sissy crossed her arms. "It's out of juice, so quit your bellyaching."

Jed squinted to read the rest of the letter, but couldn't. Satisfied he'd found what he was looking for, Jed folded the soggy note and placed it in his pocket. "Come on, let's get home before Hap comes home."

"But you haven't found God's eye yet."

"No matter. This is enough."

"I'm scared." Sissy didn't stand.

"Come on. He won't find out. Don't worry."

"No, Jed, that's not what I'm scared of. I've got this funny feeling someone's watching us."

Jed reeled around. As another flash of lightning lit the open door, he could see something obscuring the doorway. Whatever it was dashed away in a wink. Jed's throat tightened. He wanted to holler, but his voice left him.

Sissy didn't have that problem. She screamed.

"Come on!" Jed found his voice, grabbed Sissy by the arm, and ran down the center aisle of the church and out the door.

A figure at the base of the steps darted toward the tree line.

"We're next!" Sissy screamed. "He's out there!"

Jed grabbed her by the shoulders. "Listen, it'll be okay. I'll protect you."

"You can't protect me, Jed. You're no match for a man!"

Thunder growled. Lightning shot to the earth. On the edge of the woods, a man's silhouette flashed briefly—the same one he'd seen near the woods by Daisy's dirt grave. So much for the killer being in Mexico. Jed wanted to holler like Sissy, but he kept it to himself, swallowing his fear—though it felt like swallowing a too large jawbreaker. "Run!"

They ran through the open field toward home. Jed pulled Sissy faster and faster, and to his surprise, she kept up. He didn't look back for fear of seeing the stranger gaining on them. All he could do was look forward and pull Sissy almost faster than her legs could go. Faster they raced through tall, wet grass. The clouds had run clear away, so typical of summer storms, leaving muddy ground and winking stars behind. Jed loved the moon, then. Loved how it brightened the night.

In a flash, Sissy's hands slipped from his. She hollered.

He spun around. Sissy had tripped on something and lay flat on the grass. She pulled herself up. Behind her Jed saw the man, walking slowly toward them—a hundred or so yards away. Slow and deliberate he walked. One foot in front of the other. Jed couldn't make out his face. He didn't want to.

"Come on, Sissy." He grabbed her hand.

"Wait." She bent to the ground.

"We need to go. Now!"

The man came closer. Jed squinted to see the face, but the moon backlit him. The figure raised slender arms heavenward as it walked—the gait of a woman, but the plodding of a man—arms touching the sky and not a sound from its mouth.

"I found it, Jed!" Sissy put something in her pocket, then turned around. She stared at the ghostly image. "It's you."

"Sissy!" Jed tried to grab her hand, but she eluded him.

Glued to the earth, her voice quiet, she said, "That's the one who tried to take me."

Jed grabbed Sissy's hand again and pulled her through the pasture, but she stumbled. Fell again. He lifted her up. The shadowy figure gained on them. He pulled Sissy along. She tripped.

"God, help!" Jed yelled moonward, fear now grabbing hold. He pulled Sissy up again. This time she ran without tumbling. They ran and ran, the swift in and out of their breath and the pounding of their shoes against the grassy field their only noise.

They ran past Ethrea Ree's bleeding Jesus. When they finally made it into their backyard through the rickety gate, Jed turned. He thought for sure he'd see someone right on their tail, but no one was there. It was as if God had taken an eraser to the chalkboard of the night, blacking out whoever it was who'd been pursuing them.

Quiet as a cat prowling for birds, they snuck back into the house. Jed tiptoed Sissy back to bed. She took off her shoes. "What'll we tell Mama?" she asked.

"Not a thing," Jed whispered.

"Shouldn't we tell the police?"

"We will. Sissy, please tell me what happened—with that man. What did he do?"

"He scared me."

"I could see that. But why'd you leave a locked car?"

"I don't know how he did it, but that man unlocked the doors with his mind. All at once, they unclicked. So I hightailed it out the backseat." Sissy's voice shook.

"I don't remember much after that, other than running home. But I could hear him."

"Hear him? You mean his footsteps?"

"No, his breathing. It didn't sound normal-like. More like a gurgling, wet breath." Sissy's eyes showed fear—lots of fear. She trembled.

Jed touched Sissy's elbow, his attempt to steady her. "How did you end up in the rosebush?"

"That's just the thing. I don't rightly know."

"How do you know the man chasing us was him?"

"I just do, is all. He walked the same." She gave Jed a world-weary look. "I'm tired. Do you mind?"

Jed turned his back as she put on her nightgown.

"You can turn around now. Guess which hand."

"What?"

"Which hand? I have something for you."

Jed chose her left. He was wrong. She uncurled her right hand, revealing God's eye staring right through him.

"Where'd you find it?"

"When I fell, my hand touched something smooth. And this was it. If you ask me, I think God wanted us to find it."

"Maybe so." Jed took the marble from Sissy and rolled it in his hands. He dropped it into his pocket.

"Maybe God used it to protect us," Sissy said.

Jed didn't know about that, so he kept quiet. "You get some sleep, you hear?"

She slipped into bed. Jed tucked the covers around her. "Told you I'd protect you."

"You did. Thanks."

He watched their escape like he was an angel looking down from heaven. The faceless man and his plodding. The scream of his sister. The strength Jed felt in his arms when he pulled her to safety.

"Jed?"

"Yeah, Sissy?"

"What else did Daisy say in her note?"

Jed had forgotten all about the note. He pulled it out of his pocket. Sissy clicked on her night-light. In the dim light, they read Daisy's words.

"I've told you before that your family ain't normal. And it's true. But mine isn't either. And your daddy's too. (By the way, quit calling him 'Hap.')"

Sissy poked him. "Hey, she agrees with me!"

"Shush!"

"But here's what I think. I think we can get better, despite it all. Otherwise, what good is Jesus? I mean, yeah, He's good for taking our sins and all, but maybe He's good for taking others' sins too. Like your dad's. I have to believe He can make us new. Otherwise, I'll turn into my mama. Don't get me wrong. She's doing the best she can. But I want to do better. I don't want to take drugs or run around with men, Jed. So make me a promise, okay? Promise we'll do better, will you? Your future bride, Daisy Marie Chance."

"You two were getting married?"

Jed stood. He folded the note and put it back in his pocket. "That's what Daisy thought. Doesn't matter much now."

Sissy's face fell. "You loved her, didn't you?"

Jed remembered where the Daisy note had been. In between the love chapter. The Scripture he'd memorized for Hap one summer, then recited from the pulpit to cheers from the congregation. Did he love her? Had he been patient and kind with her? Had he rejoiced when she succeeded? Yeah. He had. Even so, he couldn't mouth the words to Sissy now. "Good night," he told her as he opened her door.

Hap stood there, tall as a church steeple against the Defiance sky, arms flexed across a broad tie-adorned chest. "You were out?"

Mama haunted Hap's shoulder. He turned, looking at her.

"He did it for me," she said in a hushed tone. "I needed some aspirin." She shielded her eyes from the dim light.

Jed fished through his pockets, producing the bottle of aspirin. "Here it is, Mama," he said.

Hap grabbed it, then hurled the bottle across Sissy's room. It hit the wall and broke, pills scattering everywhere. Nostrils flaring, neck muscles tight, Hap growled, "Go to your room, Jed. I'll see to you later."

Forty-Eight

Once again, Jed shrunk back to his room, leaving both Sissy and Mama in harm's way. Crashing glass came from Hap's and Mama's bedroom. Mama cried. Jed heard Hap's rummaging, a line of yelled swear words escaping. Jed sprang to the door, ready to take on his father, only to have it flung back at his face.

Still in a suit and tie, Hap looked like the kindliest pastor there ever was. But his eyes told another story—and not one with a happy ending. Jed backed up.

"So, you were getting aspirin." His words were slow, quiet.

"Yes, sir." It was the truth.

"And you took your sister?"

Sissy shimmied into the room. Jed shot her a look that said go away, but she didn't obey. "Yes, I made him," she said. Sissy ran to Jed's bed. Jed scolded himself again in the electric silence. He shouldn't have let Sissy come along. He felt pathetic then, staring into the eyes of his enraged father. He tried to make a fist, but fright kept his fingers from curling in on themselves.

"No one makes a Pepper man do anything, Sissy. Unless he's weak willed." He turned back to Jed. "Have you no sense? You could've been—" Hap's voice cracked. He pulled in a heavy breath, then wiped his mouth. "Tell me this, Jed. What took you so long? Your mother sent you out at eight, and you came in an hour later. What took you so long?"

339

Jed backed up until the bed hit the back of his legs. He sat next to Sissy. "We stopped in at the church." Jed readied himself.

"You wandered off to that church in the dark?"

"Yes, sir." Jed's heart beat against his rib cage.

Mama appeared in the doorway. She held the left half of her face in her hands. "Hap, let them be," she whispered.

Hap pivoted. "You keep your trap shut, Ouisie." Hap took another measured breath. "Did it ever occur to you that you're their mother? That you're supposed to be taking care of them, not the other way around?"

"It was only to fetch some aspirin."

"Ouisie, look at me!"

She did, but Jed noticed her trembling.

"These kids are all we'll leave behind in this world. And you've treated them like something that can be easily thrown away. You hear me? Sending them out in the night when someone's out there ready to take them? Geeze, Ouisie, what on earth were you thinking?"

"I wasn't," she said. "My headache, it—"

"Enough about your stupid headaches. They're an excuse. You know what?" Hap's voice grew louder. "You're no better than Miss Emory, neglecting our kids. It's a wonder they didn't get taken, that they're not pushing up daisies right now!"

"You're right," Mama said, her voice raspy. She grabbed her temples. "You're absolutely right. What was I thinking?"

Jed's mind tangled. Maybe Hap was right. Maybe Mama wasn't such a great mama after all. With all those headaches . . .

Hap stepped closer to Mama. "That's it, isn't it? You weren't thinking," Hap spat, his words ice-cold. And for a moment, Jed understood those chilling words, saw a bit of his father's frustration at a wife who holed away in her bedroom. Jed looked at his hands, then at Hap's eyes. For a moment he was captivated there, held by the stare of a man he thought he never understood. In that moment, he shuddered.

Sissy whimpered. Clementine barked from the other room. Hap inched closer to Mama. She grabbed her head again. "You're hopeless, you know that? Pathetic." He lowered his right fist to his waist, then threw it northward to Mama's jaw. A sickening crack reeled Mama backwards. Sissy screamed. "That'll teach you to protect our kids," Hap growled.

Jed remembered how he'd pulled Sissy away from the unknown man but never confronted him, never turned to fist the man in the face. He hadn't then. But he hoped he could now—facing a man who hit his wife, however deserving she was.

"You kids should've known better than to go out when they haven't caught Daisy's dad." He raised a hand high above Sissy's head.

"You're right, Daddy," Sissy said. "Please don't hit me."

Sissy wept, sucking in huge breaths. Hap grabbed Sissy by the shoulders. "Why did you say that? I would never hit you, Sissy. I only discipline you so you'll learn like the Bible says." He shook her, hard.

Jed tightened both fists. Enough. *Enough.* "Leave her alone." Hap let go. Jed caught her frightened eyes and motioned for her to leave the room. Now. This time she obeyed.

"You think you're a man?" Hap screamed his words, his face turning blood red. "Try being a father, a pastor, a husband. Just try it, Jed."

"No, thanks." Jed stood as tall as he could, trying not to flinch. With one violent motion, Hap shoved Jed to the floor. His jaw cracked on the nightstand corner. Hap kicked his shins, then his middle. Dizzied, Jed tried to stand, but he couldn't. He spat blood, tasting copper.

Clementine crashed into the room, barking. She jumped at Hap, grabbing his suit sleeve in her teeth. He shook her away.

"Leave us alone!" Sissy screamed from the hallway.

Hap lunged toward Sissy and grabbed her arm. Clementine bit Hap's hand. Blood sprayed across the room.

Jed tried to stand, but he couldn't. He knelt near his bed. God's eye rolled out of his pocket onto the floor. He grabbed it.

Clementine growled at Hap. Hap stepped back and pulled Sissy. She screamed. Jed clenched God's eye and threw it toward Hap's head with every muscle in his body. He roared with every ounce of anger inside him. God's eye hit Hap square in the right eye.

Hap reeled back and let go of Sissy. He crashed to the floor like a felled pine tree, toppling over Clementine. Sissy grabbed Jed around his middle, squeezing hard. Jed let out a long breath. His heart beat a frenzied rhythm. He realized his hands were still fists, that every muscle in his body felt like those fists — tight and ready to unleash more fury.

Hap lay still, Clementine silent beneath him.

Jed felt empty. He'd worked his muscles, prepared them for this moment, only to see his father crumpled on the floor, covering Sissy's best friend. Jed didn't feel victorious. He didn't feel anything but Sissy's embrace, and even that didn't satisfy. Jed stood and pulled Sissy into the hallway, away from Hap, away from what he feared was a lifeless Clementine.

"You thaved me, Jed! You thaved me!"

Forty-Nine

Officer Spellman paced the Pepper living room. "Your dad's eye is pretty bad. They're taking him to Tyler."

Jed said nothing. Felt nothing. Not even relief.

"What were you thinking, dragging your sister out at night when a killer's on the loose? What's gotten into you?"

"I saw someone. Near the woods. He followed us."

"Who was it?"

"I don't know." Jed tried to steady his voice. "It was a man. I've seen him in the woods before. Sissy too."

The events of the night sharpened in Jed's mind, like a camera lens when it's turned and suddenly everything that was blurry comes into focus. He could've died. Sissy too. And if she hadn't found God's eye ...

Mama walked over to Jed, placed her hand on his shoulder. She looked at Officer Spellman. "I think it's best you leave now. You can imagine how things've been since Daisy's death."

Officer Spellman walked to the front door, his shoes sounding on the bare floor. "Be careful, okay? We haven't found David Carter yet. No one's safe until we do." He pulled out a picture, showed it to Jed. "This is him."

Jed saw Daisy's eyes in the face of this man. Her dancing eyes. Was this the barefooted man? He didn't know.

"Is that the man you saw?" He showed it to Sissy too.

"I don't know," Jed said.

"Me neither." Sissy shook her head.

"I best be going." Officer Spellman put the picture back in his pocket and left.

Mama sat on the couch. Jed put his face in his hands. "Nothing's going to happen to Hap," he said.

"No," she said. "Nothing."

"Maybe the church?"

"We'll see. I'm sure the elders and deacons will meet."

Jed heard Sissy crying. She was in his room, arms splayed over Clementine. "Dear Jethuth. Dear Jethuth. Dear Jethuth," she prayed.

"I'm sorry, Sissy." He put an arm around her.

Sissy looked up. "Don't thay that. Clementine'th not ..."

"You're lisping."

"I alwayth have."

"No, you haven't."

"Where ith Mama?"

"In the living room."

"Crying?"

"Yep." Jed stroked Clementine's fur. He could feel her warmth, thank God.

"Will Clementine be okay?" Sissy pet the great big head. She pulled open one eye. Clementine stirred.

"It looks that way, but we should take her to the vet."

Clementine shook her head, then wobbled to her feet. She looked at Jed with those knowing eyes, like she'd seen Jed's rage and didn't approve.

Sissy cheered and hugged the dog tight.

Clementine licked her tears.

Fifty

Jed woke up, thankful for sunshine. Sissy lay on the floor beside his bed, curled around Clementine. He watched her sleep. Though he still wondered about a God who called Hap to be a preacher, over the last few days he'd made a little peace with God. At least God gave him the strength to protect Sissy. At least He plopped His eye into Sissy's hand. There was always that.

The elders and deacons sent a letter, signed by all, including Officer Spellman. Jed read it yesterday. With all sorts of King James English, they pretty much said Hap was tired and he needed a personal retreat with Jesus, but that the church was fully behind him and anticipated his return to the pulpit. The letter told how Mama needed to work harder at mothering, cleaning the house, and controlling her kids.

Hap was on day three, relaxing at Piney Cove Retreat Center. Day three of one month. Truth be told, Jed'd never felt happier. Clementine became her old self on day one and Mama stopped having headaches—all three days. Maybe hurling God's eye had been worth it.

Next to his bed sat a tangle of flowers crammed into an old jelly jar. He quietly sifted through them so as not to wake Sissy. He saw Mama's writing on the petals of a daisy, one word on each petal.

Instead of he-loves-me, he-loves-me-not, Mama wrote, "I'm sorry. It'll be better now. Hap needed rest. Love, Mama."

Jed placed the flower back in the jar. Poor Mama. Poor, poor Mama. It was a good thing Jed was around to help her see she was a good mama. And to protect her from Hap when he returned. Jed scooted around sleeping Sissy and Clementine. He pulled on shorts and a T-shirt. In the hallway, he dropped to his hands and feet and pushed up and down one hundred times. A man had to stay in shape, he told himself.

A quiet knock tapped the front door.

Hixon.

Jed went out on the porch, careful not to wake the sleeping women.

"Muriel's real bad," Hixon said. "She's asking for you. She's staying at my house now."

"I need to ask permission."

Mama appeared around the corner, Sissy-like. "As long as you're with Hixon, I know you're safe. Just be careful, you hear me?"

"He's safe with me," Hixon said, nodding to Mama.

Hixon's home, usually bright on the inside because he didn't like shades, felt like night. He'd nailed thick blankets to the window frames in the living room where Muriel slept in a hospital bed. "The doctor arranged to have this bed sent here. I'm so grateful," he whispered.

"Quit your whispering. I'm not dead yet." Muriel pushed herself up.

Hixon added a pillow to support her. "I didn't want to wake you."

"Where's Jed?"

Jed walked to Muriel's side. She took his hand. He let her. He noticed how thin her skin seemed, with spots dotting her hand and veins roping through like city highways.

"First things first. I heard about your dad."

"His eye—"

"Don't worry yourself to talk about that. I want to tell you something." She coughed, then wheezed. Hixon wiped her mouth with a soft cloth. "Now come closer."

Jed bent near.

"Your father, he has some good in him. It's real hard to see, I know."

"I shouldn't have—"

"Stop it with the shoulds and shouldn'ts, Jed. You listen to me." She coughed again. Hixon brought a glass of water to her dry lips. She drank, then nodded. "I said he had good in him, but that doesn't mean he gets to hit his family."

"But the Bible says to honor your father."

"You forgot the last part," she wheezed. "And your mother. You honored your mother when you tried to protect her."

"But Hap—"

"Hap is hurting, so he lashes out. That doesn't make the lashing right. Sometimes parents don't act right. Sometimes," she swallowed, "they flat-out do the wrong thing. If you let them wallow in that sin, don't oppose it, you're not really loving them, are you?"

Jed hadn't thought of it that way.

"Sit me up, will you, Hixon?"

Hixon cranked the bed higher. He adjusted her pillows.

She pulled Jed's face to hers. "You did the right thing by protecting, Jed. I'm proud of you."

Muriel's words choked him up. A boulder the size of Hixon's porch rolled off Jed's shoulders. He pulled away, then held Muriel's cold hands, saying nothing.

"Sometimes you gotta protect who's weak. You gotta give them a voice."

With those words, he remembered Sissy. "But Sissy's lisp, she started—"

"In due time, it'll go away. You're praying for her, aren't you?" She heaved in a breath, then wheezed it out slow.

"Yes." Jed squeezed her hand.

"Here's what I need from you. Can you do me a favor? A great big favor?"

Jed nodded.

"Hixon needs help." Her voice rattled. She pulled in another breath. "He can't finish that mural by himself. I need you to help him."

"But that's your job. You need to finish it."

"I've done all the painting I can do. You go in my place. As a substitute." She raked in a breath. "Like Jesus did for us. He took my place on that cross. And now I'd like you to take my place at Muriel's mural. Can you do that for me?"

"Sure."

"Thank you, Jesus," she mumbled. Her eyes fluttered closed, her breathing was shallow.

"She sleeps a lot." Hixon petted her forehead. "I'm afraid to leave her. But she's a stubborn one. Muriel wants that mural done. She made me hire a nurse to come in today so we could finish it. You and me painting the mural is a divine appointment, she tells me."

Jed painted Daisy's face. He pulled the brush over her skin, hoping to make it just so. He could not get her eyes right, but he kept at it while Hixon went crazy splattering paint on a section of the mural that looked like modern art. When the noon sun poked its head out from a fluffy cloud, Hixon declared a lunch break.

They sat under the large tree near the mural. Hixon pulled out lunch from his old cooler.

"You're painting Daisy." He chewed on a tuna fish sandwich.

Jed ate some Fritos, then took a long drink of Hixon's lemonade. "Yep."

Why didn't you walk her home skipped in his head like a broken record. You're no good. You're a terrible friend. It's all your fault. Over and over the sentences chanted in his head, blurring his eyes. How could he paint the friend he betrayed?

"Are you done?" Hixon asked.

"Done?"

"With your guilt trail. I feel it."

Jed looked at the mural, wondering if he should quit and head home. "I don't deserve to paint her."

"God says otherwise." Hixon laughed then, not the sort of cautious laugh someone does in the woods at night to clear the silence, but a daytime belly laugh you hear in the movie theater from someone who doesn't know how to laugh right. The kind of laugh that makes you laugh despite your nervousness. A cackling, hooting laugh that'd wake up kingdom come.

Jed held his own smile inside. Hixon laughed again, like God was telling him jokes inside his head. A snicker burst from Jed—laughter that cleaned his insides out.

"Laughter is the language of heaven," Hixon said.

Jed looked at Hixon. "She said she was going to marry me." His voice cracked.

"I have no doubt about that. Girls are a mystery, aren't they?"

"Hixon?"

"Yes?"

"I heard you in the old church. You were talking to Muriel. You said you were going to do something there. What was it?"

Hixon looked away. For a prophet-type, he sure looked unsure. "It's a secret."

"I don't like secrets."

"I can imagine. My secret's a little embarrassing."

Jed took another drink of lemonade. "Come on, tell me."

"Miss Emory. I think God wants me to marry her."

Hixon could've said he was going to be an astronaut to Venus and it wouldn't have surprised Jed more than this. "Marry Miss Emory?"

"I know it sounds crazy. It is crazy. But I love her. She doesn't know it, of course, me being a chicken and all." He took another bite of sandwich.

"You're not a chicken. You're a prophet."

"Like I said to you before, that's what other folks say. I doubt I'm anything near a prophet. Truth is, I don't always tell the truth."

"Hixon, I need to ask you another question." Jed's nerves made his hands shake a little.

"Don't ask me why I love her, because I can't tell you."

"I won't. It's not that. It's your tree."

Hixon looked away.

"I climbed your tree."

Hixon picked paint off his fingers.

"And I could see where Daisy was, clear as day."

Hixon's eyes met Jed's. They were moist. "I'm sorry, Jed." He coughed. "Like I said, I don't always tell the truth."

Jed tried to picture a menacing Hixon wrapping a brown hand around Daisy's mouth, dragging her kicking and hollering and biting into the woods. He watched Hixon's hands choke Daisy's gasps to nothing. But when he looked in Hixon's eyes, the picture vanished.

"It's not what you think, Jed. I told you the story about my tree because I wanted you and others to think I was holy. That I spent hours and hours and hours in a tree with Jesus. I saw that tree one day and I longed to spend time with Jesus there. I really meant to climb that tree, really meant to talk to him there, but I never did. I talked it up like I did, and I'm sorry."

Jed swallowed another swig of lemonade. Sissy'd said Hixon

was practically Jesus, and here he was admitting to a big fat lie. Jed didn't understand. So he took another drink.

"I'm so sorry, Jed. But I never did see where Daisy was buried because I never did climb that tree."

Jed watched Hixon's face turn into sadness. It was something he'd never seen Hap do — admit to making a mistake, to say, "I sinned." All his life, Jed knew the world was wrong because of him, that his house was not normal because he didn't do things right. Could it be that adults made mistakes too? Admitted them? Jed'd always thought adults got it right the first time. Now he wasn't so sure. "Hixon?"

"I did spend time with Jesus. I did. Just not there." He held his face in his hands. "I don't blame you for hating me. I hate myself. I'm so sorry for lying to you."

Jed put a hand on Hixon's shoulder. "I don't know what to say."

Hixon's eyes leaked. He put his hand on Jed's — the one resting on his shoulder — then released it. He stood. "I guess it's like those talent shows at Defiance High. You ever seen one?"

"Sure." Jed remembered a few good singers, a juggler or two, then the endless line of kids who sang like crows. It was the town joke; everyone knew it.

"I'm like one of those kids who smiled their way through the worst solos ever imagined."

"How so?"

"Folks told me since way back when that I was a prophet of sorts. I started believing it. Just like a mama tells her child he's the best singer this side of Nashville even when he makes the dog howl with his singing. So I started putting on 'prophet' like it was a suit tailored only for me. Truth is, I'm like you, Jed. A struggler. Someone who doesn't always feel God. On stage I'm a horrible singer thinking I'm Waylon Jennings."

"So, you're like Hap ... in a way?"

Hixon hung his head. "Yeah, I suppose you're right. I'm

hiding stuff like he is, and sometimes I pretend something I'm not."

The words formed in Jed's mind. He thought of Mama's mousy ways, how all she ever needed to hear were words of forgiveness from Hap. Or encouragement. Instead Mama clung to David Carter's words about her, stored them away in a box because they seemed to give her life. She wrote words to Jed on fragile petals. And now Hixon needed Jed's words, his encouraging words. Jed swallowed, looked into Hixon's deep brown eyes. "I forgive you, Hixon."

For a moment, Hixon said nothing. He wiped his mouth with his hand, then did it again. He looked to heaven, raised his hands to touch the sky, then applauded the clouds. He laughed. Jed looked at him, not sure what to say or do.

Hixon danced a jig, then turned to Jed, looked right through him. "A weight's been rolled off my back. I've always known I serve the God who sees. Who was I to think he didn't see my lies? He saw me walk around that tree months and months ago. He saw everything. And now you see too, and you offer forgiveness. Just like Jesus."

It was the second time that day he'd been praised. Once by Muriel, now by Hixon. It felt like a letter of grace had been written to him from heaven. Jed only wished he could put it in a picture frame to hold as proof later on when things grew dark again. Mama's notes faded as fast as cut flowers. At least he had Daisy's note. And God's eye. Tangible proof that he mattered to someone.

"Let's finish this mural," Hixon said.

Hixon painted nearby now, catching up to Jed in the middle, where he still puzzled over Daisy's eyes. Muriel's portion of the mural was done. According to Hixon, she'd worked herself to near death to finish it. Hills and valleys and trees and people strolling on meandering paths made Jed smile. On one of the paths, winding through dark mountains, Jed saw the three of them. Tall dark Hixon, bald Muriel, and Jed, nearly as tall, walking hand in hand toward a fading sunset. He looked closer. Something about it niggled him.

Then it hit him. This was the spot where Jed painted the darkness. Where the three of them stood was Bald Muriel's white dot. She'd made something hopeful out of his despair, brought to life the death he painted, electrified Ezekiel's dry bones.

But life couldn't turn out so perfectly, could it? People walking off together into the sunset? How could it, with Daisy's killer still lurking and Bald Muriel's life coming to an end?

Jed looked at his painting of Daisy. He worried if he finished Daisy's eyes, Muriel's mural would be complete, making Muriel walk into the sunset alone, without the two of them. If he painted the last stroke, would she stop breathing?

"I don't want her to die."

"I don't either." Hixon took out a hankie and blew his nose. "But I'm afraid it's going to happen despite our painting."

"I've had enough pain," Jed said. And, oh, how he meant it. "I can't have her die. I need her to help me ... with Hap."

"Clementine was her dog, you know."

Jed nodded. He'd suspected from the moment he met Clementine that Muriel had given that dog to them. To save them, in a way.

"Look at that road Muriel painted." Hixon pointed to the sunset scene. "When she finished painting it, Muriel told me our life is like a winding path with a deep ditch on either side." He pointed to either side of the path the three walked on.

"I didn't notice that. I see the ditches now."

Hixon pointed to one. "One ditch is our full-fisted rebellion. The other, she said, is our response to someone else's rebellion. She told me, 'The Devil couldn't care less which ditch we fall into, he just wants us off the road.'"

"I'm on the path, holding her hand. But when she's gone—"

"You have *me*. Plain old un-prophety me. I'll help you. You'll jump off the path if you let your daddy's anger make you an angry man. I understand that. And I aim to help you."

"Thanks, Hixon."

"Now, let's finish up this mural and make Muriel proud."

Jed looked into Daisy's blue blue eyes. He couldn't get them right. He squinted, trying to remember the way Daisy's eyes danced and sassed. When he opened his eyes, he knew. Daisy's eyes were missing Hixon brown. He dabbed a blunt brush into tree trunk brown, lightened it a bit with cloud white, and added small brown lines to Daisy's irises. He stood back. Yep. That was Daisy, all right.

"You painted her perfectly." Sissy's voice startled Jed.

Clementine licked the back of Jed's knees. He laughed. "Thanks, Sissy."

Hixon joined them. They backed up to drink in the mural.

"It's splendid," Sissy said.

"She'll be proud." Jed wiped sweat from his forehead.

"She is proud. I know it." Hixon gathered up the last of the paint cans and piled them on the side of the road for the garbage man to pick up. He grabbed the cooler. "Let's go tell her we're done."

They walked past Miss Emory's house.

Hixon set the cooler down. The curtains closed, the yard in a mess, it looked like Miss Emory'd gone on vacation, though Jed knew it wasn't true. He'd seen her a few times around town.

"I need to do something," Hixon said. He picked leggy flowers from Miss Emory's brambled yard. Breathless, he asked, "Can I have your ribbon, Sissy?"

"Sure." She pulled the blue and white ribbon from her hair and handed it to him.

He tied the ribbon around the flowers. He took off his shoes and tiptoed up onto the porch like a little kid trying to spook his sister. He stuffed the tangle of wild flowers into the mail slot so their heads stuck out, their feet poking through to Miss Emory's living room.

He came back.

"Aren't you going to knock and make sure she gets them?" Jed asked.

"Sometimes giving quietlike is enough."

Jed noticed a flutter of curtains but didn't see Miss Emory's face. Just a white hand.

Hixon picked up his shoes in one hand, grabbed Sissy's hand in his other. Sissy took Jed's. Clementine followed, wagging her tail. Shoeless Hixon and a paint-weary Jed sandwiched themselves like Wonder Bread around Sissy. No ditches flanked their route. Together they walked a shaded path through Defiance, never letting go.

It was a picture Jed comforted himself with for the rest of his life. He recalled Muriel's sunset whenever Daisy's "You never did say good-bye, Jed Pepper" haunted his memory. Because the truth was, he never did say good-bye. Never could. Those blue eyes, veined in Hixon brown, stared at him when he shut his own, still beckoning him to return to Crooked Creek Church to meet her there.

The mystery of who took Daisy and why unfolded in the most excruciating way. He seldom let himself trace over the remembrance. Some things were better left in God's hands—a bit of Hixon's advice Jed kept close to his heart all these years. Missing shoes, a faceless man, Daisy's hand pointing heavenward—these Jed locked away. He didn't want to remember her that way. Couldn't bear to.

Standing on the ruins of the toppled church, Jed closed his eyes, the evening sun keeping the darkness there bright. "I'm here, Daisy," he said, while the sun slipped behind the piney woods of Defiance.

"I'm right here."

Hixon stood on Miss Emory's porch, wildflowers in hand, she on the other side of the screen door, clutching its handle. She, with her red-rimmed eyes and tight-lipped grief. He would not be able to hold her, to press out the grief.

"You can leave the flowers on the porch." She spoke the words in such a matter-of-fact way, as if Hixon were the milkman and she was merely conducting a business transaction. "You been here recently?" He heard fear behind those words, couldn't make sense of them.

"No, not until now."

"You sure?"

"Yes," he said. "Why?"

She looked away. "No reason. Just wondering."

Hixon put the flowers on a small table next to Miss Emory's porch swing. "Miss Emory, I'm—"

"Don't say it. I'm sick of those words. I'm sorry," she hissed. "Sorry? Like you have anything to be sorry about. Life stinks. Bad stuff happens. Don't be sorry."

"But I am. Sorry for your sake." Hixon took a step closer.

She let go of the screen door, the barrier between them, and stepped further back into her house. "I don't need your pity."

Hixon put his hands in the air. "I don't mean to pity you.

Just offering my condolences. And my help. Is there anything you need?"

She touched the screen's handle again, inching a hint closer. "One thing."

"Anything."

"I can't abide Hap Pepper preaching my Daisy's funeral, you know? Would you do it?"

Hixon looked at his feet. He smiled, but then thought the better of it, placing a hand over his mouth. He wiped that smile away, then looked into Miss Emory's ice-blue eyes. "Of course. It would be my privilege."

She nodded and shut the front door, leaving Hixon with a remnant of hope and a lump in his throat.

He walked down the stairs, remembering the time he'd spent at this house, how he and Jed scraped away peeling paint, primed it, and made the house preen white. So much like Miss Emory, a shock of beauty, startling in its brightness. And yet, no one really knew what went on inside the white house, nor did Hixon know what lit Miss Emory from the inside. He'd looked in her eyes, craning his neck just so, only to find her curtaining the windows of her heart. Sometimes her beauty alone was enough to sustain him for days, weeks. But a wry smile from her pink lips was simply a tantalizing enticement to something he'd never know—Miss Emory's soul.

Hixon tried to whistle his way home, but his lips were too dry to keep any long notes. With each step, his thankfulness to preach Daisy's funeral—the privilege of being asked—waffled into dread. What if he didn't remember Daisy proper? He pictured himself in a pressed suit—his only one—standing before Daisy's small coffin, unable to speak. He saw Hap Pepper smiling his way to the pulpit, gently pushing Hixon aside, determined to preach about the girl he barely knew. Hixon prayed as he walked, asking Jesus to please give him words, the right words, to make Daisy smile from heaven, and give Miss Emory the gift of a life remembered perfectly.

He turned the corner and headed home. Behind closed curtains, Muriel, his adopted mama, would be waiting for him. She'd be heaving in cancerous breaths, talking about Jesus between rasps. It wouldn't be long before he preached another funeral, his second in one year.

The front door creaked as he pushed it open. Muriel lay propped on a hospital bed, eyeing him. Though dark circles bagged underneath, her eyes still danced, her mouth upturned like praise. "You give her the flowers?" she asked.

Hixon closed the door. He nodded as he adjusted to the darkness of the room. Light gave Muriel headaches something fierce.

"She asked me to preach Daisy's funeral." Hixon held Muriel's hand. "What should I do?"

"What your heart tells you to do," Muriel rasped.

"I told her I'd do it. I'm just afraid is all. I'm worried I'll freeze up with sadness." He squeezed her hand and let it go.

"That poor girl."

"I still can't believe she's been killed." Hixon went to the window, pushed away the blankets for just a moment, to remind himself that the world continued on as usual in the bright daylight.

"Not poor Daisy. She's dancing in heaven, son." Muriel took a breath, let it out. She smiled. "I meant poor Miss Emory. Your future wife."

Hixon turned. In the light of the opened drape, he noticed Muriel's gray lips, upturned to the ceiling, a laugh nearly escaping. "Quit your teasing," he said.

"I'm not teasing. Just stating fact."

"Some things are better left unsaid."

Muriel coughed, then cleared her throat. "You told me Jesus ordered you to marry her."

"I know. But maybe I was wrong. Maybe it's my crazy mind thinking impossible things."

"Impossible things are God's business." She coughed so weakly Hixon rushed again to her bedside. He lifted a cup of lukewarm tea to her mouth, but she shook her head. "No. I'm fine. Sit me up more."

He adjusted her pillows, propping her as best he could.

"You'll marry her, son. But it won't be the way you imagine it." She looked at Hixon then, eyes full of the world's sadness. "She may break your heart—she's so broken herself."

"I understand broken folks," he said.

"I know. I know." Muriel closed, then opened her eyes, her eyelids a theatre curtain that closed on a tragedy then opened to a comedy. She smiled, but even if she hadn't, he'd have known she was smiling by the dance in her eyes. "And she'll understand someday. It's my prayer, Hixon. You know that, right?"

He nodded.

"Preach hope at that funeral, you hear me? Daisy's gone to wide fields where her Creator lives. Life can't get any better than that."

Hixon nodded. She was right. Always right.

"Hixon, look at me."

He obeyed. Ever since she adopted him as her own son, he'd done everything he could to accommodate her, taking her into his home, implementing what the doctors said, and then some. "Ma'am?"

"I need to do it." Air stumbled over the rasp deep in her lungs.

"Maybe it's time to rest."

Muriel closed her eyes, even that small movement seemed to weary her. She moaned, breathing air that sounded like soup as it passed through her lungs. Gurgling in. Gurgling out. She didn't bother with the red wig anymore. Even so, Hixon knew her head got cold, so he'd given her his black stocking cap to warm her shiny head. It slipped off.

Hixon fitted it gently back. He sighed. How much longer? The news of Jed finding Daisy's body leeched the breath from Muriel while at the same time re-igniting one last flicker for another dream. Painting the mural on the rendering plant wall was her dying wish, but that hadn't been enough. No, one more thing, she'd told him. One last way to make her mark on Defiance, Texas—an eternal mark, she'd said.

"It's time," she said.

"But the wall—it's all that's needed. The whole town loves it. It's a testament to your kindness, to God's beauty. Can't that be enough?"

Muriel opened clear eyes. "No," she said. "Not enough." She inhaled, then exhaled. "The Lord said—"

"I know what the Lord said. But what if you can't do it? What if it takes everything out of you?"

Muriel's eyes looked beyond him to a spot on his wall where a cross he'd fashioned from scrap metal hung crooked. She pulled in another labored breath. "Jesus." She smiled.

Hixon turned to look at the cross. No Jesus. But He may as well have stood right there, smiling his shiny Jesus eyes on Muriel in Hixon's shadowy living room. What with the way she beamed, it may have been so. Or maybe she was so close to seeing Him in the next life, He'd chosen to appear to her in this life, like a heavenly concierge service. "What is it?"

"He's not finished," she breathed, "with me yet."

Yet? Hixon didn't like that word. It meant there'd be a The End to Muriel's story. Though he'd mourned his mama's death, something inside him knew grieving Muriel would snuff him clear out, flatten him like roadkill, leaving little opportunity for resurrection. He looked at Muriel, her eyes still shining, and nodded. "Now?"

"I'll need your help."

"Sure, of course."

"Well, then, let's get to getting. If He's not finished, I'm not finished."

QUESTIONS FOR GROUP DISCUSSION

1. When you first meet Daisy, what is your immediate impression? How does your opinion of Daisy change throughout the book?

2. How does Jed's view of God's protection change throughout the book? How does "God's eye" serve as a symbol of his journey?

3. Discuss Hixon. What were your feelings about him early on in the story? Did they change by the end of the book? How does he grow, or help Jed to grow?

4. Considering the cast of characters, who do you think killed Daisy?

5. Family secrets play a significant role in *Daisy Chain*. Who is imprisoned by them? Who is set free? Do secrets always bring bondage when kept, and freedom when revealed?

6. Talk about Hap. Did your feelings for him ever change throughout the story? What makes Hap who he is? Could there be salvation for Hap?

7. What role does Ethrea Ree play in *Daisy Chain*? What surprises you about her?

8. What role does Clementine play in the Pepper family dynamic?

9. What redemptive elements do you see in *Daisy Chain*? Does any good come out of the tragedies of Defiance?

10. We are told that Sissy has a lisp at the beginning of the book, but Jed can't hear it. Do you think he chooses not to hear it until the end? Does he really hear it then?

11. Jed lives with deep feelings of guilt and regret. What does his story say about living like this? How have you learned to deal with your own guilt or regret?

12. What images—the mural, God's eye, Ethrea Ree's roses—accentuate the book's themes the best? Which resound the most with you, and why?

13. Why do you think Hixon lied about the Jesus tree?

14. What does Jed want more than anything else?

15. If you could change one thing about one of the characters in *Daisy Chain*, what would it be?

16. Who serves as Jed's best mentor? Why? Does Jed mentor others?

17. What are your feelings toward Ouisie? Can you relate to her?

18. How does Emory cope with her loss? How does her relationship with Jed change over the course of the book?

For more information about the author,
please visit www.marydemuth.com.

Share Your Thoughts

With the Author: Your comments will be forwarded to
the author when you send them to *zauthor@zondervan.com*.

With Zondervan: Submit your review of this book
by writing to *zreview@zondervan.com*.

Free Online Resources at
www.zondervan.com/hello

 Zondervan AuthorTracker: Be notified whenever your favorite authors publish new books, go on tour, or post an update about what's happening in their lives.

 Daily Bible Verses and Devotions: Enrich your life with daily Bible verses or devotions that help you start every morning focused on God.

 Free Email Publications: Sign up for newsletters on fiction, Christian living, church ministry, parenting, and more.

 Zondervan Bible Search: Find and compare Bible passages in a variety of translations at www.zondervanbiblesearch.com.

 Other Benefits: Register yourself to receive online benefits like coupons and special offers, or to participate in research.